A

VICTIM

OF

JUSTICE

Taboo

"A Victim of Justice"
- Taboo.
"Free Taboo Publishing LLC."
Copyright © 2022

ISBN: 979-8-9865779-0-6

Preface

In no way does this author or Free Taboo Publishing, LLC. wish to glorify or promote gangs, drugs, or violence. Kids should take it as a warning, of what could happen, as well as what those consequences can be, and adults should teach the kids to avoid drugs, and gang activity, and to know the value of life. Do not throw your life away. All life is precious.

That being said, this book is a work of art, fiction, and meant to be entertainment. None of the people or names are real, nor are they intended to resemble anyone in real life. It does include real places to make it more real, as well as some real situations. It is FACTS that Congress has passed the First Step Act bill that takes the stacking out of the 924(c) stacking law, yet they consciously made the decision to allow all of those sentenced under this draconian law to stay imprisoned under this outdated and unfair sentencing enhancement. There are tens of thousands of people sentenced to hundreds of years, just like this author is currently sentenced to 91 years for non-violent, victimless drug and gun possession charges.

The current average federal sentence for murder is 22 years. This author was sentenced to over four times the national average federal murder sentence. Just for possession of things.

3

Not for anything violent. Not for any victims. Not for using the guns. He could have committed four murders and gotten less time.

Our sitting congress this year, 2022, has the SAFE Justice Act, the First Step Implementation Act, and many more bills for criminal justice reform just on hold in front of them. We need Congress to act NOW! Stop these unfair and ridiculous sentences! I encourage all of you who believe that the 851 and 924(c) laws are unfair to call or write to your Congressman and ask them to pass these bills! Ask for a change in this Criminal INjustice System!

TABOO

Dedication

To my amazing daughter Desiree (an avid reader).

Your name might legally be Charley.

But you will always be "Desi" to me.

Acknowledgment

All thanks to my Lord Jesus Christ above all else. Also, to my readers and fans who are in love with my work and support my dreams. My mom Kathy and stepdad Dave Evans, for raising my son to be a good person. Lindsey for raising my daughter, you've always had my heart, and always will. My sister Laurie, for always being there for me. Mike Lee for ridin' this bid with me. Shane and Travis Stubblefield, my brothers from another mother.

Thanks to Vini for pushing me to achieve my goals and her artistic influences on me, and for being a great friend. My family Big Eric, Lil' Eric, and Mikey. Dina for always making me smile, Cashwell, for always making me laugh and being a good friend.

To Kira and Bella, to Carmen and Melissa Bezares, Bladimir, and Roger. Jose and Leti Rodriguez, Fransisco and Jessica Alejandro, Michele "Momsdukes" Warner, Breanna Klein, Momo, Niki Hill, Craig Williams, Janel, Heather Campbell, Tiffany, Tammy, Chad Lobsinger, Cassie Cabrera, Tasha Diaz, Bobo, Zack, Fallon, Laura Mathis, Ivy, Rico, Lori & Athena Bailey, Ena Weeks, Brandi Carter, Randy Abott, Budda, Miss Cheryl Yeary-Eisen, Jamie & Debbie Barrow, Natalie, Brat, Stephanie & Nicole Lewis, Stephan & Livi Smith, Paulie, Allyssa, Samantha, and all of the homies in the Penitentiary: Dizzy, Chance, Bankroll, Money Mark, Gutta, Al, Revenue, Fat, Bogie, Zoe, Tank, Iceman, Run-Run, D, Truly, O, Herb, Nard, Cheeks.

To all the dead homies, gone but not forgotten: Savannah Balcom, (who saved my life when I got shot 3 times), My father Mike Yeary, Jovan 'Wolf' Gomez, Chris 'Chuck' Waters, Leighton Peale, Todd Reynalds, Christian '561' Scott, Eugene 'Chico' Simon, Manuel 'Slim' Valbueno, Jaime Medina, Paul 'Big Daddy' Martinez, Charlie Kline, Dave Barrow, Charlie Shultz, Miss Debbie Yeary, Brandon Gilcher, Tenesha Faria, Rick Marsh, and Maria Castro.

To Congress: Thank you for passing the First Step Act, so my 91-year sentence for non-violent, victimless crimes has now been illegal for 3 years, we need for you to make it retroactive! Pass the SAFE Justice Act immediately!

To the best lawyer besides Mike Salnick, my guy Mike Smith who fought like hell to give back these 91 years, even though we lost I loved his fight! Good guy!

Prologue

City of West Palm Beach, Florida
June 16, 2008

The city of West Palm Beach is located just north of Miami in Palm Beach County, Florida. It is one of the richest communities in the world. It has some of the most beautiful beaches, exotic locations, and people. It's also known for its most diverse population, though home to some of the poorest and most dangerous neighborhoods as well as people.

Life in Palm Beach County can be so different, depending on the neighborhood, or even the people that are around you. It isn't easy for everyone to live in harmony, knowing that the person less than 5 minutes walk from you has a multimillion-dollar house that is right on the beach and a car that costs more than most of the normal people's houses. Some just cope with it, some give up and accept the failure, and then again some will rob, steal, and kill to obtain that which is their neighbor's, just so that they might have the same quality of life as the next man. This is the never-ending-battle, the never-ending-story of the classes. The only way to find true justice, is to not become a 'Victim of Justice'.

Janel was a beautiful and well-built dancer, which was really just a politically correct way of saying that she is a stripper. She has worked her last 3 years as a dancer, and actually was one of the few girls there that wasn't there to get her fix. She actually loved to dance, as strange as it sounds to some. She thoroughly enjoyed her job at T's Lounge, a gentleman's club which ironically was located right across the street from the Gun Club County Jail, Palm Beach County's main jail.

Janel didn't even use drugs as most people would assume because of her chosen profession. But that was just the stereotype, she would always say. Not all dancers got high. Not that she had anything against it, to each their own and all that, she couldn't hate on those who partook because her man was actually a drug dealer, as cliche as that was. It just wasn't something Janel had ever enjoyed doing.

On this particular night, Janel could not even partake in alcohol, though she actually enjoyed alcohol, but not tonight. Tonight, she was sober. She was sitting on the couch watching the big screen plasma television, 'Daddy's Little Girls' was the movie playing. It was a movie that she had loved; kind of a hood love story, she thought to herself.

Gabrielle Union was beautiful, and Idris Elba a great actor, and the way they portrayed their own struggles touched something inside Janel. She was already emotional because of her circumstances, and then she was also waiting on her man to call her. He was in jail so the jail calls weren't as easy as when she could just dial him up on her cell. She had to wait, and she would because his calls were the one thing that would get her through the tough week at the club. She was just sitting and thinking about him, not even really paying attention to the movie, she already knew it by heart, all she wanted to do at that moment was to talk to him and let him know that she just found out that she was pregnant. Once he had accepted that and depending on his reaction, she wanted to tell him that she couldn't wait to get him out of there and out here with her, so they could start a new life together and raise their child.

She had never told him, but she was in love with him. She had been in love with him since almost the first day that they had met and spent time together on Lake Worth Beach, at the bar located right there on the pier at the beach. That had been the best day of her life and she would always cherish those great memories and the time they had spent there, getting to know one another.

The knock at the door brought her out of her thoughts. She wasn't expecting any guests, one reason being this wasn't even her condo, another being that nobody knew where she was, only her man knew. Well, he had left her in charge of the condo while he was locked up, so she was going to have to see who it was.

Janel never lived here when he was out. They weren't actually a real couple, they were more like friends with benefits, as well as sleepovers, but she wanted more. She actually *needed* more, especially not that she wasn't the only one, she now had a baby to care for and think about as well. She was madly in love with him and had been planning on doing it tonight.

"What time could have been better to tell him that she was pregnant with his child and in love with him, than tonight?" she

10

thought. She was getting up to answer the door when a loud authoritarian voice came through the door. She was now just a little bit scared. She knew what had gotten her man into jail in the first place, and she knew that the dirty, corrupt cops had been involved.

"Open up! It's the DEA/ATF task force agents, and we need to speak with you Miss Pierre! Immediately! Open the door!" said the voice calling her by her man's last name. That actually comforted her, making her feel a false sense of security with the corrupt cops, and that was a mistake that she would have to regret forever.

"Hold up! I'm coming! Damn ..." she said as she started to open the door. Instead, the door came at her, pushed open, pushing her back and onto the floor.

"Hey!" she had shouted. But nobody was listening or even caring about her wellbeing.

The agents filed right in, past her. The one that pushed the door open tried to help her up, but not as carefully as she wanted, he was overly rough with her. All she could think about was the fact that she had a child growing in her belly. Her man's child in her belly, and she had to protect it from whatever this might be. He yanked her arm, pulling it almost out of its socket while pulling her back up and closing the front door that they had all rushed in through.

"What the hell is this? You can't be doing things like that! I have rights!" she said, screaming at the top of her lungs while trying to push away from the big guy who was now holding her,

11

restraining her. he clamped his bear-sized hand over her mouth, then pulled her back into the bedroom, which the other corrupt cops were already searching. It was her natural instinct to bite down on the hand that was being held so roughly over her mouth, so she did so.

"Fucking BITCH!" shouted the dirty cop, as he slapped her down so hard that she could hear her ears ringing. She again fell to the floor, this time hitting her head. She hit her head on the desk in the bedroom and it knocked her out like a light. She was completely out of it, much to the cop's satisfaction.

"Get this place empty, take everything that is remotely personal! I don't want anything left here that could have belonged to her!" said the lead corrupt cop. They started packing her clothes up, her pictures and personal effects as well. Anything that belonged to her was taken, leaving no trace of her at all.

Out of the blue, they got interested in the attire she was wearing, which was an extra-large T-shirt, riding up around her stomach and allowing them a view as she had had no underwear on. They saw her vagina and how it was shaven clean. Then one cop bent down and started to touch her there, playing with her vagina with his index finger. He was aroused when he felt her body's involuntary response to his touch. He wanted to go further, thinking that it was his touch that had done that to her body.

"Hey!" said their leader, Task Force Officer Hermanson. "Not right now! We do what we came here to do, and you can play around later." The last part, he said with a knowing smile. The cop

12

placed his handcuffs onto her wrists, then proceeded to pick her up in a fireman's carry and take her down to their government issued Suburban. The other officers quickly packed up all of their "evidence" and joined their leader in the truck, so they could get out of this condominium building before they were seen by anyone. They needn't worry, as they weren't even noticed by the only neighbor that Janel had befriended.

It was all done and over with in less than twenty minutes. They were gone; traces of Janel were also gone with them long before friends and family had finally got the super at the building to open the condo to do a wellness check on her. Janel was gone. Nobody would ever know where. But she was gone ...

Chapter One

PRESENT DAY

Wicks could feel the full effect of the bitterness hit him like a mack truck as he was getting settled in his little hiding spot in the bushes across the street from the dive bar that his target was rumored to frequent. Every couple of days he would duck away, making sure he wasn't being followed and that nobody even suspected the hidden intentions that he had, while doing personal surveillance on his target. He would take the city bus 'Palm-Tran', to the courthouse, and then follow his target from there on foot to a local dive bar called Margarita's. He awaited an opportunity every couple of days when he stalks his target, but the target would always leave the bar with a prostitute; a witness.

Wicks wanted no witnesses, as well as no evidence that he could possibly be connected to his target, so he kept his waist length, almost wrist thick, yellow dreads pulled back into a compression sock meant for diabetics, that he keeps hidden under a black jacket with a hood. His black jeans are baggy, but not too baggy. He needed them to be that way for the things that he was carrying in them. His black Rebook Classics tennis shoes, along with all of his gear was purchased in a Wall-Mart, located in Miami Gardens, which was a half an hour from where he now stood in West Palm Beach, home to some of the richest people in the world. Also, home to the poorest, like Wicks. But unlike most, riches did not matter to Wicks, only freedom did. Nothing else.

Wicks was now ducking down in the bushes as he does every time he is stalking his target. But when he stands, he does so at a slim 6'2, at 190lbs. He hasn't been out of prison long enough to put on any significant amount of weight. But even if he were out long enough, his 9 to 5 job at minimum wage would continue to starve him anyways. So, his ribcage is going to show either way, but luckily for him, so does his eight pack abs and wiry muscles on his slim arms and legs.

His complexion is "red." Red is a Southern term in Florida for someone who is of mixed races, or redbone, like the song from Childish Gambino. Not the gang color. His father is of Irish and Italian blood, from Chicago, his mother, Haitian, born in South Florida. One of the reasons that he is starving right now is because he took the offer of a white friend of his father who did him a favor by giving him a job at his MDH printing shop, at minimum wage to keep him out of trouble and employed. Which was a good thing overall, just not very motivating.

"Some favor starving me to death out here, but shit anything is better than prison, that's for sure."

Wicks had been given an emergency release from a Federal Penitentiary after 13 long years of ineffective appeals. All it ended up taking was a bust of the dirty ATF Task Force agents, who were participating in a criminal prostitution and drug ring, to spark off an investigation. They were investigated for their illegal investigation tactics, overzealous criminal grand jury indictments and over charging documents altered to look worse than they really were, as well as the ridiculous sentencing enhancements such as the 924(c). They are all under grand jury indictments themselves now, so I have the last laugh. Well, all but his target tonight, Vincent Rodriguez Jr; a fucking RAT. A cockroach that needed to be exterminated.

§§§§

Wicks had been a small potato on the street level cocaine dealer scale. When the agents and prosecutors Jeff McMillan had started to press Wicks into giving up his "Haitian Sensations" connection that he would buy his normal four and a half ounces of cocaine from, Wicks snapped and spit in the prosecutor's face. It wasn't his brightest move, he is quick to admit, but he would never turn rat, and he was thoroughly offended that they would even try him like a rat. So, he never regretted his move. "All those dirty ass pigs are in jail now," he laughed to himself, "and I'm out here."

It had been a crazy trial though, all the people that he loved and had taken care of, had turned rat and pointed at Wicks from the stand. That showed him what loyalty in this game would get you, just like Plies said in "100 Years." So, because of his determined refusal to provide "substantial assistance," as they called it, or rat, as Wicks would call it, he was continuously threatened and had many times been superseded, or had charges added to his criminal indictment. So, with his drugs and guns possessions charges, a normal citizen, as his jury thought, would not be facing a lot of time, in theory, but in the feds, all theoretical ideas are out the window, as the saying goes. The feds deeply believed in trial in "trial by ambush," where you would find out who was testifying against you the night before your trial would commence.

Wicks ended up with an all white jury, in which case, what more could be said? He ended up with an 11 year sentence for all of the drugs and guns possessions charges, but then because of his refusal to cooperate with the government, was overcharged and over-sentenced to some 924(c) charges, which in the feds means they can enhance the sentence by adding the guns and drugs together, alleging that the guns, although not used, were somehow protecting a drug enterprise, and therefore predicating the 924(c) enhancement, creating a whole new category of crimes that they can charge a 'Victim of Justice' with.

"Possession of firearms in furtherance of drug trafficking?" Wicks had angrily asked his rat lawyer, Vincent Rodriguez Jr. at the time.

"Yea, man," said the rat lawyer, "there's nothing I can do, you won't cooperate with the government, so they filed three 924(c) charges on you, that is 5 years for the first one, and then 25 years each for the second and third, plus the 11 years for the guideline sentence, so the judge cannot give you anything less than the 66 years in the Federal Penitentiary."

Wicks couldn't believe that this was how it worked in the FEDs, not until he saw this with his own eyes. It wasn't until later that he found out what had really happened.

"What y'all mean she can give consent to search my condo? She ain't even much live there! Ain't even no female clothes in the closets there! It was my certified bachelor pad!" Wicks yelled to his rat lawyer.

"Yes, but they assumed that she resided there because she answered the door," answered the rat lawyer smartly, justifying the agent's illegal actions.

"Man, Janel told me she told them that she ain't give them any permission, and she even told them it wasn't her condo!" he snapped back at him.

"Well, Mr. Pierre I'll have Mr. Peters look into that immediately, and if she is willing to testify to that in our Motion In Limini on Friday, then we most likely can get that excluded. Mr. McMillan won't want to go forward with a trial without that evidence, so we can get a low plea deal for a couple years and avoid a trial," said the rat lawyer, making Wicks feel confident in his position after so many months of feeling down in the dirt.

Little did he know that after the rat lawyer and naive private investigator that were working on his case left, Vincent Rodriguez told the investigator Peters not to pursue a conversation with Janel until the next day; a day late.

"Why?" asked Peters, "What possible reason could we have to delay in our talking to the one witness that could kill the government's whole case against our client?"

"Oh, don't start getting all self-righteous on me Peters, always remember the hand that feeds you. You would still be stalking spouses in divorce cases if not for my connections and my push for you into the criminal side of things, so you let me worry about the best interests of our firm," said the rat lawyer.

"I thought we were in it for the best interests of the clients," Peters replied indignantly. Later on, after that awkward conversation with his investigator, Mr. Peters, Vincent called a buddy of his, Agent Hermanson. It was not a coincidence that Hermanson was also the same agent who had illegally searched Wicks' condo many months earlier.

"Hermanson," the agent answered his cell phone while driving his unmarked Crown Victoria.

"Hey Herm, Vince here, you have a problem with that Pierre case," said the rat lawyer, easily betraying his client's trust and his oath.

"Oh yea. Is that right, what's that?"

"That stripper Janel, the one that answered the door when you went into Pierre's condo? Yea well, it seems that she doesn't seem to remember giving you guys the consent to search. Says she told you that, I guess you forgot that little detail, huh?" stated the rat lawyer laughing conspiratorially.

"Is that right? I don't seem to remember it that way ... " replied the agent.

"Yea well, its not a problem you can't get around, my guy

Peters is going to see her and take a formal statement from her tomorrow, so maybe, you can ... ahh ... refresh her recollection tonight, huh?"

"I'm on it, a little hottie if I remember correctly, right? Maybe hot enough for my team, huh?" laughed Agent Hermanson.

Unbeknownst to Wicks, that same night, while he was blowing up Janel's cell phone to tell her that the investigator would be coming by in the morning to get her statement, she was being raped, beaten, and kidnapped, by the dirty ATF Agents Hermanson, and several others that participated in their prostitution and drug ring. It almost broke Wick's heart to find out when Peters came to tell him that his girl, Janel, had disappeared, and her phone was not connected to any cell tower anywhere. Janel was gone. She was his only hope and she was dead, he could feel it in his heart. The absence and pain.

There was nothing in the world that could stop Janel from trying to get her boy, Wicks out of this hole that the dirty ATF and DEA agents had put him in. Even though they were mere "friends with benefits," they were truly friends, and they loved and cared for one another. Janel knew that Wicks had sex with other girls and that it was just a man being a man, but she knew that she was no "jump off" and she knew that Wicks cared for her as a person. Likewise, although Janel wined on the pole and popped her ass in the club, Wicks knew that he was not just a random dick to her. She also cared, it was mutual with them both.

Loud screams and cheers brought Wicks back to the present. He also readjusted his position in the bushes as he noticed his leg had fallen asleep. His target was rushing out of the dive bar as many of the black patrons were cheering the jury's guilty verdict of the dirty cop Chauvin, that had murdered in cold blood the famous and loved George Floyd in Minneapolis. Wicks, at the time, wasn't aware of what everyone was cheering for, he only had eyes for his target, who had, for the first time in months of Wicks' constant and intense surveillance, finally left the dive bar alone, to get away from the excited black people, who made up a good portion of his client base. He didn't notice that Wicks was following him, as Wicks was silently cursing his leg for limping, possibly drawing attention to himself.

Wicks had his throw-away snub nosed revolver .38 concealed in his right hand back jeans pocket. Wicks also had a small knife as well. He was hoping not to have to use any of his own items though, as that would make his crime premeditated, and he wanted it to look as if it were a crime of opportunity, not planned. Planned, it would limit the potential suspect list, and might ultimately cause his target's clients to come under suspicion, as well as his former clients. To avoid that, Wicks scanned the block in front of the dive bar for possible alternate weapons. He quickly settled on a rusty fence post from an old fence that had fallen into disrepair.

Wicks picked up the fence post and quickly crossed over to the other side of the street to the side that his target was currently walking on. Wicks had already had his gloves on, but as it turned out, he didn't need them. The fence post was very rusty. It would most likely not even hold any DNA or prints anyways. He was barefaced because he wanted his target to see his face and remember. He slid his Corona virus mask down and sped up to catch his target before he left his seedy surroundings. It was very important to Wicks that the crime happen near this dive bar that was frequented by many johns and prostitutes. An area his target, as a married man, a pillar of the community, and a respected officer of the courts, had no business being around. One of the reasons the target would leave his car in the courthouse parking lot, and walk down the street to do his dirty deeds, cheating on his wife of twenty plus years.

The entire area of the downtown West Palm Beach is right next to a hood known as Tamerind Avenue, and apparently the gentrification plans there by the city had been unsuccessful as nobody from the middle class wanted to live downtown and near the Tamerind Avenue area. It did however serve the purpose for the dirty lawyers and judges who wanted to go and "trick off" or "slum it," because all these dive bars and prostitution houses were within a quick walking distance.

Being that the West Palm Beach County Courthouse, and the even more serious Federal building on Clematis Street, as well as the dirty lawyers' own law offices are so close with these prostitution trade and drug trade's location of business, it had blossomed into something special downtown. For Wicks, this made his mission even easier, killing two birds with one stone, taking out his target while simultaneously exposing his target for his own extracurricular activities for the world to see when they track his movement back to the dive bar and the area known for the drugs and prostitution transactions.

"Hey I know you, don't I?" yelled Wicks as he caught up to his target at the corner behind the little Arab store, and the alley that backs the store. His target flinched as he looked at the tattooed face of a hard man that was looking intently back into his soul. He wasn't able to respond, or even register who this goon was, before he felt a blow to his jaw and he heard a ringing in his ears. He felt someone grab a hold of his ankle and drag him back into the alley behind the store before he even knew that he was on the ground.

This was exactly why the target left his Rolex watch at home and wore his much less expensive Movado when he was working out of the court, as he would often trick off after work. He never neglected to respect the fact that he was walking through a dangerous area in downtown West Palm Beach. He knew the possibility of being robbed always exists so he planned not to buck and just give it up to this tattoo faced man. It had happened so fast that he never had the chance to wonder why someone who had tattoos on his face would rob him barefaced without so much as a Corona virus mask on.

Wicks got his target in the alley next to the walled in dumpster area for the corner store. He tested the fence post by

23

hitting his target as hard as he could, directly in his left ankle. The target's eyes bugged out and he tried to scream from the excruciating pain, but Wicks had intentionally broke his target's jaw with the second swing of the fence post, so much that all that could come out was a garbled moan. Wicks didn't care. He needed his target to listen, not talk, and listen he most certainly would.

"Look at me! Look at my face!" Wicks yelled in his target's face. "Take a real close look at me ... Nah, Mr. Lawyer-man, not the tattoos, but think back to before I got these tattoos on my face marking my oppression ..." Wicks reveled, smiling in his revenge. Finally, some justice for Janel, some accountability after all this time.

Wicks could see the recognition in his target's face, and he smiled with the knowledge that he had the ability to finally accomplish his goal and get accountability for Janel, as well as close the chapter in his life that had been keeping him more of a captive than his 6 x 12 cell, in which he had spent the last 13 years of his life. He smiled with his gold "slugs" shining in his mouth as he pulled an old, faded picture out of his pocket. He slowly turned it so that his target could see the image it captured. His smile grew. He could see that he was getting through to the old lawyer.

"Now you can see that what you did 13 years ago did not go unnoticed, and now you can make amends for causing her death," said Wicks.

The target's eyes bugged as Wicks hit him in the ribs, and then on the side of the head. Ribs cracking and head bleeding, he was trying to say something. Wicks hit him again and opened up another cut above his left eye. The target was now out of it, in and out of consciousness, and rolling his head left and right. Wicks was very strong, his blows causing the maximum damage after so many years of strenuous working out, and meticulous training in close quarters combat, in small prison cells, fighting for his life. A never-ending battle inside the belly of the beast.

"To you she was just some stripper, some witness, an obstacle in your way to get what you wanted, but to me she was my friend! She was special!" snapped Wicks, following up with his kick to his target's face for emphasis.

Wicks took a look around his area and saw that he was well concealed, the trash dumpster wall blocking any vantage from the alley or the street. He looked at his target and his already damaged ribs to ensure that he was conscious, still looking and paying attention to the photograph of Janel and suffering for his crimes against her. Wanting to project his pain to his target and cause the damage equal to that in which his target had caused him and Janel with his selfish actions, he smiled.

"Yea, I guess I can admit it to you since you are my target and won't be telling anyone anytime soon, I loved her. She was my best friend, my partner, my homie, and I loved her but never told her. So now you can understand why I've come back after all these years, you can know in your heart why I'm not wearing any mask to conceal my face, I. Don't. Need. One!" he yelled each part as he swung the fence post at his target's shoulder as he said each word, breaking his collar bone clean into two parts. The target moaned as loud as his broken jaw would allow, but he was already beyond the point of feeling any pain, his pain threshold long past, agony having put him out.

"You think I enjoy this?" Wicks asked. "I don't enjoy this job set before me, but I'm finna finish what you and your crooked ass agent friends started. Piece of SHIT!" Wicks kicked him again on cue when he said the last word even louder than before.

The target mumbled something as he cried so desperately, begging for mercy, and then Wicks set down the fence post dramatically, making the target to hope it's done. "It's only just getting started Mr. Lawyer-man," laughed Wicks again.

Wicks reached into his target's pockets and emptied the contents onto the ground. He grabbed the target's wedding band and Movado watch and placed them into his own jean pockets, along with the cash and credit cards out of his wallet. He then threw the wallet into the dumpster, thinking that the target wouldn't be needing it where he would be heading to ...Hell.

The target's face was full of the physical pain that he was being exposed to. It was the most excruciating pain he had ever endured in his life. He tried to roll onto his side but couldn't move. Wicks reached into his own pocket and pulled out a Lifestyles small condom. Fear showed on the target's face, him uncomprehendingly thinking the worst. Wicks noticed and laughed aloud.

"Ha ha ha, don't worry Mr. Lawyer-man, it's not what you think," said Wicks laughing hard, and finally enjoying himself, despite the task set in front of him. He took the condom, wiped it on the target's hands, and then placed the wrapper all over his fingertips to apply his prints onto the wrapper. He then did the same thing with the bag of heroin that he pulled out of his pocket, all for the benefits of the CSI that would later find this planned scene just the way Wicks wanted it to look for them. Wicks dropped the condom wrapper by his target's hands, and the actual condom closer to the rear of the dumpster, intending to make the scene look like a prostitution and robbery gone wrong. Wicks looked all around the area to make sure he didn't leave anything that wasn't a prop for his intended scene. Nothing that shouldn't be there and everything that should. Nothing that could ever come back to haunt him later. He considered himself an expert after all the time spent in prison watching the real crime shows, learning how someone could get away with anything, mostly murders.

Wicks took out the bag of heroin and opened it up, then he placed his other hand over the target's mouth. The target's eyes bugged out as he struggled to breathe through his nose. Wicks allowed for the exhalation, and then placed the baggie under his target's nose. He tipped it just as the target desperately sucked in for air, and in turn, the heroin, into his nasal cavity, almost making him choke on it. The target's eyes rolled into the back of his head as the heroin hit his blood stream. Wicks let the bag fall away. He dropped it next to the pocket lent and change that had come out of the target's pockets. Wicks wished that his target had just left Janel alone, never involved her with his situation. He even lightly blamed himself for even calling her as a witness in the first place, but this target in front of him was the main reason for her death and there could be no excuses for that. He would have to pay for that.

Wicks stood up. He looked around again seeing that everything was where he wanted it to be. All except a living, breathing target. He leaned down and grabbed his fence post, took one last look around, and moved next to his target's head. He thought back to a fight he had seen in the penitentiary yard over a decade ago. A white guy on the softball field had swung a baseball bat at another guy, who was later identified as a "chomo" or a child molester as they are known in prison, and hit him full in his larynx as he had moved slightly up, missing the much harder and actual intended target he was aiming for. An accidental anomaly, but a fatal one for the chomo, as he had died in almost two minutes after being struck in the neck and having his larynx crushed, preventing him from breathing. An amazing anomaly, but a fatal one all the same. But here Wicks had every intention of making this one look as accidental as the one he himself had witnessed years ago. He loved it because it was so simple and yet possible.

Wicks had not known exactly how things would play out when he finally did catch his target alone. He knew that he did trick with known prostitutes, but he wanted to make sure that he had drugs in his system in one way or the other, hence, the heroin. He had many different scenarios in his mind, after all, he had been planning and plotting on avenging Janel's death for almost 13 years. Dreaming and thinking about how he would handle his target. Now that the time had finally arrived, and he was staring at the man responsible for selling him out, and more importantly, his girl Janel's disappearance and presumed death, and now it would have an end. There would be closure, but the pain would always remain with him. Forever. A never-ending agony.

Wicks tensed himself. He raised the fence post about his head and took a last look at the living, breathing, target lying there in a heroin induced semi-coma, and regretted that his target would leave this world in such a peaceful coma. He should have to suffer, feeling every terrifying and agonizing moment of this reckoning he more than deserved for his participation in the taking of his beloved Janel. What he took from Wicks cannot be replaced, Janel is gone forever, and his reckoning is here. This was a retribution, for her. For him.

"JANEL! !" Wicks screamed as he brought the fence post down right dead on his target's neck. The target's larynx was instantly crushed and he was completely suffocated within three minutes while Wicks watched, looking into his eyes until the very last minute. The target was no longer breathing. He was no longer alive, he could do no more evil. Wicks let out a breath and dropped the fence post next to the body, filled with relief.

"Rest in piss Mr. Lawyer-man," said Wicks as he started his walk towards the bus stop for the Palm Tran. It was time to move on, but he would never forget her.

Wicks took off the gloves, turned his jacket inside out in case of any blood splatter, and put the gloves into the pockets. He was relieved that it was finally over. His target was finally dead. The Rat Lawyer was dead and gone. Rest in piss Vincent Rodriguez Jr. Janel can rest now. He was done, he walked away satisfied.

Chapter Two

Detective Nash was not completely cynical. She was more of a realist, and as such, she knew her Vic had no business anywhere near this area they had found him in, if he wasn't into something illegal. He doesn't belong.

Shelby Nash is a Detective in the Palm Beach County Sheriff's Office: and was just given a chance in the Robbery-Homicide Division in her new Department. She had received a lot of praise in her handling of the infamous arrest in the "Romeo and Juliet" cases out in Miami-Dade a year and a half ago, and was just now getting her chance at a reward, her reward being the promotion to the more elite squad. But nobody could feel her pain. The case was widely known, having been covered on nationwide news, and she, made to look the hero. But nothing could make her whole again. Nothing could replace her Tomas. Her love, her life, her partner. Tomas Nash had been her husband of 3 years. Her Soulmate and now he was gone, never to return to her.

They were such opposites, it was a small miracle they could even stand each other, but Shelby's taste was a perfect example of the old saying "Opposites Attract", as she had always liked what was different and challenging. She was 5'2 and 135 pounds with a bubble butt, powerful legs, and thick thighs from riding her motorcycle all the time. She had a beautiful face and a small, petit upper body frame. But she was every bit as bad as any video vixen in a Rick Ross or Kodak Black video, and even at the age of 29, she could dance as well as them too. He on the other hand, had been a lanky 6 feet and 175 pounds with very little muscle mass, and was very uncomfortable on the dance floor. She a detective, he a journalist. She an avid Trump supporter while he was a certified and proud Democrat who likened Trump with Lucifer himself. She was a beautiful dark skinned Haitian, and he, Cuban and white, pale faced, and awkward with a capital A, yet a very talented writer.

Somehow they fit like a hand in glove though, and quickly fell in love and got married. Only one thing disturbed their marital bliss, and that was the discussion of procreation: He wanted kids and she wanted to pursue her career. But besides that one thing, everything else they differed on was just background noise in their relationship. They were perfect.

Shelby Nash wore her hair flat ironed and pulled into a bun in back, ever since she had started sparring with her ex-Mossad Israeli friend, Sonja, and she taught her that it was the best way to keep her hair while being so active. Her friend, Sonja who was nicknamed "Gal", not because of her resemblance to that of the gorgeous actress, but because of being ex-Mossad, and having an accent similar to that of the real Gal Gadot. She had taught Shelby the art of fighting by way of Krav Maga, in which she could use her small size to pivot and use numerous types of arm bars, locks, and pressure points to end a fight within 3 moves. Shelby loved her Krav Maga and missed her friend Gal. After losing her Tomas, she could no longer stay in Miami-Dade. She was offered a position with the highest paying Police Department in America, the West Palm Beach branch of the Palm Beach County Sheriff's Office, and quickly accepted, mostly to start over fresh and to forget her pain.

It had been a normal day in Miami and she and Tomas had been in his Toyota Camry, driving together to catch lunch. They tried to have lunch together at least two or three times a week, or as much as their busy schedules and careers would allow. He was driving that day, as she rode a bike normally as her every day driver, and at a red light down town, a federal prison bus going to FDC Miami pulled up behind his Camry. He didn't even register the gun shots before Shelby was jumping out of the passenger seat of his Camry pulling her police issued .40 caliber Glock, model 22 semi-automatic service pistol. As Shelby chased the first suspect she saw, she didn't see the other suspect, a female, and didn't know what the other gunshot she heard would mean a few split seconds later.

It had all come out later, a 16 year old kid had single handedly taken on the prison bus to free his 14 year old girlfriend from custody. He had shot three federal BOP prison guards, two of which were fatal. He had gotten her cuffs off of her and ran out to check on his get away car, but he had hit the prison bus from behind to get the guards to open, making them think that it was a simple traffic accident, so the front end of his stolen vehicle was totaled. He was then confronted by the third guard, the one who had lived, and shot him five times in his vest. That's when Shelby came out and caught him off guard, forcing him to duck behind the rear of the bus and crashed car. Shelby quickly gave chase, unknowingly leaving her husband, and his Camry, open and vulnerable to the second suspect. She was a 14 year old Cuban girl, who had taken one of the guns from the dead guards on the bus, and pointed it at Tomas' head intending a carjacking.

Shelby followed the kid who had shot the guard in front of her in his vest, but she went behind the car that had rammed the bus from behind, which in turn gave her a clear view point of the kid running toward the bus' front end. It also showed her clear view of the little girl pointing the gun at Tomas while pulling him out of the Camry as he was trying to talk her down, not knowing that she was a cold-blooded murderer as well.

Everything slowed down for her, it was as if she was hovering over her own body, and not even participating in the actual horrors she was witnessing first person. She screamed for them to freeze. In that same instant, the startled girl accidentally pulled the trigger of her stolen deputy gun. Shelby shot twice, sending two of her .40 caliber, full metal jackets, through the girls center mass. She was so small that her little teenaged body flew 10 feet back into the intersection. The boy quickly turned, and with no apparent visible emotion, he fired at Shelby. Shelby fired back. His bullet went wide, Shelby's bullet struck home in his upper chest, ending the confrontation, and Tomas' life in less than a five second window of time. Shelby ran to Tomas, but all in one look, she could see by the opened eyes and hole in his forehead, that Tomas was never going to smile his goofy smile at her again. She would never again awake to a sweet smelling breakfast he had made lovingly as he would serve her in bed. Never again would they argue over kids or make love in their pool they had built in their backyard. Her beloved was gone. Now, so was the good half of her. She felt like dying in that moment, and every moment since then.

Later, when she was being debriefed about the confrontation, the coroner was removing the little 14 year old girl's body, and the 16 year old boy had been rushed to the hospital, she found out the details about Jose "Disco" Rivera and Barbara Alfonso. The boy was sending his girlfriend to go and flirt with dope boys, and while she would distract them with her pretty face and teenage body, he would slide up behind them with his Remington 870 shotgun, loaded with 12 gauge slugs instead of buckshot pellets, and rack the slide for effect, while Barbara would take all money, jewels, and drugs, leaving some very mad victims of the set up behind them, along with some empty pockets as well.

But one time, one of the drug dealers' homies had gotten control over the situation when he had walked up unexpectedly on Disco armed and had taken his gun from him. They had then proceeded to continually rape Barbara, taking turns, and made Disco watch. They then made the mistake of thinking that Disco and Barbara, whom the media had dubbed "Romeo and Juliet Killers" for how Disco would come and "save" Barbara, were just harmless kids, so they let them go. Disco wanted to kill these guys who had raped his girl and disrespected them both, and he wanted her to see him do it. But it was to his astonishment, when he finally did make his move, that Barbara let her trigger go before he ever could. They took their first four lives that day; together.

So after those killings, they agreed to just murder their victims because they were all guilty of raping Barbara just by looking at her teenage body. Soon thereafter, Barbara had gotten nabbed on a fluke. A truancy officer who had seen her out of school with her backpack on and he surprised her, then noticed blood on her shoes and arrested her. By then they had left over 15 bodies at nine different crime scenes behind them. Her backpack was subsequently searched, uncovering jewels, drugs, and the guns she had used in their last robbery. Disco and her had separated, and so Disco remained free and awaited her transfer to the Federal Detention Center in Down town Miami from juvenile placement, for his attempt to rescue her from captivity, as serial killings were considered to be under Federal jurisdiction. Neither of the kids had any family to go to, and had met in a group home and walked away together, so they were all the other had, and so Disco felt he needed to save Barbara. Only nobody could have guessed an off duty Shelby would happen to be at the same red light and would end up putting a stop to their crime spree, and take Barbara's life, while also losing Tomas' life all in one instant.

The more that Shelby grieved her loss of Tomas, the more obsessed she became about the "Romeo and Juliet" murders and robberies. Shelby studied psychology, then researched child placement policies of DCF, or Department of Children and

Families, and tried to figure out how this could have happened. How the system could have let these kids down. Let her down. Let Tomas down.

She couldn't live with herself, not only because of the loss of her husband, but also because she had shot two teenage kids. It would haunt her and wake her in nightmares as she tries to sleep, how she almost had killed Disco and certainly had taken Barbara's life. Although Barbara had taken Tomas from her, she didn't see it that way, she saw it as the failed system had been the one responsible for taking Tomas away from her. If the system had just done its job, there wouldn't be kids like Babara and Disco running the streets with guns and taking lives. She had seen it. Thus began a hurtful blaming of the system. When she had taken Babara's life, Disco turned and fired at her. There was no anger, no sadness, no hesitation, it was weird, it was as if he was an empty shell, he had no emotion at all showing. It was unlike anything she had ever seen, nothing like any book or movie, just a cold absence of humanity in him. He was now at Terre Haute, Indiana, on death row, for all of the lives that he had taken. He had never given a statement, never said a word. It was like Jose "Disco" Rivera was no longer amongst the living, he was dead already, a victim of this system; a 'Victim of Justice'.

Shelby had done extensive research and investigations into the DCF, group homes, orphanages, and how the policies and guidelines had changed over the years. What she had found astonished her and changed her whole perspective, not only on the practices of those in charge of wayward kids, but also on immigration and criminal justice as well. She started making noise amongst her colleagues and her friends, and moved on to local politicians and state officials or representatives. Her assistance and dedication paid off when she was called upon to testify about the Romeo and Juliet murders in the judicial committee upon Capital Hill in front of Chuck Grassley and Jeff Sessions for the vote on the criminal justice reform. She was one of the ones that had been a major push behind the First Step Act that had passed into law on December 18th of 2018, signed by President Trump. It had paid off again when her experience in the Romeo and Juliet cases, and her pursuit into their lives and the circumstances in the system, made her a virtual expert in the field. So, she turned it into an obsession, and continued to try to understand what had contributed to the events that had ended Tomas' and Barbara's lives, and so many other kids' lives whose stories go untold.

Shelby could not find any solace in anything she did and eventually made for West Palm Beach, to start a new life without the harsh memories caused by that hard time in her life. She did everything that she could in Palm Beach County in order to help make her community a better place. She joined Special Task Forces, gave time to talk at meetings and classes, but she never could find any comfort after seeing the evils of the system up close and personal. All that changed when her only living relative, her big sister had reminded her of all the happy times they had had in their Miami Youth Center, not far from where they had grown up in Little Haiti.

"You should maybe go over to the closest Youth Center in Palm Beach County, and be to the kids there, what Miss Mable was to us when we had lost Daddy, and Mama was struggling with two jobs to provide for us, remember how much we loved going over there Shell. All the fun that we had?" her sister asked.

Shelby and her sister Antionette had lost their father in a car accident when they were in their teens, and it had left their mother with many bills because the family car didn't have any insurance. It had been especially hard because their father Antione had doted on his two little girls whom he had adored, and their mother was a hard woman by comparison. So they had found themselves welcomed at the Youth Center, and especially by Mable Watson, better known as "Miss Mable" as she preferred to be called. They had been taken by all of the love and caring that Miss Mable had always shared with them. She had been like a Grandmother the two Haitian girls had never had. Being Haitian at that time was especially hard on the girls when Haitians in South Florida were treated like outcasts, often put down for their strict households, morals, as well as their immigration status. So Miss Mable had made the sisters feel right at home at the Youth Center, and they would never forget all of the kindness she had given them.

The sisters credited their motivation, persistence, and their ambitions all to Miss Mable, who had worked with the small girls in their respective extra-curricular activities; ballet for Antoinette, and gymnastics for Shelby. To Shelby, gymnastics turned to track and then to boxing, which had ultimately turned her into a cop. As for Anoinette, she did ballet back in the Youth Center and now she was an amazing ballerina, renowned going from France to Russia, and from Iceland to Greenland, for the most exclusive ballets in the world, sometimes as many as 6 or 7 performances in a single month.

Shelby had always wanted to make a difference in her society. She had grown up dealing with more than the average black yankee. As a Haitian, growing up was harder.

Shelby was born at Jackson Memorial in Miami, but her father had always told her about growing up in Port Au Prince. He had taught her to be very grateful to be in this country that their whole family loved so much. But Shelby still wanted to make her community better, and so she was determined to be a cop and protect those who couldn't protect themselves, and to serve those who needed help. She took it as seriously as possible. To protect and serve. It was more than a slogan to her; more than a concept. It was her motto and she lived her life by it, and it was how she wanted to spend her life. She honestly wanted to leave the world in better shape than when she had entered it. How many people could honestly say that? She thought to herself. That was one of the many things that made Shelby special, made her different from anyone else. She was dedicated to her service of others and vowed to bring change to a dying system. She was pure, in that she wanted the best for those around her.

"What do you have for me Jones?" Shelby had just walked

into a crime scene and now was talking to the CSI Tech after the coroner had taken the body away to the medical examiner's office.

"Sorry Nash," answered the CSI Tech, "I literally have nothing here! The murder weapon? It's a damn fence post with more rust than a 1930 Model T. It won't hold prints on all that rust, and forget DNA! It just pulled the cotton right off of the swabs we used so I doubt we can get any DNA off of that. I will run the condom wrapper and the plastic ziplock drug baggie also, just maybe our perp touched them, but I'm doubtful ..."

"Hey Nash, is this your first time catching a solo case?"

"Yea," answered Shelby," but I'm sure that Bill will be nearby to assist me."

"Shitty case to start with ... shit, well good luck Nash," and with that, the crime scene technician was gone, leaving Shelby with her thoughts, shitty case and all.

Jones reported and relayed that he had already cased the area and found no cameras that might help them identify their doer. The ones inside the Arab store were all located inside and so would do no good he had said. No good. She had sent some uniforms to talk to the nearby homeless and street walkers, it would be no surprise to her if in this neighborhood nobody saw nothing. Hear no evil, see no evil, speak no evil was the slogan for this area and anyone who broke that silence knew what would happen to them. The general consensus among all of the officers further backed that opinion upon completion of their respective parts of the grid that they had worked on.

Shelby decided to go to the medical examiner's office to see about the autopsy and to get a TOD or time of death, so she could check the store's cameras to see who had gone into the store around that time. Her killer might have bought a pack of cigarettes after the murder and she just needed to know when that was. Yea right, and she would get a diamond Lamborghini sent by a long lost relative! She wasn't very optimistic, she knew, but she could only hope to catch a break on this first case.

After the M.E.'s office, she had an appointment with the activities director at the Youth Center in West Palm that she was hoping to start volunteering at. Her sister had never before led her astray, and by suggesting she go there, Shelby knew this would be a great step in curing her pain and helping her soul. It might even help to start the long process of helping her hurting heart to start healing itself. Again, all she could do was hope and pray. She could have never guessed that this one move could help to change her whole life and her actual thoughts and views on life itself.

Chapter Three

The Morzella family was a solid and good family of five. There was the father and husband Eric, the mother and wife Laurie, and the kids. The two grown sons were Eric James, also known as EJ, and then the middle brother Mikey, and the youngest and most beloved son, Lil Ray, as in "Ray of Sunshine". They called Lil Ray that because although an unexpected child, he was loved no less, and his little personality at eleven years old, was a Ray of Sunshine for real, and bigger than life despite his small stature.

Both of the older brothers were proud Marines and serving in Afghanistan, much to the family's pride. But little Ray was home and kept the family busy. Ray was very active. He loved sports and loved boxing even more than any other sport in the world.

But one thing that he hated about boxing is that, with his sweet nature, he could never allow himself to hurt his opponent. In boxing though, unfortunately, that is a necessity. So little Ray's Uncle Jean would work with him, and a few of his friends as well, a few times a week at the Youth Center. His uncle would also talk to some of the bigger kids there about his history and about selling drugs and the time he had spent in prison for his crimes. Almost all the kids at the Youth Center listened and respected Ray's uncle. He had been through a lot, so he had a lot of knowledge and experience to share, so Ray wasn't the only one that was always looking forward to his uncle's visits to the Youth Center, there were quite a few of the kids that also liked and looked up to him as well.

"Stick and move Ray! Work those feet! Move around Ray!"

Ray's uncle was shouting at him from the sideline as he watched Ray spar with a small kid about ten or eleven years old. Ray could easily spar with older larger kids because his uncle was always spending time with him and working with him. So Ray's hands were known to be futuristic compared to kids around his age, making him a real contender.

Ray got the other kid against the ropes, and then he backed off a little bit with a few jabs, allowing the other kid to gain some ground on Ray. It was something that never failed with Ray. He was a better fighter than this kid, better athlete, faster and stronger, despite his smaller size. He always eased up when it was time to end the fight, it was something that was increasingly frustrating to Ray's uncle, as he couldn't understand Ray's mountainous mercy.

"Ok, time! Ray get over here," said Ray's uncle Jean.

When Ray broke off, headed toward his corner, and his uncle, he was smiling big at his uncle Jean.

"I got him good, didn't I Unc?" Ray asked, barely catching his breath from the work out.

"Yea buddy, you got him, but we need to have that talk again about following through ..." his Uncle Jean couldn't help but smile though, knowing how Ray was about pressing his opponent or mostly from his fear of hurting him.

Ray lowered his head as his smile faded, realizing that he had once again let his opponent off of the ropes when he had control of the fight, and could have pummeled the other kid against the ropes, but failed to follow through.

"But you said to respect the sport, and not to try to end a fight too quickly or get greedy," replied Ray sadly, afraid of disappointing his uncle.

"No, you did alright buddy, but when a victory falls into your lap, you take it, and don't let up when you got em on the ropes! That was your fight buddy! If you are going to win your golden gloves, you gotta stop letting up on these junior league fights, you are way better than you been givin' Ray...and you know this maaaann..." Jean said the last part to lighten the mood, by trying to imitate Ray's favorite character off of his favorite movie 'Friday' called 'Smokey'.

As he was walking with Ray, his attention was suddenly drawn away as he saw Sammy, the head administrator of the Youth Center, walking with the most beautiful and absolutely stunning, ebony beauty that he had ever seen. Her hair was pulled back into a no-nonsense bun, but her eyes were amazing and inviting. Her full lips were parted just slightly enough to show her pearly white set of teeth. She seemed to notice Jean as well, and saw him looking back at her. She had a body that was short and thick, with strong, thick legs, and an amazing apple bottom. She had on an athletic grey sports bra, and compression leggings that accentuated her body, almost causing Jean to walk straight into one of the heavy punching bags that were randomly located around the gym. He corrected his direction, silently laughing to himself about how

45

a woman hadn't commanded his attention like this in a long time.

She had B-Cup breasts that sat up high on her chest, as if proud to be a part of this moving art. Jean was locked in, completely mesmerized. As Sammy noticed Jean's attention and Little Ray continued on to the locker rooms, Jean started over towards the pair under the guise of checking a scheduled event that he had already confirmed. Sammy knew this, but played along as well.

"Hey Sammy, excuse me ma'am, what day is that event I need to have Ray and Los ready for?" asked Jean while taking a closer look at the beautiful ebony queen. Los was Ray's best friend from school that Jean was also training.

"Oh, hey Jean, I was just looking for you, let me introduce you to Shelby Nash, she is planning on joining us here at the Youth Center. Shelby, this is Jean Pierre, he is one of our best volunteers and mentors here. He works with a lot of the kids on boxing and basketball, and hopefully soon, football, if we can ever get the gear we need, as well as a photography program that he intends to start, which is being delayed due to lack of the funds and equipment," said Sammy, introducing them and making her aware of his contributions and inspirations to the kids.

"Nice to meet you Mrs. Nash, it's great to get any help that we can around here," said Jean truly meaning it. Aside from the fact that she was completely beautiful as well as bad to death, Jean was always impressed when volunteers come to help without pay, only seeking to selflessly help the kids, to make the community a better place, and to keep the kids away from the streets and drugs.

"Oh ... " Shelby was astounded, "nice to meet you as well Mr. Pierre, have you been here for long?" She couldn't help but question why they would allow some gold-toothed, tattoo-wearing, basic street thug around all these poor kids.

"Yea, I been here round six months or so, ever since I got out of prison, but I been coming here since I was a shawty, so it's like a second home to me," answered Jean. He was starting to notice her apprehension and started to say something but luckily Sammy beat him to it.

"I've known Jean for a very long time, seen him come and go, and then change, and I can assure you he is all about the kids and has made remarkable changes in his life just so he can help the kids stay off of the path that he had taken," explained Sammy.

"I'm sorry Sam," said Jean, "did I miss something? Is she some sort of auditor or something?" he asked looking at Shelby. He just wasn't understanding why Sammy was trying to explain his motivations in working with the kids, when it was so obvious to others the selflessness he had inside of him.

"Nah Jean," laughed Sammy in an attempt to soften the blow, "Shelby Nash is a detective with the Palm Beach County Sheriff's Office, and she is probably wondering about your status since you mentioned being incarcerated." He then looked at Shelby, "Am I right Mrs. Nash?"

"Yea," answered Shelby tentatively, "the thought did cross my mind for sure." With that being said, she looked Jean up and down suspiciously, and a bit rudely for Jean's taste.

"Well," snapped Jean, "let me assure you that I came here to help that lil' boy over there, my nephew and I do this here for him, and all the other kids in the system. *Your* system, Miss Police Officer, since it has let down and given up on them, so don't you worry about why *I'm* here, you gots to worry about why you are here, Miss Officer, I'll holla Sam, have a good one."

Afterwards, he turned and went to the locker rooms steaming about that confrontation with the damn cop. Here he was thinking that she was so beautiful and fine, and it turned out that she was a damn cop. No less as bad as those dirty cops that had set him up with the ATF and killed Janel. Jean was now in a bad mood thinking about Janel and all those dirty cops. He went to the parking lot to his 1979 Buick Riviera, the one with the 403 Olds while he awaited his nephew Lil' Ray, his original reason for getting involved with the Youth Center and these kids in the first place.

"You want to tell me what that was all about?" asked Shelby after she watched Jean, who in her opinion looked like a complete thug, storm off, and her and Sammy walked toward his office. Sammy sighed, then searched his desk drawer for his volunteer file on Jean. He found it, then quickly handed it over to her and said, "Jean 'Wicks' Pierre." Shelby took the file, then started to glance through it.

"He was set up by those dirty ATF agents and task force officers, I'm sure you've heard about it on the news. He did 13 years of a 66 year sentence for non-violent victimless crimes. 924(c) charges are what they were called, and until the fatal shooting of an unarmed black man downtown, and the subsequent investigation after the ATF agents were trying to cover it up, planting evidence on him, saying he was armed was fully exposed, he was sitting in prison."

"The Johnson case? Jesus, he was one of the cases those dirty cops had overcharged and over-sentenced with 924(c) counts federally? Wow, no wonder he reacted like that finding out that I was a police officer," said Shelby while her mind tried to imagine what he could have possibly gone through and what he must have felt while he was going through it.

"Yea," responded Sammy, "now you see why we try to keep him around here as much as possible, have him focused on the positives such as the kids, and use him to keep them off of the streets. These kids look up to him so much, as he represents every single thing that they have to deal with on a daily basis ... guns, drugs, violence, but then they see all he has been through, and he is there for them, and works with them in sports, talks to them about his struggles, and listens to them about their own struggles and relates to them in that way. He is truly an asset to our center, and a big brother to all of these kids."

"That sounds great, " Shelby said, handing back the file, "I hate when a group of bad apples make the whole apple tree of law enforcement look bad and dirty." She looked into Sammy's sad eyes, "I'm sorry I judged the book by the cover, that's not usually my way, and I usually am a good judge of character," she said with conviction that even Sammy could tell.

"It's all good Shelby, you will have a chance to get to know us as you spend time here at the Youth Center, he is always here when he isn't working," said Sammy truly proud of the man that Jean had become, and all that he did there.

Shelby wasn't sure how to take Jean's response to finding out she was a detective, but she was a good cop, and soon he, and the rest of Palm Beach County would see that not *all* cops were bad. There were some who were trying to do some good. "Hell," she thought, "why else would she come to donate her time at the Youth Center but to help these kids?" She hoped the police as a whole could eventually earn the trust of the community back. After all the damage and broken trust those dirty cops had caused, she knew it wouldn't be an easy task, but she wasn't scared of hard work, she liked anything to take her mind off of her Tomas, and anything to help her community in Tomas' name.

"Shell, it's been two years sweetie," said her sister Antoinette, "you've got to try to move on, you can't keep putting yourself through this. But I am happy that you finally went to the Youth Center, how is the one up there?" Antoinette still lived in Miami with her husband of almost a decade and her kids, two boys; aged 5 and 8, whom Shelby adored as if they were hers.

"Oh, it's cool," replied Shelby, "nice people there, a lot of great kids that need help just like we did at that age, and a guy that looks like he could be a gangsta out of a Rick Ross video, gold teeth, face tats and all."

"Sounds interesting," said Antoinette, "I'm sure he is pretty amazing if he is volunteering there and they are letting him around the kids."

"He was...I mean he is ... "

Later that night though, Shelby couldn't sleep and kept pondering about Jean. Just like she had done so much research and investigation into the "Romeo & Juliet" case, she wanted to understand this Jean, she wanted to know what made him tick, and how he came to be such a valuable mentor at the Youth Center. He had nothing to do with Romeo & Juliet, or her loss of Tomas, but yet he was the victim of the same failed system that her loss had stemmed from. The broken criminal justice system, Department of Children and families, and Immigration, all parts of a bigger picture and deeper problems in society. Systemic racism she had seen within the system she was a part of. She always felt she could make a difference though, and she knew one day she would. She would change it from the inside. She is inside. "A change must come from within," she thought to herself.

Chapter Four

"Lil' Fade" had just finished his workout with his cousin Demetrius "Big Meet" St. Clair. He was trying to get ready for the competition to win his golden gloves level event, and was well on his way, since Big Meet was training him. In Haiti, there was almost nobody that was a better boxer than Meet, and there was absolutely nobody that would get into the ring with him. He was known for head butts, elbows, and even sneak, below the belt blows, when he could get away with it, and he was teaching Lil' Fade to go even harder. He was also teaching him the dope game, and using him to recruit his little friends to sell heroin and coke, all out of the Youth Center gym and their schools in West Palm and Lake Worth cities. He paid them only enough to buy some Jordans or Airmax shoes, but to them, it was a lot.

Big Meet was one of the lieutenants in the "Haitian Sensations" street gang or cartel, depending on your view point on that issue. They believed that there wasn't a drug that was not worth trafficking in. From weed, to heroin, from GHB to anabolic steroids, if it was a drug, then the Haitian Sensations network were on it. Coming from Haiti, and then landing in Bahamas, using fishing vessels to trick the Coast Guard, they smuggled it into the Boynton Beach inlet. From twenty miles offshore, hiding the dope inside the bellies of huge tuna, and anything big enough to hide the packs in; they did it. They were very ingenious and creative. They actually landed 9 out of 10 loads, while the Gulf Cartel was only landing 7 of the same 10 loads across the gulf from Matamoros, Tamualipas.

To say Big Meet was well connected, or that Haitian Sensations was a big drug operation, were both understatements of the century. Lil' Fade adored Big Meet and wanted to be just like him. He wanted "32 Forgiato rims on an Escalade of his own with ten T.V.'s playing at all times. He couldn't wait to put in work so he could become a member of the Haitian Sensations movement, so he would do anything his cousin would tell him to do, like running a crew of kids dealing drugs. Lil' Fade was 14 years old, but he had kids as young as 10 to 11 working for him and was always looking for more, as that would mean a faster chance to get in position in the Haitian Sensations Cartel.

"Hey Fade," called Matt, one of the kids Fade fronted work to.

"Hey Matt, what's good my Z?" Fade hollered to Matt as they were walking towards the locker room together, using the "Z" for "Zoe," as many Haitian kids did these days in South Florida. A trend that went even harder and farther, as the explosion of South Florida's own, Haitian rapper Kodak Black took to the streets with the "Z" moniker, making "Z" an instant hit, trending all over America now, instead of just South Florida.

"Ain't shit my Z, man a nigga need a see you an re-up, I got them $500 I owe ya, and I need another pack, you know I'm tryna get like you Z!" said Matt.

"Fo Sho my Z! I got ya right here," said Fade as they got to

Fade's locker. Fade counted the $500 Matt handed him, put that away in the locker, and only then, gave him another pack, street value of $750. Matt would again sell the bundles of heroin, pocket his $250, and then bring Fade the $500 re-up money back as always.

Fade had made a crucial mistake though, and one of the packs had fallen on the floor as he locked his locker back and walked off with Matt. They separated in the parking lot as Matt walked off, and Fade walked to join his cousin in Big Meet's Escalade, smiling about being one step closer to sealing his place in his cousin's crew, and 'getting to the bag' or becoming rich, as it was known.

It was just a coincidence that Ray happened to be the first into the locker room after Fade and Matt had left. All Ray could think was that he had "come up," or profited by coming across the drugs he found on the ground in the locker room. He also knew that he was wrong, after hearing so many times about his uncle's past, but like any kid his age, he couldn't resist the temptation that greed caused. He had no idea about how much it was worth, but he figured his homie Los could tell him, since his brother was a boss in the Haitian Sensation Network. He figured at least he could get a video game or two with his profits, little did he know it was the biggest mistake of his life. The environment that he and so many kids like him were growing up in, was dangerous and it only seemed to get worse, no matter how hard Sammy and people like him tried at the Youth Center to change it. It was a cycle, and every year statistics would rise for kids and more of them would die.

Chapter Five

At just about the same time that his little brother Ray was making a big mistake, picking up and pocketing drugs that he had found on the floor in the locker room, EJ Morzella, Jean's oldest nephew on the Italian side of his family, was stepping off of a plane at Palm Beach International Airport. He planned on surprising his family as President Biden had surprised him in his first hundred days of office, he signed an executive order recalling all the U.S. troops from the Afghanistan region. EJ was so happy to be back in the sunny South Florida, and couldn't wait to hang out with his family after almost 3 years over in Sandland, eating greasy camel burgers. He desperately wanted some of his mother's good Italian food but was scared to what such rich food would do to his stomach after so many years of greasy camel meat that they seemed to put in everything over in there in Sandland.

EJ was a marine sergeant and was known as the best of the best in demolitions, special weapons and tactics, known as SWAT, hand to hand combat, First Sniper, and Recon Division. He was the one who they called to lead the team when shit hit the fan, and he loved being a Marine. They had offered to retire him with full benefits when a stray bullet had taken his eye, but he was a warrior and couldn't imagine life as a civilian. As a non-combatant, a regular joe. He was a damn marine and proud of it. That would never change. It was who he was.

He bought a burner phone as he left the airport on his way to the taxi stand. He fired off a text message to his uncle Jean in the cab on his way home to his parent's house, where all of his belongings were. "Meet me at the crib Unc, and keep it on the DL!"

He always stayed with his parents when he was on leave since having a house on his own while he was on tour was pointless because he would never be stateside to enjoy it. "Oh, shit! On my way Neph, just gettin' off work!" Jean replied back on the text. EJ smiled as he watched out of the cab window noticing a lot of changes and many businesses being shut down in the wake of the Corona scare. It was so good to be home, even if things were bad over here, it was like being in heaven compared to being in Sandland. You never knew when you would wake up dead over there, but here, at least you knew who your enemies were. They were usually the ones with the guns, not the suicide bombs attached under some long dress you wouldn't be able to see through.

He pulled into the driveway and paid the taxi driver. He was "off grid," so he was unable to use Uber, his phones had always been burners when he was stateside, and he didn't use any phone apps because he didn't want to be traced. He had already let his best friend, a CIA operative who was still in Sandland but on his way home, know his burner number so they could link up when he was back. Tyrone Bass, known as Ty to his friends, was EJ's best friend over in Sandland, and now his best friend, period.

The fact that they were both from West Palm Beach had made them become friends immediately over there in Sandland, where finding things to talk about to pass the time was hard.

Ty was the Station Chief at the American Embassy, and had met EJ when he had brought the first of many Taliban informants to Ty to receive payments for any information that they might be able to provide. Ty, soon after began to like and trust EJ, and started giving EJ some of the targets to lead his team on when they would hit.

Their friendship proved to be beneficial to both parties as it became a one-two, as they got informants then planned and executed strikes on the Taliban's many cell's operations, putting major dents into their meager and inferior forces.

EJ rang the doorbell. The door opened after a minute and his mother's scream could be heard all the way down the street from them. She teared up and EJ embraced his mom. "How ... what. .. Oh my God! You're home!" said Laurie shaken.

"Yea mom," replied EJ still embracing her, "President Biden just recalled us all, we are officially withdrawn from Afghanistan and done over there, I'm home for good this time!" He stepped inside to his new life at home, which would soon become a war even far greater than the one he had been fighting against the Taliban, and even more alarming than anything he had faced thus far in his life.

Chapter Six

Shelby can't remember ever being as frustrated as she was right now. She was riding her Yamaha R1 down I-95, going a cool 120 MPH and trying to forget the week she had been having.

First, her murder case that she had caught, turned out to be a prominent public figure, as well as a well known defense attorney. But what really sucked was having to explain to the wife and kids how he had come to be found robbed behind a dumpster, probably by a hooker and or dope fiend who had apparently accidentally killed him while trying to knock him unconscious to complete the robbery. She had had to explain to them how his car had been found in the courthouse parking lot but yet he was physically in the dangerous neighborhood that he was found in, with his pants unzipped. She had to answer questions from his wife about why he had been in that bar that they had tracked him back to, a bar frequented by prostitutes, and what he had been up to.

Shelby had talked to everyone who had been at that bar, looked at the camera footage, and found out from the bartender that he was there a lot and usually left with a prostitute, but hadn't on that day. Is that why he was found like that? She wondered to herself. Did he decide to try a street walker and instead just became a target? She literally had no suspect, and nothing to go on, but something just didn't feel right to her. I mean this guy was a well-paid lawyer. He normally would meet his tricks at the bar, and then take them to the pay-by-the-hour motel next door. He was known for this. It was his habit and that was ok with her, it happens. But finding his body by a dumpster in an alleyway in a dangerous hood like Tamerind Avenue downtown, was a bit off, in her opinion anyway. But she really had no alternate theory to go on either.

There was that on one side, then things down at the Youth Center weren't going great either. It wasn't that she didn't love being down there, seeing the kids and helping out, because she did. She absolutely loved it, and was there everyday but she just couldn't seem to find her niche in the program. She was just doing the same established routines that had already been in place there for years. She wanted to start something different, try her own idea, something new, something special, like Jean had done with his boxing. She wanted something special too, something she could share with the kids, something she could be good at, just like Jean was. It was crazy how much that she had grown to admire Jean and his great accomplishments with these kids. Who wouldn't?

Well, that was another problem, she was really frustrated about that as well, it was Jean. She couldn't get him out of her mind. He was a convicted felon for God's sake! How could she even be seeing him like that and out of context? It was insane! It had to stop, although she had secrets and broke laws, it was a necessary evil with her job. She made a difference when she broke the laws. He was a drug dealer when he did it and he profited from the sales, she did it for community benefit. His motives had been capitalism, hers the betterment of the community and people.

She found herself sympathetic as Jean seemed such a changed

person. Yet then she sensed that he was down quite a bit lately. She also took notice to seeing less of Ray, who was Jean's pride and joy, and she could see it was bothering him. She hoped that it wasn't anything serious. To hell with it, she thought to herself, I'll just give him a call and find out what was going on with him. She hit her phone on her dashboard of the R-1 she was in love with and always rode. As she allowed the bike to slow back to the speed of the flow of traffic at about 80 MPH, she let her helmet bluetooth connect, and called Jean's phone from her contacts. He answered right away.

"Yea," answered Jean seeming distracted.

"Hi, Jean. It's Shelby. You remember me from the Youth Center?" she asked.

"Oh, Hi, how are ya?" he asked in reply curtly, still distracted.

"I'm ok, I was just wondering if we could meet up?"

"Ah ... I'm sorry Miss Shelby, but what for?" he asked bluntly, she having got his attention and he was telling in his responses.

"Well ... um. .. wow, I guess I didn't think this through, ah ... you know what? Never mind, I'll just see you the next time at the center, ok?" asked Shelby.

"Agh ... look, I'm sorry I am being so short with ya, it's just that I saw the way you looked at me when we first met, and I didn't think you had any interest in me besides putting those handcuffs on me, and that's really not my thing, so ..." Jean replied and left the rest unsaid, trailing off. Although she was a beautiful woman, he had to continuously tell himself that she isn't a woman, she is a cop, and out of his league. So he wanted to get off of this call with her, but something held him.

"Ok, I deserved that, look, it's about Ray and a few other kids at the Youth Center, can we meet for coffee?" she asked, humbled.

"Well shit, if it's about the kids, I'm down, you call it," said Jean.

"Ok, Starbucks downtown? I'm right around the corner," she replied to him, smiling.

"Ten minutes Miss Shelby," he said and hung up.

§§§§

When he showed up, he had an MDH Printing uniform on from his job, and she thought he looked tired and stressed out. Probably from working a regular job. Shelby almost immediately was attracted, and she was incredibly surprised by this, he had tattoos on his face and gold teeth for God's sake. No, that wasn't attractive at all. She had never seen Jean in his work uniform, and he looked like a hard worker, as worn as the uniform looked, and as tired as he seemed, walking towards her table in the back. He has changed, she thought. She had to keep reminding herself of that fact while seeing him, and that was hard as she usually would see them going *in* to the system, and the only time she would see them coming out was when she was re-arresting them. Jean was the first one that she had seen who had successfully made a significant change, and strove for a new life, as well as making effort to not go back into the system.

"What's going on Miss Shelby?" asked Jean as he sat at the table across from her. "Shelby is just fine, I'm not old, you don't have to call me "Miss" Jean," she replied with an ironic smile on her lips. His politeness was cute though, she thought to herself, even if it was sarcastic in his deliverance.

"My bad, I keep forgetting we bout the same age, I guess it's the nature of your chosen profession that keeps me in my place," he responded ironically in a witty comeback.

"Yea, I know that you feel a certain type of way about my reaction to meeting you, and I have already apologized to you for the way I reacted when we first met, I am sorry again, would you like that I go ahead and continue to do so every time that we meet as well? I mean, I didn't know Jean, ok?" asked Shelby smiling at him in irony.

"Nah ma, it's all good, I see you got jokes, but it's all good, I'm over it, I guess I asked for the negative attention," he said trying to be a good sport.

"Well, you said it, not me, but can I ask you something?"

"What's good?" he asked.

"Well, I mean... " Shelby started, hesitating, "you are done with that life style, right? So, why wouldn't you get rid of the golds and start getting the laser on your face tattoos?" She waited for him to take offense but strangely he didn't.

Jean looked away for a moment. He wanted to vocalize his

63

thoughts on this issue, but it was not very likely that anyone would understand how he looked at himself in the mirror, or the good that can come from the bad. "Let me ask you this Shelby, you been shot before?" His face a composite of seriousness.

"No, I haven't, thank God!" She answered appalled that he would ask such a thing. "Why do you ask that Jean?"

"Well," Jean started, "God forbid it, but imagine if you had been shot in the line of duty. Now, do you think that you would want to remove those scars? Or would you use them as a reminder? Something to learn from? Something to remember your struggles by?"

"Wow, well I never really thought of it like that, but no, I'm pretty sure that I wouldn't get my scars removed ... "

"So Shelby, when I walked into that Youth Center, I had a plan to get rid of all this shit that makes me look like a monster ..."

"I don't believe you are a monster Jean," she said earnestly.

"Well... look honestly, it was the kids reaction to me at the Youth Center, they can not only sense that I've been through some shit, Shelby these are *my* scars in *my* line of duty, and they can see that and pick up on everything in me. These kids listened to me Shelby! On my first day, these street smart kids, these tough ass kids listened to me ... it was amazing, Sammy said some of those older kids didn't listen to anyone, even their gang leaders couldn't tell them nothing, but when they saw my scars," he used air quotes with two fingers on each hand for emphasis, "they could relate, they know I can understand, and they know they can trust me, ya dig?"

"You really *do* care, don't you? It's amazing ... " Shelby said.

"Of course I care Shelby, and I wish I had somebody who cared when I was that age, but that's why I want to give back, to stop them from making mistakes I made, so that's why I scare away a real relationship with a nice girl, the kids need to see my scars and learn from me and my experiences so they don't end up in that revolving door."

Right then a pretty blonde white girl came, completely ignored Shelby and smiled brightly and beautifully at Jean asking if she could get him anything more.

"Just another coffee, thank you," Jean said to her without so much as making any eye contact or smiling back at her. He completely ignored her.

"Do you want sugar or creamer? My manager tells me not to but I'll hook you up with real milk if you want," she said prettily with a wink and smile that also went ignored by Jean, yet Shelby had indeed noticed it all. The whole exchange stuck out to her.

"No ... just black, thank you ... " he answered politely again without looking at her. She smiled again and then left. Shelby was really confused now.

"So anyways, to answer your question, hell yea I would normally have wanted to get rid of ... Why are you staring at me like that?" he asked.

"Are we going to ignore that this girl just tried to almost take you home with her and you didn't even seem to notice?" asked

Shelby, clearly astonished.

"Huh, wha ... what are you talking about? That waitress girl?" He was confused.

"Wow," said Shelby, "never mind ... " She was flabbergasted.

"She was just being nice," said Jean with a smirk, "And if I didn't already know you were a cop, I would think you were jeally!"

"I'm not!" She said and threw a crumpled napkin at him, "and what does my being a cop have to do with anything?"

"Well, as if you would look twice at a thug ass nigga like me when you put away my type. Remember how you first looked at me when we had just met, that's usually your real feelings and--" Jean started, but was interrupted quickly by her.

"I already apologized for that, I am not often wrong, but I *was* about you Jean. Now that I know why you have kept the face tatts and gold teeth, and your reasons are admirable I've seen, I can say you are a good guy Jean, which is why I've asked you here --" she was interrupted.

"I thought that you just wanted my company," he asked.

She laughed a good healthy laugh. Her eyes smiled, he saw it and he liked that about her. "Yes, among other things Jean, yes you are good company."

"So Shelby, what's wrong, what's going on? Why did you want to meet up?" he asked.

"Ok, look Jean, I know you've noticed a change in the way things are at the center lately, hell, even Sammy mentioned something about it to me, little Ray and Los haven't been around much lately, I've seen that black Escalade with the big wheels here a lot lately. Those kids; Fade, Matt, and D have been doing a lot of in and out to the parking lot, I know you ought to have noticed --"

"Hold on Shelby," said Jean seriously, "am I under some kind of investigation? Is that why they sent you here? I can't believe I let you cops set me up again! I ain't got nothing to do --" He was getting loud now, mad about the accusation.

"No! Jean, calm down, I don't think you got anything to do with it, I believe what I said, you are a good man. I'm just asking for your help, I ..." She was trying to calm him down, knowing how sensitive he would be to something like this.

"So, you tryin' me like I'm a rat? I ain't no informant ass nigga! I did my time! I knew this was a bad idea! Meeting here with a damn cop, no matter how pretty she is, yo, I'm out ... " He stood to leave, but hesitated.

"Look Jean, sit down and take it easy, ok? Let me talk.."

He was standing and posed to leave feeling insulted but he could see something in her; something real and honest. She was unlike any cop he had met, beyond simple beauty, she shined from the inside out. It was her inner being that shined like that. He could see that she was special.

He sat down, "I'm listening ... "

"Ok, thank you, and look, I know you got the bad end of the stick with those dirty cops --" she started to say.

"Bad end of the stick? It was 13 years of my life that I can never get back!"

"But it made you into the strong, hard working, dedicated man you are today! Yes, it even gave you the scars, but those scars made those kids listen to you! What happened to you was unfair and it is tragic, but if it didn't happen, then how many of these kids that you do reach, would it be happening to, huh?" Shelby said passionately, trying to reach his kind, more understanding side.

"Look Shelby, I'm not sure bout what's going on, are you some kind of undercover, or some ..." Shelby interrupted him laughing because to her it was not feasible.

"I'm undercover? I told you and everyone else who was at the center that I am a detective, I wouldn't be very good at undercover if I told everyone, would I?"

"So then, who are you after? I'm a street nigga, I don't give cops information, so why don't you tell me what's up and I'll look into it, I'll talk to the kids and see what's up, ok?" Jean asked a little bit more softly, the kids being his only concern.

"I think that Mr. Escalade is using the kids to sell dope for him out of the center and their schools, I ran the plates, it comes back to Demetrius St.Clair, I shouldn't be telling you any of this, but I believe that I can trust you, DEA got him listed in their files as "Big Meet" and a top dog in some gang called the "Haitian Sensations" or whatever they call themselves," Shelby said in almost a whisper.

Jean froze. He said nothing to betray his being shaken. He couldn't allow her to know that he had any connection with the

Haitian Sensations. It could all be a trick, he thought to himself, to get him to say anything regarding his old crew and plug, was how he was thinking and stressing about it. One look into Shelby's beautiful eyes and he knew it didn't have anything to do with him, she genuinely cared about the kids, and wanted to help them. He felt exactly the same. He stood up. He couldn't do things in her way. He had to do this on his own, he knew.

"Look, I gotta bounce, I'll holla back at cha bout this tho," he said turning to leave. She grabbed his arm to stop him, but he was a man on a mission and could never be stopped once he had something on his mind.

"Wait Jean! You know something, I can tell!" she said excitedly, knowing.

"Look Miss Shelby, I'm sorry, I gotta go, but I *will* call you later, ok?" With that, Jean rushed out of the Starbucks leaving a $10 bill on the table next to the check. Shelby looked at the check. Despite the seriousness of their conversation, and the abruptness of his leaving, she smiled looking at the check on the table. The little white girl had actually put her number down on it with a little heart near it.

Shelby got up and left the coffee shop, wondering about the mysterious Jean, but also worrying about the kids in the Youth Center. She hoped she didn't make a mistake by letting Jean in with the information about the DEA knowing about Big Meet. She could lose her job if details ever became known about her telling a convicted felon about an ongoing investigation with the DEA, especially someone he might very possibly know and consider a friend. He wouldn't do that though, would he? She asked herself. She had never been in this type of situation or a position like this.

Shelby didn't see that as a possibility though, not only did Jean obviously care about these kids, but something in him was worthy of her trust, she could feel that. There was a goodness in him. She could feel what was in his heart, and as a detective, dealing day in and day out with the scum of the earth, who she had no doubt about the motives, it was nice to see some genuine selflessness in someone who had changed. She actually was seeing his past as just that, his past. He was doing everything in his power to change his life, pay back his debt to the society, and he was giving back to the community enormously. She hated to admit it, or maybe she didn't, but she was very overwhelmed with admiration. She was proud and honored to know him and as impossible as it seemed, she was starting to even entertain the idea of a real friendship with him. She smiled to herself. His motivation to make a difference and his dedication to the kids, along with his inner being was starting to make her think about possibly being more with Jean Pierre. He is special, there was no doubt, and he was also the opposite of what she should be dating. But so was Tomas at first as well. She had a memory of a magazine article she had once read that she thought was so sexist at the time. It was basically saying that a woman would know if she would sleep with a guy within 2 minutes of meeting a guy. She had thought at the time it was incredibly wrong, but now she wasn't so sure. The fact that she even considered this guy as a potential suitor was amazing. But she felt like somewhere up in heaven Tomas was watching her and wishing she gave it a chance. Tomas giving his approval was what she had pictured in her mind's eye. Could that be true?

"Is that it, Tomas?" She asked her husband up in heaven, "do you want me to move on?" She was so overwhelmed with emotion that she started to cry.

"Nobody could ever take your place Tomas, you will always have my heart and soul forever my love, always ... " She closed her eyes and allowed herself to begin the process of letting go. It was time. He wanted her to, that much she could feel from him. So she would, no matter how much it would hurt to let go, she would.

Chapter Seven

Wicks was on a borrowed white Ducati 998 following the blacked out Escalade on "32 Forgiato rims blasting XXXTentacion's mixtape that had been released post-humously. XXXTentacion, the Broward County rapper was killed not far from where they were now driving in West Palm Beach during a robbery outside of a Ferarri dealer in Broward. As Wicks pulled into the plaza, the Escalade pulled to the barbershop and Wicks continued on to the Bud's Chicken, located in the same plaza with many other stores. Wicks, played it cool and slid off of the Ducati and went inside of the restaurant to make himself scarce from his target's vision.

It was an hour that Wicks was sitting and watching the last of the customers and the barbers leave the shop, and still his target hadn't appeared yet. He was getting a little bit restless when he saw a black Yamaha R1 pull up and the fine shape of a short girl get off. His mind was completely blown when the helmet came off and... he gaped. "What the fuck?" he thought to himself, it was Shelby! Was she another dirty cop? He was stuck. She calmly walked to the barbershop as she was oblivious to his presence, as the target was opening the the door to leave. From Wicks' point of view, he could see words were being exchanged, and then they both went back into the barbershop together. Wicks was now blind. He needed to change position. He walked quickly towards the side of the shop. There were bushes there on the side of the place and he went to those bushes to hide while getting a view through the window. He then ducked under the window to look until he heard a glass break. He frantically came out from the side of the shop, expecting the worse, but not knowing what he would find.

Now knowing what to make of it, he brought out his snub nose revolver that was his throwaway piece that he hadn't used in the rat lawyer's murder, when he had put in that work. He aimed it in front of him and proceeded to the door. He went in fast and hard, and he reacted immediately to what he saw there before the target or Shelby knew that he had even come inside. He placed the revolver to his target's head, as he was on top of Shelby, fighting for control of a futuristic looking gun. Wicks didn't think or try to understand what he was seeing, he just did what was natural in his situation, he pulled the trigger. The hollow point .38 went into the left side of his target's temple and detached the whole right side of his head.

Hollow points were designed to expand once it entered into the soft tissue of the human body, and this one was no exception. It simply "blew his noodles out" as it was called when a shot to the head would push all of the brain matter out of the skull. It ended up spraying the whole area with blood and grey matter.

Shelby screamed as the blood and grey brains were sprayed all over her face and mouth. The Haitian Sensation lieutenant was slumped right on top of her. All 220 pounds of his rich, drug dealing body were dead weight right on top of her almost tiny frame. She almost immediately stopped screaming to be able to get him off of her, and then stood up. She was livid, not to mention confused, as she didn't have any clue that there was anyone else around.

73

"What the fuck are you doing?" Shelby screamed at him while drawing her service pistol and pointing it at him. He could tell that she was visibly shaken.

"I thought that I was saving you! Why you draw on me for?" he yelled back.

"That suspect was in my custody, now drop the gun!" she shouted to him.

"Yea," said Jean sardonically, placing his gun into his pocket, ignoring her demand, "he looked like he was in your custody while he was about to kill your ass! What the fuck are you doing in here alone with him without backup?" shouted Jean to her suspiciously while calmly backing up from her, keeping her out of reach.

"Get down on your knees, place your hands behind your head, fingers interlaced! Now! Do it!" yelled Shelby as she had her gun trained to his head.

"The fuck you say? I just saved your ass! God only know what kind of back door deals you got goin' on, but I ain't with it!" yelled Jean accusing her of corruption.

"Get down now! I mean it Jean! Do it!" screamed Shelby visibly shaking now.

"You might as well shoot me Shelby. The chances of me going back to prison are absolutely zero, so do what ya gots ta do girl ..."

Jean held his hands still at his side and was looking directly into Shelby's eyes. He was hoping that she could read his emotions and know he meant what he said about going back, he would rather die in these streets than to go back to that place ever again. It wasn't going to ever happen. He hoped that she wasn't dirty though, that she wasn't here to take her cut from Big Meet, covering up for them. If so, then he would be dead in about the next few moments anyway, and she would set him up, posthumously, as those dirty ATF and DEA agents from the task force had done so many years earlier. He doubted that though, there was something so pure and good about Shelby, he could sense that she was not corrupt. Something in her was just so hard to resist. He saw a flicker of doubt cross her face, and so he decided to take a chance with her, and he very slowly, started to approach her.

"Don't!" she said abruptly, although without conviction or force in her words.

"Trust me Shelby, I will never hurt you, just please lower your weapon, ok?" he said as smoothly and soothingly as he could, while inching towards her.

He slowly reached his open palm non-threateningly, and gently placed it on the side of her hand, and gently pushed her gun hand downwards. As she allowed him to do so, she was still visibly shaking. Once the gun was no longer a threat, Jean grabbed her and hugged her to him tightly. She began to cry softly in his arms.

"It's okay, Shelby. It's over, we're okay now ... it's okay ..." he said calmingly.

Shelby allowed herself to be hugged and used the offered shoulder with which she was given to cry even more. She had had a flashback from when Tomas was killed and she was forced to kill Barbara. She felt safe in Jean's gentle arms. Wait a minute, she thought to herself, he just saved my life! It was unbelievable! It had happened so fast that she hadn't realized the implications of what had just happened or the ramifications of the scene to Jean. She had to get him out of there.

"Jean, you gotta go! Give me that gun! You have to get away from here now!"

"Calm down, Shelby," said Jean with intense gentleness and caring, "nobody could have heard that shot, and if you had called backup, by now they would already have been here, what the fuck are you doing here alone anyways? Don't you know who this is and how fucking dangerous he is or was?" He looked seriously into her eyes making her to calm down and think straight for a moment.

"He, I ..." Shelby stuttered, "I'm so sorry, I ..."

"It's okay, Shelby. Take a second here, clean your face off while you catch a breath," he said handing her some paper towels to clean herself with.

She took the paper towels and started wiping off her face and neck. She was starting to calm down and was back to breathing normally. She began looking around outside the shop and noticed Meet's truck in the parking lot besides her R1 parked closer to the barbershop. She checked walls and light poles, looking for surveillance cameras, but didn't see any.

"Don't worry, Shelby, I already checked for cameras, there ain't any in the plaza, but we gotta check this shop, is this his place?" he asked her.

"Yea, it's his shop, but look, you need to go, I need to call this

76

in and do a lot of explaining, he is under DEA investigation, they are going to want to know what happened, and be involved in the investigation ... why are you staring at me?"

"Shelby, you can't call this in! I am a convicted ..." he started.

"I am a homicide detective, Jean, he tried to kill me, I have to call this in, I can't just ignore it, this was a justified use of deadly force, don't worry ..."

"Shelby! 'Don't worry'? Are you fucking crazy? Nobody is going to know why you came here! It's going to look as if you were taking a pay off being here by yourself with no backup! There is no explanation for why you were here, and especially *me!*" Jean yelled to her trying to get her to see the obvious, then more softly he added, "look ma' let me take care of this here, ok? I got a guy who owes me a favor, let me take care of this for us, ok?"

Shelby wasn't sure if she was more touched by the fact that he was trying to selflessly protect her or the fact that he said the word 'us' as if he was a part of it when she was obviously the one responsible for all this mess. She had made so many mistakes here tonight. Not going through the DEA, who she knew for a fact had an open investigation into Meet; not calling in her movements, not asking for a timed 'check in' with dispatch for her safety; and finally going into a sealed off place, as well as a dangerous situation with him without a plan, and then letting him get the drop on her. That was the worst part to her, she was pissed about that the most. If Jean hadn't come along when he did ... Wait, she thought to herself, how did he know I was even here? Was he following me? She started to panic.

"Jean, did you follow me here?" she asked him fearing the answer he might give.

"Come on, Shelby, how would I have already known there were no cameras in this plaza? I been sitting here in the Bud's Chicken for an hour before you even pulled up over here! I been following *him* so I can see if he got anything to do with what you told me at the Starbucks, and I was wondering why *you* were here when I saw you pull up ... you need to trust me Shelby, I'm trying to protect you and the kids!" said Jean passionately, and convincingly at that.

"I know, I'm sorry, Jean. I came here to talk to him and when I told him that I will bring him down if he didn't stop selling to those kids, he pulled the 'ghost gun' out, you know the kit gun they build themselves, that has no serial number on it? Well, he caught me off guard, and I was fighting him for control when you came in, you know I *did* have him under control, right?" Shelby asked knowing the answer, and knowing just as well in her heart that he would lie to help her feel better.

"I know you did ma, I just wanted to protect you even when I know you can protect yourself," he said and then smiled to her hoping to help her even more, as he knew that everything that he could do to make her cope, make her feel better would be appreciated. He only wanted to help her get past this moment, knowing how hard it was to take a life and then be responsible for the taking of that life. He wanted to take the brunt of the pain and responsibility from her, do anything to make her time easier. He really liked her already.

Chapter Eight

John Jay, also known as "JJ" to his friends, was sitting in his chair at his 1800's era desk, located at his family's alligator farm way west of Miami, near the Florida Everglades. He had just had a call that he knew would come one day, he owed a favor out, and he would of course honor this favor. The favor given to him was definitely worth any favor he would have to pay back, and he was still grateful to the owner of this favor that he owed out for his favor given to him about a year ago.

His mind drifted back to when he was in prison at a maximum security Federal Penitentiary Canaan; USP in Pennsylvania. It was about a year ago and he had been assigned a roommate that needed to be dealt with, but he was such a big motherfucker that he just couldn't fight him as a solution. Plus, JJ is white, Italian really, but in this world, the prison world, if you are not black, you are considered white. The roommate had been an Indian, or 'Native' as the politically correct term in prison was. At the penitentiary level, there existed an understanding, a non-negotiable policy amongst the convicts, who were the ones who in all actuality ran the prisons. The policy was called the hands off policy, and it was understood by all gangs, cars, or races. Cars were basically just the group of people that you rode with. Your gang. Your group. So nobody of one race, car, or gang, could touch any member or any different race, car or gang. If that rule was ever broken, then the entire car would go, or fight, the entirety of the other gang, car, or race. So, there could be one on one fights, but only with another member of your own car, race, or gang. This was the law, and everyone in the Federal Penitentiary all lived by this and respected it; it was the rule.

So, JJ said something one day to his friend about this situation that he found himself in. That friend just happened to be Wicks, and although it was frowned upon to befriend or hang out with other members of other races, cars, or gangs, it wasn't completely unacceptable. So, JJ, being from South Florida, and the fact that Wicks happened to be a member of the Florida car, made them get along well despite their difference in cars, upbringings or economic backgrounds. Wicks told JJ that the hands off policy did not apply for his roommate since he was claiming to be on "man time". Man time was some shit they had at the mediums and the low security prisons, where there were no rules about conduct. Rats and Chomos were all accepted there. Man time basically meant that he didn't want to be a part of any race, gang, or car, but be by himself. This also meant that he was ripe for the picking and there would be no gang repercussions if anyone in any car robbed or killed him. He was a Chomo for sure, or in other words, a child molester. See, in the penitentiary, each car would read all the other member's paperwork from the courts, such as sentencing transcripts, docket sheets, judgement and commitment papers, to make sure that they aren't child molesters, rats, or rapists. If they were found to be either of them, two or three members of that gang, car, or race, would jump him off the yard, meaning they would jump that person, forcing the administration to transfer that victim. The prison policies dictate that one victim from a multiple fighting incident must be transferred. One on one fights were let back out onto the yard when the time in the SHU or the box was up.

This was the only way that the convicts were to ensure that they were surrounded by those who were honorable, by street standards, and those who weren't sick in the head like those who preyed on children. Because of the whole, gang-has-to-stick-together rules, they wanted to make sure that if they put their lives on the line that it would be for only those who deserved their help and not some scumbag chomo, or even a rat. So, these were the rules governing the prison population and what kept them away from those "no good" inmates that weren't worth fighting for.

So Wicks, knowing of, and concerned about, JJ's impending release date, and the plan that they had agreed on for JJ to send in the mail back to Wicks for the rest of his 66 year sentence, the synthetic drug called K-2 and Flaka. The plan would be beneficial to them both as they both were aware of how much money there was in the sale of the drugs applied onto paper in the prison environment. For this reason, Wicks decided to go ahead and handle the chomo situation himself. Wicks had a 66 year sentence at that time with no expectation to get a release at any time in the future, and so, seeing no release date in the near future made him care less about a murder charge on a chomo, who he felt deserved to die anyway. He was already most likely going to die in prison anyway so what more could they do to him except to run any additional murder rap concurrent with his current sentence for the guns and drugs, meaning that the sentence would be served together instead of one after the other. The funny thing was that he would probably only get about a quarter of the sentence that he received for the guns and drugs for the murder. Or not even. The government would obviously care more about him not paying taxes on his drug money than they would about him killing another prisoner who was a chomo anyway, as well as another federal inmate. Everyone hates the chomos, even the administration.

So, even though Wicks didn't care about a murder sentence, he still didn't want to go to the SHU, which was Special Housing Unit, or what they call confinement in the FEDs. So he took a few precautions on his own to ensure the successful completion of this mission without capture or suspicion.

It wouldn't have been very hard either way to disguise himself since the Corona pandemic scare had just happened, and United States Penitentiary, Canaan, was already requiring that the inmate population wear face masks whether they believed in this Corona scare or not. So all Wicks did was add sunglasses, scarf and snowcap, although not all at once. He knew that JJ went to work in the kitchen and his shift would start at 5 a.m., giving him a concrete alibi, so he made his move at breakfast. He went with his unit to the chow hall wearing a short sleeved shirt and had his gloves, sunglasses, scarf, and long sleeved shirt hidden in his pants. On the way to breakfast, along with several other inmates, he disappeared into the pill line window in the medical section next to the chow hall, where people could go also for sick call. Knowing that this was the only place on the yard that didn't have any cameras, he waited until after the last inmate had left, and the pill line window had closed. He then quickly donned his scarf, snow cap, long sleeved shirt to hide his tattoos, and his sunglasses to assist the face mask in hiding his facial features. He then started back to the unit where JJ lived and blended with others who were leaving from the chow hall after eating their breakfasts. He walked into the unit where JJ and his target lived and went straight to the mop closet, and immediately closed the door. He took his lock out of his left boot, then tied it on to the laundry loop used for holding clothes together during laundry day. The loop he had already tied to his wrist so that it wouldn't come loose. He took his shank, or prison made knife, out of his right boot and carefully tied the attached string to his right wrist, since he was right handed and wanted to be able to jab with the shank using his most dominant hand. The lock was because of the size of his target, he had to have something to disorient his target before he could go to work on him and finish him off. The strings tied to both of his wrists were because of a long ago target. His target had gotten a hold of the lock and tried to take it from Wicks, almost causing him to fail his mission that time and lose the fight. He would never make that mistake again.

Most convicts are very observant, especially in the penitentiary, where life was always in jeopardy in any situation that might pop up at the drop of a dime, and they can easily sense imminent danger, or tension in the air. So, many of the other predators noticed immediately that Wicks didn't belong, and didn't recognize him as

JJ's friend with his disguise on, but they knew that something was going to go down. Some got their shanks ready, just in case there might be some danger for them, or in case some long ago misdeed had finally come to catch up with them. Or in case it was something with one of their homies that was in their gang. Others went directly to the showers in case whatever might transpire might cause a prison wide lockdown, in which case there would be no showers anytime soon. The former was wrong, the latter was right. Wicks walked past JJ's cell, cutting his eyes as he went, to the window on the door looking into the room. Empty. The chomo must have still been in the chow hall. He would be taking his time as well, big and hungry as he was.

Wicks slid into the room and hid next to the door, in between the toilet and the wall. He then readied his weapons in his hands for his upcoming battle. He didn't have to wait long when the door opened, and as soon as the massive Indian was parallel to the sink and couldn't back out, Wicks swung his lock and hit him once, twice, three times. It had the desired effect, causing the disorientation that Wicks had been hoping for. Just like a drunk, the target stumbled further into the cell towards the bed. Wicks was elated at his work so far, but couldn't stop.

Wicks went in for the carotid artery immediately. He stabbed his target in the neck five times. As soon as the blood splattered the bed and the walls, Wicks backed off in order to keep a minimal amount of blood coming his way. Some got onto his federal issued black boots, but that wasn't a problem since they were already black and wouldn't show the red blood. He carefully checked himself over then went to check on the body. He was dead, but he had produced a lot of blood. Gallons of it in fact. It was starting to pool under the bed. Also not a problem, as long as it stayed there. He still had to do one more thing to send a message as well as to keep the blame off of JJ, even though he had a solid alibi. He hated it, but it was necessary to throw off any investigation into the murder. He opened the pants of the corpse. He took the genitals and cut them completely off of the body. He then took them and shoved them into the mouth of the big native Indian, as was common with child molesters who were killed for their sexual preferences, and or perversions. Good riddance, thought Wicks to himself.

Wicks hid in the room for about another 20 minutes until the yard move was called on the intercom on the whole compound, letting everyone know that they were now allowed to move around on the compound to and from the yard. The yard move was the green light basically for the inmate population and guards to know they were going to be moving to units, yard, or to their work or school assignments, or even medical.

Wicks went back to medical, got in his little camera-less corner, and lost the long sleeved shirt, the scarf, snow cap, and sunglasses, throwing them all into the trash can in medical, that also contained biohazard waste, so would be disposed of more regularly than that of other trash. He quickly went from there towards the yard, blending in with the rest of the inmate population who were just then leaving medical on the same yard move. All he had was mere minutes to get to the yard.

The lockdown wasn't implemented until 4p.m., when they had a "stand up count" time every day, and the body was discovered. JJ wasn't due back from work until after the count time, and so was completely alibied on camera, in the kitchen the whole day, and since the chomo did report to the pill line window that morning to pick up medication that he took, it left the investigators and S.I.S ., (secret squirrels), who weren't all that smart to begin with, baffled as to how the culprit could've fooled their cameras in such brazen and cunning way. But like everything else in the Federal Penitentiary, if it doesn't bother the staff or affect them, they don't care if the convicts kill each other all day until the last man standing. So, the lockdown stayed in effect for three days, until the cell could be properly cleaned and sanitized for the next lucky guest, and things went right back to normal. The one thing that did change was the lack of a camera in the pill line corner. That mistake wouldn't happen again. Not the same way anyway.

JJ wasn't even questioned about his alibi since he was a few months shy of his release date, so nobody even suspected that he would have anything to do with a murder in prison. He even got moved to Wicks' unit. That was a fluke though. Just because of the overcrowding in the prison, there was only an open bunk in that dorm where they could put him while he was out of a cell, and he had just asked to stay there, where he was already comfortable, and since it saved work for the guards ...

JJ smiled to himself as he remembered the whole episode.

87

Damn right he would help his friend, he would be glad to, especially after Wicks had turned him onto the right people to send the K-2 and Flaka to in the prison system, after Wicks himself had gotten surprisingly released. Since then he, JJ, a simple gator farmer, had been making $25,000 a month just applying chemicals and wasp spray, which got people high as space cadets, to the pictures that he would then send in the mail to the inmates, who then would sell microdots of that same paper for five bucks a hit.

John Jay reached for the phone on his desk and wondered if he would be feeding his gators any beef tonight. He knew that beef was definitely on the menu if Wicks was calling for his help, and he had no problem being Wicks' chef's assistant, as his gators did love some beef. He would find out soon enough though.

JJ called his wife Tasha, who was from the Bahamas. He told her that he needed her to tell her brother to get him a van as soon as he can, and that it was important. They would be driving to West Palm Beach tonight. Tasha's brother, who went by the street name of 'Smack' lived in Fort Lauderdale, which was on the way, so that he could have his van waiting for him when he got there heading towards West Palm Beach. Smack was a master car thief, so JJ had no doubts that his van would be ready when he finally arrived in Lauderdale to pick it up. He was reliable.

"Boy, why you got me up this late anyways?" asked Tasha grumpily.

"I gotta help my boy Wicks, you tryna ride with? I gotta bounce right now."

"Boy bye, with all that rushin' me! Come on and get me!" said Tasha smiling.

When he got to Smack's house, there was a nursing home van in front of the house ready to go. JJ smiled to himself at the reliability of his brother-in-law.

"Bruh, you got till round 9A.M. when they finna see it gone and report it, so get done before 8:30, ya dig?" said Smack, in his urban way of speaking.

"'Preciate it brother-in-law, I got ya," said JJ.

"All good Jay, you know I got ya my white, Black Boy!" laughed Smack at the dig.

With that, they were on their way. JJ got his cutter from his truck to open the safe Wicks had told him about, along with a canvas to wrap up the gator food that he would be carrying back with him when the job was done. When they arrived at the barbershop, it only took a few minutes to pop the safe, being such a cheap Sentry model, but to comprehend what was in it was what took a few minutes for JJ to catch his breath. What wasn't in the safe is what JJ was wondering, he had cash, sure, but there was everything in the drug world known to man in here, thought JJ to himself. There weren't just bundles here either, there were 2 kilos of heroin, a kilo of flaka, meth, coke, crack, and some more shit that JJ couldn't even sit there and contemplate. This was not what he had expected when he had come on this mission, but still he shoved it all into the garbage bag that he had found under the sink. The guns he put in the canvas bag with Big Meet and loaded it all into his van from the back door of the barbershop. He told Tasha to take the Escalade to Smack's chop shop homie in Perine, and then he did another check around the barbershop to ensure that he had left nothing of any consequence. All was good, nothing there to connect him or Wicks to this place. He knocked over the alcohol glass vase that had the scissors in them, all over the floors. Obvious arson, but with no connecting evidence or body to identify, he couldn't care less about it. He just wanted no trace evidence.

JJ lit a cigarette, headed towards the back exit where the van was in the alley, checked the surrounding area, then went back in the shop. He flicked the cigarette he had lit already, watched as the sparks catch the paper towels, which in turn caught the alcohol, and finally the walls and ceiling. He needed to see the walls catch, because that was where the blood and brain fragments had been sprayed with the shot fired. He locked the back door, got into the van and pulled off as calmly as he could without drawing attention. He was back on the gator farm before sunrise. What a beautiful day it was. He texted Jean about the need to meet up with him to discuss the contents in the box, and didn't want to put that on a phone or text, but he received no response. But he would eventually. He knew that he would, as he always did. For now though it was back to feed the gators that he loved so much, another day.

Chapter Nine

They were doing "a buck forty" riding on I-95, meaning that they were speeding at 140 MPH. They mostly stuck to the HOV lane, or the High Occupancy Vehicle lane, but sometimes had to slow to 110 or 120 just to weave through the traffic in other lanes. They were using their helmet bluetooth systems that were linked together so that they might be able to talk on a continuous line that was open between them. It was three in the morning, so there wasn't so much traffic on the roads once they were north of Palm Beach County, it was an unincorporated area through which they were riding. Shelby was on her R-1 and Jean was on his borrowed Ducati 998. Shelby was a better rider because she used her bike as an everyday Vehicle, but since the Ducati was such an amazing piece of machinery, they could easily even out, riding at an even keel on the long dark highway. Allowing the miles to ease the transgressions of the last hours that they had faced together, the trip was a life saver.

When they had left the barbershop, after Jean killed Big Meet to save Shelby, it had been like pulling teeth to get Shelby to trust him enough to let him save them, dealing with it in his own way, using his own methods and people. He had called in a favor from a friend of his that he had done something huge for a long time ago and completely trusted him. Ever since he had seen the gators at JJ's place and what they were capable of, he had seen the gators eat actual live humans or in all actuality, rats because that's exactly what they are. Either way, Jean knew not a bone or particle of DNA would

91

ever be found.

JJ would take the Escalade to one of the many chop shops in Perine, just south of Miami, and get any money that he could, so the Escalade would be in a million small pieces before nightfall tomorrow. Jean also hadn't told Shelby, since she had been so frantic, but he had noticed the floor safe in the back room of the barbershop, and had told JJ to quietly empty the safe and set the place on fire when he leaves. The body was gator food, so JJ had put that into the van, and let his wife Tasha drive the Escalade, which she had loved since it was sitting so nicely.

"Ready to turn around?" Shelby's question returned Jean to the present. They were all the way to almost Melbourne, which was about an hour north of Palm Beach County, but they had made it in less than half an hour, which had to be a record.

"Alright, let's get some gas first, ok?" he said.

They made it off in their bikes to the gas station and Shelby looked at him intensely. He opened his arms just feeling the power of her healing in them. She stepped into his offered embrace and held on for dear life, if only for a few minutes, it was an amazing feeling.

"Thank you Jean," she said as she looked into his dark eyes gratefully.

"You don't have to thank me Shelby, I'm sure you would have got him, I just saw ... and I reacted, I know that you can take care of yourself. I'm sorry I took that away from you," he said, meaning it more than he could imagine.

"It's not something I am used to. It scared me, took me out of my comfort zone, and I am sorry for the way that I reacted to you, but I gotta admit, it doesn't feel too bad to be protected," she said hesitating, then added, "and cared for." She looked down shyly. Jean couldn't help but become mesmerized by her apparent innocence and vulnerability. It was refreshing to him.

"I got an idea Shelby, there is something I want to show you -- no, share with you, follow me," he said, and then got back onto the Ducati, after they had filled their tanks at the gas station.

On the ride back, they went a little bit slower, but still made it to Palm Beach County within forty minutes. About that time, JJ and Tasha were almost to Perine, and the fire at the barbershop had attracted all the usual fire trucks and lookie-loos trying to see what had happened there. The flames at that time were just starting to come down a little bit. No matter what was going on in the world, Jean and Shelby were both in their own respective thoughts, and were silent on the way back. Since they were coming from the north, Jean led the way, getting off I-95 on the Palm Beach Lakes exit and cut over to downtown from there. Shelby followed.

Once they got to the bridge that crossed over to Palm Beach Island, Shelby started to worry. The run down shitty houses over here on the Island started at ten million dollars, so what could he possibly have in mind coming over here? She wasn't sure, but she knew she needed to start learning how to trust Jean. She knew that it would be hard to open up, but she reminded herself what he had been through with those task force agents from the DEA and ATF, and how hard it must be for him to trust *her*. He was trying though, and he was trying very hard too. "But why?" She asked herself. Why would he allow her around him after what he had been through? All she could think of was he was doing everything he did for the kids. She was the one who had figured out what was going on at the Youth Center, and he wanted to fix that for them and to protect them from the danger. That's what it had to be, right?

When Jean pulled up into the Flagler Museum parking lot, and then turned toward the side of the building, stopping next to a big tree in the hard packed grass with a beautiful view of the intra-coastal waterway, Shelby was more than curious. But as they killed the bike engines, the amazingly silent night was in deep contrast with the night they had had so far. It was as quiet as when your head went under the water in the beach. Then she noticed the view! From where they stood, the Flagler Museum was to their right, and then to their left was a small sidewalk that ran along the water. It was meant for access, yet it also separated the multi-million dollar houses, and their backyards from the waterway, the owners' corresponding docks and respective boats tied to their docks. But even all that, as interesting as it was, had nothing on the view of the city on the other side of the water. It was downtown West Palm Beach, and it was stunningly beautiful when the noise of the city was silent, and couldn't pollute the ears as it didn't at this spot that Jean had found and brought her to. It was like watching the huge city all lit up on television, but pressing the mute button, allowing the silence. "It's absolutely stunning, Jean," she said at loss for words.

Jean nodded in agreement with her, he already knew. They were leaning against their bikes, taking in the view of the lights of the city reflecting off of the almost still water, as there weren't many boats out at this hour of night. They were quiet for a while before Shelby couldn't hold herself back any longer and reached her arm into the crook of his elbow. He didn't turn his gaze away, but allowed her into his space gladly. By that time, they both knew and felt it. They both wanted the same thing and would attempt to open the door for that eventuality. There could be no denying it, as it had crept up on them both like a thief in the night. Both had been robbed by that same thief before, and were both scarred, as well as scared to open up again, only to be hurt again. But by this time it was too late. They were both unable to deny the feeling, it was as clear as daylight.

Jean leaned in and kissed her tentatively. She moved her hand under his long dreads onto the back of his neck, and pulled him even closer. She wanted, no, she needed, him to be closer to her, nearer to her soul, her heart. Jean put his arm around her slim waist and pulled her in the same way, as close as they could get to each other was what they both wanted. He was so hard beneath his pants that she could feel him. She felt her insides melt, her fire burning as they continued to kiss and caress each other's tongues, making a slow passionate love, inside of their joined mouths. She was moving slowly, almost caressing his hardness against her stomach, as she was so short in comparison to him at that close range. He solved that problem as quickly as it had developed. He broke their kiss and embrace, and gently lifted her up and placed her facing him, but sideways onto his Ducati, and started the embrace all over again, kissing on her as if he was on an expedition to find treasure in her mouth. One that he found very shortly.

Shelby felt under his shirt to his washboard stomach, ab muscles lined up like they were late for something. She began to pull up his shirt, and he allowed her to continue, and pulled it off. She kissed his neck, his shoulders, down to his pecks, and then began to tongue down his nipples one at a time. Jean pulled away and began to pull her shirt over her head, she helped him along with great need overcoming her. Jean started to caress her amazingly perfect B-Cup breast with his hand, while kissing her neck and licking in and around her ear lobe. With his right free hand, he unclasped her black lace bra and let it come apart. He parted long enough for her to allow the bra to fall off of her arms. He then palmed and caressed her right breast, while licking, kissing, and sucking on her dark, small, bead like, left nipple sweetly and gently enough to give her a tease while pleasuring her as well.

A sweet moan escaped her lips as she succumbed to his touch, and she was slowly grinding on the seat of the Ducati, her mind in another world, a world where only she and Jean existed, a world where her body was becoming one with Jean's body, and they were both in their own heaven together. She felt like never before.

Jean continued his attack on her nipples with his mouth and tongue until she began to rub his erection through his pants. She wanted more, needed more. There would be nothing that could stop her now. She wanted all of Jean inside of her immediately, this moment. She could feel all of her juices going through her panties! Damn! She was absolutely soaked! She was rubbing, touching, even grinding herself on the Ducati seat. Her control of herself was completely uninhibited and relaxed.

She felt beautiful, amazing, and even happy, and Jean was the reason.

Jean could take no more of her rubbing on him. He would lose himself if she kept it up. He wanted to make this last forever, never let it go, so he placed his left hand in between Shelby's legs, and felt how wet she was through her jeans down there. She was more than ready, so Jean rubbed her there on her clit with his left thumb and index fingers, while unbuttoning her jeans with his right hand. She put one hand on the Ducati's gas tank and the other on the rear seat, lifted her beautiful ass up, so that he could slide the pants down her legs and then off, after removing her riding boots one by one first. He knelt down in the grass and pulled her to the edge of the seat of the bike. He pulled her black matching panties to the side and was introduced to the most beautiful and lovely pussy that he had ever seen before. It was all so dark and perfect. It looked like a dark straight line, yet when he parted her lips with his tongue, and began to slowly kiss it, he saw the bright and light pinkness of her inner folds.

As he was licking and kissing the button and lips, she began to move around and moan. He started to tongue into her opening, and then back to her button on top. Back and forth, he went like that, driving her crazy, she had put her calves onto his shoulders at one point, and now seeing as she tightened her grip on his neck in between her shins, he could feel her about to come. "Oh shit, Jean!" With that, he started tonguing her harder, and felt all of her juices spill into his mouth, as she relaxed her grip on him. He stood and kissed her deeply, allowing her to taste all of her own heavenly juice that she had already shared with him in his mouth.

"I want more," she said as she began to unbuckle his belt, "I want it all, and I want it right now, Jean." She kissed him more slowly, yet passionately, and allowed his pants to drop down to the ground. Still kissing him, she started pulling down his boxers. She put her hand on his full 8 inches and slowly started stroking it while kissing all over on his neck. He was trying to go slow, but he had his hands on her hips and then put his fingers under the elastic of her black lace panties. Slowly and sensually, he pulled on her panties. She again opened the gate and lifted up for him to pull them all the way off and expose her love flower. It was beautiful.

She put one hand behind his neck, kept the other on his 8 inches and gently pulled him closer. Always closer was what she wanted. He allowed himself to be pulled closer to her. He kissed her while taking the head of his dick and rubbing it up and down her pretty pussy lips, in between them, and all around, getting her juices all over himself and his dick to lubricate their love to come. She was moaning at the way he was making her feel, teasing yet possessing her. She was so close to another orgasm, and he hadn't even entered her yet. All precautions were in the wind as they were both caught up in their mutual pleasure, and amazing ecstasy, they never for once contemplated birth control. Didn't even think about it. They felt so close so fast, almost as if they were meant for each other all their lives and just now was let in on that very special secret. They were elated.

He took full advantage of her closeness to her orgasm, and continued to kiss and tease, until she could take no more, grabbed him and guided his full length into her soft wetness of heaven. He slowly began to stroke her, so that she would be able to adapt to his girth, and he felt a sense of calm, a feeling of being complete with her. It was perfect to him, not too tight, but he could tell that it had been a while for her. He knew it because he knows her, inside and out. Was one with her; connected with her.

He looked into her eyes as he was slowly stroking, still going at a slow pace, a loving pace, and he was just hypnotized by her beauty, along with the amazing way he felt around her. He felt no need to show off or put on a performance with her, he was just there with her, one with her. Just living in the moment was enough, and he wanted it to last forever. Keeping a slow, sweet pace with him, Shelby was about to come again. She gripped him tightly, with all of her might but stopped, allowing him to be in control, allowing him to control his and her motions, all with love in her eyes.

"Oh my God, Jean, I'm about to come again! Ah ... oh shit, baby ... you feel so damn good ... ah ..." Shelby mumbled as she started to come again. They began to kiss some more, and Jean started to speed up for himself to get ready to come, as he was looking into her eyes, seeing her staring back into his.

"Shelby, it feels so damn good baby, damn ..." he says as he is feeling her walls start to tighten around his dick. She wrapped her legs behind his back at his hips and he started to speed up even more. "Baby, I'm going to come, oh damn you so good Shelby!" he said still stroking her, in and out, watching the whole bike moving back and forth like a see-saw. "Come with me baby! I'm coming right now!" Said Shelby, moving her whole rhythm with him, even matching his. "Oh, baby," he said and the strokes started to get longer and harder. Jean finally let go of himself and exploded inside of her and held onto her tight like she was his only lifeline in a world of chaos. She came with him at the same time and gripped him just as tight. They both held onto each other in that same position for a while, neither willing to let go of the other, just catching their breath.

Moments later, or it might have been more like hours later, they stayed in each other's arms comfortably. The sunrise started nearing the skyline and it looked absolutely amazing. It was just the perfect cap for their night. They were in paradise, in heaven. They were in love. That fast. That deep. It was something very special, something incredible in fact. They were both one. Complete.

"It's so beautiful Jean," said Shelby, still hugging him as they were seeing hints of the light coming over the mansions east of the intracoastal.

"I'm looking at your beauty," he said staring into her eyes.

"Don't be corny, Jean, " she said as she giggled into his arms. "I know what's up." She then began to get dressed, but she was smiling at him. "I know you downplay what just happened between us as something that just happened after a serious life or death situation, but it's more than that, and I know you gotta be feelin' it too, what's between us, right?" Jean asked as he also started to get dressed, knowing that the sun would be coming all the way up momentarily. She only smiled at him.

"Come on, I wanna show you something," he said to her smile.

He took her hand and led her towards the path to where all the docks were located at. They held hands as they were walking along the path on the intracoastal waterway, taking in all the beauty of the morning.

"I know you've been hurt, Shelby, me too, but I'm here for you, and I would not ever hurt you. I want you to know me and I want to know you all the way on the inside, ya know?" he asked.

She was silent for a few seconds to collect her thoughts. She was on the fence and it was killing her because she was a cop. He was a good man, she knew, and had changed his life, but he was still a felon.

"Let me ask you something, Jean," she paused as he raised his eyebrows waiting. "How many girls have you brought here? It is too beautiful of a place to keep to yourself ..." She was walking and staring into his eyes to see if there could be any deception in them. In him. "I can understand why you would ask me that, but the answer might surprise you, I haven't brought any girls here, you are the only one." He was looking right back into her eyes. Into her soul. She was taken aback, she detected nothing but complete honesty in him. No deception at all.

, "Okay, I see why you look like that, I'll explain, let's go over here and sit for a minute," he said, leading the way for her to an empty dock where nobody would mind them sitting there. They reached the end of the dock, he removed his shoes and allowed his feet to dip into the water. She wrinkled her nose at the dirty water in the intracoastal waterway, but she came, sat down, and followed suit. He smiled at how pretty and small her cute little feet were. Beautiful as the rest of her.

"I was with a girl, a friend, Janel, and she was the one who showed me this place when I was going through a rough time, sometime ago. She was who I was with when the ATF and DEA agents set me up. Actually, "with" is a bit of a strong word, we were more of close friends, yet we had feelings for one another that neither of us were ever able or willing to address. We were young and wild, and I guess, why fix something that isn't broken, ya know? Anyways, right after I was arrested, she disappeared, and nobody ever saw or heard from her again ..."

"Oh my god! Jean, I'm so sorry ..." Shelby said with all the empathy that she truly felt in her heart for this man.

"Well, its almost 14 years, so I've had time to heal, time to live with what I had caused ..." Jean started, blaming himself as always.

"What do you mean "caused"? How could you have caused anything like that when you were in jail? That's crazy, right?" she asked, interrupting him.

Jean paused, looking out at the water as the sun was rising. Like a phoenix rising afresh out of the old ashes, new and young, trying to start over, Jean wasn't sure if he could go on, as it could call into question his responsibility for the rat lawyer's murder that he had committed just a month ago. He decided to take a leap of faith, and share a piece of himself, with the only girl besides Janel, that he had felt this close to in his whole 38 years on the planet.

"Well, I didn't mean it as if I was directly responsible, but I called her as a witness, so yea, I caused it, no doubt about that. Once those dirty ass agents from the task force realized that she could prove she didn't give consent to search, and take down their whole case, Hermanson, the leader of the dirty cops kidnapped and killed her, I know it in my heart," said Jean. He was focused far off, as if not even in this moment anymore, he was actually back in that day, that moment, reliving his loss all over again.

They sat quietly for a moment until she finally spoke. "Jean, there is no way that you could have known that that was going to happen, it's not --" she started.

"What...Not my fault?" Jean snapped interrupting her. "I should've known though.

By not even knowing, I'm responsible for her death." She looked him in his eyes. "I got my husband killed, Jean. I live with the guilt day in and day out, I understand, and accept how my choices, my mistakes, caused his death, but my own circumstances are so much different from yours. There wasn't any fault to what you did Jean, and you shouldn't be having to live with this, facing all this on your own. There is nothing you could have done differently. You can't shoulder all of that, Jean. You just can't," she finished.

"I could've taken that plea, 25 years to life and she would still be alive," he said. He made no other sound or move and yet she noticed a lone tear falling out of the corner of his eye. Her chest tightened with empathy, her own pain crept in, but she allowed him to have his own moment. His own pain present and ever powerful.

"So, what happened to your husband?" asked Jean sincerely wanting to know, to be able to share in her pain as she had shared in his, to give her his shoulder, as she had given hers so freely. He genuinely wanted to know more about this amazing woman, this strong woman. She didn't answer right away and he sensed a strong desire to hold it inside of her and not share it ever with another soul. She would though, as the sun came up, and the boaters began to move up and down the inter-coastal waterway, happily oblivious to the anguish that each of them were there feeling, and their respective suffering mutually shared.

"It was an attempted prison break from a Bureau of Prisons, or BOP transport bus. Tomas and I just so happened to be in the car that was in front of the prison bus, unknowingly actually, blissfully unaware. I didn't even know it was a prison bus until I got out of the car after hearing the shots. I fucked up, Jean.

I chased the male suspect because I had seen him shoot, who happened to be the only guard who survived, five times in the chest. He had a vest on actually." She paused, trying to put herself together, but she couldn't stop the flood of tears that came falling down. "I chased him around the back of the bus, allowing for the girl that he was trying to break free to get a gun from one of the *dead* guards, and she, she ... she killed him right as I rounded the corner of the bus, and I didn't stop her... I should've stopped her! I should've protected him, I ..." She broke down, she couldn't go on anymore, it was just too much for her.

Jean pulled her in close, hugging her, and as he did, she began to cry deep, into his chest that he had offered her. "SSHHH Shelby, it's okay, I'm here for you. SHHH..." Jean said, trying to comfort her, holding her and hearing her heartbeat as it pitter pattered, feeling her tears soak into his shirt, and allowing her to draw on his strength to keep her strong. They stayed like that for a while, until she was calm enough for him to try to speak. "Shelby, you've got to know that it ain't no where near being your fault! You gotta understand from a rational perspective, that you saw and pursued the only threat that you could identify! Tell me what person, what cop, would see this guy shoot another guard five times and then not chase him, but instead go to check the bus, just in case there is another gunman? Come on, Shelby, your husband would be heartbroken if he could see you blaming yourself for something you could never have seen or known. There was no way that you could've prevented that ma, no way ..." he said.

"But when I say it about Janel, you still blame yourself, even though there is nothing that you could've done ..." Shelby pointed out to him.

"You know what?" he asked, "You're right, and sometimes it takes you to see it from someone else's point of view to see it rationally, so I guess I can reassess my view and try to see it from another perspective, as long as you can agree to do the same about your husband's shooting." He smiled at her, hoping to convince her.

"I can try, Jean, that's all I can promise ..." Shelby said finally.

"That's all I ask for," he said pulling his feet out of the water. "Come on, let's get out of here, do you feel any better?" he asked, truly caring about her answer. "I do," she said, "thank you, Jean, for everything."

"Always, Shelby, that's what I want for you, just to be happy and heal, no matter how hard things are, I'll be here for you always."

Chapter Ten

"Oh shit!" exclaimed EJ from the van provided by his friend, Ty with the Central Intelligence Agency.

Ty hadn't been back yet for a full month, and the CIA had already heard some chatter within the Taliban cells, about a big contributor to their cause, or to ISIS, in or around Boca Raton, Florida. Boca is an upscale rich area in southern Palm Beach County. Many people are unaware of the fact that the actual radicals that flew those hijacked airplanes into the World Trade Center, actually took their flying lessons at Boca Raton's airport because of Boca's affluence and reputation for wealthy class. They were there among the regular rich people, just blending in plain sight and they pulled it off. Nobody even suspected them. Not even the after interview where the neighbor is always like "he was quiet and weird," or "I always knew that something was wrong with him," or the like. They blended in as intended.

With so many rich people in Boca, nobody thought anything out of the ordinary of the new affluent oil sheiks, as they were portraying themselves to be while they had been taking their flying lessons. In fact, before September 11, 2001, America's awareness as well as alert levels weren't what they are today, 20 years later. We in America, are all too familiar with what the terrorists took and what havoc they brought to our innocent civilians. That is why Ty does what he does for the CIA, he is the terrorists worst nightmare, their crippler, and EJ is the hammer that he was using to cripple them with. He was a serious threat to their existence.

"What you got, EJ?" asked Ty, his full attention on his trusted friend.

"I know who that is, I mean on the white Ducati that just pulled in behind that Maybach. Looks like targets in Maybach are unaware of the tail following behind them," answered EJ on their shared communication unit, or COMS for short.

"He's got a damn helmet on, how you going to know who that is under there?" asked another team member that had been on continued surveillance on their target, and who had received the actual reliable intelligence that the person actually in control of funding for this Taliban cell operating in the U.S. was going to be in attendance tonight. Apparently, there was a lot of chatter about this meeting, and that this guy was a big player and supporter of their cause, making him a target. The money was supposed to be in the target's possession and they wanted to get that money, not only to use it for fighting terrorism, but to cripple the Taliban as well.

"I know it cause ..." EJ trailed off, as he was watching the bike closely going after the blacked out Maybach had stopped. "I know it, cause he is riding *my* damn Ducati, and my bike is customized, dropped and stretched, with the frame polished that I did myself! Fuck is he doing here?" he said almost to himself. All of their attention was brought back as the Taliban big shots came outside to greet their guest, which allowed the van's video monitoring system equipment to record all of their faces. All the data would be analyzed real time back in Langley by a team of specialists standing by, just for the purpose of using the facial recognition software to identify these new players in this dirty terrorist game.

The driver of the Maybach got out of the car and opened the trunk before going to the passenger door, opening the door so that the Big Man could get out, and as he did, the driver went back and took out two suitcases and handed them to the first Taliban man, then grabbed the last two and handed them to the remaining guy. They were some metallic aluminum cases and looked very heavy. They could be carrying dirty bombs, phone books, or even dirty clothes. They were slightly upset that they had no indication as to what was in the cases, but were certain they would know soon enough.

The bike parked farther up the street, so EJ intended to find out just what the fuck was going on. He stepped out of the van in his all black tactical gear, and he blended right into the shadows of the night. He doubled back around the block and saw that the bike had been abandoned. Wicks stepped from the shadows of the bushes that he was hiding in when he saw EJ's face, and knew he wasn't a threat. He had a questioning look on his face, so EJ said "follow me," and then led him back to the van as quietly as possible so as not to raise suspicion. Wicks being just as silent.

"Fuck is you doing here, Unc?" asked EJ when they had made it safely back to the van. Ty had already come aboard the van since he was the operations specialist on this mission, and needed a status update, or sitrep on the ongoing task.

"Fair question, 'Unc'," said Ty looking dead at EJ. "This is your uncle that I met before at that barbecue?" he asked EJ, a little bit dumbfounded.

"Yea," answered Wicks, "I'm his uncle, who the fuck are all y'all? Some type of narcs or some shit? EJ, what you got goin' lil homie?"

"Look, Unc, I need you to just answer me first, why are you here following that Maybach? What are you doing?" asked EJ, imploring him to answer him.

"Look, Neph, you tryna see what's up? You wanna holla at me, all good, ya dig? But I don't do no talkin' in front of no damn police, ya heard?" replied Wicks calmly.

"Gentlemen?" EJ said looking at the rest of the team. They all immediately moved so they could get out of the van and allow EJ to find out what was going on with this new turn of events. As far as the team knew, EJ's uncle could quite possibly be working with the money man, the Big Man, following him as an independent security agent, as could just be trying to protect him from the jackers. They just didn't know.

Once everyone was gone, save for EJ, and Ty, whom Wicks had met before at a family function, they waited for Wicks to answer. He still looked uncomfortable with Ty in the van but he decided to trust his nephew enough to take him at his word.

"I'm following "Richy Rich" Baptiste to see if he is doing anything that contributes to the sudden rush of drugs and money comin' through the Youth Center by the kids. With all this extra money floating around, dope, just the kids acting weird and being less like kids-including Lil' Ray-had got my attention," said Wicks.

"Wait! You saying that my 11 year old brother fucking with drugs?" asked EJ loudly, as he was appalled to hear that his brother had anything to do with or was even around some drugs.

"That's what I'm tryna find out nephew, but yea man, that's how it's looking right now," replied Wicks. EJ slammed his fist against the side of the van. The door opened as an operative heard the bang and wanted to make sure that everything in the van was going okay. Ty nodded and signaled for everyone to come back in and to get back into their respective stations.

"Jean," started Ty, since he was the one in charge of the Op," your nephew and I are here for the national security. You say this guy is into drugs, that's fine, we don't give a fuck about that. We are only here to stop another terror attack on our country, we ain't twelve' ya feel me?" Wicks nodded, he knew this Ty was a street nigga too, so he could respect that. "So, what we need, is to know what the fuck a drug dealer is doing, meeting with islamic radicals or terrorists." Wicks is confused, he can't imagine any reason for that type of relationship to exist.

"Man I can't help you there, bruh. But man, Richy Rich ain't just some ordinary drug dealer. He and "Big Head" are the only ones left in the leadership of the Haitian Sensations Drug Cartel, and they are the actual sons of two of the main founders from Port Au Prince, back in the late 1980's, so their power, their infamy, their ... shit man, they employ their own mercenary army in Bahamas where they bring their products in from... man this would be a Fortune 500 company if they were legit, ya feel what I'm sayin'? They got more money than God..." he trailed off watching collective expressions and knew he had hit a nerve. He started thinking about it.

"Fucking crypto!" yelled EJ, "fucking bitcoins!" He looked excited.

"Fuck you talking about?" asked another asset looking confused."Very good, EJ, you're on target with this, " said Ty smiling at EJ.

"Man, it's fucking crypto currency," said EJ, trying to explain to Wicks and the rest of the team how his thinking was going. "It's untraceable, reliable, and it doesn't have to be laundered like most drug money! See, Richy Rich ain't here to support their cause as we had heard at all! Shit, he's just dumping off the dirty cash that they have, and they probably don't know what the asshole he's meeting up is doing with it! Shit, if we hit them both once Rich leaves, we will stop that cash from being used against America, and we can also capture Rich's crypto accounts, and use it to finance our war against them, more operations without having to go through Congressional Oversight Committees."

"I love it when you talk dirty like that!" said the lone female asset there, as she smiled at EJ nodding her approval. Her name was Samantha and she was crushing on EJ.

"Good call EJ! Ok, let's get suited up! We will breach when Rich pulls off, I'll contact the locals to grab Rich! Let's make it happen team, we want them alive, but do we really care about some terrorists? So weapons free, just bring me one mouth to talk to, beyond that, let's have some fun team!" Ty said as he racked the bolt on his MP5, indicating that he was ready for action.

Wicks and EJ quickly stepped outside for a brief talk, before they had to make their move. EJ had already been suited up and ready to go, so he did have a moment to spare while the rest of the observation team prepped themselves for the action about to take place.

"When the fuck was you finna tell me this shit about Ray, Unc?" asked EJ peeved.

"Neph, I got this under control, I already handled the nigga who I know was giving the work to a few of the kids at the Youth Center, so I'm assuming he was the one giving work to Ray, but I'm there almost everyday and there is a nice lady who comes in now, and she's actually the one who hipped me to what was going on. So, I will be watching and I'll keep an eye on Ray, by the way," Jean started smiling, "you should slide through over there and put your gloves on, let's see if you still got it." They both started laughing, remembering the fun times they had there.

"Unc, you know I still got it! Ain't no question about that!" EJ said, and then paused a moment thinking, "Alright Unc, you keep an eye on him, and let me know what's good, and if y'all need me, ya dig?"

Wicks nodded at him and he glanced around. "I see you enjoying my bike too, Unc... " EJ said smiling. "Sho nuff is," said Wicks smiling back at him. "Well, Unc," said EJ, "don't worry about this fool Rich no more, we gone take him to a black site, find out what he knows, and then it's off to Guantanamo for his ass, never to be seen or heard from again. We get all his bank codes and crypto holdings, and we will put his drug money into good use protecting our country, it's all in a day's work, and thank you for the assist too, you know we were completely off track with that one."

"Damn nephew, that shit's cold bruh," said Wicks shaking his head at the irony.

"Patriot Act homie, it's a blank check to do whatever the fuck we gotta do to protect the country, ya know?" said EJ seriously, "so anyways, I'll check you out later, gotta go kill some terrorists for my country, be easy Unc." They dapped up and hugged. "Fo sho, nephew," and Wicks got on EJ's Ducati and got away from the upcoming slaughter that he was sure was about to take place.

EJ came back and got into the van, but everyone else looked like they were ready to go on the breach, so he grabbed his M-16 and pulled the bolt back, putting a round into the receiver, and then flicked the selector to three round bursts.

"Smith, you breach, Jonesy you're point, remember, leave me one mouth to do the talking, and, ok here we go, the Maybach is pulling off, locals are already on him, so let's go get the terrorists, work call!" said Ty with his little pep talk.

All of the team's assets surrounded the upscale two story house. It made the job harder that in Florida there are no basements to break into for a better surprise attack. Only front, back, and sometimes, garage doors. This house was no different, and the stairway going to the second floor was a narrow, straight hallway, almost like a shooting range lane. Impossible to miss a target in the lane, and nowhere for the targets to hide while they were in that lane.

Team two was at the back door, and a two man Op was at the garage door. The CIA asset Jonesy went in first through the front door since his marksmanship was unquestionable and in a class of its own. There were two tengos on the couch that were apparently watching Al Jazeera on the big screen television, who both, within three-tenths of a second had holes put into their radical heads, before they could even register the infidels coming into their lair. Jones moved right to the next room, and several more shots could be heard, as the rest of Team one filled in the front door. Simultaneously, Team two and the two men on the garage Op, also breached their respective doors, rushed into the house clearing rooms as fast as their weapons could fire, and cleared their share of the first floor. "Living room! Clear!" said one asset.

"Kitchen! Clear!" said another asset.

"South Bedroom! Clear!"

"North Bedroom! Clear!"

Many assets yelling to one another that their respective rooms were cleared was all that could be heard besides the actual gunshots throughout the house, until the whole bottom floor was cleared and every terrorist dead. "EJ, bring that shield, Jones, switch to non-lethal, let's clear the top floor now!" yelled Ty.

EJ was last in, and not engaging because of his status as a Marine support agent, not an actual asset, so he handed off the shield. It was an electrified bulletproof shield, so if a target touched its front, they would be electrocuted. All of the assets switched to their secondary weapon systems, such as tasers and paintball guns, shooting chemical agent, or mace filled balls that would burst upon contact with a target. EJ stayed lethally armed, as he was bringing up their rear of the combined teams, and therefore could stop somebody from attacking them from the back.

Before Jones could even start to go up the stairs, an Arab terrorist came out, and without so much as aiming, he started spraying the ceiling and walls of the house. He was quickly disarmed by a taser at the end of the arm of Samantha, the female asset who had earlier flirted with EJ. They quickly followed Jones, holding the shield, leading them up the stairway. At the top landing, they split their teams back up, and the lone radical lunatic was cuffed quickly with the plastic zip ties, then gagged as well as bagged, where a black bag to prevent spitting was placed over the head. The positive side effect being that the terrorist can't see anything at all. Sensory deprivation. It can also be used too in a tight spot for waterboarding, a CIA tactic used to extract information valuable to them from reluctant targets.

EJ was backing up the stairs while still covering the whole of the bottom floor, and then posted himself at the top landing while Teams one and two started clearing the upstairs rooms and shouting their "clear" signs as they went along. It wasn't until he heard the hostage sign come over the COMS that he reacted. EJ had but one eye, but as a marksman, he felt, and it was evidenced that he didn't need it at all, since he only required one eye to aim a rifle. The proof was in the pudding, and he actually shoots better with the one eye than most people with both eyes intact. It sucked though when he was trying to get to the target. This tengo had an AK-47 assault rifle pointed at a beautiful grey eyed light skinned girl in a hijab. EJ didn't hesitate to put a 5.56mm green tip NATO bullet right through his skull and dropped him with less care than sweating a fly. He then ran to the girl and ripped the hijab off of her head to see her to safety as she was screaming hysterically, trying to get away.

After examining her whole body, he confirmed that no visible wounds had been inflicted on her, so he quickly dismissed her to the other agents who were to lead her down to the bottom floor and away from the uncleared floor.

"Got suitcases of cash!" one asset had shouted. "Are you ok?" asked another agent to the girl as she escorted her to the stairs, and EJ noticed at that time the beautiful eyes that struck him as special as she was so out of place in this situation. "Me ... ok ... me okay!" she said as she descended the stairs with the other female agent, who led her to the new cleared zone downstairs where they were questioning others who had been captured.

EJ joined Ty and the other assets who had located the cash in one of their top floor bedrooms. The room was full of computers and other technical looking equipment, as well as a table with chairs, on which the suitcases that they had observed being removed from the trunk of the Maybach laid open, displaying all its contents for them to see. "Did you open them?" asked Ty. "Fuck no, I ain't opening no towelhead's fucking suitcase! I look like a damn rookie?" answered

117

the asset who found them in the room, who was ironically, the only Arab on the team. "Good work fellas, we've got their hard drives, and their money, 'I've got to say today was a good day." Ty said, quoting Ice Cube's hit song from back in the 1990's. There was smiles and some nervous laughter for the moment.

Suddenly, there was some loud screams that could be heard, and one in particular, was that of Samantha, their female asset, and it was haunting. "Oh no! Get Down!" Her scream was cut off by an incredible and powerful explosion. It was an almost impossible noise. As soon as it ignited, all noise in the background went completely silent; the ear drums of those upstairs were destroyed and bodies downstairs, it was devastating. EJ was standing at the window wondering to himself how these terrorists, who aren't the sharpest tools in the shed to begin with, could have gone undetected for so long in such an upscale neighborhood.

He could not comprehend what was happening neither did he notice that the window in front of him, was shattering outwards in front of his eyes. It felt like he was now being propelled by some invisible forces who threw him out onto the lawn, fifteen feet down and ten feet out. He never got the chance to figure out what happened prior, as he was now flying through the air. The darkness came and took him. He never knew what had hit him, just as the old saying goes.

Chapter Eleven

"Big Head" Jimmy Joseph was cruising on his 35 foot Sea Ray Sundancer leaving Nassau, Bahamas, on his way back to West Palm Beach, Florida. He was pissed that he had been called back from Port Au Prince, Haiti, while he was overseeing the building of his 12 bedroom mansion, on a 50 acre estate, just outside of the infamous city. He has to drop off his wife and the kids back at his other compound, on New Province Island, near Nassau. His compound had many buildings, along with his house, some for storage of many different types of narcotics and many arms as well. Others were barracks for his personal militia that he had kept as protection from not only the jackers, but also from sovereign or government armies. Big Head was like the Costco or Sam's Club of drugs. He was also working his way into the niche of guns and military weapons systems but that, he was just starting to get his feet wet in. He was trying to fit into the arms dealers world; he would eventually do so if he could only make some more of the right connections. For that, he was dependent on his partner "Richy Rich", and his association with some of those radical ISIS idiots or whatever they were. He didn't care, he only cared about progression in his world. As far as he was concerned, the only color that mattered was green and the only damn religion was the worship of money. That was the extent of his morals.

All he knew was that Big Meet was missing in action and now, so was his own damn partner Richy Rich. He was pissed. It was either Rich trying to pull a coup, which he really doubted, or it was the Mexican Gulf Cartel finally making a move, after damn near two decades of them being in competition with them. Either one was a very bad look for Big Head, as he could do without either of those type of problems.

Oh hell, he thought to himself, a cartel he could always deal with, but inside his own organization, it would be hard not knowing who had betrayed him, as well as how far the pollution of his team might have gone. That was the worst thing, not knowing. One thing in his favor was that Richy Rich was scared to death of being in Haiti, scared of ever leaving Palm Beach County all together, so the militia was completely under Big Head's control, and nobody, even Mexican Gulf Cartel, could build even close to a strong enough army to come for him.

Some of those kids, he had got off the streets and given a home to. He had given them training, family, money, and something to protect. That's why he almost knew for a fact that it wasn't a coup, they would have to go through Buju, Antione, Richy Rich, it was just crazy to think. He had too many people in between him and the touchables. He had given them all something to fight for. Rich knew how effective Big Head's militia could be as well, since he had been on board in a distraction boat, many years ago, to witness the event when U.S. Coast Guard boats and helicopters, had descended on a load boat while they had been running in distraction boats. Danzi and Scarab boats, typically known as "go-fast boats" or cigarette boats, were used to get the Coast Guard to chase them. As the load boat, most of the time a slow fishing boat would be able to get by, with all the action on the distraction boats. Rich had seen the ten militia men alone with SAMs, or surface-to-air missiles, take out the helicopter, and two coast guard cutters in 45 seconds flat. They also got the load successfully to the Boynton Beach Inlet with no casualties to any of his men at all.

That was the awesome power that Big Head possessed, as well as his influence with the politicians and government officials that he payed, and owned, to keep things running smoothly, and keep that incident with Coast Guard from repeating itself. So, it had to be that Mexican Gulf Cartel and Ascension Felix, who he had always had beef with, out of Matamoros, Tamaulipas, a state in North Eastern Mexico. It had to be them making a play on his team for exclusivity for the South Florida area. They had been trying to take over since his father had been killed by Baptiste in Port Au Prince, Haiti, many, many years ago when that regime was in power there.

See, Big Head had no problem staying away from South Florida and keeping himself on the islands. That was a reason that he and Rich, as well as their fathers-before-them-had such a good system as partners. Big Head had muscle and influence, with his political connections, but Rich had all the little youngsters pushing the dope for him, in addition to his much bigger clients. Rich had the means to move the dope, charismatic as well as a hood legend, he was an intricate part to their money printing machine. But so was Big Head. So, one couldn't run the operations effectively without the other one. They needed each other. More than ever, now that he was about to make this six million dollar arms deal, with those Taliban motherfuckers. He had already brokered the deal with an associate in Trinidad, who in turn had acquired the grenade launchers, M-60s, and SAMs from his contact in the soon to fall Venezuelan government, from which Trinidad was off the coast of.

It seemed to solidify the suspicions in Big Head's enormous cranium, that this had to be the work of those Mexicans in the damn Felix Family and the Gulf Cartel. What he couldn't figure out, was why his mole in the DEA, Raines, couldn't find anything at all definitive about Big Meet or Richy Rich's disappearances. Nothing at all! Big Head was pissed as he pulled his boat into his docking at his grand Manalapan house, just east of the city of Lantana. Agent Raines was waiting on him on the dock when he stepped off of the boat in his Versace suit and Red Bottom boots. He kept his signature machete in his hand for the visual effects and the theatrics he was known for. He started walking up the walkway from the dock, with Agent Raines in his wake, as the Big Boss lead the way. His right hand man, as well as assistant, Antione Jean, walked with him, leaving his body guard Jojo, in the boat to gather all of the luggage and belongings.

"What ju got fa me?" Big Head asked Agent Raines, in his thick Haitian accent, once they were inside the house and safe from any outside ears. His house, a five bedroom mini mansion, right on the inter-coastal waterway. A step down from the huge mansion he was building in Haiti, even from his house on the compound near Nassau, but still a multi million dollar estate, in the richest community on the east coast.

"DEA, ATF, and the FBI has nothing. Palm Beach County Sheriffs has nothing, and they are the ones on the Task Force as well. I went down the list, every informant I have, offered bonuses, everything I could do, Jimmy, and all I got were remote suspicions about the fire at Demetrius' barbershop. Nobody knows nothing! If it was the Gulf Cartel, I would know about it, plus, they don't care who knows it when they do their shit. So, we would have found at least a head or some body parts, cuz the bodies don't disappear all the way with them," said Agent Raines.

"Ju stupid beech! Fa why I pay all these monies, huh? I pay ju- I get nothing! Get the fuck out of my house beech, you go find who do these to Haitian Sensations an ju bring to me they heads! Ok? Cuz if ya no do ... I find men who *do*! Now ju get out!" yelled Big Head, as the scared to death agent ran out of Big Head's house on the double, wishing that he had never gotten involved with these crazy Haitians.

"Who the fuck walks around with a fucking Machete, anyways?" he wondered to himself.

Antione and Big Head later pulled up to a stash house on 5th & K street North in Lake Worth City. The two Portuguese brothers, Pookie, and Mookie, were with their cousin Steff, there in the trap, next door. Pookie and Mookie were both just under six feet tall, and average size, tan-skinned and both with over 20 gold teeth permanently implanted in their mouths, as 'plates' or pull out teeth that weren't permanent weren't accepted in south Palm Beach

County. Anyone who had the plates, were a punch line in the hood if you weren't a child or a girl. Even pit bulls in Palm Beach County, as a popular culture, had permanent gold fangs. But if a grown man wore a plate or the pullouts of golds, the homies would ride them mercilessly, making fun of them until they take the embarrassing things out. It was not cool or fashionable as it was in Texas, where plates were cool. In Palm Beach County and South Florida, if you were in the dope game, you were in the game for life or not at all.

Steff, Pookie and Mookie's cousin, was only 5'4 and maybe 160 pounds, soaking wet, but he packed a mean punch, he was the real muscle in the group. As being quick tempered and spending three days a week at the shooting range, Gator Guns, made him the Haitian Sensations' most dangerous member. He had nine bodies under his belt and was always quick to add more, as he would shoot first and ask questions later.

The last guy he had killed had been a Zoe Pound gang member, and he had just started having dinner with his wife, some oxtails, rice and black beans. After Steff shot him in front of her, he sat there eating this guy's dinner with his wife sitting fearfully across from him at the table. He literally didn't give a fuck. Growing up, if you beat him in a one on one, he would get a stick and come back. You beat him with that? He comes back with a knife. But that had been before he had discovered the miracle of gunpowder propelled lead. He was never the same afterwards. So he lived at that shooting range since then, spending all of his time there. Steff had put his first body in the ground at the age 15 and vowed to have a hundred bodies before his 30th birthday. He was 19 and had nine bodies so far. He knew the Haitian Sensations would have him there in no time though, and he was ready.

"Steff, what's good in the hood? How's things in Lake Worth, lil' homie?" asked Antoine as they settled into the living room of the house.

"All good homie, jus' been bumpin' an grindin', tryna get this money and slay these niggas be in da way, ya dig?" said Steff.

Steff led Big Head and Antoine, whom he usually deals with, if not Richy Rich, into the safe room. The room was reinforced with rebar, and had an electronic barred entrance, and a seven foot tall safe. An Italian job.

"What's goin' down big homie? Y'all lookin' all stressed out and shit, my count on point, ain't nothin to be stressin' fo," said Steff trying to ease the tension that he was sensing from the moment Big Head pulled up on the scene, which was rare. But Antoine put a reassuring hand on his shoulder and said, "It ain't you Steff, Big Meet and Richy Rich both been MIA and we don't know what's up, so we are checkin' all of the homies, just to see if anything been goin' on, and when the last time anyone had seen either of them."

"Aww shit! Nawl bruh, I heard bout the barbershop burning down an shit, but I ain't seen neither of them for a minute, ya know? What y'all thankin' tho, bruh?" asked Steff, truly concerned about the situation.

"We ain't sho, but it could be the Felix Family," said Antoine.

"Awl shit, man they been bitin' at our heels for a good minute, so I wouldn't put shit past 'em, but I ain't had no problems out 'em in a minute. They mainly stay out west, which don't bother us cuz we hustlin' in da city, so ... I just don't know, but I'm with you, I'm bout that action if you need me!" replied Steff.

"Das' good lil' Steff, I let ya know, ju jus' be on point an watch good an let we know what ya hear ... " said Big Head in his thick Haitian accent.

"Ok Head, fo' sho'! I got ya!" said Steff.

After Antoine handled their business and let Steff know he would be doing so from now on, he locked the safe back and made the final plea of what they had come to do; Investigate and warn.

They then slid on to the next house that they had on their agenda to do the same with. Both kept in mind how Steff had not only always been loyal, but also such an efficient killer. They might need him sooner than later if some things were not figured out soon and their missing guys found. It wouldn't be pretty either.

They then visited the rest of their crew members in the six other dope houses that they used for crack and heroin distribution. Only one report of a small confrontation between an 11 year old and a 14 year old distribution kid. It was Big Meet's nephew in fact. So, being as this was the only incident where anything was out of the ordinary, it allowed them to concentrate fully on the issue. The fact that it involved the nephew of one of the most valuable as well as a missing member, it caused even more attention to be placed onto this issue.

"Wha' happon'?" asked Big Head when they had finally gotten Lil' Fade alone.

"Well, I was missing some of my dope. A bundle out of my locker at the Youth Center was missing, so I had been askin' round, till one a my licks tol' me he had bought da same color bags as mines wit da Z on em! So, I put in that work fo' my position! I wanted to be a Haitian Sensation and now I be done put in that work, so I'm in now ain't I? Right? I'm a Haitian Sensation like my Unc, right?" asked Fade with all of the eagerness of the 14 year old that he was. A kid that wanted his toy.

Antoine and Big Head just looked at each other. After they heard this story from two others, and then finally from Fade himself, they weren't so sure about this. There could be no way that an 11 year old being shot by a 14 year old could have anything to do with two of Haitian Sensations' top ranking members going MIA, could it? They were both thinking that it was a coincidence. Plus, it didn't make any sense for Richy Rich to be involved in any of the actual workers. Richy Rich was above the lieutenants such as Big Meet, who were above the workers and the prospects as well. All of the available information just didn't make any sense to them. None.

"Do ya uncle know you lose a bundle? You tell him who you suspect at all? Anything?" asked Antoine as Big Head nodded in agreement.

"Nawl, my uncle ain't been round too much lately, I handled my business soon as I be done found out who be done got my shit, so I'm in now ain't I? I'm Haitian Sensation since I put that work in?" he asked again, relentless about it.

Big Head and Antoine left and went to see Leo, on the South

Side of Lake Worth, to see if he had heard anything. Leo Fuentes was a Miami Cuban, but had moved to Palm Beach County to be closer to his family in West Palm Beach. Leo ran his group out of Lake Worth City's South Side, which was opposite of Steff's operation on the Northside of town. Leo was short, and stocky, but he was no joke. His whole mouth was filled with gold teeth after he had, on Miami Beach won his Golden Gloves title.

He actually had got his first body in the ring when he was just 17 years old. He had caught his opponent so hard with a left hook to the temple that he was knocked out cold and ended up going into a coma as a result. He had some brain swelling and no matter what the doctors did, they just couldn't stop the swelling, and he never again woke up after that blow. Leo was infamous in Miami for that fight, hated even. But it wasn't only that fight that he was known for, he was also known for who his father was as well. His father, Manuelito Fuentes, had been one of Castro's top officials in Cuba, in charge of his security force, until one day he uncovered a plot on the former dictator's life, and knowing Fidel so well, he stepped aside and allowed it to take place. It obviously failed, and Manuelito fled Havana with his family. He ended up settling in South Florida; first Miami, and then Palm Beach County, where they have been since.

Antoine and Big Head arrived at the Lake Worth operation's base, a house off of 12th Avenue South, where many Haitians, Jamaicans, and Cubans, called their home.

After their knock, Leo opened the door and invited them in. Although Leo was Cuban, like many Cubans, his skin color was black. Along with his gold teeth, his skin color allowed him to fit in to a black or Haitian neighborhood without being out of place. His fluency in Spanish allowed him to deal with all of the hispanic clientele that Lake Worth had, as well as the Spanish speaking gang members looking to break away from the cartel that the Felix Family ran, and their long reaching tentacles. He was considered a great asset to the Haitian Sensations cartel, and was constantly pursued by the Felix Family to join them. Leo knew his place though. He respected the 'gangsta' of the Haitian Sensations members who went and took the sentence given to them when they were caught. Felix's Matamoros Cartel were always dealing with rats, and when they would kill one, three more of the rodents would appear in place of the dead one. Leo had no respect for an organization with so many weak links, and so he would always stay loyal to the Haitian Sensations.

"Antoine, what's good?" asked Leo as he dapped paws with him, "Big Head, been a while my friend, good to see ya, what's goin' down?" He pointed to his Italian Latuzzi couches for them to be seated. Once they had sat down, he joined them in his own, Lazy-Boy chair that was his favorite, facing them. Even though Leo was only 20 years old, he was addicted to nicer things, and he kept his base of operations house-full of them; furniture, electronics, even his dishes were Versace. He offered them a drink. He was sipping on Hennessy, his favorite, on ice, as always.

"Nah, we good Leo, only we come fa to check on ya, see is all goin' good wit' ya in da L-Dub?" asked Big Head, using the hood name for Lake Worth City.

"Yea Head, everything be good over here. Always on da lookout, always got my head on da swivel, ya dig?" replied Leo, not knowing, yet sensing that something was amiss, just waiting for them to get to the issue at hand.

"Okay, okay ... " said Antoine, looking into his eyes, "we got a lil' problem going on an we tryna figure it out, so we talkin' to everyone ... "

"Oh, Yea?" replied Leo, "what's going on then?"

"Big Meet, Richy Rich, dem missin' ..." said Big Head getting straight to it.

"Dey missin'?" asked Leo, confused, "Missin' like, dead missin', or missin like dem done run off missin'? Cuz it's a few kind of missin'."

"We ain't know Leo, but dead dem might be, cuz we not hear nothin', an Big Meet dem barbershop burned down ... " started Big Head as Leo's phone started vibrating on the table. "Nah," he said when Big Head asked him if he needed to get that phone call, seeing that it was his little brother Los on the phone, "Jus my lil' bro, I'll hit em back later, so damn, Big Meet's shop burned down? Damn ... " he trailed off, not knowing what more to say beyond that.

"Yea," said Antoine, "last night we get the call to come back, but that shit happen two nights ago, both been missing since then."

"Well, shit I ain't even much heard anything, but you know I stay in the L-Dub, and I only be goin' to Miami, never to West Palm, so I wouldn't know anyways, but that's crazy! Shit, what y'all need me to do?" asked Leo, not knowing what more he could say or do, but wanting to know the purpose of the visit since they should know he would've called Antoine first if he knew anything at all anyways.

"Nothin' can be done, just stay on point, and get at us if you hear or see any things that are strange, it might even be the Felix Family, so just stay eyes wide, and keep the operations tight," instructed Antoine.

"Alright, fo sho, you know I'm always on point, I'm tryin' to keep this money machine movin', so I'm on it. Holla at me when y'all know what's up, or if you need me, I'm down fa da cause, ya dig?" Leo said to them as he walked them outside. He noticed that his phone was vibrating again as he was walking them out. Something was up, for his little brother to be blowing up his phone like this, so he was hoping that it was nothing to do with his family. Shit, he had enough stress worrying what Big Head and Antoine had dropped on his plate, he didn't need any family type of emergencies getting him any more pressure than he already had going on.

After they had pulled off, he saw a few of his workers coming up the block from their shifts on the corner, so he had to do their counts, and give them their re-ups, before he even had a chance to call his little brother back. But when he walked into the living room to grab his phone, with the intention of calling Los back, he saw that his phone was already vibrating with an incoming text from Los. It read: "Lil Ray been shot! We @ St. Mary's downtown."

Lil Ray was his little brother's best friend and sparring partner. Although Ray was a bit younger, unlike most adolescent kids, their age difference only made Los look at Ray as a little brother, which in turn, made Leo look at him in the same way, as if he was Leo's own little brother. Except that Ray would be a 11 year old little brother, so how had an 11 year old kid ended up getting shot? Leo didn't know, but he got into his white Denali with the white matching leather interior, and sped off to St. Mary's hospital as fast as he could, without risk of getting pulled over. When he arrived, he was astounded at the story that Los was telling his friend's mother, Miss Laurie, who had also just arrived. Miss Laurie, the white Italian lady, was balling her eyes out, and Los was covered in his friend's blood. Apparently, Los was there when it had happened, and his quick action and his balls, had gotten him and Ray a fast ride to the hospital when he had flagged down a car nearby the Youth Center that they had been walking from. That ride by no doubt was what saved Ray's life and his mother was grateful for that, although she still couldn't comprehend how her 11 year old son came to be the shooting victim and her standing here worried to death if her son was to survive or not. Los couldn't tell her the details, only that the shooter and his friends had taken off running after the shots, not having seen Los inside the Arab store buying snacks, and that mistake had allowed Los to see Ray's shooter and his friends. But that was something that he would keep to himself, and what he would further use when the time for retribution came. That way nobody would be looking for the actual shooters, only who they thought were just random kids shooting at other random kids. But the day would come when they would pay for their misdeed, and Los was willing to help them see the errors in their ways.

Chapter Twelve

"Jean! Get your ass down here to St. Mary's hospital! Ray been shot over by that damn Youth Center and my baby is in critical!" cried Laurie into her brother, Jean's ear in his bluetooth. He was required to use the bluetooth at work at the print shop where he was employed because of safety precautions.

"What the ---sis what you mean that Lil Ray been shot? He fucking 11! How the fuck could he be shot?" yelled Jean as he started to walk towards his boss' office away from his own work station, which drew some attention from co-workers.

"On my way, sis. Try to stay calm and just pray for him and I'll be there in a few minutes!" Jean told her as he walked to his boss, Mr. Travis' office. Mr. Travis was the family friend of he and Laurie's father whom had given him the job there.

A friend of his family, so it was therefore not a problem when there was a family emergency.

"Mr. Travis, Lil Ray been shot, Laurie called me from St. Mary's and wants me to be there with the family, would you-" Jean started trying to explain before Mr. Travis interrupted him, confirming his affiliation with their family by saying simply, "Say no more, gone down there man! My prayers are with y'all and lil Ray ..." Jean was so lost as he jumped on the Ducati and left some rubber on the pavement peeling out of the industrial street. He broke every law, but he got to St. Mary's in six minutes flat. He found Laurie, Los and a few others in the waiting room of the ICU floor of the hospital. Laurie ran to him and hugged him, crying on his chest. He hugged her back as he caught eyes with Los. He knew that Los knew what was up since he was so covered in blood, it could only be Lil Ray's. Los gave him a nod and then nodded towards the door so he would know that he needed some privacy to talk to him, and Jean nodded back to him immediately agreeing.

"It's ok sis, he gone be alright, just keep praying sis, Ray is a strong shawty, and you and I both know he too stubborn to give up ... let me go an holla at Los and see what the hell happened," he said releasing her.

"Jean, don't you do nothin'!" said Laurie, still crying her eyes out, "I don't need you going back to prison, just let the cops handle it, ok?"

"Okay ... okay, sis," he said patting her back, "nobody goin' back to damn prison, I just need to hear from Los why this happened, I love you, I'll be right back." As he released her, Los took his cue and led him out through the door and into a stairwell. "Who?" asked Wicks with a murderous look. He was no longer Jean. He had immediately allowed for Wicks to take control and be the one to pursue the ones responsible for the shooting. He had to find out who, but Wicks had a target to get, and as he never before failed, he wasn't going to start failing now. Especially when his family is involved. Wicks would get his target. He always did. Wouldn't stop.

"Man check it, they ain't know I was inside that lil' Arab store. So dey won't even know that we know, but Unc, it was Matt, Lil' J, and Fade, dem! Fade pulled da trigger man, I'm sorry, I-" Wicks

135

interrupted him though.

"Man, don't say sorry Los, wasn't shit you could do, but damn lil' homie, dem lil' niggas just kids! Fuck!" Wicks was pissed, but he was not convinced he could go and bust on some 14 year old kids. They were only a couple years older than Lil' Ray himself, to Wicks, being 38, they were all the same age. They were just kids.

"For what tho, Los?" asked Wicks, genuinely confused, "What da fuck dey wanna bust at Lil' Ray for?!" It just didn't make any sense. Lil' Ray didn't offend anyone.

"Unc, he made me promise not to say nothing, but I know I gotta let you know at least what's going on. .. he found a bundle of dope in the locker room at the Youth Center. I told him them 'Z' bags was for Fade's shit, but he wanted to hit a few licks and try to help out with you and his family, ya know?" said Los respectfully. Everyone knew that Wicks had paid his dues, put in work, and earned the respect, but for Los, he was even more respected because of the knowledge Los had about Wicks. When Wicks had kept his mouth shut and took 66 years after going to trial rather than a plea or turning rat, only a few people were privy to the information that Los was an insider to. It really had been Los and Leo' Uncle, Damaon 'Diamond Dozen' Fuentes, whom the ATF, DEA, and Task Force agents were really after because they could never find out who he had been paying off to get the Haitian Sensations the Government protection that they had so clearly enjoyed all of these years. It was a protection that went far over their heads and they wanted badly to get to the bottom of it and find out who their crooked agents were.

When Wicks couldn't be bribed, threatened, or persuaded into talking, the pissed off dirty cops, who the whole time were just trying to make sure that they got their cut, went after Wicks, hoping to be able to break him. They couldn't and they didn't. So they overcharged him and set to make an example of him. But he still never broke. So the respect that the Haitian Sensations had for him, as well as the whole Fuentes family as a whole was immense. Los would always look up to Wicks and respect him, and his gangsta. He had most definitely earned that much from everyone connected to the Haitian Sensations.

"What he mean to help me and his family? I got a job, and his dad has a good contractor job, and they are doing good! What the fuck was he talking about? What was he thinking with this shit? After all I been through? He didn't learn?" asked Wicks, seriously confused on this.

"Well, you know," Los said and paused, "Everyone always talkin' bout how you should be sittin' high, big crib, you know, after all you done and been through, niggas wanna see you on top this shit, ya know?"

"Lil' homie, I'm not 'back on top' as you said," said Wicks angrily, "cuz I choose *not* to! Cuz prison is where we end up. All that shit you buy goes to the next nigga in line man, it's a set up, a fucking revolving door. Ma-fuckas want us to go back to prison, and that's my reason for not being back on top the bullshit drug game Lil' Homie, cuz it ain't worth it, and I beg you Lil' Los, as I would beg my lil' nephew in there on ICU, man leave all that shit alone man, the whole drug game is for suckas! When you alone at night, when they lock dem cell doors, they got complete control of you. If they decide not to feed you one day, guess what? You finna die. Simple as that. No amount of money in the world can buy your way out of that shit then. No money in the world is worth being locked in a cage like a fuckin' animal. But if y'all at the Youth Center don't start listening and thinking for your own selves, y'all will find out soon enough. I pray not though, I don't wish that shit on anybody, not even my own enemies ... not anybody ... "

"What happened to you in there unc? You ain't the same no more," said Los.

"Let's hope you don't never find out lil' Los, cuz they put us against each other in there, make us stab and kill each other for their entertainment. We do it too, cuz it's like eat or get eaten in there man, kill or be killed. Ain't for us lil' homie, so what it takes a lil' longer to buy a lil' smaller house? It's a small house that they can't take away from you man, ya dig?" said Wicks, trying hard as he always did to drop some jewels on the youngsters at the Youth Center and keep them away from following his path. The wrong path, the path that he regrets the most.

"Oh, thank you Jesus! Thank you Jesus ..." Laurie was saying as they walked back into the waiting room. The doctor was just walking away, and from everyone's happy expressions, Wicks could sense that Lil' Ray was going to be okay. He silently gave thanks to God, along with everyone else there to support Ray, also praying for him.

"Hey, Sis, what's good? What did the Doctor say?" asked Jean.

"They removed the bullet that was near to his spine! That's why it was so serious, cuz it could have paralyzed him, it was so close. By the grace of God, he will be able to walk again. Thank you Jesus! The other two bullets went in and out, one though his leg, the other went through his shoulder. Neither of those did any damage at all that was life threatening, so he will make it--thank you Jesus!" said Laurie with tears running her mascara down her cheeks, tears of relief for a mother worried.

"Good sis! Thank God for that! When can we see him?" asked Jean, with Wicks having been replaced with Jean now and Jean's worried heart taking control.

"He's still out, they said in a few hours he should wake up," Laurie answered. Just then Sammy and Shelby walked up. Sammy said "I'm so glad he ok, let me know if there is anything that I can do to help —" but Laurie interrupted, "You can stay away from my son! This shit happened right when he left that damn center! I'll never let him back over there!" said Laurie angrily towards Sammy. "Wait sis, now you can't blame Sammy for anything, he's only trying to help the kids, it's not his fault," said Jean in his defense. "No, it's okay Jean," Sammy said, then looked to Laurie, "if there is anything I can do or help in anyway, please give me a call, I'll go now." With that he turned and left. Shelby gave Jean a hug after Sammy had gone. "I'm so sorry Jean, is he okay?" Shelby had tears in her eyes as she asked this, but refused to let them drop, as if by them dropping, it would somehow seal Ray's fate. "He gone be okay ma,

139

thanks for being here," said Jean holding her close and speaking gently into her neck. "Of course Jean, I came as soon as I heard," she replied as earnestly as possibly, considering the situation.

Jean and Shelby sat and held hands for a few minutes. Shelby had heard around her department that the Haitian Sensations were expecting to war soon. Many of her senior colleagues had snitches that had been telling them Haitian Sensations was pissed about their two high ranking members going missing and were gearing up for a war. So, all the Palm Beach County law enforcement agencies, even the municipalities were all notified and expected to be ready in case anything jumped off with any of the gangs. Shelby was on call but had been spending every free minute that she had at the Youth Center or on her laptop doing her own investigations. She had been doing a lot of soul searching as well and had come to somewhat of a conclusion. Her decision could jeopardize her life and her career, but she could only follow her heart and pray for the best. She also thought that her career was nothing if not for having the power and ability to help people and make a change in her community.

"Jean, I need you to come with me, I have to show you something, and I need to know if you trust me...I mean completely?" Shelby was shaking now, and Jean could sense the desperation in her voice. The need that existed in her.

"Well, Lil' Ray gone be alright, so I guess, let me tell my sis I'm finna bounce but will be back," said Jean if not a bit reluctantly, but as he examined himself, he found that he did indeed trust her with his life obviously. He had bodied Big Meet in front of her, and allowed her to not only witness, but participate in a conspiracy to destroy evidence, get rid of the body, and commit arson at the barbershop, all in the name of righteousness, if not justice. So if she was anything hot, she would have given him up for that and he would be in jail now. So, he figured she was trustworthy, if anything, she was definitely that.

After he had explained to his family about his reasons for having to depart from them and promising sincerely not to kill anyone involved in it, and to let the police do their jobs to his sister, he met Shelby by his bike, where she had also parked hers. "Where to?" Jean asked as he slid onto the Ducati. "Follow me ..." she said and then with that, she started her bike, kicked it into first gear, and then began to burn off, quickly leaving Jean to play catch up.

She pulled over at a mini-plaza in Lantana, off of Federal Highway, that had a bondsmans office and accounting firm in it, and parked on the side of the building. There were woods located behind the plaza, and Jean followed as she led him down the path after leaving the bikes and helmets behind. They walked for about 5 minutes down the path until there was a tree that was burnt and dead, obviously one that had been struck by lightning. She then left the path and stopped at a haunted looking clearing, a bit off of the pathway. Jean noticed a distinct area with a six foot by three foot area that was covered by some rocks and such. He was astonished. This was obviously a grave site. The burial for something, or maybe someone. Shelby noticed the look of recognition in Jean's facial features. She still couldn't get over the fact that underneath all of his facial tattoos, he had a gentleness about him, a kind and handsome face. She thought that it might have been a contribution to his decision to actually go through with tattooing his face. After all, a man couldn't look gentle or kind in prison, could he? He would be constantly tested and have to continually prove himself to everyone, but with the facial artwork, he had a look that said he was outright dangerous. She brought herself back to why she had brought Jean here in the first place. To show him that she trusted him with her life.

As she stared at the grave, Jean looked questioningly at her, waiting patiently for her explanation. She was sure about what she was doing, she trusted him but the words would be some that she had never spoken before to another soul. To Jean, it seemed so wrong, so out of place, with birds chirping and animals living around this certain death, it was unfair that whoever this was, got to stay in such a beautiful and peaceful place, while he lived in a world where dirty cops can get you 66 years in prison for non-violent and victimless crimes. Wicks was back now. He couldn't sit aside while death was so near to him. His 11 year old nephew sat in a hospital after being shot over some drugs. He couldn't stand that this beautiful and very special girl could be living in a world so full of pain, Jean struggled with his thoughts without allowing Wicks to assume control. He didn't like that Shelby sat here in pain. It was another injustice visited upon an imperfect yet amazing world. Unjust.

"Andre Wells," she said finally. Jean knew it was coming

142

before she even said it, he knew it would be justified. Wicks type of justice. Either street justice or God's justice, either one was okay by him and Wicks.

"A heroin dealer and sometimes photographer. He caught a young girl, Savannah, 14 years old, beautiful, stunning actually. He said all the right things and told her how beautiful she was, and how she could be a model, that she was special really, which by the way was the only thing that he didn't lie about. He was a wedding photographer by profession, she met him at a distant aunt's wedding, and he happened to be working that event, the rest is history. I never knew how he did it, but he started by taking pictures, telling her that he could help her get her little brother, her family, out of the poverty in which they had lived." As Shelby spoke, her eyes radiated the hatred as she stared at the grave of a guy worse than a simple chomo, he was a monster preying on a little girl's love for her own family.

"She fell for it, and then ultimately for him. You already know the story, he then got her on heroin, the pictures he took turned into porn which then turned to tricks. She never stood a chance. I arrested him for murder, read him his Miranda rights and had given him the Miranda card so he could sign it saying that he had been read his rights, but somewhere in the confession, he either didn't give it back or maybe someone lost it, either way, his shyster lawyer got it thrown out on the 5th amendment violation of his Miranda rights. Yea, even though I read him his rights, I didn't start recording the interview until after I had done the card. It was my fault ... " Shelby stopped talking and looked into Jean's kind eyes.

143

"His lawyer was right on top of it. I think you might know him. Vincent --" Wicks' eyes got big as the realization hit him and he interrupted her.

"--Rodriguez, Jr." He said it almost reverently. Almost like a prayer.

"Yep. So, when I found Vincent Rodriguez's body a few months ago, I thought nothing of it, but when Sammy handed me your file, I saw how big your case was, and I was curious, so I looked into your record, and when I cross referenced his name with your case files, I got the link between Marlow and Rodriguez on their twitter accounts. I happen to know that scumbag, Marlow from when he worked in Miami robbery homicide division, just before he had joined ATF and had relocated to West Palm Beach. Seeing that Marlow had several sexual harassment complaints in his file, one of which was from me, it wasn't hard to imagine him involved in that ATF-DEA task force drug and prostitution ring that got taken down. Every dog has it's day."

"So, back to this. Ultimately, Andre Wells pleaded guilty to possessions charges and they dropped the murder of Savannah, which just killed her mother's heart and the rest of her family, her little brother. So I waited the year and a day that he was sentenced to, followed him, tased him, and drug his skinny ass here, gagged and tied, dug this hole in front of him, and then happily pushed his chomo ass in, and started filling in the hole with him still and intensely breathing air he didn't ever deserve."

Shelby looked at Jean seriously and intensely. "I wanted you to know that I know what you did with Rodriguez, who was a bad man. He was involved with Marlow and Hermanson in that drug and prostitution ring. I also wanted you to know what I do to bad men, men that the justice system doesn't work on. Men like Andre Wells, men that have to pay for what they've done." Shelby stopped talking and was looking expectantly at Jean.

"But you were so grossed out when I blew Big Meet's noodles out! I don't get it!" Jean was laughing yet very confused. He had a lot to figure out. This woman was like a deep sea of secrets, some he might never know. But he would accept the challenge before him with her. She was worth it, he knew that much.

"The reason that I was so grossed out, was that you got brains in my hair! You know how hard it is to get brain matter out of a black girl's hair?" Shelby punched his arm laughing along with him. Sharing the moment. Somehow after all this and after the secret that she had shared with him, he was so impressed, he was reassured. He now knew that everything was going to be okay with them. They were going to make it and they both could feel it in the air. It was special.

Chapter Thirteen

After the explosion at the ISIS Taliban safe house, the full strength of the CIA had cordoned off the block, transferred all the living victims to a special trauma floor at Delray Medical Center, and told the press that it had been a gas leak. The press were of course idiots. They didn't even have gas in that neighborhood, but press would run with whatever sensationalized the story and made it more outrageous, so that's what they got. The incredible.

EJ, Ty, and the two other assets were the only survivors inside the house. EJ woke up in the hospital with a light concussion as he had been propelled out of the window by the explosion and had hit his head on the next door neighbor's wall and air conditioning unit located where it was facing the house that blew up. Ty, and the other two CIA assets were suffering from minor cuts and bruises but they all had hearing loss from the explosion's powerful force. The suitcases of the money were all recovered as the actual fire didn't spread into the upstairs area. Ambulances had already been in route before the explosion because of the casualties and victims of the breach and the following fire fight directly afterward.

All the terrorists and assets that had been in the downstairs section of the house, were all pronounced dead on the scene. The Fire Department's investigators had found the remnants of a C-4 enabled suicide vest which they believe the 'hostage' had been wearing. The Haitian grey-eyed beauty had been faking her captivity in order to be surrounded by the most Americans, or infidels, as they saw us, when she then would detonate, and take as many American lives as possible. Another evil so dark, that it was unimaginable. These were the same people, same animals, who had crashed planes into the World Trade Center Twin Towers, taking countless innocent American lives. Even a visiting class of innocent kids had been killed in that crazy act of cowardice. Now in another cowardly act, this brainwashed girl had killed all of the innocents in the same way, these infidels that she had killed, had been the same great and brave people who had moments before, put their lives on the line in order to save hers. Fucking islamic radical terrorists. EJ could never see or understand how they could just brainwash people into believing their rubbish. It was a mystery to him, one he would never be able to figure out no matter how hard he tried. They were from another planet almost, mostly like Aliens to Earth.

EJ moved as though he wanted to get out of bed and Ty was there immediately to stop him. "Whoa there playboy, you got a concussion, they are holding you over night for tests to come back, relax ..." said Ty. EJ sighed, but he laid back. EJ always trusted and respected his friend and mentor, so he relaxed and laid back.

"How many did we lose, Ty?" asked EJ bracing himself for the answer he dreaded.

"We lost eight of ours, Samantha was one of them, I'm sorry, I know you liked each other. We also lost the four of them that we had captured upstairs, so we are all suspended for the following investigation ... it's a really big clusterfuck, bad news all around," said Ty resigned to the worst case.

147

"Anything at all positive come out of this shit?" EJ asked, upset.

"Well, we did catch one sneaking out of our custody, thank God for small favors that he got as far as he did, cuz he's unhurt and can talk, so that's the best news yet," said Ty.

"How much does he know?"

"Seems like we got the head of this terrorist cell, so once we lay into him, waterboard his ass real good, we should get all the accounts and crypto currency they had. Fortunately for us, his hard drives and the cash that Richy Rich had brought him weren't damaged in the explosion ... so, yea we lost a lot of good people tonight, but at least they didn't die in vein, we got what we were looking for, we also got Richy Rich and his body guard as well ... " explained Ty.

"It's my fault man, Ty it's all on me ..." said EJ in a whisper.

"The fuck are you talking about? Man, keep it together!" Ty said angrily.

"If I had pat her down, then I would've felt the vest," said EJ.

"You're kidding me, right?" Ty said exasperated, "so, let me get this straight, you think that in a hostage situation, in the middle of a firefight, you would have thought of patting down the actual hostage?" asked Ty incredulously. EJ answered by putting his head down, saying nothing. What more could he say? He felt it.

"Ok, I see, we feel sorry for ourselves? Ok, how's this then," Ty paused to find the right words. "Let's say that we didn't have you to take out the guy who was holding her, or even say that you did pat her down and feel that vest, do you know what happens?" Ty asked rhetorically. "Either way, she detonates upstairs and destroys the hard drives! That means that we are all dead for nothing! We can't save lives like that EJ. There was nothing you or I, or anyone could have done differently, and the sooner you stop second guessing yourself, the sooner you accept what happened wasn't your fault, the better off we will be, okay?"

"Yea, I feel you, I just can't believe that they are all dead ... " said EJ.

"I know man, I know ... " Ty put his hand on EJ's shoulder and squeezed, then walked out of the hospital room, leaving EJ to his own thoughts.

§§§§

The next day, Ty picked him up when he was officially declared fit to leave, by the doctors. They were in an unmarked Yukon and headed south on I-95 towards Miami. EJ was glad to be out of that place, he hated hospitals, even though they had saved his life on more than one occasion. He was just ready to get out of there.

"Where are we going to?" EJ asked him as they drove.

"To an undisclosed location that the Justice Department uses for an office, basically to have meetings that shouldn't be on the record," said Ty cryptically while concentrating on his driving.

EJ just sat back and tried to mentally prepare himself for a very rough debriefing that he knew would be forthcoming.

They pulled up to a nondescript office building, surrounded by many other plain looking office buildings as well as warehouses. He pulled the Yukon up to the garage that seemed so out of place, it looked like a nonfunctioning model, but a small metal box on a pole with a small speaker and even smaller button gave it away as a government building. Ty rolled down his window and hit the button on the little speaker box, which in turn answered him loudly.

"Certified Innovations Attorneys, how can I help you?"

"Certified letter from President Trump, sir. It requires a signature for delivery," said Ty as he pulled up closing the window.

"Really, Ty? Certified Innovation Attorneys? CIA ..." EJ was laughing as he was saying it, "and a letter from Trump? Could you CIA folks be anymore dramatic?" They had a laugh together as he pulled in the open door.

"You ain't seen nothing yet! You will soon though ..."

They parked the truck once the garage door had closed, and got out. Ty led EJ to a small room with a conference table at the center of it, and four very serious anal retentive type suits sitting around it.

They all stood and Ty introduced them all to EJ. Steve Sutton, FBI; John Smith, CIA, (obviously with a name like that); Jim Miller, DOJ; and a Marine Major, Jenks. The Marine Major saluted EJ, which he returned in a formal manner. Always and forever proud to be a Marine.

"Gentlemen, you called this meeting, I brought him to you. You got the floor," said Ty as he and EJ found comfortable seats at the table.

Jim Miller began, "We asked you here because we had several reports of your actions two days ago at that ISIS cell in Boca Raton."

"Sir, I know what I did was ..." EJ started, trying to accept responsibility for the explosion and loss of lives that he deeply felt was his fault, but was interrupted before he could even start.

"There is an elite task force made up of all of the best of all of our agencies put together, to execute with extreme prejudice, any and all possible threats to our Nation's security. It's a multi-agency, multi-jurisdictional task force, and nonexistent on any records, oh," John Smith said, purposely interrupting EJ's cop out, "best of all, you only have to answer to the Patriot Act, so you are to be 'weapons free'."

"I, ah, I don't ..." EJ was unsure of himself all of the sudden. Was this real?

Major Jenks chose that moment to speak up, "It's an inter-agency task force. Task force assignments have to be volunteered for, we can't assign you, military don't do investigations on U.S. soil, so the ball is in your court, Sergeant."

"Ah, gentlemen, I do appreciate the offer, and I am flattered that you would even think me qualified for something like this, but I just don't know ..." said EJ.

"Think of this EJ, after all of out talks over in Sandland, all that you wanted to do to help our Country, all that we *have* done to make our Country a safer place, how we have protected its citizens with what we were doing over there. This will be the same, except that we will be doing it right here, where we will actually see the results and know the people that we have saved. Don't you still want to make a difference? You can man, this is your chance! Man, do this with me, EJ, you are what we are missing on our team, this is your chance, don't pass it up ..." said Ty passionately and sincerely.

"Ok, fuck it, I guess I'm in. We go after the same people, just over here now?" asked EJ seriously.

"Of course! This is where we make the difference."

"Ok, let's do this ..."

Chapter Fourteen

- War Ready -

It was midnight and she was dressed in all black. She had armed herself with an AK-47 as well as a Glock 27 sidearm that she had taken from one of the crime scenes that she had worked in the Southside of Lake Worth. They were most definitely not the service weapons that were issued to her. Not when she had to use them for what she was planning. She also had a grenade and was very nervous about it because she had no idea whether or not the damn thing even worked, but she would be finding out soon enough. She was falling. No, not falling while she was here creeping in these bushes at the 'El Toro Loco' club on Military Trail. She was falling in love, and she was worried that she couldn't even do anything to stop it. The past few months of being around Jean had brought her out from under the rock that she had been living for all these months since losing Tomas. For that reason, for Jean and the kids at the Youth Center, she was about to set aside her oath as an officer of the law. She was not only going to set aside her oath to uphold the law, she was about to break the very laws that she was supposed to be upholding as well.

It was not like she hadn't broken the law before, even in the name of Justice taking a life, but never recklessly. Never like this. Never without a clear meaning. But there was no other way, they were never alone, yet always protected. Elizebeth and Jose Renteria were a team that DEA files had labelled 'Double Trouble'. They were siblings and both dangerous, but she especially, so having been sent

153

to Cuba at the age of 16, to train with the Special Forces Operatives who were ex-patriots and a 'for profit' enterprise. Only she excelled so much so, that she outgrew her very own teachers, and then ended up killing them as a type of self test to see her skills, and what they were capable of. After several more trials, her father could find no trainer who would take her on as an apprentice. She was now a family sicario, or an assassin, as well as right hand and protector to her brother Jose. She was the Felix Family's finest sicario because she didn't look anything like an assassin, so beautiful, so lovely. Her brother was the South Florida face of the Gulf Cartel and the Felix Family. He was the head of operations in Florida and answered only straight to the 'old man' himself, Ascension Felix, Jr ., which makes him the number two man. It was all in the files Shelby had called in several markers and favors to get a hold of through the contacts that she had in the Miami Beach DEA field office. But it was well worth every marker she gave out and every favor that she called in.

Shelby now had complete and detailed investigation files of both the Haitian Sensation and Gulf Cartels, and every member in them. Her immediate plan was to take out the Renteria siblings in such a manner to where their family could only conclude that the gangbanging Haitian Sensation zoes had finally decided to take them out and try to expand their enterprises further west of Lake Worth City. But it had to be done just right. Exactly how these zoes would do it if it was really their plan, it had to be an attack of their nature. Which is the exact reason that Shelby's unproclaimed love and partner in this venture was five miles north on Belvedere Road at the restaurant the 'Taqueria' which was one of the Gulf Cartel's strongholds and stash spots. It was more sensitive than most of their spots because the old man himself was the actual owner and used it to launder money into this and many food type legal businesses. There were the slaughter houses, chicken farms, meat packing houses, and the cheese and dairy farms he also owned and operated. The legal meats and cheese distributors, were actually doing very well, making the illegal enterprises even that much harder to launder for. It was for that very reason, that they had at that time, so much currency stored in the attic on this very night. Bad news for the cartel, good news for Shelby and Wicks.

§§§§

Wicks had spent the whole day near the Everglades, having to spend time dividing the proceeds of Big Meet's safe, as well as picking up a murder vehicle to hit the old man's Taqueria with. He had taken the Tri-Rail train to Miami where JJ, Tasha, and Smack had picked him up. After telling Smack in person what he needed, they dropped him off in 'Murder Gardens', Miami Gardens newest nickname for all the homicides that often happen there. JJ had given him the weapons and money in the safe, after Wicks had explained the situation to him and what he would be using the money for. He was waging his own war against enemies of the kids at the Youth Center. All the money and proceeds from the war would go to the kids there. He didn't have any need for any money or material things anymore.

He remembered back then, when he was hustling and he laughed. At the single sight of all this money, he would have immediately gone back to Dr. Kelly and dropped some more golds in his mouth, gotten a '73 Chevy Impala drop top and went to Power Audio, and dropped TV's, some slump in the trunk, and some Asanti rims so he could sit tall in the dunk. He would have never thought to use the money for good, to fund a war between two cartels that were tearing the city apart and hurting the kids. But now, he was going to use it to protect the kids that he and Shelby cared for at the Youth Center. He laughed to himself. Times have changed. Most definitely have changed a lot. Money was no longer the root of all evil. For the *love* of money was. Wicks no longer cared or loved the money, nor did he care for it. It was all about his little nephew Ray and those kids. That's all that mattered now.

He was sitting in a rimmed up Grand Marquis with Haiti's flag sticking out on small plastic poles, fixed to both of the rear windows, allowing everyone to see that this was a car that was definitely owned by a Haitian. He was strapped up with an AK-47, Smith & Wesson bulletproof vest, and two 'baby nines' or what the Taurus PT111 was known as. He also had the ghost gun that Big Meet had tried to use to kill Shelby when Wicks had saved her by blowing Meet's brains all over the walls. Wicks didn't know if any of the weapons would trace back to the Haitian Sensations, but by them just having the chance to do so, they had agreed to leave the ghost gun in the car in the parking lot when it was done so the cops could find it. Smack had stolen the 'most Haitian car' he could find in Little

Haiti, and was hoping just the flags alone would do the job of implicating the Haitian Sensations in the robbery and murders. The fix was in, as they say in the movies.

After going to Gator Guns shooting range and making sure that all the guns were in working order and could fire properly, they finalized their plans at Chili's across the street. Sipping two for one Patron Margaritas, they agreed to take out the Gulf Cartel's muscle and money all in one shot. Shelby's intelligence reports from the DEA's files said that they had been told by confidential informants that the restaurant had been storing all of the ill gotten gains in the attic and were looking for more cash investments after their purchase of 12 food trucks had been a great success. Shelby and Wicks agreed that the best way to implicate the Haitian Sensations was to kill two birds with one stone and burn the whole place to the ground. They would destroy all the drug proceeds, burn their storage convenience, while simultaneously blaming the rival gang that they wanted them to fight with. They were waiting until after midnight so that collateral damage would be at a minimal. The restaurant would close, and most of the upright citizens at the El Toro Loco would have absconded, retiring to their beds, while leaving many more criminal element there for the main event to be introduced.

After the last three restaurant workers had locked up and left the parking lot guard by himself, Wicks scaled the fence opposite of the guard's line of sight. He knew the security on the building itself would be top of the line, knowing the content of the attic, as it also explained a 24 hour parking lot guard at a restaurant that closes at midnight. His best bet was to break in through the rooftop, so he climbed the walled in garbage dumpster and jumped to the roof without much difficulty. He had a chisel and hammer, but immediately saw that he wouldn't be needing it as there was a roof access hatch. "Were they serious?" thought Wicks.

Wicks pulled up the gas can from the dumpster and went to the access hatch. He used the crowbar, and as quietly as possible, he pried open the hatch and crawled in through it. Immediately he could see how unorganized these people were. There were pallets of cash everywhere. Every inch of the storage area was filled to the ceiling with the ill gotten gains. They didn't even have a sequence or form, it just looked like they pushed it in every corner they could find and didn't even care that stacks of cash had fallen all over the place. He went down the staircase and into the kitchen. After locating the gas line, he broke it loose very gently with the crowbar. Propane immediately was shooting out into the air as Wicks walked back to the stairs and ascended back into the attic where he had left the gas can. He took some stacks of $100 dollar bills and removed the bands from around them and placed them loose into his backpack. Once filled, he strapped it on and began to pour gasoline into every corner of the attic. He took his can with him and climbed back outside, onto the dumpster once again. As he walked away, he threw cash in every direction until his bag was empty and he was safely back to his car. He put the gas can in the back seat, the grenade on his lap and called Shelby.

§§§§

"Yea?" Shelby asked answering the ringing phone.

"Please be careful bae ..." said Wicks, then hung up.

Shelby stepped out of the bushes that she had been hiding in on the back patio area of the bar. She looked inside the bar. There were three different bars inside and then the one bar outside where the mechanical bull was located at. The middle bar was a circle bar, with chairs surrounding it. The other two bars were against opposite sides of the walls, and then there was a big dance floor in between the circle bar in the middle and the bar on the wall closest to the front door. Shelby was at the back door though, coming in from the back patio bar. She looked around and spotted the Renterias standing by the circle bar in the middle. She had the AK47 hanging from a strap up under her Burberry trench coat. She was wearing the Haitian flag bandana on the top of her head, where she donned a blonde wig. A Versace corona mask was what hid her pretty features from the cameras.

Timing seemed perfect since the Renterias were isolated from the larger crowd and apparently having a meeting with someone with a familiar face to Shelby. He was in a heated discussion. Shelby wasted no time, whoever he was, she had to have seen his face in the files, or in the investigations in her job, so he would have to be just as guilty as they were. She pulled the pin on the grenade and allowed the handle part to flip away. She rolled the grenade in a bowling like motion across the floor towards them and lifted the AK-47 assault rifle and fired a few rounds at them to make sure that they got down and stayed where they were, ducked down. She also wanted to give fair warning so other patrons would get down and get out of the way, and thereby avoid the catastrophic impending effects of the grenade.

The explosion was even louder than she envisioned, and she flinched a little bit, the reality of the grenade actually working after all the thoughts of it being a dud. The place at the bar where the Renterias were standing was completely obliterated and there were some small fires all over the center bar and its surounding area. Out of the three bars inside of the whole club, only two and a half remained. Shelby could see some parts of the bodies and one still moving, so she fired the rest of her 30 round magazine into them as well as the immediate surrounding area, making sure to obliterate anything still breathing.

Shelby pulled the bandana off of her wig as she turned away walking off, dropping the AK-47 there, she drew her Glock 27 sidearm and fired some random shots to keep heads down. As the building was filled with smoke, there was no chance of anyone stopping her when they couldn't even see her. She dropped the Haitian flag bandana as a calling card and faded into the dark night amid screams and sirens closing in. She kept to back alley ways for two blocks until she felt relatively safe, and she came to where she had parked her bike in the Taco Bell parking lot. She took off the ridiculous wig and trench coat, put them in a Taco Bell bag and tossed them into the dumpster that belonged to the restaurant and quickly took off towards the Taqueria. She dialed Wicks on her dash phone that connected to her helmet bluetooth.

"Are you alright?" asked Jean immediately upon answering the phone call.

"All good bae, I'm two minutes out ..." answered Shelby touched by his concern.

"I'm in place now ..." said Wicks, Jean being in the back room now, since Wicks had taken control. It had been about 15 minutes since Wicks had opened the propane gas lines at the restaurant. That was plenty, he thought to have allowed the Taqueria to fill with the flammable propane gas. Shelby pulled her bike into the apartment complex which backed against the rear end of the Taqueria, and she parked next to the black Grand Marquis with the big rims and stupid looking flags hanging out of the rear windows. So damn conspicuous, it was perfect.

"Really?" she asked, laughing as she got into the passenger seat next to her man. His bonnie, she thought to herself, smiling.

"Shit, it'll get the job done, are you okay?" he asked her as he kissed her lips tenderly and looking her body over to reassure himself she was unhurt.

"I'm good bae, done and done, let's go finish this shit."

Wicks nodded as he put the car in gear and pulled off to go finish the night's activities and give these damn cartels something to really fear and stress over.

Wicks pulled into the Taqueria parking lot, fully allowing the security guard to see his car, and drove almost even with the front glass doors, but still far enough to protect them. The security guard started his security truck in their direction, thinking this is just another person trying to get a late night bite of good Mexican cuisine. He had every intention of just telling them to get lost since the restaurant was already closed for the night. He had dealt with plenty of drunks, looking for a late night bite to eat, they were always harmless. Not this time. He was almost 50 feet to them when Shelby opened fire on his vehicle's engine block, as well as the tires, with Wicks' AK-47. It was important to use and leave these ridiculously outdated and inaccurate AKs at each scene because they were so popular with the Haitian Sensations, they were almost a trademark with them. A calling card.

As the security truck took heavy fire from Shelby's carefully aimed 'warning shots', the guard didn't even attempt to mount a defensive position. Instead, he immediately ran into the middle of the road in an attempt to keep himself out of the line of fire. Shelby dropped the AK-47 once she saw the guard was safely distanced from the restaurant. She and Wicks then started running in the opposite direction, towards the rear of the restaurant which backed into the apartment complex where Shelby's bike was parked. They ran past the big glass rear windows, and as they did, Wicks threw his grenade as hard as he could after he had pulled the pin, arming it. The whole window pane broke unexpectedly as the heavy grenade had passed through it, shattering it into a million pieces. Shelby and Wicks ran harder, faster.

Seconds slowly passed and they finally reached the fence that separated the restaurant rear parking lot from the apartment complex. They climbed it together, both in the best shape of their lives, and upon reaching the top of it, they both were stunned when they were propelled forward from the force of the explosion caused by the detonation of the propane, lit by the grenade's ignition. Both were thrown off of the fence, but only Shelby tucked and rolled with her forceful landing.

They looked back at their night's accomplishment. Burning money was beginning to drift upwards as the breeze only strengthened the already strong flames, overtaking the entire building. The fire was already greater than either of them could have imagined or hoped for. The fully engulfed building was so hot that not just the Grand Marquis, but also the security truck, which had been parked even further, had both been touched by the roaming flames. Their job was definitely completed and mission accomplished, they both continued onto where the bike was parked. They both got on and started back to Shelby's condo, where they had been spending a lot of their time lately. A honeymoon of sorts.

Shelby had obtained a very popular and hard to come by condominium in the Moorings of Lantana, located on the Federal Highway, and Dixie Highway split, right on the border of Lake Worth City and Lantana Township. It was located right on the inter-coastal waterway, ironically less than a 7 minute walk to Big Head's, the leader of Haitian Sensations' house on Manalapan, the town directly across the bridge from Lantana, on the beach side of the inter-coastal. Even less in a boat. Shelby loved her condo, and since Jean had been staying there with her, she loved it even more. It finally felt like home. Jean made it feel that way. Jean loved it just as much and had always wanted to live there again after so many years away in prison. It was just irony that he had lived here when he had been indicted by those dirty task force agents. That just goes to show what a world we live in. Enigmatic.

They had accomplished so much this night and were ready to rest. They knew they would need it for the upcoming war they had spent all this time and money to ignite between the factions. This would all be to the bottom line purpose of saving the Youth Center, and making their community a better place to live.

Chapter Fifteen

The streets were crowded with a lot of people, a crowd actually. Pedestrians filled all of the wide sidewalks of El Centro in Matamoros, the city in Northeastern Tamaulipas, Mexico. Some younger girls walked in the mandated navy blue skirts with white knee high socks and white blouses of their respective schools. Others, older girls, walked in bright, colorful, and tight dresses heading to the different discos all around Centro, the main strip of the city.

Two of his body guards walked in front of him, and two behind him. All four had bluetooth ear pieces in their ears and communicated through the jawbone microphones, greatly resembling the American Secret Service agents, if not for the visible tattoos on their hands, neck, and on one, his face. They all had serious, no nonsense looks, as well as the killer look in their eyes. They were constantly on the lookout, observing everything and overlooking nothing. Anything and everything was a possible threat, every person a suspected Sinaloa sicario, with whom they were currently and always beefing with. An ongoing war was always in place.

El Senor was walking along side his favorite Grand Niece on the main street of El Centro and stepped into the La Victoria supermarket. He had just bought this particular franchise as a gift for her graduation celebration. She was going over all of her ideas, modeled after the Publix Supermarket chain that was exclusively for Florida, where she had been going to school at Florida Atlantic University or known better as FAU. El Senor, also commonly referred to as El Jefe,

165

Ascension Felix, had promised his niece that he would match her one for one on her La Victoria markets chain. He meant that he would buy another store for every store that she herself had earned with her legal proceeds. Elizebeth Felix was ecstatic. It was a deal made in heaven, and Elizebeth, Liz to her friends, knew her mother's favorite uncle would deny her nothing. She knew that he had every intention of spoiling her to death until the day he was in his grave, as he always had, her mother before her.

El Senor was a medium height, somewhat chubby Mexican with dark skin and beady eyes that made him look all the more dangerous, especially with reputation of quick temper and cruel manner. Not to Liz though, to her he was a teddy bear and the sweetest uncle a girl could have. Liz, on the other hand was beautiful. Liz had the fair skin of her father and green eyes, like the color of the forest. She was also very small, petite even, 105lbs and 5'2, yet pretty enough to model, which she had done while attending FAU in Boca Raton. She thought that her favorite Tio was unaware of that, but just as El Senor controlled the whole Gulf Cartel, he controlled everything that involved any of his family members as well, even if they were away at college. Once he had been made aware of the fact that Liz was dating her photographer, Phil Flash, he had them watch her even more closely. Then when he was apprised that Phil Flash had put his filthy hands on his grand niece, he immediately ordered for the demise of the scum Phil Flash, with prejudice.

He would never deliberately hurt his grand niece either, so he ordered it to be an accident, and in front of a speeding Tri-Rail train he went, or 'fell', even though he had never taken or had reason to take the Tri-Rail. All went smoothly after that. Liz spent a few weeks heartbroken, but she was already about to graduate, and so it was something she had soon gotten over when she got back to her uncle's compound and was ready to put her business degree into good use. It was her dream to put together a supermarket chain that valued family and awarded its employees with stock options and used stocks as bonuses or rewards, exactly how the Publix Supermarket chain did. Her dream was to get her uncles and parents out of the illegal side, into her movement towards a legal enterprise that her whole family can get in on and involved with. Something she could be proud to say that she was a part of. El Senor understood her up to a point, and even respected her ambition. He would love to have more legal businesses to launder his drug proceeds with, but he would never be able to leave the drug business, no matter how much he wanted to make his niece happy. He couldn't do that. He could never relinquish the power of the Gulf Cartel, never step down as El Jefe. One of his many sons would eventually have to step up and kill him, just as he had stood up over his own brothers and killed his father when he felt that he was ready enough to run the cartels well.

He kind of held back, kind of slow walked, his security team having spread out to clear the area, and admired Liz. She truly was something magnificent, something special. Amazing really, she was even now giving compliments while simultaneously directing her new employees as to her plans and her preferences. She kind of had a way about business. A way to sell ice to the entire village of Eskimos, while all the while making them feel special, making them feel as if they had won the best possible prize imaginable. Damn it, how he had wanted to get her involved in his operations. Imagine the deals that she would be able to strike and the officials that she could bring to their side, the politicians that she could compromise. But for now, she was happy, and that meant a lot to El Senor as well, as he didn't believe that the men in the family were more valuable than the women. Didn't think that the women belonged in the kitchen just because they were women, not if they had skills to contribute to the family. Liz had taught him that. She had taught him a lot and he was always impressed with her abilities as well as her motivation, her drive.

His satellite phone rang, bringing him from his woolgathering. He knew that it was very important since it was not his normal private touch screen Galaxy phone that he usually used when not in flight or on one of his many boats.

"Bueno," answered El Senor. He listened for a moment with a serious look on his face.

"Mande? Cuando? Y que ... ejo de la puta madre ... si ... chinga su ... si ... mevoy ahora ... ok, orale," He hung up cursing.

"Ignacio! Ignacio, come," said El Senor calling his right hand man.

"Si, Senor, what has happened?" Ignacio was El Senor's son's best friend since childhood, and had risen to become El Senor's Chief of Staff, as well as his own personal enforcer.

There was not a man feared more in the Gulf Cartel's organization, as he himself had been battle tested in the wars against the Sinaloa's Cartel, and its infamous head, 'El Chaparro'. But on top of that, he was a liaison between El Senor and 'Dos Zetas' who were the armed forces behind the cartel. So he could literally call in an air strike against anyone, or any organization, he felt might be a threat to El Senor or the Gulf Cartel. He had a navy as well as an army and airforce in the Dos Zetas. The 'Z's. The last letter in the alphabet. All Mexicans were aware of and avoided Dos Zetas. They knew they might be found somewhere with their heads missing or hanging 50 feet in the air from a bridge if they didn't cooperate with Dos Zetas. Even the Policia as well as government knew not to mess with or bother with the Gulf Cartel, and were paid very well not to. They were all aware of their place. There could be no mistakes with Dos Zetas, or heads would roll.

"Jose and Elizebeth were both killed last night in Florida. It was an attack on a club. They were meeting with a new contact on their team that they had just brought in," said El Senor, perplexed.

"Do we have any information?"

"Nothing, as of now," said El Senor. "I might need you to go on down there and take care of things until I find some replacements for them."

"Whatever you need Jefe," said Iggy humbly.

"Jonny says we currently have no open beefs about anything that might have instigated this, so I am at a loss for words, but I've always had in the back of my mind about these damn Haitians, they have been a pain in the ass for over 20 years. If you find anything supporting their possible involvement, I want Jonny to immediately initiate an investigation into them so that we might strike back efficiently and send them back to that God forsaken Island they had come from," said El Senor with terror in his voice. The decision was made. A war could be started in a blink of an eye. That fast of a decision could end lives.

"Si, Senor, I'll go to our plane and fly over there right now, if you wish."

"Orale," said El Senor as he started walking towards Liz.

"Tio, is everything okay? You seem bothered," said Liz once he had rejoined her and Ignacio had headed to go to the airport.

"Si, Mija, it will be, soon enough, " he replied, smiling to himself watching as Ignacio was leaving. Ignacio thought he was smarter than El Senor. He smiled more.

§§§§

On his drive to the airstrip, close to El Senor's compound located in nearby Rio Bravo, Iggy's Phone rang. "Si," he said when he answered the phone to the 561 area code in America. He listened for a little while and then, "El Senor will be greatly displeased to hear this report, I suspect that you hold that guard until I get there to question him." There was nothing more to say.

The report Iggy had just received had informed him of the total loss of El Senor's Taqueria restaurant, and theft of an unknown amount in cash in the single digit millions. There had been a trail of bills left from the restaurant, which told him that it had been a great amount of cash, which meant a great amount of people to carry so much weight in paper money. A coordinated effort. Organization. Numerous bodies to carry the money . He deduced to himself that it must be either a government agency, or some gang or cartel.

When Iggy looked at it in combination with the attack on his organization's representatives in Florida, it looked as if another group, gang, or organization, were trying to make a move to take their territory and started to move right in the heart of things, in South Florida, where the loads mostly go to.

Although Iggy himself had full authority over the Dos Zetas, he couldn't simply bring them into the U.S. The Estados Unidos laws were very strict, and the borders, very real. Very guarded. Shipping kilos was one thing, and many border agents patrols didn't pursue it if it wasn't done in front of their faces. But human trafficking was different, and especially moving military men like Dos Zetas were out of the question. There would have to be planning, payment to officials and a clear date. None of those were available at this time. So, he simply didn't have access to his Zetas. A few Gulf Cartel sicarios he could use, but if his enemies were a large group and organized, he would be in an uphill battle.

Iggy was convinced that he would need to be very careful and fully investigate any enemies before coming up with any action to El Senor. He would need to fully appraise all of his options, but he was sure there would be action. Of that he was sure. He would make sure of that. The Gulf Cartel would not, no, could not, allow the deaths of the Renterias to go unanswered. Iggy would have to move on those responsible for those lives taken and that money missing, whether he wanted to react at all or not. He couldn't look weak at a time like this.

Three hours later Iggy was stepping off of the G-5 at the Lantana Airport as he couldn't get clearance to land at their usual Palm Beach International Airport. Jonny Tapatio, Chief of Security team for the cartel in Florida, was standing beside a plain black Suburban with 2% tints. Jonny stepped forward and embraced his second cousin on his mother's side, Iggy, who had brought him in from the tough barrios in Matamoros, and Reynosa that he had grown up in.

"Good to see you primo," said Iggy.

"You too, primo, it's been too long," Jonny and Iggy got into the backseat of the Suburban, and its driver quickly took off. Driving these streets that he hadn't seen for a while, Iggy could sense that there would be a change coming about. He didn't know exactly how it would pan out, but the change was definitely coming. Jonny could feel it coming as well. There would be politics, there would be infighting and there would be many, many deaths. That was something for sure.

"You know this situation being unanswered for so long is making us look weak," said Jonny trying to gage Iggy's reaction, position, or any hint of either one. Iggy showed nothing on his poker face, but said from behind Versace shades, "So primo, the question is; do we proceed with the plan or do we try to pursue some shit about which we have no clue about?"

"What about Ricky? Shouldn't he decide in which direction we should go? He wants to be El Jefe, so shouldn't he decide?" asked Jonny, testing his position.

172

"Or primo," said Iggy, "he feels like we are useless and replaceable if we can't even run the Florida operations while he is busy dealing with the whole rest of the country? If he thought that we needed his input, I'm almost certain that Ricky Felix would have at least called to let us know where he stands and give new orders. But maybe he sits back to see how well we deal with this alone?"

"Okay, primo," said Jonny, "then what are my orders?"

"Officially, you are to go find out who is responsible, as well as investigate and find the weakness of those who killed the Renterias. Report back and we can go from there." Iggy paused and looked deeply into his eyes. "But unofficially, nothing gets in the way of money, not family, not revenge, nothing. Money is the only reason that we are here, so fuck Jose and Elizebeth's murders, there are more important matters at stake here, so don't forget that primo ... now take me to question this guard from the Taqueria, we can go from there," ordered Iggy.

They started the trip to go question a guard who could not tell them anything, not only because he was unable to tell them anything but because he knew absolutely nothing and he would surely be dealt with because it had happened on his watch. Even when they knew that it wasn't his fault, he would still have to be made a scapegoat, simply because they couldn't allow anyone to think they could take a loss and live to see another day. They would all be a lot more cautious now, pay a lot more attention, and bust their guns a whole lot more after this. This was a one time thing, it would never happen again and wouldn't be tolerated.

173

Chapter Sixteen

Several weeks had passed and EJ's family were all happy to have Lil' Ray back home safe. His healing was a miracle. The doctors had tended to him in the hospital so well because he was everyone's favorite patient, he had that way about him. He could melt even the coldest of hearts. He was upbeat and optimistic despite his injuries. Doctors told him that he had some serious prayers behind his recovery and he should be grateful for that. Now, his only problem is getting his mother to allow him to go back to the Youth Center that he loved so passionately. He plotted, bargained, and begged daily, all to no avail. Up until now, his mother still blamed the whole incident on the Youth Center. She wasn't easy on him.

Once EJ had found out about the situation, he had come immediately from his training in Langley, Virginia. He couldn't believe that he and his little brother had been in the hospital at the same time. His phone had been destroyed when he was thrown from the second story window in the explosion, so he hadn't even known until he was provided with an agency touch screen Windows phone for his training and he had been able to call home. He couldn't believe what they had told him had happened.

EJ had called Ty and explained the situation, which in turn, had earned him an exemption from the training that they had all agreed that was really unnecessary in his case anyways. He was already considered the best of the best in his field of operation. EJ was given an agency condo downtown to occupy while he was in the city, and it was a perk that he could definitely appreciate since it was the first time in his life where he was allowed to have his own space. He had been bunking in bunks for so long that a condo alone, was a novelty. EJ was still grieving all of those lost in the explosion at the ISIS cell house, and still felt personally responsible, even though the General Review Board Committee had cleared him of all responsibility in the loss of lives at the house.

Something inside EJ tortured his dreams at night of the explosion, over and over again, making him relive the painful incident every night. He began to avoid sleep for fear of his dreams like a Freddy Kruger movie, only sleeping when he would crash out from exhaustion after days awake at a time. It was getting so bad that he had to take some Xanax bars sometimes just to ensure that he didn't have those dreams and be brought back to that fatal night.

EJ began researching the reports of the shooting of Lil' Ray in order not to only take his mind off of his own survivor guilt, but in order to investigate into the shooter or shooters as the case may be, with the intention of finding them. He would eventually want to be the one to bring to justice those who were responsible for hurting his little brother. So far, the reports were saying that the detectives had reviewed a surveillance camera's digital footage outside of the store where Ray had been shot, and had not been able to see the shooter's face from the angle in which it was facing. So they had basically kicked the case back since Ray hadn't talked to the detectives and only indicated that he didn't know who had shot him.

What EJ himself had discovered was a big shocker. The detectives had missed all his findings because of their laziness as usual. However, he decided to move on with this information immediately before a more thorough detective came along and made the same connection. Yea, he thought, like that would ever happen. These cops didn't care about a kid getting shot if he wasn't pointing the finger and doing their job for them. Typical cops. EJ had used his CIA credentials in order to gain access to Palm Beach County Sheriffs Office computers and then viewed all of the surveillance cameras footage. What he found had surprised and confused him. He knew right then what was up.

Lil' Ray's closest friend and schoolmate, Carlos Fuentes, could be seen clearly on camera at the exact moment of the shooting. You could see clearly with no mistake that Los actually saw who the shooters were because of his change in facial expression, and then his running out of the store with a determined look on his face. The rest of the story was in the original responding officer's report when he responded to a call of GSWs at the hospital, or gunshot wounds as they were known by medical staff. It was a Florida law that all gunshot wounds be reported to the law enforcement for a police investigation to be initiated, and followed up by detectives to determine if filing charges is appropriate, or if it was an accidental shooting. Always, either way though, investigators were brought in.

EJ discovered Los had basically saved Ray's life with his quick and decisive actions. Getting Ray to the hospital so fast was what had bent the odds into his favor. EJ planned to keep that in mind when he got to talk to Carlos, and he was most definitely going to talk to Los, ASAP.

EJ drove to the Youth Center on his Ducati that his uncle Jean had reluctantly relinquished control of back to him. There weren't many cars in the parking lot since it was going on 8p.m. on a school night. But he knew Los had a fight coming up and would be there training and getting ready to take on an older and far more experienced boxer. Los had always had a good work ethic, always trained hard.

He found Los training alone, without even sweating, and hitting the speed bag. EJ grabbed some focus pads off of the bench nearby and started strapping them onto his hands as he walked over to where Los was just now noticing him. "Wanna hit the mitts a lil' bit?" asked EJ.

"Sure," said Los as he turned away from his speed work.

"Give me a jab, cross, hook, and parry," said EJ putting his hands up with the focus targets on them ready to work.

Los jabbed his left into EJ's left mitt, turned his hips left, threw a right cross, spun his body right and swung a left hook, finishing with a left spin with the crook of his right elbow guarding his right ear. A perfect parry. "Again," said EJ restarting the set. They did it over again a few times, changed combinations, and ran that one for a while.

177

"I saw the surveillance footage inside the store from when my lil' brother was shot ..." Los stopped his set and looked into EJ's eyes. Searching. He said nothing.

"I want to know who shot my lil' brother," EJ continued.

"Man big homie, I ain't ... look, just let me handle this shit in my own way, and I'ma have dat nigga bodied soon, it's my problem," said Los.

"Nah, Lil' Los, it's my problem, he's my lil' brother, and I'm going to get whoever did this to him," said EJ in the most persuasive way.

"It's a 'Z' problem EJ, we gone handle this shit, Wicks know whaddup," answered Los, trying to get EJ to back off him on the issue.

"Wicks ... so, my uncle knows what's up then?" he asked Los perplexed.

"Man big bruh, I can't talk about this shit, all I can say is man it's finna be handled, so don't worry bout it, we got it," said Los with a little bit of an attitude, and with that being said, he turned and headed for the showers.

EJ was angry, but thought to himself that he could actually respect the lil' nigga's gangsta since he was a citizen and Los was gang banging up under the 'Z's in the form of the Haitian Sensations. But what really pissed him off was what Los had let slip about his uncle Jean having knowledge of it and not putting him up on game, or at least allowing him to participate in the take down that he felt that he deserved to be a part of or at least aware of, if nothing else.

He got on his Ducati and dialed his uncle Jean, on his dash and his helmet bluetooth gave the ringing tone in his ears.

"Yea," answered Jean in his ears.

"Where you at Unc?"

"Over to the Moorings of Lantana, at Shelby spot, what's good bruh?"

"I'll call when I'm downstairs," said EJ and disconnected.

§§§§

Sensing something amiss while speaking to EJ, Jean told Shelby that he was going to the recreation room right next to the gym and left, so that he could speak to EJ alone. After receiving a call from Los with a heads up, he already knew what this was going to be all about when EJ got there. He also knew how he was going to react to being told to stand down. He knew that EJ wouldn't take it so well.

When he got to the Recreation room, he racked the pool table and put the 12 pack of Heineken into the refrigerator that he had brought down from Shelby's Condo after taking one out for himself. He walked outside towards the water and stared at the beautiful inter-coastal waterway, watching the boat traffic as they slowly made their ways to and from various fishing expeditions, snorkeling or SCUBA adventures, and even jet skiing. It was hard to believe, just looking down in the water, and seeing a manatee passing, looking up at the boats and happy people enjoying life. Just less than a year ago, he was in a maximum security Federal Penitentiary, serving a 66 year sentence, for non-violent, victimless crimes.

His phone's vibration alert brought him back from his thoughts. He said a quick prayer of thanks to God, in Jesus name, for his freedom as he did every day, on his way to the front to let EJ in. When EJ had his bike parked, he followed his uncle to the Recreation room. He accepted a Heineken as the small talk continued.

"Man, Unc, this shit here nice! Right on the water too," said EJ.

"Yea, it is nice here, gives me an opportunity to be grateful for being here today. Makes me appreciate family, love, freedom, and all I have here today. But just remember, only a year ago, I was sitting with a 66 year sentence," replied Jean.

"Love?" EJ was surprised. "You love this detective?"

"Yea, nephew, I guess I do," said Jean. "Crazy shit, huh?"

They didn't say anything for a few minutes as Jean broke the silence by breaking the pool balls that were racked on the pool table. He followed up by shooting a few shots, sinking some 'large', which is what they called stripped balls, as the solids were called 'small'. Finally, EJ chose this moment to speak.

"Look, Unc, I gotta holla at ya ... " EJ attempted to compile a convincing argument, knowing that Jean would not like or agree to it.

"Neph, we finna handle this here bout Ray, ok? The less you know, the less you have to worry about, and the better. This ain't Sandland, EJ. When bodies go to droppin' over here, niggas go to First 48 and shit, rats tellin' everything. With that comes indictments, man you think I ain't finna get them niggas who shot Ray? He my family Neph, I need ya to step off, ya dig?" explained Wicks, as Jean stepped back.

"Look Unc, ain't nobody takin' shit from you. I know you put your work in, and did your bid, but I have training and experience, I can do shit street niggas only see in the movies. Don't shut me out, he my lil' bruh," said EJ heatedly, yet forcefully so he would be heard, knowing what he was capable of.

"Man, this some street shit EJ, street niggas handle shit in da streets, it ain't like no movies, we live by a code, so when I fall, I can take my life sentences, you got your whole life ahead of you, bruh, I ain't bringin' you in, you out nephew, sorry, but I got this here, so don't you worry bout this here ..." Wicks said, speaking firmly, closing the door and making it final.

"He's right Jean," said Shelby as she eased into the room from the hallway that led from the gym. "He's got tactical training that we don't have, and we need that with what we're going to be up against."

Both EJ and Jean were caught off guard. Wicks allowed Jean to deal with her. They were surprised as they had thought that they were alone in the Recreation room.

They both paused for her to approach the pool table.

"You can't bring him in on this, he a good kid, and let's not forget a fucking Marine! I just won't jeopardize his future, this is street shit and ..." Shelby interrupted Jean, "and I'm a cop, but I'm in this with you." Jean looked at her, "You were already in it!" his face incredulous.

He looked at EJ, back again at Shelby, and could see the determination in both of their faces. He was torn, but finally Jean decided to acquiesce to their seemingly already made up minds, or they might take on the mission without him.

"Alright, fine, damn, what is this? Two against one now?"

Shelby walked up to Jean, put her arms around his neck, and gave him a sweet kiss," The more preparation and skills we have, the better chance of us all making it safely home and with the conclusive result that we need," she told him.

"Unc, you really don't even know or have any idea of how good I really am, I've done over 80 something raids of ISIS houses. I'm talking about fire fights, weapons free. I've killed 43 of the Taliban myself, and I am considered to be the best in my field. I really know what I'm doing and I am an asset to your team, cuz no matter what you are planning, I'm sure I have done more and gone harder. Plus, I wouldn't insist if I wasn't completely confident in my skills and abilities to get results," EJ concluded.

"I know Neph, I just didn't want to risk anything happening to you or your future when we can handle this, but alright Neph, just please be careful or your mother will kill me!" said Jean smiling, now that the awkwardness had been replaced by the love and familiarity. EJ relaxed. He was in.

They enjoyed the rest of the beer and took turns playing the winner on the pool table until EJ agreed to develop a plan to breach and came up with some ordnance with which they could breach with. The justice would come. Only EJ didn't know that they would be hitting not exactly the one who shot Ray, but the ones that were ultimately behind the issue because they had been the ones that gave the kids the drugs which caused the fallout and attack on Ray. Justice would be served, just not on the one who had pulled the trigger. The one who put the battery in the back of the trigger man was good enough.

Chapter Seventeen

"Hi, I'm Elizebeth Felix and I'm here to see Mr. Mateo?"

"Oh, sure. Please go on to the back, he is ready for you," said the secretary, a skinny blonde type. Not the airhead blonde type though, she seemed like the smart kind of blonde, and of the former, Liz had seen plenty after four years in college at Boca Raton, Florida, the home to Florida Atlantic University. FAU was where many students were privileged blondes with their daddy's money to blow; to party first and go to class second and that's definitely if there was no party to be at while class was ongoing.

Liz had it even easier than most of them money-wise, but she always remembered where she came from. Rio Bravo, Tamaulipas, Mexico. She had an extended student visa, as long as her uncle kept paying the right people. Oh, and as long as she stayed enrolled in classes at FAU. That was the easiest part because all the classes were online due to the Covid-19 scare and everyone not being able to be there in person. So, she just used the skype-like app and logged in everyday when nobody would be on there and left her laptop going, so they would log her hours even without being there. She had already earned her Associates degree in business, so the classes she was now enrolled in were just to keep her Visa, and her application for her dual citizenship in play. She would never risk losing that one.

"Miss Felix," said the Regional Director of the Publix Supermarkets chain, Matt Mateo. "So nice to finally meet you, my daughter has told me so many wonderful things about you."

"Thank you so much for your time, sir. Samantha always spoke about you when we were roommates, she is my best friend here, so it's a pleasure to finally meet you, and please, all my friends call me Liz." In fact, Samantha had told her nothing but bad things about her father, but who was keeping count?

He smiled like a wolf, taking in every bit of Liz's 5'2 petite frame, as he tried to picture what was under her brown Prada business suit, white blouse, and Red Bottom heels with the discrete spikes on the sides of them. Liz had purposely used the term 'best friend' to further entice her ex-roommate's father, after her ex-roommate had made a drunken confession one night in which Samantha had admitted a long running affair that had been ongoing between her ex-bestie and her father. It had both grossed Liz out and embarrassed her for having that knowledge, but it still wouldn't stop her from using that to further her plan of tying together her La Victoria brand with his Publix Supermarkets brand. That was her ultimate goal.

Liz had put together a whole business plan just short of an all out merger of the two big corporations. She was currently investigating international laws to see how far she could go to tie her La Victoria to his Publix Supermarkets without going too far into the merger process. Her main obstacle though besides the fact that she didn't actually own the La Victoria Market chain herself, well maybe not yet, she only owned one franchise, was that Publix was a family based company, and they only did things through

Matthew Matteo's recommendations. Hence, her visit to his office to try and give him her pitch.

"... can appreciate your proposal of a 23% discount on all meats, cheeses, and produce," he was just saying, "but I am very skeptical about these promises, and especially the possibility of longevity in your ability to provide ..." she interrupted him there, before he could make any more assumptions on her ability.

"What I didn't include in my proposal is the fact that my family, the Felix Family, owns Felix Bakery, Felix Packing Houses, Felix Meats, Felix Cheeses and Diary, oh, and by the way, we've just acquired Peru Trucking as well, so we will be that much more of a safe bet to move our product to every venue available, and are expanding our interests into the rest of the Southern States. My point is," she paused here for the dramatic effect, "We are an unstoppable force, and because of my relationship with Samantha, as well as my great admiration for the Publix Supermarket brand, I've agreed to extend this offer to you."

In reality, it was the other way around, Liz had actually been the one to pursue Samantha since the day she had found out about her Father's role in Publix, and hounded her mercilessly ever since. Liz had befriended Samantha and had actually asked to be her roommate, even though she could easily afford her own apartment off of the crowded campus. She had studied Publix, and admired the family oriented atmosphere, and finally begged Samantha for this introduction to her father in spite of her estrangement from him. Liz did nothing in life without a goal in mind, a means to an end in business so to speak. This was why all of her teachers as well as the other students, knew that she would one day be successful, while they also felt sorry for her in a way, for not having a personal life after Phil's death, outside of her business interests and her goals.

"Well," he said while looking into her eyes, "while I myself may be the gatekeeper to corporate in Lakeland, I would have to do a lot of politicking and convincing to get your proposition even heard. I would be willing to consider it, why don't we discuss it over dinner tomorrow night, yes?" The wolf grin came again.

"Sure, it would be a pleasure," she said trying to keep her body language from betraying her insides involuntary cringing, while praying that her own facial expressions would not betray anything negative to him about her true feelings.

After her meeting with Mr. Matteo, she drove down to the Delray Beach Semitary. She spent some time with her first love, Philip Lans, her boyfriend as well as photographer when she had modeled, better known as 'Phil Flash' in the industry. She still couldn't believe or accept that he had died and that he was gone from her life forever. Her heart ached for him, but as soon as she had composed herself, she got back into her rental, a white Ford Explorer. She then headed north, to Delray Beach's North side. Heart aching and still worrying about her plans for the introduction of her family's business venture into the American capitalist market with Publix Supermarkets, she was headed to the only place that she had ever felt at home in America: Her real best friend's

187

house, in the Delray Beach version of Little Haiti. She drove to Marquita's house, well her mother's house.

Liz arrived at Miss Sadie's and parked her rental behind the old Toyota Corolla that was in her driveway which was Miss Sadie's trusty car. She refused to buy a new car when her car worked just fine, she was always known to say, much to everyone's amazement, being as though it barely worked at all. But it did work, of that there was no doubt. When she stepped out of the Explorer, Marquita was already out front with Smack, both puffing on a blunt with enthusiasm. Immediately Liz's mood began to lift, she wanted to hit the blunt of whatever exotic breed of Marijuana that Marquita had personally grown and designed herself this week. Liz knew that Marquita grew different and exotic breeds weekly and experimented with all kinds of lights and irrigation techniques. She knew, just like every other person that knew Marquita, that she would not be disappointed. She never was.

Liz and Marquita had met and become fast friends after hanging out at an FAU 'foam party', which is a party where the dance floor was waist high in foam bubbles, and had smoked a joint of some Grandaddy Kush. Marquita's great sense of humor and upbeat personality had lifted Liz's spirit while her and Phil were on a break, after a big argument that had ended in a physical altercation.

Marquita wasn't just beautiful, Liz had thought at the party, with her big bubble butt and thick thighs and legs. Her boobs, double D cups, sat proudly and high up on her chest, and her pretty face got a lot of attention from the boys at the school. Liz soon found out that Marquita was also a genius. She had already designed and had patented a lighting and irrigation system that powered itself, and that was before she even started going to FAU for her agricultural degree that she now used to specialize in certain strains of 'Cannabis Sativa' and cross-breeding strains. She was very motivated and ambitious not to say the least, a talented girl.

Marquita now worked for the government, producing the most effective medical marijuana to help with many different cancers, as well as glaucoma, and also the best ways to make them target specific areas. She had become an expert in growing technology and lighting, as well as irrigations. Her side hustle though, of course was creating the most popular recreational weed recipes in South Florida. It was only natural that she and Liz were to be best friends since Liz was a heavy consumer of recreational marijuana, and Marquita an expert in the same field, much to their mutual pleasures. So they just clicked, as the old saying goes.

Marquita gave Liz a hug when she had stepped onto the porch, and passed her the blunt, which she immediately hit before even speaking to her friends.

"Hey, girl," said Liz finally after a deep coughing bout.

"Hey, mama, I'm so glad that you are back! How're things back home?"

"Oh, things back home are great!" said Liz, "I got to see my family and I closed the deal on the La Victoria store, so I'm officially a merchant! or should I say a grocer? I'm not sure which!" Liz giggled as the weed took a good effect on her.

"Girl," Marquita laughed with her, "you so crazy!"

"Hi, Smack," said Liz making him blush, while kissing him on his cheek, "what have you been up to? Visiting Moms' and staying out of trouble I hope?"

"Of course Liz, how can I get you to marry me if I'm in jail?" he retorted with a sly smile, hugging her extra tight to try and relay his feelings to her. Since Liz had been coming here to Miss Sadie's house and staying with Marquita, she had grown to know and love her family as her own. Marquita, Tasha, and Smack all loved Liz to death and although Smack and Tasha didn't live here with their mother, Miss Sadie, they were always there on and off hanging out and helping their mother with things around the house as a real family did. Miss Sadie had always welcomed Liz to stay there when she was in town and wouldn't hear about her staying in a hotel, even when money was not the problem in Liz's case. Miss Sadie's house was as small as the houses that surrounded it in the area known as Lil' Haiti in Delray. But she kept her three bedrooms spic and span, and her small kitchen immaculate. Even though Liz was used to living in her grand uncle's mansion on the 300 acre estate and having a bedroom bigger than Miss Sadie's whole house, it was cold and empty at her Uncle's. Living here in her best friend's family home, eating Bahamian food and feeling the family vibes and love, had meant so much to Liz. It had allowed her to feel at home for the first time in her whole life. She was so very grateful for their love and warmth, and she loved Marquita like the sister that she never had growing up, and this she cherished the most.

"So girl, you tryna hit Clematis Street tonight and go clubbin'?" asked Marquita getting ready to go out already.

"Nah," said Liz, "my uncle got some shit going on, and the only way I could get out without 'Creepy Carlos' the body guard from hell, was that I had to promise to stay away from Lake Worth and West Palm. So, no Clematis Street."

Clematis Street was a downtown hotspot for partying with younger adults because of it's back to back clubs, bars, and restaurants turned clubs after midnight. It was the trendiest place to go on Thursdays, or 'college night' as it was known.

"Okaaay ..." said Marquita, thinking. "Jazz on the Ave, or Club Boca?"

"Definitely not feeling like walking around Atlantic Avenue with a bunch of drunk dudes tryna grab and feel on me, so no Jazz on the Ave ... " responded Liz.

"Aw, shit why y'all 'ont come with me," said Smack, "I'm going to that all night bowling spot in Boca, ya know? The one by the Town Center Mall?"

"Oh yea! Let's do that 'Quita! I remember we used to go there before we were 21 and could drink legally, when we were going to FAU, remember that?" Liz clapped excitedly like a kid, while laughing happily.

Marquita pointed at Smack, laughing at him because of his age.

191

"Oh, you got jokes?" Smack was asking, trying to keep a straight face. "I am turning 21 in three months, sis! Damn!" he started laughing when he couldn't hold it in anymore.

"Okay, Okay lil brother, we can slide with you there, I guess."

"I'm only a year and a half younger than you, Quita!" retorted Smack.

"Yea, well, you still my LITTLE brother," Marquita replied smiling, as she knew that he loved their attention and being a part of their lil' clique.

Chapter Eighteen

EJ was ready to leave to go on his first date since being in the U.S. again. He was meeting her at the place she suggested near her family's home in Boca Raton because she apparently didn't like motorcycles. "They are very dangerous," Lindsay had said at that time when he mentioned picking her up on his. She felt so strongly about it, that she apparently was going to try to convince him to get rid of his and not ride them anymore.

The only reason that EJ was entertaining Lindsay's eccentricities when she was so obviously not his type- she was too bourgeois- was because all through his high school years, he had been crushing on her, while she wouldn't even notice his existence. So, he figured he would give her the benefit of the doubt since she had DM'ed him on his Facebook page asking how Lil' Ray was doing after the shooting. The message had warmed his heart after he hadn't heard from her in so long and had awakened his old crush, enough for him to ask her out on a date.

He parked his Ducati at the all night bowling alley, where she had suggested they meet, and went inside to see her. Inside was like a club atmosphere, black lights, strobes, fog machine, and loud Hip Hop music on the loud speakers. Da Baby was rapping about having a threesome with Ashanti and Megan The Stallion. There were many teens there, but most of the population there were made up of 20 something college kids from FAU, and about evenly mixed races between black, white and hispanic. All looked like they were having the time of their lives. It was obvious to EJ that ex, molly and flaka were all popular, as well as the ever present weed. EJ didn't partake in any of that stuff. Alcohol was enough for him.

EJ looked for, and finally located his date. She was one of the ones actually dancing at a bowling lane. She even had her own bowling shoes on. That wasn't the first thing he noticed though. It was that there were several other people sitting there, all in bowling attire, while he had on motorcycle boots and a helmet in his hand. He felt as out of place as Kanye at a Democratic Convention.

"Hey everyone, this is Eric, he is a marine, Eric, this is my friend, Leslie, she goes to FAU. This is John, Mike, Sara, and my boyfriend, Donny."

"Nice to meet you all, Donny? You're Lindsay's boyfriend," he looked to Lindsay, who looked clueless, "nice. Not exactly what I was expecting, but it is good to meet you all," EJ said graciously, playing it off, yet still pissed. He was not going to stay pissed long though as he was aware that Lindsay wasn't at all his type. She had pretty eyes, sure, but she was a bit overweight, though with big boobs, where he stayed very fit. She was so clueless, she obviously didn't even see the position that she had put him in, while Leslie, the intended ambush of a blind date, as well as Donny, both caught on immediately to his reaction.

EJ just sighed and made himself comfortable, feeling like it would be a very long night here. "I'm so sorry," Leslie whispered, "It's so obvious that she didn't tell you anything about me, or

Donny, for that matter ..." She looked embarrassed. She was quite pretty, ash blonde, blue eyes, pouty lips, about 5'5 and athletic looking. By her legs and butt, he took her for track or a gymnist.

"Well, it's ok," he said laughing, "obviously for the best, right?"

They ended up playing several frames, and bowling the night away. Lindsay drank a lot, became obnoxious, so Donny took her home. EJ actually had a very good time after Lindsay was gone, Leslie and her friends were actually very good company. So they had some drinks, bowled, danced, and enjoyed the night.

When everyone was tired around 4A.M., they decided to head home, or back to campus in Leslie's case. EJ walked her to her car, exchanged numbers, and accepted her kiss on the cheek, followed with a quick one on the mouth.

"You're very sweet, I can see now why she was trying to set us up," said Leslie smiling from her seat in her Honda Accord.

"Thank you, you're pretty great yourself," said EJ. "Drive safe, Leslie."

"You too ..." With that, she pulled off into the night. EJ smiled. He decided to go back in for one more drink before heading home.

The dark parking lot looked like it was still pretty full, but there were a few couples walking to their cars; a single small girl, and then a group of guys by a black Escalade who looked as if they were having their own tailgate party right there in the parking lot. Some Vincente Fernandez song was playing, something about what a shame it was. They were Tejanos, most likely Mexican better yet. They were a bit rowdy, he heard a bottle smash after being thrown a distance away, and that is what drew his attention closer to them.

EJ could not say exactly why he kept his eye on them other than maybe a sixth sense. He felt something coming. Something bad. He also noticed the small lady, very well dressed, on her phone walking in their general direction. She was either so engrossed in her conversation and did not see them, or she actually knew them. EJ guessed the former because of her appearance. She dressed classy, so she obviously came from money.

EJ was still slowly walking towards the front entrance of the bowling alley, yet simultaneously, he was keeping his peripheral vision on her. Somehow, he knew what was coming, he had seen it before. A few too many drinks could turn a man from simply 'trying to holla' at a girl, to thinking that he could handle her into his arms and then take. It could be worse when all of his friends were there and instigating the whole event.

"Hey, Mamita!" said the big one with the Cowboy Hat on.

"Mamacita, ven mami !" said another.

"Hey baby, don't you hear me? Come here!" Cowboy Hat again said.

EJ heard all the catcalls and the shit talking, and then watched them trying to follow her, grabbing at her, and then attempting to force her into their circle. By then, EJ had seen enough. He started walking their way, and cracked his neck as he walked. The last

196

thing he needed right now was more attention, more unnecessary attention, but he always had considered himself too principled of a man to allow these assholes to accost a small helpless girl, even if it did mean drawing more attention.

"Hey stop it! Don't touch me! Get off of me!" she was very calm though in her manner of speaking, was the thought that was stuck in his head, yet he picked up his pace anyways, just to make sure she was safe.

"Aw, come on mami, come and dance with me!" said one along with a lot of laughter among the others, especially Cowboy Hat, ever the instigator.

"I'm warning you! Let go of me!" she said as EJ was almost there to help her.

"Aw mamita, you warn me? AWW you warm me so good! I love -- " that voice was rudely interrupted suddenly. EJ could hear a scuffle.

"Hey! What chu doin' to Jose?" said another voice as EJ rounded the corner of the truck and saw the most unexpected scene.

The scene before him would be laughable if he had just seen it on TV instead of in person. There she was, the most beautiful girl that he had even seen before, sexy, pretty, and petite. Just the way he liked girls. He did have a type and she was most definitely it. She had her right leg around his neck at the joint, her left leg behind his neck, and her ankles crossed, locked with his left wrist in both of her hands, pulled across her right thigh she basically had him in an arm bar. It was a Krav Maga move. Something that he

197

had seen a lot of from Mossad, Israeli intelligence, who often used it in their hand to hand combat. Something like that was perfect for a girl of her size, so petite. It used their small stature, their body weight, to initiate locks and holds that could end a fight before it is even started. It was obvious to EJ that this girl had used it to remove this pushy guy's hands from wherever she didn't want them to be. EJ was fighting a laugh.

"Uh uh, y'all step back now," EJ said to this asshole's friends who were trying to pry her off of their buddy, but actually had made her tighten her grip on him.

EJ grabbed the biggest one's shoulder and yanked him back from trying to pull her legs— which were gripping his friend's neck— apart. The asshole was actually going to sleep from her hold on him. Comical to EJ. He had to punch the big guy's nose to keep himself from laughing, causing his hat to fly off. Now he *did* laugh. "Hey man, what the hell is wrong with you? I'm trying to break it up!" he said.

EJ pulled another guy off of her and hit him in the throat, instantly incapacitating him, as he curled into a little ball coughing, trying to breathe.

"All of you back the fuck off!" EJ yelled as he pulled the last one off and pushed him towards the other three, who were now just over the whole thing, putting their hands in the air trying to get away from him. Well, except for the one with the bloody nose. They were all sobering up really quickly as realization was hitting them that they were all participants to what might be perceived to others as a possible attempt at a rape. They all wanted no further part of that and started all backing away. Then they turned and ran full on into the dark parking lot. Idiots.

"It's ok ma'am, you can let go now, he is almost certainly unconscious and you are safe now the other ones are gone," said EJ in an attempt to calm her down. Little did he know. She let the guy go and stood up looking around with confusion on her face.

"Shit! You idiot! You let them get away! I was going to get on their dumb, ignorant asses next, and you let them go!?" she asked jumping up onto the hood of her victim's Escalade truck, still looking around everywhere, pissed.

"What?" she said when he looked at her confused. "You thought that you were going to come over here and what? Save me?" He said nothing, stunned. Her slight accent was beautiful and a bit sexy to him. She sounded Mexican or maybe Guatemalan.

"Like some lame ass damsel in distress or some shit?" she asked. But he didn't know what to say or even how to begin to form a response to her with, but he did feel something though. Just what that was, he wasn't sure about.

Finally he said, "I knew by the Krav Maga that you weren't a damsel, I just thought that you could use a hand, well, and I also hate bullies, go figure" he said.

"Oh, so you know Krav Maga by just one move?" she looked dubious.

"Well, yea, I've worked with Mossad before. In Afghanistan."

"I was trained by an ex-Mossad agent in Cuba," she replied.

"Cuba, huh? Wow, well I'm EJ, sorry to have interrupted," he said laughing.

"Liz, and it's okay, you saved those assholes some serious hospital bills, so they should really be grateful. You said you had been in Afghanistan. Are you in the Army?"

"Marines. And you?" asked EJ expectantly, as she had to be military or Defense Department with all of her training.

"Just an FAU student wishing to have a night without being felt up on without provocation," said Liz laughing. EJ laughed with her. It was a moment.

"Well, maybe I could help you with that. Do you think that you might want to go out with me sometime?" asked EJ even surprising himself with that question.

Liz hadn't felt butterflies like this since she had first met Phil. She knew that she was definitely attracted. He was cute, and strong. The way he pulled the big guy off was so sudden, so violent, so powerful. Liz definitely liked him. She liked how he wasn't intimidated by her, like most of the men she knew were after seeing her fight.

"Yes, I think that I would like that very much," she answered smiling, feeling like it was definitely the right decision that she was now making. She knew there was something here, something special. She had the same feeling with Phil, so she knew it was real.

Chapter Nineteen

Big Head answered his phone as he sat in his small office in his Manalapan home. "Yea," he said without looking at the phone display to see who was calling.

"Big Head, this is TFO Raines, I'm calling as a courtesy to let you know that I'm out, I'm done, I can't work with you anymore, I'm sorry."

"Yea right, ya out when me say ya out. When ya lookin' at the inside of a pine box ya out. Ya don't tell me no 'ting bout ya bein' out," said Big Head.

"NO! Mr. Joseph, you don't get to talk to me like that anymore, I'm not in this anymore, I'm done!" He said it with finality, then added, "Do you even realize what you have done? You've even got the Gang Task Force focusing their attentions on you and Haitian Sensations! You got their attentions now!"

"What foolishness is this? What I've done? I not know for what crazy foolishness ya talkin' bout and ya better start talkin' cop! Ya fa piss me off and ya not like ya dish I serve to ya, do ya hear me?!" shouted Big Head to get his point across.

"Look, Big Head, I'll give you a heads up now. But that's it. I'm out after this. You fucked up taking out the Taqueria and the Renterias. The Felix Family has a lot of pull in all of the right places, and now they are putting all of our Task Force resources, as well as any, officers to investigate you and the Haitian Sensations and any, and I quote, "all possible connections to the

Renteria murders, and or connections with the ordnance used in such murders, or the arson of the legal business, the Taqueria," well you know how the rest goes, I am sure I need not keep going," this he said with a bit of attitude. "On top of all that, we still have no evidence whatsoever the Felix Family had anything to do with the disappearances of either Rich or Big Meet, so you might have started a war with them and they could possibly have had nothing to do with this shit!"

Big Head was reeling, so he stayed silent. He had no idea what in the hell was going on, but he couldn't allow the dirty ATF agent to see that he was in the dark. No good leader could allow himself to look weak as this will make him look and remain leader for very long. So he had to play the only card he could play in order to continue to look in control; indifference. He did that very well, as usual.

"Ya not done 'fore me say ya done, and me let ya know when ya done, wit ya dirty ass! Ya understand me pig?" This he said as deadly and as serious as he was known to be. He kept up his reputation then.

"Look here Joseph! I worked with Richy Rich, not you! He is gone now, and since he is gone," the dirty cop paused dramatically, "so am I!"

Big head was laughing. He even clapped his hands a few times for effect. "So passionate! Such a dramatic speech! Did ya practice dat in front ya mirror at home?"

Raines didn't know how to respond. He was definitely thrown

for a loop.

"Let me tell ya 'fore ya piss me off ... ya want lil Billy and Amy to stay playing soccer at St. Andrews? Ya want lil miss Pretty Alicia to stay a chiropractic assistant at Dr Quams office?" He laughed again. "Ya see, ya might have only *seen* Richy Rich, but ya been *my* durdy cop da whole damn time and ya work fa me, not he, but fa ME! So don't ya forget who da fuck ya work fa and who ya talkin' to, Pig. Me not fa play no games wit cha! Me call ya when me need ya!" With that Big Head hung up and immediately called upstairs to Antoine Jean.

"We got fa be on point wit dis shit. I ain't tell nobody fa do no 'ting, but da man sayin' that they got many Task Force dem fa come fa us fa da murder! But me not tell fa nobody fa murder dem Mexicans!" Jean was there seated in Big Head's office while he was pacing back and forth, obviously very upset, and for a good reason too. They were being blamed, and having heat placed on them, for some murders and arson that they didn't even know about. It was a first for the Haitian Sensations leader, as being blamed for murders was nothing new, but they were usually the ones who actually had committed the offenses they were being accused of.

"Well, from what I got from everyone I've talked to in the streets, the Felix Family was robbed for tens of millions in cash and then the restaurant was burned down to destroy the evidence. Except that there was a car at the scene stolen from Lil Haiti in Miami, and then the Haitian flag bandanas left at both scenes, it's so damn retarded looking that even those idiots working the Task Force are not even taking our money and are trying to cut ties with us. It's not only that, but Head, man everyone really thinks we did this, and were stupid enough to leave all this damn shit at those scenes leading right back to us. It's fucking embarrassing to us, it makes us look unorganized and sloppy as fuck. Not only that, but we are losing some of our big buyers because of all this heat on us. We need to do something here. Cops aren't telling me shit, and won't even take our money..." Antoine trailed off and ran his hand down his face at a loss for words. Just frustrated, he couldn't say much.

"Ok, so me goin' back Port Au Prince and ready 400 Mawazo soldiers dem, you fa take over here, and we fa continue wit no Richy Rich. You fa gone make all Richy Rich contacts. Keep dem trap house goin', we can't lose no more. Stay here as you been doin', me fa take me Sundancer back fa Port Au Prince, handle tings ... " He finally stood up and began to gather his things.

Antoine thought right then about just blowing Big Head's brains out right there and then, then dealing with the aftermath later himself, but it would be just too complicated at this time. It wouldn't get the point across either, and that was important if he was to take over things. Richy Rich had had his own plans for the future with a move like this, along with Big Meet and some others, it was inevitable that someone would smack Big Head and take over. Such an arrogant fuck, thought Antoine. But no, he would allow him to continue to think he's in control, until the day that his friend in the 400 Mawazo could pave the way for his coup. This was one advantage that he had held above Richy Rich or Big Meet, he had inside help with the Mawazo. A coup would just be impossible without one. Richy Rich and Big Meet had been presumptuous to think they could have pulled this off without him, and the minimum of help with the 400 Mawazo soldiers. Everything had to be planned, checked and double checked after checking again. It was not going to be easy.

Once Big Head had left in the Sundancer, Antoine got in his own 1984 Toyota Corolla, his favorite car, and headed to a bar downtown Lake Worth called Sneakers. He saw his man, Steff at the pool table running down his balls. Steff was known and hated for playing $100 games of pool, and in the event that he would win, which he usually did, he would then set his opponent's $100 bill on fire, much to all the broke nigga's hatred and amazement. But it did make all of the little barfly girls love him and chase him even more. Which was why he did it.

"What's good my nigga?" Steff asked and dapped him up.

"Shit, a lot, but we can get to that in a minute," said Antoine. He went to order a drink. Hennessy & Coke, and two shots of Patron. He came back to the pool table and handed Steff one of the shots. They touched glasses, touched the table with the glass bottoms, and then downed the smooth clear tequila. Steff chased the smooth shot with a sip from his Heineken, Antoine sipped his Henny and Coke, then sat down sighing. He was so tired and stressed. He needed a few more shots.

Immediately Steff dismissed his current barfly company, a blonde, both in hair and in personality as well. He sat down in the booth opposite of Antoine and listened for two more drinks each to everything that Antoine had to tell him. They were both baffled as to who was behind not only the murders but also the disappearances as well. All of the information that Steff had been hearing on the streets, from strippers he slept with, to cops that he paid off, were all in agreement that it actually *had* been his crew who had pulled off the move on the Mexicans. It was actually giving them even more street cred that their already murderous reputations had been rumored to be like. The rumors were now also saying that the amount of money stolen from the Mexican's Taqueria was at 25 million dollars. Shit, thought Steff, if that had been true, we would have been able to retire very early.

By the time the bar was closing, Steff and Antoine had agreed on a tentative plan that might be able to benefit all of those involved. They wouldn't be able to appease the Gang Unit and the Task Force cops screaming for their heads, but there was a way to calm things down between factions and keep their money trains rolling. It was the only way really. They had to talk to the Mexican plug.

§§§§

In the evening of the next day, Antoine went and paid Richy Rich's house a visit. It was a big six bedroom two story house in the Black Diamond neighborhood out West. Black Diamond was in the Township of Wellington, just west of Lake Worth and West Palm Beach. It was an upper middle class suburban neighborhood most commonly known for its access to the equestrian circuit and same lifestyle, as well as the famous Polo Club. Antoine could see why Richy Rich had moved out here, you definitely weren't going to run into any of their associates or enemies way out here, but damn, he was thinking, he would stick out like a sore thumb.It all came into focus, gave Antoine a clearer picture when a pretty blonde girl with blue eyes opened the front door of the beautiful white stucco mini-mansion. Antoine stuttered for a second before correcting his slight slip up.

"Is this Rich's house?" he asked her.

"Yes," she said, her eyes puffy from crying and now watering up all over again.

"Oh, I know you. You're one of the guys from his club right?"

"Uh, yea," he said, immediately catching onto what Richy Rich must have told her to explain away his felonious looking associates. "I've come to try and help to find him and get him safely home to you," the last part he tried to say as sincerely as possible, and with confidence, even though he knew that it wasn't even going to be a slight possibility finding Rich. If Rich was even alive, he would have made some sort of contact with either Antoine or his own family. Of that he was almost certain of. So that was proof enough that Richy Rich was most definitely dead.

"Ah, thank God," she said rushing forward and hugging Antoine. "These cops are so damn stupid! They say that they think that he might have run off somewhere and left us! They think that he might have gone to Haiti, but I'm pregnant with our second child, and he already just adores Jr.! So, there is no fucking way that he would leave us, but knowing that scares me even more, cuz now I'm sure that something has happened to him," she sniffled, "oh, I'm sorry, please come in."

"It's okay," he said stepping in past her, "I'm here to help in anyway that I can." He noticed immediately the marble floors and chandelier above them that looked strikingly like a genuine Tiffanys & Co. addition to the house, very good tastes, that's for sure. Very good indeed.

She led him into a large living room area with Latuzzi imported Italian leather couches, and a remarkably huge LED Television hanging on their wall with a cute kid around the age of four or five playing a video game on it.

"Jr., go play in your room for a little while, okay sweetie?"

"Okay mommy, when's daddy coming home?" Big innocent eyes looked into the inner most part of Antoine's soul. But he couldn't let on, no matter what, he kept it up.

"I don't know Jr., but this nice man is going to try to help us find him, okay?"

"Please find daddy," said the little boy running away before Antoine could even compose an answer to reassure him with. The mother stayed crying quietly to herself. "He's such a good boy. Smart as hell too," she said.

"I'm really sorry Mrs," Antoine said since there was nothing more that he could say. He left it open though, questioning.

"Debbie," she told him.

"Oh, sorry, I'm Antoine," he said smiling to her.

"I remember, you're the one whose daddy started the whole club, right? I met you one time at John Prince Park, at a barbecue, about a year ago maybe?" She smiled back at him. Friendly. Nice lady, he thought. Too bad for her bad choice of man.

"Well, my pops was one of the founders. One of the three founders of the club, that is, and yea I do remember that party. I do think I remember you too. So nice to see you again, though I'm sorry for it being under this circumstances. But that's why I'm here right now, I am trying to track Rich's movements from around the time that he went missing. So I wanted to come to look through his things and his records. I'm hoping his phone was connected to the Cloud or had a 'Find Me' app -- " she interrupted him there, before he could even finish his thought out loud.

"Shit, I can't believe that I didn't think about that! His phone, yea we have it synced to our computer and iCloud, so it could show ..." she said and started walking down the hallway, her sentence trailing off. Antoine followed her into a home office with a desk and a laptop sitting there, which she hit a key on and woke it up, then started playing with the mouse. "Shit, his location is turned off now, but his last location is in ... well that's weird, we don't know anyone out in Boca Raton ... " she said as the confusion showed clearly on her pretty face.

"Do you think that we might be able to copy his phone info to a..." he was looking all around the office for a disk or a sim card to copy it to, so that he might download the phone contacts onto, which was the real reason that he was even there in the first place.

"Oh, well how about I just give you his iCloud account info and password, and then you can just use it as you need it?" she suggested brightly.

"You have his iCloud account password?" he asked in disbelief.

"I am his wife of many years," she said laughing, "of course, I used a spyware app to make sure I know what all of his passwords are." She smiled then.

"Oh you," Antoine said stuttering, "I thought that you meant that he gave you the password." He was shaking his head now. This beautiful, devious woman, she was definitely something else. More than meets the eye, but I am never going to get married, he thought to himself with finality.

"Just bring my husband home to us," she said deadly serious.

Chapter Twenty

Iggy Rodriguez was a good looking dark skinned Mexican. He had, what they called, the 'Indio' look, and he learned to be very tough while growing up in some of the most violent places where he started his life. Mexico City, Juarez, Reynosa, and finally here, in Matamoros, Tamualipas. He grew up kickboxing in order to take out his anger. At 6'3, 220 lbs, he had a lot of kickboxing to do for a lot of anger.

He ended up fighting semi-professionally, mostly at cock fights and dog fights with him backing himself and training all alone for the fights. The fact that he was best friends with Ricky Felix, El Senor's second son, wasn't even the thing that got him noticed by El Senor at first. It was his amazing heart. Determination.

Ricky Felix was pretty tough himself, and one day after school some kids were picking on him because of the roach shaped brown birthmark on the back of his neck, as kids tend to do. Ricky, being who he was, which at the time was a grandson of a cartel boss, had bit off more than he could chew with a group of kids numbered like a soccer team. He was way outnumbered. He didn't care. He fought.

He had been getting beat up pretty bad, but they would discover later on, that it was a trick of sight. It always looked worse than it really was. Mostly, when a group of kids that big, were all fighting against one kid, they most likely would be hitting each

211

other more than they were actually landing on the intended victim.

When Iggy went to the bike rack to retrieve his bicycle and saw so many kids jumping one kid, even though he didn't know the kid from Adam, all he saw was red as he started dropping bombs on the kids from outside of the circle they had created around the one they were jumping. It was a totally unexpected move but one thing Iggy had always hated since he was little, was bullying. Once Iggy had broken the instigator's nose and he had taken off, it only had taken a few more punches from Ricky and Iggy together to send the rest of Ricky's assailants running home for their lives with black eyes and split lips.

When the Felix Family had heard about the incident and Iggy's bravery, they had tried to reciprocate by sending a car over to award Iggy for helping the Felix kid, he promptly returned it to the Felix family saying that his mother doesn't accept charity, and his bike was working just fine. This made them all respect and love him even more, welcoming him into their family, which made him and Ricky like brothers, although very few people actually knew the story, and there would always have to be some animosity from the other brothers, even though they generally accepted him.

After Jonny had taken Iggy to the guard for questioning who had been working that night when the Taqueria was robbed, he had needed to change his clothes. He had blood all over himself, and could not yet shower because his cousin had expected him to stay with him in his town house, and hadn't secured him a suite anywhere.

212

He had questioned the idiot guard for almost 4 hours and emptied two quarts of blood on the floor, as well as on his clothes, and only had come up with a few leads. One was about the stolen car that had Haitian flags and really big wheels, further cementing in his head about the Haitian Sensations angle. That fact, taken in addition with the fact that their friends in the Palm Beach County Sheriffs Office had told them about a Haitian flag bandana that was also found at the scene, tied as a mask, but had come up negative for any allele of DNA, pointed in the same direction. His problem though, was the streets. If a move by the Haitian Sensations was underway, the word would be all over the underground, and yet there was nothing there. Radio silence in the streets. That was unusual to say the least.

Another thing was that: even the police and sheriffs deputies on their pay roll had no idea about it either. Iggy knew for a fact that a few of the cops on their payroll put together, had hundreds of street walkers and snitches working for them, and the fact that not one of them had any knowledge about these murders or the Taqueria robbery, didn't sit well with him. Something was most definitely amiss with this whole situation. What, now that was the main question that he couldn't answer, but maybe he didn't have to. Maybe there was another way. His thoughts were interrupted by his phone ringing. He looked at the display and saw that it was Liz and so he went ahead to answer her call.

"Como estamos Dulce?" He was the only one that ever called her Dulce, which meant 'candy', because of how he thought she was so sweet. He smiled thinking about her. El Senor had asked that he check on her routinely and made sure to keep her out of West Palm Beach and Lake Worth, where she might be used against him if this were actually a gang style war. She was apparently returning his call.

Once he reiterated to her about staying outside of the city and as south as she could from where all the events were happening, he again begged her to allow him to send her a bodyguard to protect her. As expected though, she declined with as much zeal as her little voice could muster. He was sure the body language matched her tone. She was ... difficult. Something that he was now very used to with her. Nothing was ever easy when dealing with her.

Either way, if he needed to, he could always assign a tail on her later to keep her safe, from one of Jonny's many employees. But it was a problem for another time, as he had much more pressing matters to attend to, like a phone call coming through on his Sideline phone app. Sideline was an anonymous phone forwarding service app.

"It's very suspicious," he answered the call, "when someone is calling a number that I had given to a dead man."

"Well, it is equally bewildering to me, when I go through my missing-not dead-friend's phone, see his contacts, and I find the name 'Iggy'," answered the very educated voice on the other end of the phone call.

"Shit! What a fucking idiot," said Iggy.

214

"Yes. My sentiments exactly, because Iggy is a very peculiar name, not common among our people at all, and we both, my friend and I, only knew one 'Iggy', and if I'm not mistaken, I believe him to be some big name in the Matamoros Cartel, am I correct?" the educated voice asked, further prolonging the dramatic effect.

"So," said Iggy carefully, "with whom am I speaking? You sound like the fucking dean at Yale, who the fuck is this?"

"I am a friend I think. At least for now I am. Or until I find that you have outlived your usefulness. Oh, and I do resent the Yale dig. I actually attended Harvard Law, so I take being associated with Yale as an insult."

"You are boring me. I don't give a fuck. What do you want? And who the fuck are you?" asked Iggy starting to lose his patience.

"I am a part of the same organization as the one who you gave this number to, and if it was for the same reason that I think that it was for, then I believe that we might be able to continue the original plans that you had arranged with Richy Rich and Big Meet," said the Voice.

"Organization? You think that this was organized? Your man stored my fucking number in his phone under my actual *name*? If that's your organization, shit, what if this had been my real number? I should hang up right now! I don't even know who I'm fucking talking to, I see no reason to continue talking ... "

"No! Okay, listen, I get where you are coming from, my name is Antoine Jean, okay? Don't hang up, we can continue the talks

215

that Rich had started with you on my behalf," said Antoine, trying to be reasonable and keep him talking.

"On your behalf?" That definitely had his attention now.

"Yes, I am the one who initiated the talks. I believe if we go ahead with our plan, we can both corner our respective areas with an agreed upon pre-arranged price for each locale and item. It will in the end, provide us with a monopoly of the heroin, fentynal, cocaine and flaka markets in South Florida."

"You talk like this on a fucking phone?"

"Iggy, I bought this Trac-Phone a half an hour ago, and I will see it into the Atlantic Ocean in another hour, so I talk as I please, as I already did a reverse lookup on this number and discovered that it was indeed a Sideline Phone App number, and therefore, untraceable, as you are using Wifi. I do my due diligence."

"Okay, I'm impressed, but still, we don't know each other, so how do I know you ain't tryin' to set me up?"

"Greed, my friend," said Antoine. "We need to monopolize South Florida, as you have done in Southern Texas. All the other states on the East Coast and the south will be paying our prices. As long as we stick together and do this. Nobody will be able to go around us, except maybe from California, and trust me, *nobody* wants to go to California and deal with them. The whole eastern half of America's prices will skyrocket. We will not only raise our profit margin, we will cut out the street users as well. Only the big buyers will be able to afford us. It is again, why we have always invested heavily into rehabilitation clinics and centers, since they

216

are unregulated."

"Ok," said Iggy, "same plan?"

"Exactly the same plan my friend," said Antoine.

Iggy had taken one of Jonny's company Tahoes, as he hated the much bigger Suburban. He pulled into the town houses that were called Green Briar, where he was apparently going to be staying with his cousin. Walking in, he greeted Jonny and then updated him on the progress he had made that day, and especially the fact that the original plan was back on, and that they would be working with the Haitian Sensations again.

"So, what's up with Jose and Elizebeth then? Are we still looking at the Haitian Sensations for those murders or what?" Jonny asked him, just to be sure about the issue and clarify it all in his mind.

"Well," said Iggy, " I don't really think it matters, does it? Of course you will still have some of your people looking into it, but when we actually start putting the plan into effect, I think that it will fade into the background, as their murders will be of less importance when the old man ain't around no more. So, nah, we can let it go for now, let's concentrate all of our energy on filling our storage units with as much product as possible and start making it available for our New York buyers only, at the already agreed upon price. We can dry our city out a bit while building our relationship with our northern friends. When we turn the faucet back on here at the inflated prices, they will all run to the Haitians, who will be doing the same thing, causing everything to level out at the inflated prices. We all keep our already held territories, and the drought will be started right here first, spreading from here to all over the U.S. I wouldn't doubt a thing cuz, it will most definitely work."

"It is a brilliant idea cuz, but do you think they will catch on over in Cali? The Sinaloa Cartel over there?" asked Jonny.

"Well yea, this Haitian is a regular fucking Einstein. Whatever, it will work for us. Ricky don't care, he just wants the position and the West Coast. But as much as I know it is going to work, I'm taking bets as to what the Sinaloa Cartel's response will be." He paused, thinking, "I mean they can keep their prices low and make a lot of money with the factions that will travel that far, but with that, it's a lot of dealing with new people, so that is more attention, more traffic, and more risk. But if he raises his prices, the West Coast would even out and he would still make more money, but there would be less attention. Man, I put my money on them jacking their prices up and getting with our program."

"It's a good bet primo," said Jonny laughing.

"Now, all we gotta do is get on with the plan, find a way to get El Senor down here so we can put an end to him and place Ricky in power, then go forward with everything like that. Once Ricky is in power, he will go forward with taking care of those Sinaloa dogs, get them out of the way and take over the whole 1,954 miles of the U.S.- Mexico border."

"Once Ricky controls the West Coast border and doubles the prices over there, we can up our prices on the East Coast again, using our new Haitian friends to control prices throughout the Caribbean. It's just, if you think getting El Senor to come across the border in Texas was hard, wait till we try to get him to come to South Florida. That's the one that's going to be the real hurdle," explained Iggy, contemplatively.

"What about using the Taqueria as an excuse? It's in his name, ain't it? That could work ..." Jonny trailed off to Iggy shaking his head.

"It won't," said Iggy with certainty, "even if the restaurant wasn't in the name of a shell company out of Costa Rica, he would write it all off."

" ... and what about Jose and Liz's deaths? Can't -- " started Jonny.

"Primo! That's it! What else could command his attention? It's fucking Liz primo! The Liz that still lives! She is his favorite, he loves her to death, he could risk coming over here for his precious niece. Now, how to set it up ... Do you have an extra guy that won't be missed?" Iggy asked, with a devious look in his eyes.

"I was about to fire this lazy asshole Juanito ... He's got no family connections, would he be missed? It's doubtful." said Jonny smiling.

"Ok, put him on tailing Liz immediately, we can form a plan as we go, give El Senor a casualty, a body that protected her with his life, and we ransom her as a Haitian Sensation-400 Mawazo, and when he gets here to save her, we again make it look like the Haitian Sensations are responsible for his death, then Ricky can

219

come in, take out the Haitian Sensations leader Big Head, and then it's back to business ... no?"

"It's a damn good ass plan, primo, I'll get Juanito on Liz immediately," said Jonny, plotting and planning with Iggy deviously.

Chapter Twenty - One

Some time had passed with Shelby and Jean living together at her Moorings condo, and things had progressed very nicely between them. Their feelings had grown serious and a mutual love developed. Even their sex life had become an amazing adventure. Something they both had enjoyed with zeal and vigor, they couldn't wait until the next time they could be together whenever they were separated.

Shelby had several new cases on the murder board at work, had made an arrest in a child rape-murder case that had really affected her. Her suspect had lured a 12 year old girl on Facebook to meet him at the Boynton Beach Mall, then taken her back to his house claiming to be a movie producer, and then raped and killed her.

The only reason Shelby had caught him was thanks to her parents having her Facebook password, reading the exchange and reporting to Shelby. She then got the mall cameras from the meeting time and followed the guy's progress to the car, got the license plate, and executed a search warrant at his house, which was where she located the girl's young body. It was the worst thing she had ever seen. A heartbreaking situation, very hard on her soul. Fortunately, the guy had resisted their attempts to arrest him, so a 'use of force' report had to be filed, and an explanation given as to why he had been beaten to a pulp and was currently semi-comatose, and had his jaw wired shut.

Unfortunately for her though, his lawyer, Roberto Norvelli, had been filing motions left and right in an attempt to get evidence excluded and undo all of her hard work. Because of the use of force had resulted in an extremely serious injury, and 'attempted murder by law enforcement,' had been the vernacular that had been used in the motions. All of the heat had been coming down on her because she had been the lead detective in the investigation. All of this had been taking its toll on her mentally, and physically, in the worst ways.

"Baby," said Jean causing her to jump, "what's wrong?"

"Nothing, Jean, just a little bit stressed," she said as he started massaging her shoulders from behind her, "you know the Jameson arrest?"

"Yea, I thought you got his chomo ass, a lil beatin' ain't all that bad, they'll get over it, bae, " he massaged her even deeper, "don't sweat it."

"Nah, I know, but Jones called. Norvelli got Jameson out on bond, shit, this whole shit is a mess, I don't even know what I'm doing anymore, Jesus ..."

"Wow," said Jean. "Well, just relax and let me take your mind off of this, if only for a few minutes." He smiled lasciviously and rolled over the top of the couch, falling on top of her, causing her to giggle. He laughed with her and looked into her beautiful brown eyes. Her face turned serious. He lowered his head slowly and kissed her lips. She let his tongue enter her waiting mouth and massaged his tongue with her own.

She was so wet and her body in so much need. Shelby grabbed at Jean's belt and tugged. She didn't want foreplay, she needed her release. Jean wanted it as well and pulled her panties to the side. It was an easy access, since, as the song would say, she 'had her T-shirt and her panties on' and nothing else. Jean allowed Shelby to pull his pants as far as his knees, as he sucked and licked on one of her chocolate Hersheys kiss shaped nipples, and then another. As soon as Shelby had accomplished getting his pesky Balmains out of her way, she grabbed at his full eight inches with her half as small hands. She immediately began to guide his head into her opening, and then up to her clit, and back down to her opening again until he had her juices to wet his head up, so that he would be ready to penetrate her. Jean obliged and didn't make her beg, he himself was desperately in need of her as well.

Shelby was going to let him slide into her gently, as he would often do, but couldn't wait. She instead pulled him as hard as she could, until she had pulled his body as close as he could possibly get, and had his whole eight inches inside of her to the hilt. "Mmm," moaned Shelby as she accepted his length, feeling the warmth wash all over her body, as the tension and stress was slowly leaving her body with every stroke, so roughly doled out by her sun and stars, who had her heart totally.

"Baby, you are so good, " Jean said stroking her as hard, and fast as he could, knowing what she needed to take her mind off of all that she was going through and stressing about.

"Aw, Jean! Yes! Jean, awww." He was really digging into her

223

guts and trying to give it all to her, he couldn't slow down, not when she needed every stroke he could give her. She flipped positions and she allowed him to hit her from the back, doggie style. He gently spread her butt cheeks and pushed harder and more into her, the cheeks out of the way, giving him more access. He turned her around again and pulled up one of her legs onto his hip as he got even deeper, and then started going in a rotation. "Awww, Jean! I'm! Coming! I'm -- Ahh, Jean! I'm Coming again! Don't stop! Don't stop!" She was screaming her words and he felt them at the tip of his dick, as she was throwing her pussy back at him. He felt her grip on him tighten. She pulled him down onto her and her arms locked him into her grip. She froze her body. He kept stroking her, and he felt her water flood over his dick, as he also felt his own build up getting ready for his release. "Shelby, baby! I'm going to cum with you! I'm about to... cum!" Jean said starting to go even faster than he already was. "Come for me baby, show me this your pussy baby, give me that nut baby!" He started to let himself loose inside of her, his cum filling her to the brim.

"Grrahhh! Ahh, Shelby! Damn!" He was trying to catch his breath but couldn't.

"Aww, baby, I love you so much, Jean I love you!"

"Damn baby I love you too, I've never really felt this way about anyone before. I've never shared what we share before, you are so special to me, Shelby. I am so happy being with you. Nobody could ever compare to you baby, I love you Shelby, I really do. It's nothing like the time I've spent with you."

"Aww baby, thank you. I'm so glad that you are telling me cuz I didn't want to be in this on my own, I can't lose you Jean, you have changed my life and you don't even know it yet. You mean the world to me," said Shelby smiling.

They were both curled up on the couch and Jean had kicked his Balmain stonewashed pants to the floor and shared Shelby's comforter with her. He glanced at the television, a 55" Sony LED curve, and saw what movie was playing: 'Running Scared' with Paul Walker and Vera Farmiga, who were trying to chase down their son and his friend, who had stolen a hot gun, and were in a lot of danger because the mob who used the gun wanted it back from them. Jean laughed as he saw what part of the movie they were at. "What, bae?" She glanced at the movie, and uncomprehendingly, looked back at Jean in askance.

"I want to give you something no other man can give you and seal our relationship for life," he said looking at the movie. He smiled. On the big television screen, the movie was at the part where Vera Famiga had run down on these chomos', or child molester's house, and found the little boys in the play room, minutes away from getting molested.

"Please! We're sick! We just need help, that's all," said the lady chomo in the movie. Vera Famiga didn't even blink when she shot both chomos in their heads without a second thought. She got the boys and got out of there.

"I can give you Wicks, let Wicks do Jameson, and he will never be able to do something like that or hurt any kid anywhere but in hell. I really want to do this for you bae ..." Jean told her sincerely with all of his heart.

"Okay," she said without argument, "then I want to give you something too. I'll work out a plan for this Lemonhead character. He is the only one that I could find that was connected to Big Meet, but the thing with him is, every file I've seen has nothing on him, no info at all, but on the streets they are all saying that he is the one in control of the flaka and heroin, so he was the actual one who had supplied Big Meet, and thus Lil' Fade, Matt, and the whole crew that was involved with Lil' Ray's shooting. So he is the *real* one who was responsible for Lil Ray's shooting, if you look back to the source, and once we take him out, we can be done with this and go back to just doing our part at the Youth Center, right?" Shelby looked into his eyes expectantly. "You're not having second thoughts about staying clean, are you?"

"Baby, no," answered Jean, staring right back into her eyes, "I am not going to go back to that. *Ever.* I don't care about the money, I thought that I showed you that with the Taqueria! I only want a future with you, with us. And a future for these kids at the center. You never have to worry about me going back, that is not going to happen. Trust me Shelby and never doubt me, I've never felt like I do with you, and I would never risk losing that for anything in the world. I'm with you a hundred bae, don't trip, okay?"

"Okay, but talk to me if you ever have doubts, I know what you have been through and I would never want to pressure you, okay?"

"It will never happen baby! I'm in this for da long run, ya heard?" said Jean.

§§§§

Shelby met EJ at his condo downtown West Palm Beach at City Place. It was a 23 story building and EJ's condo was on the more affordable 12th floor, since Uncle Sam was picking up the bill for it. When he opened the door and invited her in, she was surprised to find that it was already furnished very nicely, as it had been Shelby's impression that he had just moved into this place without any furniture of his own, being that he hadn't had a place of his own. She knew that he had always stayed with Jean's sister, Miss Laurie, when he was normally stateside.

"It came like this," said EJ to her unspoken question. "It was some kind of a safe house for defectors, was my understanding of what this place used to be."

"It's very nice EJ, and I see that you have all of your toys laid out."

"Far from *all* of my toys," said EJ laughing, "this is just what I have planned for us to use tonight ... "

Shelby's eyes widened. "All of this?"

"It's common for a breach team," said EJ, "but since it's only you and I, we'll have to improvise ..." Shelby just nodded as she examined the tools of the trade. There was even a battering ram, which they could use to forcefully open any door without much

227

effort, a shield, vests, and bulletproof trench and helmets, to name a few. There were HK MP5 sub-machine pistols with wet suppressors, Sig-Sauer P229s, also with wet suppressors, which used eight plastic plates surrounded by petroleum jelly to contain all of the fire and powder that comes with pushing a bullet out at the speed of sound. Unfortunately, in real life, it wasn't like the movies, suppressors actually affected aim, so they could only be used in closed quarters work. Shelby was taken aback.

"Where did you get all of these?" She continued her visual inventory.

"All shit marked to be destroyed when we all pulled out of Sandland -- ah, I mean Afghanistan, and well, most of us keep our breach equipment because it has been tried and battle tested. It is all in good working condition and all very accurate. I've taken good care of all of them and maintained them expertly, what?"

Shelby was looking at him smiling, "Nothing, you're just so passionate and intense about this stuff, I don't see this type of stuff very often and it's just so obvious that you know your stuff. I'm glad you will be there to have my back."

"Well, it's you having our back going along with this, I know this isn't how you usually handle things in your profession, but if worst comes to worst, technically under the Patriot Act, Section 806.3 --"

Shelby interrupted him there. "Don't worry, it won't get to that, it ain't my first rodeo, and I won't throw up when we are done. I'm a professional as well," she retorted to him.

"Okay, Shelby. I understand what you mean with that. Gear up. We are wheels up in ten minutes!"

Chapter Twenty - Two

Wicks was back. He had parked his 1979 Riviera at the Winn-Dixie supermarket on Federal Highway and Hypoluxo Road, in the city of Lantana. He then walked across the street to the east side of Federal Highway where an upscale, well kept neighborhood was located hiding behind several condominium buildings. He had on a grey jogging suit with reflectors that were required for joggers, black gloves, and some black Rebook Classics, again courtesy of the Walmart in Miami Gardens.

He jogged past his target's house three times before being sure there were no prying eyes or cameras. He turned his jacket inside out to attempt to conceal the reflectors, and then headed toward the thick bushes that could conceal him, lining the driveway that enclosed the whole property.

The target's house itself was a two story, six bedroom, white and grey Florida Keys style that backed up onto the intercoastal waterway. It had a three car garages attached, one of those doors was opened. Wicks couldn't believe his luck, but still proceeded with caution, just in case there was a security guard on the property. He wouldn't be surprised, fact of the matter being that the news had broadcasted what he had done as well as the location of his house where they had found the girl's body. Also the fact that they had just recently released the crime scene property back to him, which was also causing some controversy in the news.

Wicks approached and could hear the television on. Oddly

enough, it sounded like the Steve Harvey game show was on. As he approached, he noticed the new Cadillac Escalade, and an S550 Benz in two of the parking spots in his three car garage. The other one that was opened seemed to contain many cameras, film, and accessories for the film and photography business. Basically everything that one might need to make a movie or photograph scenes. Maybe this asshole really was a movie producer. It didn't matter one way or the other to Wicks though. This guy was never going to be able to make another film or take another picture in his miserable life. He was a predator of defenseless kids, the worst kind of human being in the world. Anyone who could exploit the innocence of a child was an evil and ruthless scumbag who had no reason to live. The fact that this scum was breathing the same air as him further infuriated Wicks. He didn't deserve the air he breathed.

Wicks walked up to the door in the garage that led into the inside of the house. He turned the knob on the door very carefully, and as slowly as possible, so as not to alert the TV watching target, as he wanted his attention to stay diverted, but he need not even have tried. Because as soon as the door was an inch open, there was a small beep beep, that could be heard, an alert that a door was ajar in the house.

Wicks then heard a voice, " ... the hell?" Shit, an alarm system. He was so surprised that the garage doors were left opened that he completely forgot to check for an alarm. How did he miss that one? he asked himself. Oh, well, he thought.

Wicks pushed the door the rest of the way open and moved quickly into the kitchen that the door led to, and then beyond. Through the kitchen was a large opening to the immaculate and huge living room, an oversized L-shaped couch, and a gigantic television with a bandaged up asshole currently getting up from the couch, in front of it with a startled incredulous look on his face.

"Hey! Who the hell are you? How'd you get in here?" Eyes widened big.

"You left your garage door opened," said Wicks nonchalantly and then in one quick motion, he jumped over the couch and punched him right in his already broken and wired shut jaw. His words were surprisingly understandable for someone that had his jaw wired shut. This guy must have been much the talker when he was in front of people, because he talked like he had nothing wrong with his mouth at all. After the punch, the guy flew backwards towards the floor and immediately balled up, begging for his life. Wicks kicked him in his ribs as hard as he could. The guy was a complete wimp, crying and slobbering all over himself. No surprise there for a pedophile. No wonder why the little girl had not sensed the predatory nature in him, or his craziness, and trusted him enough to ride alone with him. He was acting so completely harmless, that you could forget how he had raped and then killed a little girl. But Wicks wouldn't forget. He couldn't forget. Nor would the chomo, now that Wicks is here.

"Stop! Look I got money! I'll give you everything! Please just don't kill me!"

232

"Where's the money? If you want to live, it better be a lot!" answered Wicks.

"I do! I do! Man help me up, I'll show you," he said crying, and beginning to stutter. Wicks helped the already beaten up and bandaged, crying grown man up. He was only about 5'6 or so, and maybe 160lbs soaking wet, and already having been beat up by the police, going bald and grey, with big and fat 'Chomo 3000' glasses on. He looked every bit the creep that he was. Wicks followed him into what was his bedroom apparently, and then to his big, walk-in closet, to which the door was already opened, revealing a Sentury digital safe, about two feet squared.

"Code?" Wicks asked him as he let his chomo ass drop to the floor.

"Nanana na -- you're going to kill me if I tell you," cried the sick chomo incoherently with a desperate look of pleading in his eyes.

"Motherfucker I'll kill you if you don't tell me," said Wicks calmly and then backhanded the chomo as hard as he could to get him on the same page.

"Ok ok ok, just please don't kill me, take the money and go!" he said crying, as he then leaned over and dialed in the code into the safe, then opened it, while simultaneously reaching inside. Wicks kicked him as hard as he could, right in his temple, instantly knocking him unconscious, and making his head fly back against the back of the closet next to the safe. Wicks had kicked him pretty hard. He laughed to himself as he saw the indentation that the chomo's head had made in the dry wall, it was a Mount Rushmore reverse look for his closet. Maybe it would even add some value to this terrible house that the bank would probably have to sell later on.

Wicks leaned down and opened the safe door the rest of the way and saw immediately on top of everything, a .380 Walther readily accessible to the chomo, if Wicks hadn't stopped him right then. "Wrong time to grow some balls Mr. Jameson," he said and laughed some more. Wicks was enjoying himself. He took the bank envelopes that the gun was sitting on top of and looked at them. They had receipts attached to each one of them.

The bills inside them, it turned out, were actually legitimately withdrawn money from the banks, there were even withdrawal slips from three different banks. Each one was for $10,000. So, there was $30,000 total in legal funds taken out of his accounts. It almost seemed as if it had been withdrawn in order for this chomo to go ahead and make a run for it. Well, that was the way it looked to Wicks anyway. He contemplated this for a second as an idea had struck him, and went back towards the alarm pad that had beeped when he had come into the kitchen from the garage door. Green Lights. This asshole actually had an alarm system in his house and really just didn't even activate it? What an asshole, thought Wicks. He still had the money and receipts in his hands. He put them into his pocket, walked over to the kitchen cabinets, and started searching for an item to use on his target. Once he had located what he was looking for, he quickly got back to his victim and started to stretch out the seran wrap around his upper torso, locking his arms to his body, incapacitating him. He kept going down to his feet and back up to his face. His target's eyes opened instantly and widened at now knowing that his oxygen was being cut off, along with the realization that he would soon be in hell, where other predators would take full advantage of their ability to rape and kill him, over and over, every minute of every hour of every day, for all eternity. He had to know that he had this coming. It would definitely be a lot better than prison would have been for him, that was for sure.

He was mumbling, begging with his eyes, and thrashing about, as much as the restraining wrap would allow, all to no avail. His fate was sealed when he had raped and murdered an innocent and defenseless little girl. Wicks was there, staring into his target's eyes all the way until the chomo's very life was forfeited. Wicks had made sure that he could never breathe his air again.

Wicks took one last look, picked him up, and carried him out to the garage. He closed the main garage door that had stood open, exposing the camera equipment to the world. He had an idea. He found the Escalade's keys in the damn ignition. Was this guy an idiot or what? What a fucking rich asshole, he thought to himself. He started loading all of the camera and filming equipment into the trunk of the truck right on top of the guy's body. There was so much, but he managed to fit most of it into the back, completely covering up Mr. Jameson's corpse. He decided to give the house a quick once over just to make sure. He started looking for artwork or sculptures that a man on the run would definitely take, after emptying $30,000 in withdrawals from his banks. He took two paintings that were signed 'Vini' in the bottom right hand corner, because if there were any, these were the ones that would be worth a lot of money and worth taking on the run to sell later on.

When Smack answered his text, he was already in Delray Beach, visiting his mother and other sister, so he said that he would take the Tri-Rail train to the Gateway train stop, near Lantana where Wicks was currently at, so he could be picked up easily. Wicks packed up the target's Coach suitcases with toothbrush, deodorant, shaving kit, underwear, socks, a couple suits, and some leisure ware so it would all look genuine. He found a box of pills for sea sickness and took all of the pills and left the empty box on the counter in the kitchen for the cops to find when this asshole missed his first court date. Everything had to be right to make it look like he was alive and well, but he was on the run. Wicks stopped at nothing to care for every detail. Wicks was in his element, a place where he, not Jean, excelled and felt confident in his chosen trade. It was where he belonged.

After loading all the suit cases and artworks in the car, Wicks took the S550 to pick up smack from the Tri-Rail station and allow him to drive Jean back to get the Escalade. When Wicks had allowed JJ to deal with Big Meet's remains, he paid a debt that was owed. But Wicks would never let Smack to ride with a dead body as a favor to him. He would let him chop up both vehicles for helping him though. That could make a good and healthy profit for Smack to get on with, but truth be told, there was no possible way for Wicks to undertake this complicated disappearance act all by himself. He needed Smack, no doubt about it.

When he was finally ready to leave, he didn't lock the doors and figured the unset alarm system would help the 'went on the run scene' look more valid and believable. A realistic situation that happened all the time with serious court dates and serious charges. He drove the Escalade and followed I-95 South all the way down to Miami with Smack following closely to watch his back. They both breathed a lot easier once they had made it safely down and onto JJ's Gator Farm by midnight. They unloaded the camera accessories, uncovering the target's lifeless body, and started putting them into one of the sheds that was empty and was closest to the parking lot. Once the body was free, Wicks grabbed the body and slung it over his shoulder, prepared to carry it to its finally resting place.

"Ya need some help there, Big Homie? I got ya back bruh," said Smack.

"Nah, I got him, do me a solid and get all the rest of the shit out of the vehicles. I'll catch a ride to the Tri-Rail station wit ya, and then you can do ya thang with both of these cars, just make sure they in a million parts by tomorrow, okay? No joy ridin' these murder vehicles, right?" asked Wicks.

"Both of em? Man you know how much dey worth?" asked Smack incredulously.

"Fo' sho' lil' homie, I appreciate the help," said Wicks, turning away to make sure the gators were going to be well fed tonight. He made sure he came at midnight because that was when the gators would be most hungry as they were only fed in the morning so that they would be more docile with visitors there at the gator farm, and wouldn't be a threat to any visitor. He also wanted to make sure that he watched every single piece of his target completely consumed and disposed of. There would never be any piece or even a shred of DNA evidence to be recovered, except maybe by gator feces one day.

He left detailed instructions for the film and photography equipment and left the paintings in the shed, since he would have to see how rare they were before deciding whether or not to destroy them or to give them to JJ, he could never allow them to come back and connect him to this body. Wicks didn't make mistakes. Those weren't part of the plan, and he always had a plan. Was always prepared for anything and everything that might come his way.

Chapter Twenty - Three

"Z's up! Hoes down! What's good my Z?" sang Kodak Black, the South Florida rapper, on his new mixtape called 'Da Zoe Code'.

Lil' Fade, Matt, Lil' Jay, and Post, were all at the dance club for teens called 'Chance's' out west of Lake Worth. It was in a plaza behind a Checkers Drive-thru restaurant, and it was known for having numerous fights and even a couple shootings on rival gang, as well as Cartel Members, or even different High School's members, always having been able to run into each other and clash at the popular night club.

Chance's was one of the only places that teens could go to hang out since the bowling alley across the street had put an occupancy limit on teens after they had grown tired of having to break up fights, and call the cops on fights that they couldn't have possibly broken up on their own. Chance's infamous popularity became incredibly more bolstered when another teen hangout in Lantana, the Palace Skating Rink, had closed down. That, in addition to the bowling alley being mostly unavailable to kids, is what had created a niche for Chance's, and had given teens a place to hang out at. The fact that Chance's security team had all but completely ignored the fire marshal's occupancy limits and packed the place well beyond capacity, was never lost on the city's counsel, or even the police department. But because Chance himself was basically the Suge Knight of the club world, and just as feared, they were yet to step to him, so the 'he'll do as he pleases' mentality was the basic assessment of him and his movements in the business.

Nobody knew how the whole incident had started that night, but the Fire Marshal had later found quite a few of bottles of Everclear, a grain alcohol so pure, it was basically a moonshine, broken all over the place in the club. That was mostly what had fueled the fire, but then, a 55 gallon drum full of gasoline was found as well. Apparently, the gasoline was used to fuel the security's Golf-cart like parking lot patrol vehicle, and the cause of the blaze was quickly determined.

Matt had been sipping his bottle of Everclear. He looked up and saw Kiko and his brother Juan, who were their competition in the flaka sales. They were known to work for the Matamoros Cartel, possibly related to the Felix Family themselves.

"Look Lil' Fade! There go them painchos Kiko and Juan up in here," Matt said, getting the attention of all of his homies.

"So wha?" Lil' Fade said slurring his words, as the Everclear 180 proof liquor had taken the most effect on his young 14 year old body and mind. "What you finna do about it? You ain't no Haitian Sensations anyways!" Fade went into a coughing laughter as he passed the Optimo blunt that they were smoking on, to Post, the instigator of the whole crew.

"Shit my Z, you ain't Haitian Sensations either, from what I heard," said Matt calmly trying to engage in an altercation.

"Oh damn, Lil' Fade, He ain't said that shit did he?! Damn!" said Post in an attempt to amp up this confrontation between the two homies, as he always did. Secretly, Post was always jealous of how

Lil' Fade had put Matt on, and made Post wait, while in his heart that bred envy, Post knew he was the better hustler.

"Well, at least I buss my gunsh," Lil' Fade said viciously, as he knew that Matt didn't even draw his fire when Lil' Fade had smoked Lil' Ray.

"Nigga, I'm bumpin' 1,000! I ain't gotta shoot, my Z, just watch me work y'all Zs!" With that said, he grabbed a full bottle of the Everclear out of the backpack that they had smuggled the liquor in, and walked off as the other boys stayed laughing at him in his wake. Little did they know what would become of that move. Sometimes people have more heart than they have brains, and when they do, great mistakes can be made, and with them, immense consequences can be forthcoming. Matt walked towards the booths on the other side of the club.

The club didn't have a 'bar' per se, they were teens there after all, but there were several booths lining the walls, a huge dance floor that took up most of the space in the club, and then the ten banquet tables surrounding the dance floor. The problem was that there was cheap carpeting throughout the whole place. Well, all except the dance floor itself.

The laughter continued as Matt eased his way over toward the other two brothers, who were currently engaged with two pretty little white girls in a deep conversation. Finally, Post attempted to put out the blunt that they had been smoking on, but saw the action out of the corner of his eye. The blunt, a Bubblegum Kush, crossbred with a Grandaddy strain, continued to burn on the table as Post shouted,

241

"Oh, shit!"

There were four other young Haitian kids sitting at the table, and then all of the other Zs that were also sitting with them, and all looked up at Post's loud shout of warning. They all watched the scene play out in a slow motion.

Matt held the Everclear bottle by the neck and walked right up to the older brother Juan, who was also bigger as well, and slammed the full bottle into the side of his face. The girl that he was talking to screamed as the bottle broke and glass shards as well as grain alcohol was splashed into her face. Kiko, the younger brother immediately swung on Matt with a left haymaker, but Matt easily ducked it and jabbed Kiko with his left, and then ducked Kiko's right return cross, and hit him in his neck with the broken neck of his bottle still in his other hand, severing his carotid artery.

When Post had shouted, all of these Haitian boys in their crew jumped up, and began to move toward all of the Mexicans who were starting to move towards the fight. The Haitian boys were trying to move fast to cut off the Mexicans before they could get to the fight and jump Matt.

The blunt that Post was going to put out before seeing the fight, which distracted him, had caused him to drop it on the table and then the momentum of his movement caused it to roll off of the table and onto the carpeting. When the rest of the boys who had been sitting at the big banquet table jumped up to go assist their homie Matt, the knees of some of them had hit the bottom of the table. The jolt of the knees to the table caused five of the bottles of Everclear, which is very flammable liquor to bounce off of the table. The one full bottle hit the metal chair on its way down, causing it to break and spill its contents into the carpeting, which quickly soaked in and spread over a larger area of carpet. The other four bottles landed all safely on the carpeted floor, saving them from breaking, yet allowing them to pour most of their contents out onto the big carpet, being without caps on them, thereby spreading the alcohol in to the carpet further and further.

The blunt, having been burning all the while into the carpet, was starting to catch it on fire. The smoke started to distort as so many bodies were moving so fast, causing air to flood the smoldering carpet until finally there was a small flame born. As the alcohol soaked further and further into the carpet, the diameter grew until it got to the flame and ignited into a fully fueled fire. The chairs weren't a problem because they were all made of metal, but the banquet tables were all wood and quickly went up, fueling the flames even more.

The whole building was sound proofed. The walls covered in a foam sound proofing egg cartons with curtains over them. The ceiling, foam-like tiles, and finally the carpet on top of all of the rest, all went up within three minutes when the first punch had been thrown. Already people had started trying to escape from the violence, but once the smoke started to develop, and flames could visibly be seen, they became frantic. Some kids who had fallen at the front of the line had not gotten up at all. Two were actually trampled to death.

When Matt had stabbed Kiko in the neck, Juan had screamed and came at Matt with every wild and amateurish punch that he had in his arsenal, but Matt ducked, weaved, and parried with ease. Each time Matt fed Juan a jab, just to play with him and keep him from getting within his long reach. Finally, Juan knew he had no chance with Matt on hands, so he put his head down and rushed him. This was another amateur mistake, as Matt sidestepped, and put a knee to Juan's eye, opening a large cut on his eyebrow. Juan turned and grabbed at Matt, this time actually getting a hold of him, and they both fell to the ground. Before anyone could reach them, Juan had Matt in an arm bar, his left arm bent back over Juan's right knee and was adding continuous aggressive pressure to it.

It was then that all of Matt's homies arrived at the fight scene on the ground to save Matt's arm, right before Juan's homies managed to get there. Post quickly hit Juan in the jaw with a mean hook that rocked Juan out of the hold that he held on Matt. He tried to grab Post then, but a kick to his head from Lil' Fade quickly had him rolling into a balled up fetal position as a lot of kicks rained down on him from all of the Haitian kids, there to support their homie in this new found gladiator school that had awakened the beast in them all.

Juan's homies got there in time for the other Haitian boys, that were not participating in kicking juan into a coma, to turn their fury on them. An even bigger fight ensued, between the Mexicans just arriving, and the Haitians. Both sides were taking a punishment. It was hard to figure out which side was winning. Juan was asleep, knocked unconscious by Post's kick that broke his jaw. Some of the Mexican boys who had been knocked down in the rumble, got up coughing and seemed to notice that the air on the ground was cleaner than the smoke-filled air when they were standing up. They all panicked and tried to run away.

The music stopped as the fire had spread and finally reached the DJ's equipment. It had come from the carpeting to the booths lining the walls, and then finally to the DJ booth, as well as the walls and furniture. The screams were less coherent, and the young combatants started to disappear one by one towards the front of the club. Most of the ones still fighting became disoriented and got lost in the smoke. Some of them made it out, but some of them were running deeper into the fire as they were unknowingly thinking that the front door was in the opposite direction. Those were forever lost, the fire itself began to consume anything and everything in its way. The fire didn't care if you were Haitian Sensation, or just Haitian. If you were Matamoros Cartel, or Mexican. Young or old. Fourteen kids died that night and 29 more were hospitalized for broken bones from the stampede, actual burns, or smoke inhalation. Juan was the only one that died from being stabbed to death. That was murder.

It didn't stop there though, as many smaller fights continued in the big parking lot between factions. The police then had spent hours arresting and separating teens into three distinct groups to be placed into the paddy wagons. One was for the Haitians, one for the Mexicans, and one for the non-affiliated kids. It was a complete mess, and it was a black eye on the city of Greenacres. It was a fatal blow to Chance's nightclub for teens. The ensuing lawsuits for wrongful death, the physical injuries, and endangerment of underage kids, would ultimately end up bankrupting him and ensuring that he never regained any business licensing in South Florida again. He quickly disappeared back to the Bahamas and was never seen or heard from again. His companies plead for Chapter 11 bankruptcy and only his lawyer even made any appearances on his behalf for the pending criminal negligence charges. Chance's was permanently closed that night, all because of one 14 year old, Matt, had been trying to prove his heart to his homies. It was like an episode of the Dave Chappelle Show: "When Keeping It Real Goes Wrong." It had definitely went wrong for Matt, Lil' Fade, Post, and Lil' Jay that night. Many pointed fingers in the club by the security team, as well as the other teenaged bystanders, had put all of the blame on Matt, and Lil' Fade as the leader of the Haitian crew, and they were also charged as such...

Although the Haitian kids were not yet even real members of the Haitian Sensations, nor were the Mexicans fully members of the Gulf Cartel, the mainstream news media, in their well known thirst for the most sensational story, painted the most aggravated events. The picture that they painted linked the control of the Gulf Cartel kids involved, to the Felix Family, and the Haitian Sensation kids to the 400 Mawazo in Port Au Prince, who were known for their piracy on the high seas, as well as their propensity to kidnap and ransom rich Americans. They, in fact, were already under so much scrutiny for the kidnapping of quite a few American Missionary church

246

members from Ohio that had made national news, and so they most definitely didn't need any more attention. But they still got it with this episode.

News media on every continent were already bashing and bringing too much attention to the 400 Mawazo, but now with this on top of it, things had gotten embarrassing. Calls were made, and Big Head was notified by several and their business associates about the attentions paid, which caused him to be infuriated even further than he already was about the Mexicans and disappearance of his workers and associates in the Haitian Sensations section of his Cartel. He immediately began to plan, made some moves of his own, and then got even more angry when he couldn't figure things out. What was this shit? he asked himself. Who were all these people they were saying were Haitian Sensations that were being accused of fighting at a local teen nightclub? None of it made any sense to Big Head, which infuriated him all over again, until he started breaking things and ended up kicking his "65 Sony LED Curve TV that was playing the offending news station on it. Shit, now he would need a new television to watch his Soccer games.

Chapter Twenty - Four

"Thank you," said Liz. Matt Mateo, the Regional Director of the Publix Supermarkets chain, had been holding out her chair for her. He had brought her to one of the most exclusive, as well as expensive, five star restaurants on the whole Palm Beach Island: Charlie's Crabs.

Charlie's Crabs was located on the beach in the famous Palm Beach Island, and provided not only food to revel more than any restaurant in the world, but the location provided a perfect view of the Atlantic Ocean that was breathtaking. It was a place at which only the rich and famous could eat regularly, and where even the middle class guy might propose to the object of his affection, and then maybe take her every few years on their anniversary. Liz thought that it was a lame attempt, as well as a desperate one, and it made it obvious to her that he was trying to impress her. But the same affluence that he was trying to flaunt to her was already, an established fact with her, as she had sought him out only for the overall influence that he might have had over her prospective business endeavors. But Liz knew the game and so she allowed him to put on for her benefit, but in the end, she knew that he would either agree to help her with this, or not.

"Would you like our wine menu to start with?" asked the waiter.

"That's okay Marquis, just bring me a bottle of your finest Pinot -- no, we are celebrating, que no? Make it your best champagne," said Matt.

"Very well Sir," said the waiter with a smirk that conveyed the fact to Liz that he thought her date was a douche. He needn't have wasted the thought, as Liz was very aware of the nature of the man seated before her.

"I have had my assistant working day and night since we last met to go ahead and compose a proposal to show to corporate, but first, I need her to ascertain whether or not this is even legally feasible, and if not, whether or not there are ways for us to still benefit from your offer by investing in La Victoria so we can still use your proposed financial advantages to our contracting your meat and dairy distributors ... " said Matt magnanimously smiling at Liz as if he had personally agreed to merger the separate corporations together himself.

"Well, I'm glad that you can see the advantages of doing business with all of our family companies and hopefully with my new brainchild, La Victoria. I have many great plans for La Victoria, most are modeled after your very own Publix Supermarkets, and there are so many things that I can do for the people, just your system of share rewards with your employees is a ground breaking idea that nobody had ever used before in this business. I love it actually," said Liz smiling enthusiastically, eyes lit up, and face as bright and beautiful as ever.

Matt's face couldn't help but smile along. He really was enjoying Liz's company, but something passed over his face. Liz noticed it immediately.

"What's wrong Mr. Matteo?" asked Liz fearfully for her deal.

"Listen, I don't know how much Samantha has told you about our relationship, or our past ... " He trailed off, questioningly.

"We were roommates, so we talked about everything," she said catching his meaning immediately, and letting him know that she was aware of everything that had transpired between them.

" ... well ah, I made mistakes," he said, and Liz raised her eye brows. "Ok, I made a lot of mistakes when it came to her, and ah, my daughter really doesn't talk to me and. .. ah, well that is why I actually agreed to see you, and why I brought you here -- this is her favorite restaurant. So, well, I am going to do everything that I can to help you, but I must admit that I was hoping to get something in return for helping you. .. " He faltered here.

"Mr. Matteo, I don't know --" she started, bracing herself for the inevitable.

"I want you to talk to my daughter and to just let her know that I love her so so much, and I miss her like crazy, oh God, how I miss her, and maybe you can put in a good word for me, let her know that parents aren't really perfect. I know I was wrong and I have really learned from my mistake. I would never do anything ever again that could possibly hurt my baby girl ... I ah, I just want to fix things and have a relationship with my daughter, could you? Do you think that you could possibly help me with that Miss Felix? Liz?" His eyes were full of tears and they were definitely genuine. Liz was conflicted, because of what he did to get into this position, and yet she totally felt sorry for, and believed him. She actually wanted to help him, and that was saying a lot being the fact of the act that he had committed to get himself into this position in the first place. Sleeping with a girl his daughter's age was bad enough, but to actually carry on a whole relationship with his daughter's best friend was despicable. But she would help him. She believed that he had learned his lesson. Believed that he wanted to change for her, and that he would do anything possible to make things right, repair their relationship, and never let it happen again. The fact that he hadn't hit on Liz was testament to that.

"I will do anything and everything that I can to mediate things with you and Sam, but not because of any of this business, I want that to be real and from my hard work, but I'll do it cuz I think that it is the right thing to do for Sam, and I believe that you have learned from your mistake and will not do it again," said Liz tearfully, passionate in her words, really meaning it.

"Oh, thank you! Thank you so much Miss Felix, I never want to lose my relationship with my baby girl again, she is my world, it killed me to be estranged from my only daughter, whom I adore, thank you so much, it means so much to me," said Matt, smiling happily, wiping tears from his eyes.

"You are welcome, Mr. Matteo," said Liz sincerely.

The rest of their 'meeting' went well, he had the lobster, she, the king crab, and their meals were amazing to them both, which nothing less could, or would, be expected from Charlie's on Palm Beach. They were famous for it. Once Liz was comfortable enough with him, now knowing that he wasn't trying to take her home with him, she was able to drop her guard and actually enjoy the conversation as well as his company. She could see how Samantha's best friend could have fallen for him, and carried on in an inappropriate relationship with him knowing fully about the consequences if they were caught. But Liz's mind kept drifting throughout the whole meal, back to EJ, and how she had met him. She actually could not stop thinking about him the whole time.

This was something that she hadn't experienced since her modeling for Phil-Flash, she decided to call him when she was done here with Mr. Matteo, and she planned on having a sitdown with Samantha in order to try and mediate a truce between her and her father. Before her thoughts were completed, Matt's phone rang. He reached for it, saw the screen, and went to answer it.

"Oh good, there's Grace now, maybe she has finished researching the deal and has started working on the proposal, excuse me, hey Grace," he said answering his phone. "I, well, no, I didn't, but -- well of course I wasn't aware, and ... okay then, bye. Oh shit, well damn, I don't know how to say this ... " He sounded flustered.

"What?" she asked. "What's wrong? What happened?"

"Well basically, first of all, the deal is dead in the water. I, um ... " he said while accessing his phone apps on his iPhone. "Ok, here it is, look at this," he said, handing her the iPhone 13+. She took the phone, started looking at what the Fox News app was saying. Her eyes widened when she saw the images and the bottom line that showed. "Shit! What the fuck is this shit?" she exclaimed. It was a whole story about a 'Gang War' in West Palm Beach. "Ties to Felix Cartel & 400 Mawazo: 14 deaths in gang fight at club," the small print read across the bottom line, alluding to her family in Matamoros, Tamaulipas.

"Miss Felix, Liz, as much as I like you and want to help you, my team called me about this, there just isn't any possible way that Publix Supermarkets can get involved with your family after this horrible publicity, you couldn't imagine the trouble I could be in if this had happened after a proposal had been made and I've been presenting you to my people. I'm truly sorry Liz -- " he stated regretfully.

Liz interrupted him, "Listen Mr. Matteo, I'm sure this is a mistake. If you give me some time, I can have all this cleared up, I ... " she trailed off as he was shaking his head, it was of no use, her deal was dead in the water as he had said.

Matt paid the check and then escorted her back to her car, her rental Explorer.

"Well, I'm sorry for wasting your time, Mr. Matteo, I'll be in touch when I am able to speak to Samantha about repairing your relationship, but you better not blow it again, ok?"

"You are still willing to help me with her?" asked Matt in surprise.

"Of course I am, Mr. Matteo, I meant what I said, and I believe you made a mistake and suffered for it, learned from it, and I also made a promise to you that I intend to keep. Also, I know how important a father is to a little girl and young woman, and I believe that you are ultimately a good man, and Sam deserves that, but you had better not ever make a mistake again," said Liz sincerely.

253

"I won't, wow, you are one hell of a friend, and I'm glad Sam has you to have her back, thank you from the bottom of my heart Liz ... " he replied.

"Of course, no guarantees, but I'll do my best ... "

"Thank you again ..." He gave her a big hug before she got into her Explorer and then took off back to the main land. A heavy heart beating in her chest.

§§§§

When Liz pulled off, she immediately called her Grand Uncle.

"Hey Mija, how are you sweetheart?" asked El Senor lightly.

"I'm pissed Tio, what the hell is going on in West Palm?"

"Wha? What do you mean? Nothing is happening, I just don't want you hanging around until we figure this business with your cousins out ..." he said.

"No, Tio, I'm talking about the shit at the club, and the Fox News saying our family is at war with those Haitian kidnappers over in Port Au Prince!" snapped Liz thinking that he was purposely being dense.

"What are you talking about?" asked El Senor worriedly.

"I'm talking about I just lost the Publix Supermarkets deal because of the bad publicity about our family businesses on the news about the war going on that even you apparently don't know about, damn it Tio, I worked really hard for this deal, and now it's blown away!" Liz was almost in tears. She had been working years on this deal. It was her dream to get her family out of the drug business altogether, and now her dream was up in flames.

"Liz, I have no idea what you have seen or heard, but I'm putting you on the jet back, I want you here and safe --" started El Senor.

"No!" said Liz forcefully. "I won't come back! Not right now Tio, I need some time to think, this has been my passion for so long, I can't just abandon this, I have to get to the bottom of this and see what had really happened, what caused this."

"I want you on that jet, I'm calling Iggy now and I'll find out what the hell is going on, but I did not sanction this, this, whatever this was, and for that my sweet Mija, someone will pay," he said dead serious.

"I gotta go, Tio," said Liz openly crying now. "I'll call you later ..."

After she had hung up, she was driving aimlessly, searching for some inspiration to hit her. It did as EJ's handsome face danced into her mind. She pulled up along the beach and decided to take a walk in the sand and maybe get her feet wet in the water a little bit. She was so upset, that a calm walk ankle deep in the warm Atlantic Ocean was all she needed.

She removed her heels and slid to the backseat and exchanged her business suit for jeans and a tank top. She hardly ever felt sexy anymore, and hadn't since losing Phil, but now she had that feeling a little bit. Thinking about EJ now made her smile to herself. She exited the Explorer, walked through the sea grape tree corridor down to the beach, and looked out at the water. The sun was behind her, setting in the West, making her view of the beach and the water that much more amazing and pretty. It kind of brought a new perspective on life to her. She had always been spoiled, more like blessed really, because she wasn't a brat, and she had always worked hard and done everything in her power to distant herself from her family's violent drug business. Always had wanted to get them away from it, and get them legal and straight. She had taken so many steps forward and worked so hard to get the La Victoria and Publix deal off of the ground. Much too hard and many steps to have to start all over at the beginning. She couldn't believe this. She was a few days away from closing a possible deal and now some dumbass gang shit, some shit that she couldn't control, had ruined all of her hard work and plans. She dialed EJ from her cell phone's contacts where she had saved his number. They had only traded some texts here and there and had only a short conversation since that night, but she knew. She just knew that he was something special.

"Sup, Karate Kid?" asked EJ, a mischievous smile in his voice.

"Funny, Mr. Knight in Shining Armor, where are you? Can we hangout tonight?"

"Sure, I'm ah ... at the Youth Center, but I can come to you if you would like?"

"Text me the address, I'll come by over there ... " she said ending the call.

Chapter Twenty - Five

"Ok, I need you running a distraction at the front door. I'm going to go and breach the back. My land assessment map and blueprint from the city says that it's got five bedrooms, so I'm counting on at least one or two more guns if we are lucky ..." said EJ as they were sitting in a CIA van with government plates that wouldn't come back as any particular agency and was used to transport suspects. But seeing government plates alone usually deters any regular "Bubblegum Top" cop car from investigating any further, so it was perfect for the job. They were both dressed in their tactical gear, complete with bulletproof vests and helmets, plus way more guns than Shelby thought would be necessary, but she just deferred to EJ's great training and experience, and accepted his seniority in this type of raid.

"So, cuz I'm the girl, I have to do front door distraction?" asked Shelby smiling.

"No, if you were 'just the girl', ya ass would be waiting in the damn van and here to call back-up if I needed it. Because I need your help and you have police training, I need you at the door in front so that I can breach in the back, ok? Now, we have almost no intelligence on this subject, so be very careful, alright? Okay, so are you ready Shelby?" he asked sweetly as he smiled to her.

"I'm ready, let's do this ... " said Shelby, more to herself than anything.

EJ stood up. Nothing more needed to be said, they opened their makeshift 'coms' which was actually their phone lines, connected to their helmet Bluetooth, as Shelby waited for EJ to move into his position in the bushes next to the back patio door. "In position," he said into his bluetooth. "On my way," was her quick response as she exited the van into the dark night. "Back door unsecured, so let me know when you are about to knock," said EJ, surprised after testing and finding the back door unlocked. He then stayed on standby, with his hand on the door knob.

"Copy," said Shelby, "I'm almost at the door, give me a three count and I'll knock on three, ok?" EJ mentally prepared for a fight, as he liked her plan. "Ok, one ... Two. .. Three!" EJ then turned the knob as he could hear a faint knock coming from out front. The plan, it turned out, was set perfectly as there were three individuals sitting at the kitchen table. As the back door opened into the kitchen, EJ was able to see them all as well as a forth tengo walking away towards the knocking at the front door, him looking curious as to who it could be at the door. All of the players with Double Nine Dominos in front of them also had their attention diverted to the leaving forth member and the apparent excessive knocking coming from the front of the house, EJ observed as he cleared the back door into the kitchen.

EJ took his time aiming at the first two tengos that he could see had a firearm next to their place at the table. He shot the first one in the eye, then turned his HK MP5 to the next target before the first target's brain matter stopped flying towards the kitchen sink. The second shot went through the side of the head of the second target before he even realized that his partner was, in that same instant, a corpse, just as he was about a split second later. The quick pweff, pweff, got the third target going, reaching for his gun that was tucked into his waist band. But the grey matter from the second target's head had sprayed him, and unfortunately for him, had blinded him with brain fragments and blood.

EJ spent a second taking careful aim as target three was moving. He didn't get scared about the gun, thinking that only an idiot would tuck his gun into his waistband while being in a seated position at the table. It was the quickest way to get the gun caught up in the fabric of your clothes in a jam, which target three, was currently in. EJ didn't even care about a gun, as it was currently caught up in the tengo's boxers, but he didn't want his target to give off any noise that could alert other tengos in the house, that was as yet cleared. He took the quick and easiest insurance, hitting his target with a double tap to the head. The target's brains went all over the Dominos, and when his head hit the table, it upset the Dominos and sent them into chaos. It sounded like a regular game of 'bones' and the dominos being mixed, much to EJ's relief. EJ just hoped that the four pweff sounds, and moving dominos did nothing to alert anyone else currently in the house, or the tengo that was answering the front door. He couldn't risk his target getting away and alerting Haitian Sensations about their movements.

EJ rounded the corner hearing another pweff, a body dropping, and saw Shelby easing the front door closed behind her as silently as she possibly could. She grabbed the shield that she had leaning against the wall next to the front door, and looked questioningly at EJ with her eyes, which were all that could be seen behind the helmet. "Hold it in front of you, stay low, and I'll take the targets. No matter what, do not drop the shield, ok?" he whispered to her. Shelby simply nodded.

The first door was the one closest to them, and she selected that one first because all of the other doors were on the opposite side of the house, past the living room, which they had already visually cleared together when she came in through the front door, into the living room, and he, from the kitchen.

Shelby stopped by the door, with her shield up, and allowed EJ to reach around her body and open the door about an inch, quietly. They got back into position, her with the bullet resistant shield up, and EJ, MP5 up pointing beyond her into the crack of the door. She helped the door open with her foot and he followed directly behind in a closed formation, solid, and unbreakable. The door opened to a two car garage, as they expected that it would, and it was devoid of any subjects, tengo or otherwise. They quickly cleared under the cars, a Dodge Hellcat Redeye, and a BMW X3M SUV. They then exited the garage as quickly as they entered it.

Now that their 'six' was cleared, they got in formation again, then they moved to the first of the doors in the hallway. They employed the same method and tactics as they had with the garage door, and they cleared the first three of the rooms. Two of them were bedrooms and one was a home office. When they finally reached the fourth door, they heard a moaning type of noise. Only this was no sexual moan, it was a painful moan. One that bespoke of great, unimaginable, continuous, and exacting pain. Once they had the door open, they were both horrified to find a young girl tied to all four points of a brass bed. Her hands were tied to the head board, feet tied to the foot board, and she was spread eagle on the four poster bed. She was as naked as the bare mattress that she was laying on, and covered in all the same blood and feces as it was. Her own.

The young girl's eyes widened in recognition of her potential saviors, her possible chance at escape from her personal hell, but as her mouth was gagged, she couldn't even utter a word. Shelby immediately started to lower the shield until EJ grabbed her, shaking his head in a warning. When they looked around, there were belts and whips, dildos and other sexual torture and pleasure devices, and finally there were needles and a sandwich bag of a brownish powdery substance: heroin obviously. By the color and texture of it, they could see that it was most likely the 'Haitian Sugar', which was the popular street heroin that was cut with fentanyl to make it even more potent and addictive.

EJ moved towards the door, pulling Shelby along as the victim pleaded with her eyes, begging not to be left alone, terrified. But Shelby knew it just as well as EJ, they could not even check on her before handling their primary target: Lemonhead, which was the whole reason that they were there in the first place. They would have to come back for her, but first they must complete clearing the house before dealing with anything else. There was only one bedroom left, so they both knew that this would be the most dangerous part of the mission, where they knew there would be some return fire because of the opening of the doors and the searching of the rooms had made some noise, so Lemonhead would have known of their presence by now.

EJ positioned himself again behind Shelby, who was still holding the shield, with his MP5 aimed around her and towards the hallway. They quickly passed through the bedroom door, back into the hallway, and headed finally to the door that dead ends the hallway, obviously it would have to be the master bedroom. EJ tapped Shelby's shoulder, halting her. He then pumped a 9mm round from his MP5 into the doorknob. Shelby took the correct initiative, kicked the door open, and then led with the shield into the grand bedroom with vaulted ceilings, brass trimmings, and a four poster Alaska King bed with a canopy, and an open mirrored door exposing the biggest walk-in closet that they had yet to see. It was truly a master suite, it was also very beautiful if seen in any place but here.

They immediately saw the opened window with the screen kicked out upon entering this fantasy bedroom, but still cleared the room before investigating any further, just in case there was some trickery in the making. EJ looked out, seeing it was clear and heard a car's tires squealing, but they had already sounded several blocks away, their mark had been on point tonight and had survived the attack, but he wouldn't forever be that lucky.

The house cleared, and it now being safe to move about freely, EJ slid off his assault helmet, "He got away, it sounded far away already, I'm thinking he bailed right after the knock, he's good, really smart, damn it ..." he said frustrated. Shelby also removed her helmet, "We will get his ass, don't worry, now what?" she asked, while looking around the room seeing how nice everything was, but not sure what to do.

"I'm going to search for anything to lead us to him, you get the victim loaded into one of those cars and get her to a hospital as fast as possible, and before you ask, no! Not cuz you are the girl!" EJ said seriously this time. Shelby didn't laugh or argue, she just got to it.

EJ began to search under the mattress, moved on to the end tables, and then the dresser. He quickly moved on to the closet, in which he was surprised to find nothing there. He started to step out of the walk-in closet when an abnormal indentation in the floor stood out to him. He walked back to the corner and knelt down. Feeling with his fingers along the edge of the wall, he located a small string that was of the same beige color of the carpet, but made of a different material. He thought about hidden things in the Hijab place that he had raided in Sandland, and he was convinced that there was a small compartment under the carpet.

EJ pulled on the string and lifted the corner of the carpet, revealing a one foot square safe, made by Winchester. Shelby choose that moment to come into the bedroom helping a young girl that was too badly battered to even see what her facial features looked like under the bruising and swollen areas on her face. Shelby helped her to the bed and she sat on the edge, ready to run at even the slightest provocation. She was in worse shape than he had originally thought.

"Whatcha got?" Shelby asked, since she couldn't see the safe from where she was standing at the front of the closet.

"A safe. What you got? She know anything?"

"She's been kept in that room since she was taken, doesn't know much, but she said that there were more girls like her in the other rooms on the night she was brought here. Beyond that she doesn't have any idea of what day it is ..." she said.

"Ok, well let's keep searching while I think of a way to open this," said EJ.

They split up again, the girl got up by herself and started to follow Shelby around like a toddler, expecting something bad to happen at any moment, or for someone bad to come and put her back into her room of terror, something even worse to her. EJ was looking for a desk somewhere that must have bills and identifying data, but only found some papers in a drawer in the desk, in the home office. He then went to the kitchen to get a garbage bag from around the dead bodies playing dominos, then went back to stuff all of the papers that he found in the bag and headed back to the safe. He placed the garbage bag on the bed, stepped into the closet and started feeling around the safe, hoping that it could be removed from the floor whole. It couldn't. He tested the seal, seeing that it wasn't air tight, just fire resistant. It was only the cheaper version of the much more expensive fireproof safes that were made by that same brand.

EJ headed back out to the garage and grabbed some tools. A drill, a crowbar, some sprinkler PVC piping, a cap, and finally a screw. He stopped in the kitchen and took a gallon bottle of McCormick vodka, poured it out in the sink and then filled it back up with some water from the tap.

Back at the safe, first he poured the gallon of water into the cracks along the safe door. It was slow work, allowing the water to fully collect inside the safe, and he had to fill the bottle three times before it actually filled the safe completely with water. He took one of his 12 gauge slugs out of his Remington 870, put it into a small piece of PVC that was about one inch long, making sure that it would fit. Satisfied, he then took a screw and screwed it into the PVC cap, where only the very tip of the screw was poking through the PVC cap. Just enough to touch the striker cap of the slug bullet sitting snug inside the PVC pipe.

He stuck the PVC pipe containing the slug, facing down on the door of the safe, right near the edge of the door. Now all he would need were a couple pounds of pressure in order to detonate the reversed improvised land mine. Something that he had learned and seen many times over in Sandland. He placed two of Lemonhead's Red Bottom shoes to steadily hold his work, then tossed another random shoe on top in order to hit the PVC cap, sending the pressure into the screw, acting as a hammer on the slug, which caused the primer to ignite, and the gunpowder in the slug to explode and push the 12 gauge slug directly into the edge of the door of the safe.

The water acted as a sealant, which prevented any damage to the contents of the safe.

"What the hell?" asked Shelby, running in, gun up in a firing position, searching for more targets thinking the worst when she heard the shots fired.

"Getting the safe open, had to improvise ..." he said, then grabbed the crow-bar, and fit it into the new blown open part of the door and began to pry it open. The water had mostly exploded outward when the device was detonated, but there was still several inches in the bottom of the safe compartment. There was also some papers, stacks of money, and some jewelry.

"Grab it all," he said, holding his garbage bag open for her to put inside all the items he found inside of the safe. "We need it to look like a robbery gone wrong, so we can't leave anything of value behind. Let's go ..."

Chapter Twenty - Six

Big Head was on his Sundancer with Buju, one of his frontline men in the 400 Mawazo militia, which was basically his own personal army of killers that he kept in his compound's barracks near Port Au Prince, Haiti. Buju was always his first choice because Big Head had recruited him at age 11 years old himself. Buju's father had been working for Big Head's Father back in the day and he had lost a whole shipment of cars that they were exporting from South Florida to Haiti, where his profit margins were about 600% because the cars were mostly stolen. When Buju had come to Big Head asking to join his militia, as they weren't called the 400 Mawazo yet, Big Head told him that the only way for him, the son of a fuck up, to get a job, is if he cleans the slate. "How I do that?" Buju had asked him at the time. Big Head had simply handed him an old rusty .22 revolver in answer. Ever since Buju had went over to his house and quicky put five bullets into his father's head, as the first one hadn't penetrated his cranium, everyone had feared and respected him in some kind of animalistic way. It was said about Buju, that if Big Head were to ask that he kill his own mother, sister, and family dog, that Buju would have completed the assignment before even Big Head was done issuing the order. It was well known in Port Au Prince, that all of the 400 Mawazo were considered to be just like him and maybe more ruthless, if that was even possible.

Head had 12 other of his 400 Mawazo soldiers in a Bahamian fishing boat not far behind him, as to not draw attention from the

U.S. Coast Guard, because not only were they a gang, well documented with the Coast Guard, and all subject to deportation immediately upon contact, but they were also carrying enough weapons systems and ordnance, to supply a platoon of soldiers. That, the Coast Guard would *more* than frown upon if they made contact with them, and would be more likely to sink the vessel and drown all sailors aboard in the deepest waters of the Atlantic Ocean. Luckily, Big Head had, just like Castro had in Mariel Harbor in the 80's, forcefully commandeered this fishing boat, and his men blended perfectly as fishermen with the real crew of sailors. The fact that the boat flew the Bahamas flag as its port of call was just another bonus. It would draw way less attention than a Haitian flag.

They completed the trip when they reached the Boynton Beach Inlet. They dropped the 400 Mawazo there, where Antoine and Steff were waiting on the Inter-coastal side parking lot, as so many Haitians getting off of a boat on the beach side would be sure to draw too much unwanted attention.

They all loaded the crates containing the guns and ammo into the back of their rented U-Haul, and the dozen Mawazo, warriors jumped in the back compartment after them. The house next door to Steff's trap house was abandoned due to its being condemned by the city, so all of the Mawazo carried everything from the U-Haul right into Steff's trap house. Once inside, they passed straight through the living room and right out of the back door into the back yard where all of the bushes that surrounded his yard, blocked the view from the neighbors, and then they filed right on into the back door of the abandoned house, which would be their new base of operations from now on next door.

Since the windows were all boarded up on this house because of the condemnation, it had the added benefit of making sure that nobody on the outside of the house would be able to notice them on the inside of the house. Steff had an electrician customer of his, cut the lock on the meter and reconnect the power to the house in order to make the Mawazo just a little bit more comfortable. Of course the house was infested with rats and roaches, but things like that Steff knew, they were used to from living with them in Haiti, hiding from the many different agencies and enemy gangs that were always trying to get them. Having power would be a luxury, which was more than they were used to.

"So, what's the plan now?" asked Steff when they were all alone in his house.

"Shit, we will have to wing it, Big Head brought all of these Mawazo here, but Buju is over there with him, and most of the Mawazo will follow Buju," answered Antoine as he contemplated.

"What about the Mexicans?"

"We have to wait for word from them. We can't make a move until they do, or the whole plan will fall in on itself. Buju will wait, he has Big Head's trust, so what more can be done? We wait ..." said Antoine.

They were interrupted by Antoine's ringing phone. He grabbed it, saw who it was on the display and cursed under his breath. Jesus, what now? he asked himself.

"Yea?" he asked, answering the call. After listening for a minute or so, he put his hand down his face wondering how he could have such bad luck.

"Okay Lemon, just stay down there in Lil Haiti, lay low, and I'll get back with ya," said Antoine stressing. He hung up, then said to Steff: "Fucking Lemonhead ... says they hit his house, doesn't know who, but says it was most definitely not the Mexicans. Thinks that it was the FEDs, except that he didn't think that it was more than two or three people, but he didn't stick around to find out."

They both sat back and thought about that. What the hell was going on was the question in their collective minds.

Chapter Twenty - Seven

Lil' Fade woke up in a smelly, 16 by 20 jail cell. His head hurt and as he looked around, his pride was hurt even more. There were about 20 individuals inside a holding cell built for less than 10. The place smelled like ass, feet, and stale wine. He could see why, as he noticed many of the bums sleeping on the floor. The bigger, more violent felons were sleeping on the benches lining the walls, them being on the top of the prisoner food chain, so to speak. There was one phone near the front of the cell. That wall was completely plexiglass, making the cell into a fish bowl type of enclosure.

Lil' Fade looked wildly around as an emotion he hadn't felt since he was a little kid began to overcome him: Fear. Not only did he not know anyone in here, but it looked like he was the only minor, everyone else here were all fully grown adult men. Some of them looked at him as if he were an appetizer, a small Zoe-Cake. He thought that they would've or at least should've, sent him to the juvenile facility, but yet, here he was, a 14 year old in an adult facility, which meant that whatever they were charging him with, he was being charged as an adult. That definitely was not a good look. Whatever this was, this was some serious shit.

"St. Clair!" yelled a mean looking guard with two gold teeth bringing him out of his observations. Lil' Fade got up and looked at the guard. "Come on! We ain't got all day waiting on you jit!" said the guard stepping back to let him pass.

He pointed to a row of six government chairs that were

connected to each other to prevent them from being used as weapons in a fight, and Fade saw that two of the chairs were empty in the row. One empty seat was located next to a bum who had the matted hair of someone who hadn't showered for over a month. Lil' Fade took the other empty seat, one side of which had a sleeping wino, while the other side had a slim, dark skinned Haitian looking kid with braids who looked maybe a couple years older than Fade himself.

"What's up Jit?" asked the other guy, "where you from?"

"I'm from Lake Worth City," answered Lil' Fade, "where are you from?"

"Fort Liquordale, jit. Well damn jit, how old you is?"

"14, but I be in dem streets, so ain't no jit, ya feel me? I'm Lil' Fade."

"Okay, okay then Lil' Fade, dey call me T-Zoe, 'you in fo Fade?" asked T-Zoe.

"Shit, I 'on't even know yet, we got into it at da club and shit went down, damn club be done caught on fire and shit, then I woke up here ... "

"Oh shit, Fade ... So you one of dem jits from the Haitian Sensations that got caught in that club wit dem Mexicans and all dem kids be done died and shit?! Damn, Lil' bruh, that's all people are talking about in here since last night! You know it's a lot of jits that died in that fire, damn lil' bruh, I hope dey ain't charge you wit dat shit over there!" said T-Zoe.

"St. Clair, step up here!" called the tall, matronly looking light skinned lady guard. She was standing in front of an ATM looking machine with a touchscreen in front of it and a clear glass plate with red laser lights for reading finger prints on it. It was very advanced looking and Fade was surprised that they spent this much money on things like this, he thought the government was broke for all of the crying the politicians do on their campaign ads. There was never too much money for incarcerating individuals and making them caged animals though, he guessed.

"Left hand first ..." she said snatching his hand roughly and pulling his thumb out and pushing it onto the scanner glass so that the laser beams could record his thumb print, forever documenting his arrest and charges. The rough guard lady then stretched out his index finger, and she repeated the same process with each of the ten digits as well as both palm prints. She then sent him to sit down again, and he was again able to pick his new friend's brain on how the whole process in here worked and what to expect while he was going through this personal hell.

"You got printed, now they finna take your booking picture, read your charges to you, and tell you what your bond is, that is if you even get a bond, which I doubt if they charging you with anything to do with all them deaths at that club. Then they finna put your identification wrist band on, so they know who you is no matter where in the jail you go to. I'm sure that you finna be able to ask what dorm you finna go at, but I bets that you finna go to the jit floor ... if you is, Fade, you betta have your fight game up to date, ya dig? Cuz them jits in there? All they do is bump all damn day! I mean all damn day bruh ..." said T-Zoe.

Lil' Fade continued to pick his new friend T-Zoe's brain so he could know what to look forward to and be ready for whatever they might have for him when he gets where it is that they are going to send him to. Lil' Fade had every bit of confidence in his fighting skills, but as T-Zoe was schooling him, nobody could whoop six or more opponents, and that was what he would be facing if he didn't get 'clicked up' inside with a group or a gang to ride with. T-Zoe explained that on the adult side it would be different, a man could mostly stand on his own two feet, ten toes down, and hold himself down, as nobody would usually mess with him unless he was either really soft, or he was there looking for trouble. The jit floor, he found out was a whole different animal. A beast.

When a big burly white guard was fitting his identification bracelet, he chanced asking him what dorm he was going to go to. "12th floor, jit dorm, hope you can fight kid ..." was his answer. The answer that Fade was here dreading, but he wasn't scared to fight, he was scared of facing the unknown. It was the not knowing that scared him. Not knowing any friends in here, not knowing if he has any enemies, and not knowing if he was in a lot of trouble. He took a look around him at the winos and thugs, all dumped into a cell together. All of them facing the unknown. Just like him, just like he was facing this unknown outcome. It reminded him of a saying from years ago, that the only thing that was guaranteed in life, is death. "Death is promised, life is not."

This, as Fade looked around the booking floor at Gun Club County Jail, is going to be a hard pill to swallow. After all the partying, all the hustling and getting money, having all of the same age, as well as older peers, looking up to him because he was right under Big Meet. He was almost a member of Haitian Sensations, and would be, when Big Meet comes back and sees he'll bust his gun and represent Haitian Sensations fully, and how he *did* bust his gun for his respect. How he shot Lil' Ray because he had stolen from him, from Haitian Sensations, and disrespected them all. Lil' Ray had to be dealt with, and Lil' Fade had to earn his membership to Haitian Sensations, so he had to shoot Lil' Ray.

But after all those who looked up to him, he never saw as clearly as he was seeing right now, this minute, this moment. He was here all alone. All by himself, nobody to look up to him, nobody admiring his Haitian Sensations connections. Somehow, while listening to Lil' Baby, Kodak Black, Moneybagg Yo, YFN Lucci, and NBA Youngboy, he only saw the romanticized part of the lifestyle, only the cool, fun and glamorous parts. The only parts that the rappers rap about are always the pros, and never the cons. He felt tricked, lied to. He never saw that there might be a day in Gun Club County Jail that he would have to sleep on the piss covered floor next to the bums and dregs of the streets. Never thought he would be living on the pissy, dirty floor with bums and winos, because the gangstas and thugs are taking up all of the space of the benches.

In all of the movies and rap songs he knew of, they never had to go through all of the finger printing, booking pictures, and the interviews by medical staff about his allergies, religious food preferences, even STDs. Never heard of the ways that they were being herded around by the nasty guards like cattle, he had indeed been sold a dream. He couldn't see himself going out like this. This couldn't be it. This couldn't be what the real life is like when the cell doors lock at night. This couldn't be it, not for him.

He turned to the guard and asked the one question that he had been fearing the whole time since he had woken up in this cesspool: "What are my charges?"

"Shiid, jit, y'all gone heavy out there at that club, ya got 13 counts of manslaughter, one count of first degree, arson, inciting a riot, and two counts of battery on an LEO. That's Law Enforcement Officer, if you ain't know ... and then you got the FEDs waiting to talk to you when you done here. Shiid jit, I'm surprised that they even let you keep your teeth after the battery on the LEO, but maybe they know you gone lose 'em on the 12th floor. But don't worry jit, they got something to put in there to soothe those gums of yours --" He was laughing when Fade interrupted him.

"Fuck you pig! You suck my --" said Fade before the guard smacked the words right out of his mouth, snatched him up by his shirt, and dragged him back to his pissy, smelly cell.

"Bitch ass mothafucka!" Fade screamed out of the door after the guard had locked him in and walked off laughing at how he could push the kid's buttons, and then slap the shit out of him with no repercussions. He got some free recreation with a kid that he could go now and tell his gay boyfriend about when he got home.

"Damn Lil' Fade, you gotta take it easy with these guards Lil' Homie, damn you know they who gotta feed us, and they control every aspect of our lives, the moves we make, visits, letters, everything man ... Lil' Homie, you don't show your hand before the bets is in, ya dig?" said T-Zoe in the corner, trying to drop some jewels on the youngster, trying to get him ready for this prison shit.

"Man that hoe ass cracker put his hands on me! Man! I'll fucking --"

"Lil' Bruh, take it easy, he got them keys, you wanna get him? You wait till you out there and on da same level playing field as him, ya dig?" asked T-Zoe.

"Damn big homie! Punk ass pigs! Shit! I can't believe that he tried me like that! Ain't no bitch in my blood cracker!" he said as he tried to raise his voice towards the man that had abused him and hurt his pride.

"Yea, well," said T-Zoe seriously, "you might as well get used to that shit man, it don't get no better from here no time soon, it only gets worse. Never gets better, ya dig?"

"Man I gotta get up out of here! Ain't no way to escape?" asked Fade.

T-Zoe laughed, "Yea, through the recreation yard fence in the South Tower, but the last guy that tried that shit fell from South 6 floor and broke both of his legs. You used to be able to sign up for the drug dorm at the stockade, where it's only a fence between you and freedom, but now they closed the stockade, and made it into a homeless shelter. Nah, Lil' Bruh, I say that unless you got some real big time connections --"

"Like Big Meet?" asked Fade seriously, trying to make himself sound important.

"Yea? From Haitian Sensations? How you know Big Meet?" asked T-Zoe in return.

"My boss and my cousin, he was bout to bring me into Haitian Sensations, but then I haven't heard from him, so he gone right now, really it's weird cuz can't nobody get a hold of him ..." answered Fade, melancholy.

"Well, Lil' Fade, I hate to be the one to tell you this, but in da game, when someone goes missing and can't nobody find them or get a hold of them, Haitian Sensations or not, they usually end up dead," said T-Zoe.

"Shit," said Fade starting to sit down before realizing there was a light skinned gangsta looking guy in his late 20's, or early 30's with an athletic build laying down on the bench where only about four inches were free for Fade to sit . He looked at T-Zoe.

"You might as well get used to it now, cuz this is the way it is in here and discussions are had with hands, disputes settled with violence, you already know. You gotta decide now if you are a predator or you are some prey. There's no other option. Fight or flight Lil' Fade, you gotta live up to your name that you gave yourself, ya dig?" explained T-Zoe trying to amp the kid up to see where his heart was at, see if he could even make it the first night.

Fade nodded to T-Zoe, understanding quicker than most that his gansta was being tested. Off top Lil' Fade was ready and wanted to step up to the plate to prove himself, show his heart, maybe more to himself than to his fellow prisoners. He knew what he was capable of inside of a ring. But this was the real deal, real life. No head gear, no ropes, no gloves. What he did have was anger. Anger at Big Meet for leaving him without initiating him as an Haitian Sensations member. Anger at his father for leaving him and his autistic sister on their own. Anger at Matt for starting all of this bullshit to begin with, the shit that he was now trapped in, and anger at himself for being fooled into thinking that some of these rappers had been telling the truth about their lives. Thinking that they were not just entertainers, but that they were really in the dope game and murder game. He thought that they had been rapping about their real life experiences and not just the fantasies that those entertainers really sold, like an off brand low budget hood movie. Lil' Fade was mad now, and as in his training, he channeled all of his anger. Used it to his advantage.

Sitting down in the spot on the bench, while simultaneously sweeping the light skinned gangsta's feet off of the bench, he said, "Move over man, I'm tryna sit down here."

"Man! What the fuck you think you doin' jit?" said Light Skin, jumping up all of the way off of the bench, chest puffed out and ready to 'take off' or to initiate a fight, by taking the first swing.

Lil' Fade just stood up and looked towards the fish bowl to ensure that he was not drawing attention from the guards and was clear to take off himself. Without even knowing it, his look towards the glass commanded Light Skin's attention, making him turn his whole head in that direction to see what it was that Lil' Fade was looking at. His attention was diverted momentarily, Lil' Fade decided to take the opportunity to 'take flight' on Light Skin with two left jabs to gage his distance, a right cross, left hook, and then he leaned forward for a Mexican head butt. Dazed, Light Skin dove towards him, locking him quickly into a bear hug. They were both thrown off balance with their combined weights together, causing them to fall onto all of the other sleeping bums, then rolling, and finally getting back up and falling onto the same bench that they were fighting for in the first place, then they fell again onto the ground with no chance to get back up hugged up like they were. Fade knew that he had no chance at all in a wrestling match on the floor with the much bigger, more muscled Light Skin. Lil' Fade was trying to break the hold that Light Skin had on him, but Light Skin knew that his only chance at beating Fade was wrestling him, because he had already witnessed what Fade had for him with those mean hands if he was to let up just a little bit.

Right at the last minute, when Light Skin thought that he had Fade under control, T-Zoe came off of the wall and started to stomp his shoe into the side of Light Skin's face and neck, trying to break the hold that he held on Fade. Finally, he had no choice but to let go, Fade quickly jumped up while the getting was good, and got back to his feet in a second and put his set back up ready to run it back all over again. Light Skin was getting up slowly as the kicks to his head had dazed him and he was dizzy once he got back onto his feet again.

"Told you to move over! I ain't no hoe ass zoe! Ya heard?" yelled Lil' Fade.

"Jit, I'm finna fuck you up and make you my boy!" said Light

Skin after he spit a glob of blood onto the floor next to another bum still sleeping during all of the commotion.

Lil' Fade ducked Light Skin's weak hook, came up and hit him with a two piece right and left, ducked Light Skin's straight left, and swung a hook intentionally missing his face so that instead his elbow caught Light Skin with all of the momentum of the missed hook straight to his jaw that he was trying with all of his might to break. Light Skin ate that, turned with it, swung a left hook, and was caught off balance as Fade blocked it with his left forearm. While Light Skin was facing the wrong way and Fade was under his left, over extended arm, Fade took his opening and hit his ribs, turned, locked Light Skin's left arm in an arm bar, came up from under it with an incredibly serious upper cut that caught Light Skin in his already fragile jaw. That was it, thought Fade, the fight might be over.

Light Skin stumbled and his legs came out from under him, dumping him on his hands and knees, desperate. Fade backed off to let him get up as a natural reaction from a boxer, who was used to a referee starting a count right about now at this point. But that didn't happen here, in a holding cell of intake in Gun Club County Jail, the desperate man took over. Not believing or even accepting that he was being bested by a jit, Light Skin rushed Fade from off of his knees, which was a move anticipated by Fade and dealt with by a diving punch downward with all of Fade's 160 pounds behind it, pushing the head into his flying knee, ultimately ending it all for Light Skin.

Light Skin was out of it and the guards had already 'hit the dueces', or their body alarm for the fight, drawing a flood of 20 or more guards to come in and lay everyone down on the ground who wasn't already down there. They roughly grabbed Fade, T-Zoe, Light Skin, and the two other bums who were closest to the fight to be able to do a body check and inspect their body and hands for signs of a fight, to know who actually participated in it. SIS, or Special Investigative Supervisor, was there to figure out if they were affiliated with any gangs so they knew whether or not they would have to lock down the jail due to a possible gang war. After they had cleared them all assuming that none were of any particular important affiliation, they were brought out and put in separate cells.

"This one says that he wants to kill himself, so send him to South 2-D and put him on suicide watch!" said the white guard that Fade had already gotten into it with. He then thought back to T-Zoe's words about them having all the control and them having to feed and deal with the prisoners every need. Too late though.

"Fuck you pussy ass cracker!" shouted Fade as they led him away to go to the worst possible place in the jail. The 'butt naked cell', suicide watch.

Chapter Twenty - Eight

EJ and Shelby had just finished at Lemonhead's house and were loading up when EJ's phone rang. Shelby noticed the immediate smile that formed on EJ's face when he picked up but said nothing about it, she just smiled to herself thinking about Jean, and how she felt about him.

"Sup, Karate Kid?" asked EJ, answering Liz's call, with a mischievous smile on his face.

"Haha, funny, Mr. Knight in Shining Armor, so where are you at? Can we hang?"

"Sure, I'm ah ... at the Youth center, but I can come to you if you want me to?"

"Text me the address, I'll come by over there ..." said Liz hanging up.

EJ looked at Shelby, "I gotta go, can you drop me off, and take care of all of this shit? You can just take it back to my condo and lock it all up there?" he asked, but she was already nodding, a sweet smile on her face.

"Sure, I got ya, so you want me to just lock up and leave the van in the parking garage over there? We can go over everything tomorrow I guess, right?" asked Shelby in agreement with him.

"And what about the witness? What can we do to tell her to keep this shit down low?" he asked her contemplating himself.

"Don't worry, I'm going to take her to some friends of mine in Dade County that will help her with her recovery and possibly get

283

some information out of her to help us find Lemonhead, because right now she is just out of it. I can't even imagine what she's been through, she just fainted. It seems like they have been drugging her and raping her for months, and that is going to take some time to get through and unravel, but I'll keep her safe. You ready?" asked Shelby ready to go.

"Yea, let's go ... " They both lifted the girl up and carried her to the van, which wasn't very easy, because they had parked far away, because they definitely couldn't park the van in front of Lemonhead's house. That would be a link that might connect them if a nosey neighbor just so happened to be looking out the window and saw the government plates on a van out front. Being as though they had been holding a young lady against her will for several months and nobody noticed, it was doubtful that they would notice, but not a risk worth taking, so they took every precaution to ensure their safe getaway.

§§§§

Liz finally received the text with the address to the Youth Center. She was wondering what the delay had been. Was she really anxious about going to hang out at the Youth Center with this guy? she asked herself as she drove from the beach. Well, maybe 'excited' was a more accurate description of her feelings. She had felt the sparks, and that was saying a lot to her, as she had never thought that she could've had those feelings for another again after Phil had died. Yet here she was, all these butterflies in her stomach after only one meeting and a few phone conversations. All she could really hope for is a good friend, because butterflies or not, she had to concentrate all of her energy on her new career. She had worked so hard ... then again a news flash reminded her of her dream merger being smashed only a few hours ago. Hence, her need to hang out with EJ and to have something to occupy her mind and take some of the pain away.

As she was driving her rental Ford Explorer, she noticed a car that was a few car lengths back from her. It seemed to have one headlight that was brighter than the other one was. She thought nothing more of it as she drove on thinking about whether there would ever be another chance to resuscitate her deal with Publix Supermarkets, but chided herself again for putting herself through unnecessary torture. She needed to let it go already. She needed to allow EJ to take her mind off of her work and take her away from the stress.

She finally pulled into the Youth Center parking lot, and although she didn't use much makeup, being naturally beautiful, she lowered the vanity mirror to add some eye-liner to enhance her pretty green eyes, hoping to make EJ smile. With the vanity mirror in position, she noticed a car parking across from her, back a ways, behind her location. She got out of the truck, still thinking nothing suspicious at first. She normally wouldn't have even taken a second look, but she couldn't ignore the one bright and one dim headlight that she had already previously noticed when she had been leaving the beach not much earlier, it was the same car. After she had gotten out of her truck wanting a better look, and while she was there and hesitated, a figure exited the car and approached her Explorer. She immediately took her keys out of her pocket, placed the ring of them in her palm, and pushed a few of the sharp ends of the actual keys in between her fingers in a brass-knuckle type of knife like weapon. It was her only weapon, she thought cursing herself for leaving her damn gun in the center console of the Explorer, too far to run and grab now. She was stuck with what she had available.

As the figure approached, Liz prepared herself for the inevitable assault by going on the offensive and preparing for the coming fight. As he approached her, he noticed her tension and put his open palms toward her in the universal signal of peace. She saw it right away and eased her stance.

"Es mi, Senorita, Jonny, he send me to protect you and keep you away from trouble. There's so much trouble right now Senorita, I muss keep you safe," said Juanito, in his best broken spanglish that he could speak.

"Damn it, Juanito, you can't be creeping up on people like this! You almost made me hurt you! Damn it!" said Liz breathing heavily and starting to relax after having her adrenaline pumping, thinking about the danger and being prepared to fight, win, lose, or draw.

"I sorry -- lo siento, Senorita, I only wish to protect. Jonny, he send me, he say to protect -- I protect you, make you safe ..." he tried to smile reassuringly.

"Okay, Okay I get it, Jonny sent you. But I can take care of myself! Now you can go tell Jonny that I said 'No'! They are not going to violate my privacy like this, I am grown, and I am not a part of that Cartel bullshit! Okay? Ok, now go!" vented Liz angrily as she was pushing him to go.

He just stood there confused. "I watch. I keep Senorita safe," he answered her tantrum confused.

"ARRGGG! No, I want you gone! Now!" Liz said and then turned and started to walk away, then added: "You might wanna get that headlight fixed if you want to follow people, cuz it makes you stand out, now I'm sorry that I yelled at you, but you need to go..."

She walked the rest of the way into the Youth Center, trying to take the extra time to herself to give her temper a chance to cool off before going in there. In the front entrance once she entered the front door, she saw a lot of boxing trophies, and some from gymnastics and basketball awards as well. She saw that EJ was in a lot of the pictures, alongside many kids and other volunteers that she didn't know or recognize. She smiled seeing all of the obvious affection that EJ had with this family of unrelated people, all of these young and old, dedicated to helping these kids in the program to stay on the good path and away from the negatives that are overrunning the streets where they all live. She smiled even more knowing that her instincts were completely on point, that her first impression of EJ as being a good guy was correct, and the butterflies in her stomach were there for more than just any physical attraction. He was kind, smart, funny, and he cares for and helps kids. She could admit that he was something special.

She continued into the gym forgetting about the confrontation that she had had in the parking lot thankfully, and saw some kids playing video games in a makeshift living room with a big screen projector, couches, and an old well worn, Playstation 4 gaming console. Some of the kids in other rooms were playing pool, table tennis, foosball, and Double Nine Dominos or spades. On the court, there was a basketball game going on and a weird looking guy with big yellow dreads, facial tattoos, and gold teeth, coaching the kids. She continued on around the court towards the offices located in the back where EJ should be, finally saw him and a cute little kid. They were opening up one of the boxes that were stacked up against the back wall, next to the office in back and the exit door.

"Hey, it's Rhonda Rousey! Hey, how are you doin'?" asked EJ jokingly while smiling, a huge grin with anticipation. He was obviously happy to see her.

"Hi! Mr. Knight in Shining Armor! Wow, you made me laugh and I really needed that today too! So, what are you doing over here tonight?" she asked back.

"I'm just organizing this stuff for a new program that we are starting here. Glad as hell that I could make you laugh though, that pretty smile should always be on display, lit up like a lamp! So, you are welcome to laugh at my goofy Italian ass anytime!" EJ said smiling self depreciatingly.

"Oh yea? Well, maybe I will, we will have to see about that one ... So, what is this new program that you're starting over here? I wasn't even aware this place was over here ..." said Liz looking all around at the Center.

"Well, I volunteer here, mostly for this lil' guy here," said EJ grabbing a hold of Lil' Ray and messing up his hair laughing playfully. "My lil' brother, Lil' Ray! Say 'hi' Ray, this is Miss Liz."

"Hi, Miss Liz, wow, you're really pretty, do you have a boyfriend?" he asked.

"Ray!" said EJ laughing. He turned to Liz, "I'm sorry, he's normally not so damn nosey! Are you, Ray?"

"It's okay, EJ," said Liz, "Thank you for the compliment Ray, I do appreciate that ... But no, I don't have a boyfriend." She said this part looking at EJ and laughing as EJ's eyes got big at that statement.

"Good," said Lil' Ray, "cuz my brother doesn't have a girlfriend either, and I can tell that he likes you, cuz he's always so serious and never goofy like this, until now. So, you most definitely got my blessing!" and with that said, he ran off, just looking for some more mischief to get into.

"Well, he's definitely a cutie! So, what happened to you?" she asked laughing.

"Me? What's wrong with me? Oh, I get it, you don't like my egg shaped head, huh? You biased? Well, I'll have you know that some girls actually like eggs ... ok! You got me. I'm sorry that I'm not better looking, but I make up for it with jokes on myself, and enthusiasm to put on armor and save groups of poor guys getting picked on by mysterious and violently dangerous damsels that are not in distress!" said EJ to her uncontrollable laughter, the way he was going in on himself.

She had never seen a man so comfortable that he was able to

just crack on himself like this nonstop, just to make her laugh when she was down. Actually, normally it was quite the opposite. Most guys took themselves too seriously. Way too seriously. Most of them tried to impress her with self important stories about themselves, and with throwing money around like they grew it on trees.

EJ did neither. He was here working as hard as anyone, and he wasn't being paid for it, he was doing it out of kindness. He wasn't trying to act tough or even trying to impress her, or even joke about others. He was just being himself, joking on himself in order to make her day a little brighter than it was and to cause her to smile, which made her smile even more just knowing that was what it was about for him. Nothing selfish, only caring and kindness.

"So, can I help? What's in all these boxes anyways?" she asked, curious.

"Sure, we can use all of the extra help that we can get, and it's equipment for a new photography program that I'm going to try and run, since my grandfather, Big Mike, used to be a photographer as a hobby and had left me some of his things when he passed. So, somebody else donated all of this brand new equipment for filming and photography anonymously, which almost never happens, since everyone always is looking to get the tax write off for donations. So, it's really a big blessing when that happens, and I just can't wait to start running this photography program and trying to help these kids find a positive avenue to express themselves with photography and film. So, I will be teaching the kids all about this stuff and how to use it all. It's going to be so much fun! It will be great!" he said full of enthusiasm and optimism.

Chapter Twenty - Nine

The four Bahamian contractors, or mercenaries, as they were known in the business by the politically incorrect, sat in a black Toyota 4-Runner at least a decade old that had been stolen from the long term parking lot at the Palm Beach International Airport. They didn't talk, didn't need to for their assignment. They had received their instructions for their assignment through a dead drop email address that was connected to a public library computer's IP address, which is almost impossible to trace. Once they had made contact with the client on a burner phone, two pictures were sent on it through the emailing app, one was a termination, the other, a catch and release. The latter, was only if there were demands that were met. It didn't matter to the team leader one though, as long as the funds were paid, he would do his job. He always did.

Team leader one had been militarized for so long, and had so many false names since his time in South Africa, that he couldn't even recall his given name even if tortured. It gave him an up on a lie detector examinations, on their actual machines, since given names were one of the control questions asked. But he was never asked, because he was never caught, and he always completed his assignments, he had never once failed a mission. Never would.

His three other cohorts would also do their job as trained. They were contractors, as mercenaries were no longer accepted as a description of their services, since coming back from Afghanistan contracting themselves on both sides. It didn't matter to the

Bahamians who was paying the bills. As long as someone was paying these bills.

They continued to wait, as they watched the front entrance and also, the white Explorer that they had identified as their target's vehicle. They had already terminated their first target, but they had to deal delicately on their second, because this target wasn't to be touched or hurt in any way. Only taken. But upon completed demands, later released, was the plan. The subject was very important. Very important to somebody, that was for sure, and that somebody was very paid. The men tensed when their target came into sight from the front of the building. The target wasn't alone though. The two individuals walked slowly, as if on a nature walk, but still conversing animatedly with one another, as well as laughing at the jokes of one another, as if on a pleasant date.

The client had briefed team leader on the importance of never underestimating target two, as the target had significant training and skills in combat. They would make the same assumption as to the individual walking with the subject, as birds of a feather ... or so the saying goes. So they would wait until the subject was alone and they would take her then. They had put the body of the first target in his own trunk and so, they didn't fear about his being discovered until they had already completed the taking of the second target.

The target and the 'date', as the Bahamians began to think of the individual, walked to the white Explorer, continued to talk and to laugh with each other and it was much to the annoyance of the team leader. She fumbled with her keys, but then she finally hit the unlock button on her truck's key fob, and got into the driver's seat. They continued to talk and laugh with the driver door open. The continuous flirting and playing was the most annoying thing to the team leader, this courting. He was used to just grabbing the woman that you had desired and either taking what he wanted or paying for it. Either way, he wasn't going to court or beg for it. Americans were so old fashioned that it made him sick. Courting was for those days long past, like in the Bible days.

Finally, the date turned, then began walking back towards the front of the big building, and was going, leaving their target alone. The Explorer started and she began backing out. Team leader started the 4-Runner as well, then prepared to back out, after the second target had cleared this row of the parking lot. She cleared the row, heading for the exit, so he backed out and tried to catch up as naturally as possible.

She pulled out into traffic, on 45th street, he followed. Then unexpectedly at the first red light on Broadway, she made a U-Turn, heading back the way that she had just come from, and made team leader scramble to try to make a left onto Broadway, and then his own U-Turn on Broadway, out of sight. He quickly made his U-Turn, then made a right back onto 45th Street and hit the gas in an attempt to catch up. All of the pretenses of stealth out of the window because he couldn't risk losing his target.

The chase was on. They didn't know what had happened to make the target turn around, but it was obvious that something had made her turn to go back that way. They were hoping that it was only her forgetting her purse and not because that she had spotted them.

Chapter Thirty

They had spent several hours together, sorting through and putting away in an empty storage room, all of the tools of the photography trade, such as cameras, accessories, equipment, and filming assortment parts and all, that had been donated. After all of that, they took the tour of the center. EJ introduced her to Sammy, his uncle, and some of the special kids that he was involved with, helping when he was in town. If Liz had been quietly impressed before when looking at the pictures and trophies, she was completely enthralled with him now, maybe even a little bit smitten. But she knew that it was mutual with him.

She was completely taken by the family atmosphere at the Center, the way that they all depended on each other, asked and cared about their progress and well being. It had her attention because as big as Liz was on family orientation, mutual family participation, and support, she had never been as inspired as she currently was seeing the kids, and the volunteers' interactions with them, and each other here. They all asked about, and tried to help, with their goals and dreams. Just as EJ was getting his photography and film making program started. His uncle Jean had the basketball and boxing programs, and Detective Shelby Nash, who she found out was his uncle's girlfriend, apparently had submitted a new plan in order for her to start her idea of an Explorers program. It would be for the young ladies who wanted to pursue a career in investigations or law enforcement, and would have several class meetings a month, where she would also offer ride alongs on patrols, studying closed cases for missing clues, and an eventual internship at the Sheriff's Office starting as a dispatcher. A sort of ROTC for future cops.

This Explorers program with Shelby had not been approved by the City yet, or the non-profit auditors and lawyers, but the fact that these volunteers here at the Center, especially EJ, went to such lengths to keep these kids on the right track, was such an amazing inspiration to Liz. It made her want to get involved as well, and she even went as far as telling EJ excitedly. She had been inspired, and she wanted a role to play in the Youth Center. EJ didn't know what to say, but anything that would keep her around more, was a plus for him, so he was all for it. He really liked her. He actually enjoyed the time that he was spending with her, more than any other girl that he had ever spent time with, and that was saying something. It was saying a whole lot. It was saying that she was very special.

They had finished everything they had to put away, taken a tour, and fluttered around a bit more. Eventually, they could not delay her leaving anymore, as there was nothing else left to do or say, as all excuses and small talk was exhausted. As he walked her outside, EJ saw his uncle's Riviera, Sammy's Prius, a few other vehicles that belonged to other volunteers, or family to some of the kids, but he noticed a vehicle that didn't belong and could see it was empty. So, as he walked with Liz, he kept his eyes peeled. His Marine-trained senses could detect something afoot in this parking lot. Once he got to her Ford Explorer, he kept his eyes all around while he kept talking to her as if nothing was wrong, but as his eyes moved further on down the same row of parked cars, he saw a black SUV that he was pretty sure had never been there before.

From his first encounter, he knew Liz was a sweet and honest college student who knew how to defend herself, so he allowed their conversation to get to the saying goodnight part, and instead of attempting to kiss her, as he so desperately wanted to, he said goodnight and started off. This definitely surprised her. Liz wondered why he didn't even try to kiss her when she knew they were both feeling each other. She then wondered what had made him run off so suddenly, but they had spent several hours together, so maybe EJ was just tired, she thought, or hoped. She knew he liked her though, she could feel that much.

As she pulled off, she noticed a black SUV pull out behind her but thought nothing of it since she was already aware of Juanito's presence. She got onto 45th Street and hit the gas slightly as she asked herself whether it was worth attempting to lose Juanito, or just let him follow her. She started to decide to just let him follow, and a thought just hit her, making her remember Juanito's headlights. This couldn't be Juanito following her. Her phone started ringing in that moment. She looked at her display on her Explorer bluetooth and saw that EJ was calling, and she hit the answer button to hear EJ's heavy breathing on her truck's loud speakers.

"Ok, Unc! Right now, come on. .. damn it! Liz! Listen to me very carefully, you are being followed by four men in a 4-Runner "

"Four? It was only Juanito when I came in and he was in an old car -- "

"No Liz! Turn around, right now! Come back and pick me up!" said EJ out of breath. She could hear his foot falls on the speakers, so she knew that he was running, but to where, she didn't know.

"I'm making a U-Turn right now," she said alarmed, but still not necessarily convinced about who it was following her.

"Okay, I'm almost out front, okay? Hey, Unc! Hurry up! Okay, Liz, I'm here in front of the Center, so slide through and just act as natural as you possibly can in this situation, I know it's scary, just act normal," he said.

"Okay, EJ, I'm pulling in now. .. I see you ... " she said and ended the call.

At that very moment she pulled to a stop, EJ came and jumped in the passenger side of her truck with a backpack. He was breathing very heavily. He pulled a machine pistol out saying, "Okay, take off, we are going to stop up ahead somewhere and try to see if they try something or not." He jammed a magazine into the receiver of the MP5 but kept the folding stock flipped in, so that it was out of the way in the small space of the inside of the truck. Liz reached her hand into the center console, and came out, placing her Taurus PT111 baby 9mm on her lap and trying not to panic or even show any sign of knowing that she was being followed.

"What?" she asked EJ, not knowing or seeing, but yet still sensing his look. "A girl has to keep a little bit of protection around, doesn't she?" Despite the seriousness of the situation, she still had a playful look and tone in her voice.

"Yea, but you are being followed by four guys who look very dangerous, and yet you are acting as if you are taking a walk in the park, like nothing is wrong. So tell me, Liz, why are you so calm right now?" he asked her seriously.

"I was just trained young, okay? Leave it at that, you wouldn't be able to understand it all anyways, it wasn't my choice to be born into my family. Okay, here is a red light coming up here."

EJ put his bluetooth in his ear and dialed his uncle as Liz stopped at the red light at 45th Street and Broadway, right at the same place that she had made her U-Turn earlier. They both were holding their firearms in their hands and tensed, ready to react on the drop of a dime.

"Nephew, I'm behind them now, they aren't making a move, they just followin' and watchin', might be they tryin' to kidnap and ransom and don't want any witnesses," said Wicks on the ear piece in his ear.

"Okay, we need her alone to see what they do," said EJ, noticing Liz dialing on her Explorer's dash bluetooth. The name Juanito came up on the screen in the dash, along with the ringing in the loud speakers.

"Who's that?" asked EJ, thinking about before, when he had called to warn her and she had slipped up mentioning Juanito, surprised about the truck having four occupants, instead of just one. She had expected one person to be following. Interesting, thought EJ, who was following her that she was aware of?

"Just a friend that was watching out for me ... " said Liz and then she hit the send button again, and again her call went straight to the voicemail, unanswered. He said nothing. It just wasn't the right time for intrusive questions. But he did plan on asking her eventually.

They were moving again and trying to formulate a plan to get things going, to kind of help things along and instigate a move from the opposition. All three of them had their minds working overtime, when Liz had a thought she shared.

"Put your shit back into your backpack EJ, there is a Micky D's up in that plaza ahead, you get out, I'll stay in the car, and you guys can come from behind them, wherever they park, if they don't move, I'll start over to them to distract them and you can disarm them from the rear, I'll draw, and cover the driver and the guy in shotgun, " Liz said confidently.

"It's a solid plan, Nephew," said Wicks in his ear, hearing her plan through EJ's bluetooth piece.

"No! It leaves her alone for too long for me to move all the way around the place to come out behind them, it's too risky," said EJ with finality.

"Well, I am pulling up there, and I can take care of myself!" she said angrily.

"Jesus, Liz, I'm not putting you down, I'm just saying that it is too risky."

"And I say that it's not, and that the plan is settled," she said defiantly.

"Okay, EJ," said Wicks hearing both sides of the conversation,

"It's a solid plan and we have no time, let's do this ..."

"Okay, okay, but Unc, pull up ahead of us and park in there first, she can drop me off at the front and I'll double back and come out from behind the restaurant, then she can park. It kills more time so that I can get into place and be ready faster," said EJ, and Wicks was already pulling up, passing them to get ahead of them and get to the restaurant first.

"Okay, good, slow down a bit so that he can get parked, and try to take your time after I get out, so maybe they can park first, ya know?" asked EJ.

"Okay, EJ, and thank you, I didn't even catch them in time, so I appreciate you since I would be either dead or kidnapped right now without your quick thinking, and I don't even know which would have been worse ..." Liz let that thought hang in the air between them, meaning it.

"Well, let's take care of them first before you start all of the thanking me, ya know?" EJ said quietly anticipating a fire fight.

When they pulled into the McDonald's parking lot, Wicks' Riviera was parking at an angle where the back door could be seen from his position. But because of the full parking spaces in front, it forced Liz, and in turn the opposition, to park even further away towards the back where there was lesser light and more opportunity. Liz pulled up to the front door and allowed EJ to get out with his backpack on him. Once he was inside, Liz let her foot off of the brake and drifted slowly to allow EJ to have some time to get out of the back door, but also to double check to see Wicks had already exited his Riviera and was in place.

Once Liz had delayed as much as she possibly could, she went three spaces past the Riviera and backed in so that Wicks could come up from behind the Explorer and surprise them if they decided to make their move. Which they did, about 30 seconds after Liz had parked. It all happened so incredibly fast and the fire fight became surreal, almost like in a very bad action movie without sound. That is, until Liz raised her baby 9, breaking the silence.

The 4-Runner pulled up, blocking in her Explorer. The front and rear passenger doors opened all at once, with the two assailants on the passenger side of the truck walking towards Liz. She pretended not to notice, but racked the slide on her Taurus PT111, chambering a round, and held it pointed towards the window. She then lowered the window, as if to speak to him, just as the first subject walked up, making a target of himself.

As soon as his head was in a close enough range, she pulled the trigger, spraying the midnight air with blood, bone, and brain fragments that used to be what did the thinking for the first subject. As he fell, the next one dropped with another spray of red, by a silenced 9mm round from EJ's MP5, as he came out from the back of the McDonalds walking towards the 4-Runner and the Explorer. Wicks, already at the front passenger side of her truck, and quickly moving towards the opened passenger window of the 4-Runner blocking her in, was hessitant to fire. The reason being because they would be needing information, they all knew that dead men don't talk.

"Stop! Don't move!" Wicks shouted, trying to take him alive. EJ shot the third passenger that was trying to escape the ambush. He had missed being caught up in their well laid trap, but now was soaking wet in his own blood about 30 yards away. EJ's markmanship was still incredible, even with one eye, so it was an easy shot for him.

As soon as the third target had dropped, the last living target, the driver, hit the gas in an attempt to flee. Wicks, MP5 set on three round bursts, shot three in the front passenger wheel, and three more in the back as he took off in high speed, to ensure all available, reachable tires were going to be disabled. The driver had hit the gas so fast, and was already going at a good high speed, that when he was trying to turn left and around the back of the McDonalds to get away, all the weight of the truck shifted to the right side, which caused him to flip. He immediately lost control of the situation.

The 4-Runner sits up high, so when both right side tires were deflated, it leaned all the way right. The centrifugal force shifting to the right side with a left turn at a high rate of speed, and he had a bigger problem: Loss of control.

When the 4-Runner flipped the first time, the driver, who wasn't wearing his seat belt, was thrown clear from the truck, which somehow humorously, had landed almost on top of the garbage dumpster. But when it settled, it fell off of the dumpster and into the backyard of a house that backed up to the McDonald's parking lot. It actually landed on what was left of all four wheels.

Liz put her truck in drive and pulled up next to the driver of the totaled 4-Runner. She hit the tailgate button on her key fob, and EJ, who had already ran to the thrown body, began to pick him up while Wicks started his Riviera and took off down the street in the opposite direction that they had come from. Knowing the Explorer's license plate was located on the tailgate, EJ left it up while Liz took off for the front of the restaurant, and the exit. EJ had cut strips of his shirt for the cloth to tie the driver of the 4-Runner's hands together, then the feet, then the hands to the feet, hogtying him all together.

Once Liz had made it down the road and EJ had their prisoner secured, he pulled shut the tailgate and then climbed back into the front of the truck to the shotgun seat. It was actually quite possible that the shots were not heard because of the suppressors in Wicks and EJ's cases, and because Liz's one shot had been fired inside of her truck and there hadn't been anyone outside of the restaurant when it had happened. But when the 4-Runner had crashed, flipped, and then landed on the dumpster, Liz and EJ had just barely cleared the scene before any of the nosey patrons or McDonalds employees could make it outside to see what had crashed into what. The incident would most likely be on the local news in the morning with an 800 number requesting information and clues, but there would be none.

Chapter Thirty - One

"I don't know, primo! They are not responding to my emails, but I still think that everything might be all good, because no contesta Juanito tampoco ..." and so on and so forth, was Jonny's continuous answers and excuses for his failures.

Iggy was very aggravated, but he couldn't just call Liz out of the blue and not have a valid reason without raising some suspicion. Especially if she had just been attacked, and their attack had apparently failed. She would then definitely be on the defensive and feel some type of way towards him, maybe even straight out suspect him. He needed to be careful at this point. Very careful.

"No contesta Juanito," or Juanito doesn't answer, this meant that their patsy was almost assuredly dead. There is no way Juanito wouldn't answer his phone when it was his boss calling him, and Jonny had called several times. So, he is dead for sure. So, that much of the plan had indeed worked, they had killed Juanito, and then somewhere in the next phase of their plan was where something had gone wrong.

It shouldn't even be a surprise to Jonny, thought Iggy. Shit, he helped arrange her damn training himself with the Mossad agent who had defected to Cuba and had made her into a human weapon. They had already known how extensive her training was for just this type of situation. They had relayed, well, Jonny had relayed, this information to the people that they had contracted to handle the faux kidnapping in which Juanito was supposed to lose his life in order to certify the seriousness of these supposed kidnappers and ransomers. But either they had not heeded their warning and failed to listen, or they had just underestimated Liz's petite size and frame, as well as her pretty face. They had judged a book by its cover and had lost their lives for making the wrong assumptions and judgements.

"So, primo, how do you get in touch with them? Through their email only?" asked Iggy, trying to figure out a way to verify things.

"Well, I've got a burner phone number, and I've been calling it, but no answer, I keep trying, but man, maybe they just ain't had a chance to--"

"Wait," said Iggy interrupting, "what phone are you calling their number on?" No, thought Iggy, my cousin couldn't be that stupid, could he?

"On my phone, why? What difference does it make? They not answerin'."

"I guess none, primo," said Iggy as he walked away to the bathroom so that he could gather his thoughts. He closed the bathroom door once he was inside. He ran the cold water in the sink and splashed some into his face. This should be good to help him gather his thoughts and figure out what needed to be done. Jonny had never been the sharpest tool in the shed, Iggy had always been the chess player. While Jonny was the checkers player. But Jonny had always been a necessary evil, he was brutal and loyal. Both were important qualities in a cartel security agent. But the fact that Jonny hadn't thought to buy a burner phone to call the contract carrier's phone, really bothered Iggy. Sure, people make mistakes in this business, but there was never an excuse for dealing with stupidity. Iggy could not tolerate stupidity. He would not. Some people's mistakes have major consequences. That was just the way things were in this business.

Iggy had come up with his cousin Jonny, since they had been kids, and although Jonny was a little bit older, Iggy had always been smarter. When Jonny had been doing bad in Reynosa, Iggy had asked Ricky, who was like his brother by this time, to help his cousin with a job. Ricky had his own group of coyotes, or human traffickers, on the border town of Reynosa and had immediately put Jonny to work as a coyote. He began taking groups of immigrants across the border to McAllen, Texas.

He was quick and efficient, but he was brutal. While raping some of those women that he had brought across, a few had died, mostly due to injuries dealt by their rapist, Jonny Tapatio. That would have an adverse effect on the business.

The Gulf Cartel needed their own enforcers around this time because of the original Zetas ex-military forces were having a lot of problems with the people in charge of them. So they had Jonny doing a lot of the type of brutal work that he was very good at, as well as being a sicario, or assassin, for the Gulf Cartel, and whatever other odd jobs that he would have to do to make them trust and respect him. Then came the original fight with the Haitians over 20 years ago in the early 2000's, and Jonny had been in Florida ever since doing security. From being a hoodlum to coyote, enforcer to sicario, and now security leader in Florida, to being a dead man walking.

When Iggy walked back into the room where his cousin was waiting, he did so as silently as he could and very carefully. Jonny had made the ultimate mistake and compromised not only Iggy's future, but Ricky's as well. If word ever reached the old man that they had anything to do with setting up Liz, their entire family's line would soon be hanging from a Matamoros bridge in El Centro to be an example to others what would happen when you crossed the Gulf Cartel. Jonny was sitting at his computer, with his back to Iggy, not even aware of his presence back inside of the room. It made things a lot easier for Iggy. Now he wouldn't have to look into the eyes of his cousin before he would kill him.

He pointed at the back of Jonny's head, and pulled the trigger. He had just killed his closest cousin. His best friend in his own family, and his fellow conspirator. He killed Jonny and would do so again to protect what they were trying to build.

Chapter Thirty - Two

"Man this fucking asshole is dead ... just look at him," said Wicks, checking the driver of the 4-Runner's pulse in the back of the Explorer.

"Shit, now we'll never know who sent them," answered Liz.

"Well, that's not necessarily true, check his pockets for ID, phone, keys, or anything we can run and get a lead on through the database," said EJ.

They were in the Explorer, parked in the long term parking lot at the Fort Lauderdale Airport, about 15 minutes or so, south of the airport in West Palm Beach.

They had pulled up next to an old Toyota and found it to be unlocked. Liz was going to trade in the Explorer after they let most of the air out of one of the tires, but she had to complain to Avis Rental car agency about the tire first. But they would just have to dispose of this body first, hence the Toyota, Team Leader One's final resting place, or at least his temporary resting place, at least until his body was found or stunk so bad that it drew attention to its location.

As they were searching the body, who had actually died of a broken neck, an injury suffered by being thrown from the 4-Runner without his seatbelt on. They found no identification on the body, but they found a Trac-Phone, and nothing else of substance. There wasn't really any blood except from his broken nose, and since he wasn't bleeding in her truck, because the dead don't bleed, they had very little to clean up in there. They popped the trunk on the Toyota, and carefully loaded the body into it. They closed the trunk, let the air out of Liz's back tire, so as not to affect her steering in the front, and drove to the Avis Rental desk, where Wicks and EJ waited, while Liz did the "I'm a woman and can't get the tire changed" act so they would issue her another Explorer without question.

The Explorer they issued her this time was black and had a sun roof, which Liz loved immediately. After an hour at Avis, they were finally back on I-95 headed back up to West Palm Beach, and with EJ examining the Trac-Phone that they had taken from the dead body. It wasn't complicated because it was just a burner and had no lock on the actual phone, but it didn't seem to be bursting with any information either at their first look. At the first look anyways.

"So, there is an email icon on here, but to get into it ... yea, it's password protected, which is interesting considering the fact that the actual phone itself has no password. This can only mean that the phone was a one time use burner, and this guy didn't even have it long enough to assign it a password, but the one thing he did use it for was an emailing device. Now ... look at this," said EJ, holding the phone for Wicks to see.

"No contacts are programmed into the memory, and its sim card is in here too," observed Wicks as he continued to look at it.

"Yea," said EJ, "but look at the call log ..." He handed the phone off to Wicks, who started tapping the different icons on the screen.

"Shit, no outgoing calls ... but why would they with the emailing app?" said Wicks as he continued to click. "But there are several incoming calls, and look, none of them were answered. Oh, shit! These calls have all been received in the last two hours and the phone is on silent, so we just didn't hear it." Wicks continued to examine the phone, looking at the missed calls.

"Give me the number so I can run a reverse lookup and find out who the phone number belongs to, let's hope they weren't smart enough to get a burner phone too, if not, we will get their ass," said EJ pulling out his iPhone 13 and opening his google app, preparing for the lookup.

"You can look up the number and find the registered owner? Like in the phone book, but backwards?" Wicks asked incredulously, as Liz looked at EJ and a smile passed between them. Technological ignorance was so cute, they were thinking, Wicks was just like a little baby learning to crawl.

"My uncle's been in the penitentiary in the FEDs for the last decade and a half, so please forgive his ignorance of technological advancement," said EJ laughing. Liz silently joined in, but kept it low since she didn't want to offend him.

"Over-charged and over-sentenced though," said Wicks. "A victim of Justice is what I was, a victim to their messed up judicial system, the so called justice system ... shoulda called it the *injustice* system, cuz if you really want to see some criminals, just go to any police station, prosecutor's office, or federal building at shift change! You will see plenty of criminals there!" They all had a good laugh at that one, since it was not only true, but also close to home.

"Yea I know that's right, ok, I got the app open, give me the number," said EJ.

"561-801-7203 is the number, so at least it's a Palm Beach County area code," said Wicks answering EJ.

"Ok, it's searching ... ok, here's a hit, oh shit, it's a business name, Tapatio Investigations LLP." EJ felt something coming from the driver's seat and noticed that the Explorer was now losing speed as Liz stiffened. He looked up and saw that Liz, who was already porcelain complexion, had turned sheet white and was now shaking visibly.

"What?" EJ asked her, "What's wrong? You know them, don't you? Tell me who it is Liz, they just tried to kill you! Talk to me please baby!"

"I'm ... I'm sorry, but I shouldn't have involved you guys, I need to drop you off and fly back to Mexico and let my Uncle know about this, but don't worry, at least I know now, and I wouldn't have known without your help, so thank you, both, I --" Liz tried to start but was interrupted by Wicks.

"-- No! We ain't leavin' you! He's my nephew and you're his...whatever," he said.

Chapter Thirty - Three

She only had two eyes, one gun, and a split second in which to choose ...

"Damn these little gangbangers!" said Mike, Shelby's temporary partner on the case that she was working on right now about a kid with the 'ZMF' tattooed on his neck. He had been shot so many times in his 1985 Chevy Caprice that they couldn't even calculate at the scene exactly how many bullets had struck him.

A look in the gang book verified his affiliation, but not membership to the Zoe Mafia Family, or the ZMF as it was often called in the streets. It is a very big and popular gang with many teenaged Haitian kids. Since the moment that she had been working with Mike, it had been a nightmare for her, trying to talk to any witnesses in the White Houses projects in Downtown West Palm Beach. Most people already hated the police here, and almost everywhere for that matter, but Mike made it even worse. He was just more than what was required from a detective.

Mike Chambers is 6'3, and almost 300 pounds. He used his weight to intimidate, or to try to intimidate, since it didn't work most of the time on these street tough gang members. Another reason was because he was white, and he isn't the cool white either, with somewhat Mediterranean heritage. He was Scottish with the red beard and hair. Shelby could almost tell, suspect rather, that he was not necessarily racist, but he most definitely preferred his own kind.

She thought that it was evidenced in his style of policing, especially while interviewing potential witnesses and with his attitude change inside of the black neighborhoods.

She wasn't bothered too much by him because her partnership with him was only temporary, and on a rotational schedule at that. She had been assigned a case with every senior officer and senior homicide detective. They had told her that it wasn't because of her handling of the first case that she had been assigned out of the gate, but she definitely believed that it was because of her bombing of that case. The lawyer-trick, Vincent Rodriguez, Jr. A homicide of opportunity had been her conclusion in her paperwork, and technically she still had the case file opened and marked as an OUS, or open/unsolved. But based on her training and experience, she knew that a drugged out hooker, or her pimp could be blamed for the murder. She wouldn't collar anyone for it, because she had known that it was her man, Wicks, that had done it, and she considered that to be a justifiable homicide. The world would be at no great loss, for the killing of Vincent Rodriguez or anyone like him. He was just a scumbag that deserved what he had received and the world was a better place for it. She didn't over-exert herself over things like that, he seemed like a complete sleaze ball anyways. Even his own wife had nothing to say about him that could even be considered as a positive sentiment, and that in itself says a lot about the person that he was.

"You shouldn't call them that, Mike, some of these guys are just out here playing basketball, they're not all gangbangers," said

Shelby, trying to get him to stop prejudging the guys that they were trying to interview, before they even knew anything about them, other than the fact that they all liked to play basketball at this park.

"I know that it ain't exactly politically correct, Nash, but trust me, these scumbags here are all gangbanging punks, just as soon to kill you as to look at you ..." retorted Chambers cynically.

Shelby said nothing. She knew that you couldn't necessarily teach an old dog new tricks, and any further comments would just more than likely drive a wedge in between their already strained partnership, and this was the only case that she would have to work on with him. She definitely didn't want any static, or to further clash with the brass, but she really did not enjoy working with Chambers. The apparent racism she could deal with, she had been dealing with that type of shit for her whole life growing up, but this man was arrogant for no reason at all. He wasn't even very smart, and she had no idea how he had even come to be a detective in the first place, or maybe she did. The good ole boys' network reached all over Florida, just as it did in the rest of the country.

"Why don't we split up and interview separately, that way we can cover more of the area a lot quicker," offered Shelby, thinking that they would never make any progress in this case until she could talk to someone without her idiot partner around spreading his semi-racist vibes to possible witnesses.

"Trying to get rid of me, Nash?" he asked her half seriously.

Shelby sighed, there was only one way for her to get around it, Shelby had always spoke her mind, but she just couldn't right now, she had to play the game. She couldn't win in this situation. "I just think that with our two different interview styles, we might put them to better use separately, and the case would ultimately benefit in the end, ya know?"

"Oh, well alright, but don't be mad when I'm the one to crack the case, due to my ahh. .. my interview style," answered the Senior Detective, her subliminal message clearly going over his head to her relief. He actually was an idiot, of that she now had no doubts whatsoever.

Shelby talked to a few young men and then to a young boy who eyed her with hearts in his eyes, like she had been his first ever young crush. Shelby consciously didn't wear her Palm Beach County Sheriffs Office Badge around her neck, as did the other Detectives, as she felt that it psychologically hindered her ability to gain trust with the person that she would be interviewing. In an unconscious way, while talking, it allowed the person of interest to temporarily forget that she was a detective. She never thought, that in this type of a situation, it would be a good move to continuously remind the person you are asking for help from, that you are a cop. In other situations, sure, but here she wanted to be just thought of as a normal person asking about something inconsequential. She wanted them to be at ease, and no matter how hard she had tried, that would never happen with Mike by her side.

"Yea, he my frien', we be at school, sometimes we be talkin' to da same gulls ... " the boy continued on about him and how he had known the victim and any of the random details that he was offering

317

up to her to steer the subject away from the ZMF tattoo which was what she actually was here asking about.

"But what about the ZMF tattoo? Do you know what that is?" she asked him.

"Nah, I not really know too much bout that one," he said, looking away and betraying the fact that he was lying to her.

"Now, Little Twan, tell me about it, don't you want to help me to catch whoever did this to your friend? You don't want this to happen to you or any more of your friends, now do you?" Shelby asked him. He shook his head in the negative.

"Nawl, I 'on't even know anything about all of dat ..." he again repeated.

Shelby was exhausted after questioning Lil' Twan, and had gained only a small lead of who his closest associates were, but mainly a kid named Cedric, who had been going by the street name of 'Earth Worm', as in Earth Worm Jim, because of the way he looked with his small eyes, glasses, and the worm shaped body. Shelby would have to go and find out about what this Earth Worm knew, and if he himself could be a ZMF member, and then whether or not he knew anything about the shooting death of her vic. For Lil' Twan to even intentionally bring attention to him meant that subliminally this Earth Worm either knew something, or he himself might be the doer. What if this was Lil' Twan's way of guiding her to the one responsible for the shooting and death of her vic? Maybe Lil' Twan knew that Earth Worm did it, yet couldn't rat on him, so he just gently led her to him. There was a phrase for this in the streets, and it wasn't any more flattering than the previous term. It was called 'dry snitching', but it was the same.

§§§§

When Shelby had got about as much as she possibly could from her interview with Lil' Twan, she started walking back towards where her partner's unmarked Crown Victoria was parked, at the front of the White House projects. As she passed an alleyway, she heard some elevated voices, one of which, was a very loud and authoritative voice. Another cop, great, she thought to herself, but she still started down the alley towards what she thought to be an officer that needed some assistance. She took in her surroundings. Not good.

In all actuality, Palm Beach County Sheriffs Office didn't technically have any jurisdiction being in the downtown West Palm Beach area. The whole of West Palm Beach downtown was patrolled by the West Palm Beach Police Department, and the inner city has police substations and is all governed by their own police department, the West Palm Beach Police Detectives Division. They even had their own Robbery/Homicide Division and quite a few renowned homicide detectives. But the reason that Shelby, Mike, and Palm Beach County Sheriffs were called in was because of the ZMF tattoo on the victim's neck, and the gang affiliation to that tattoo.

The gangs in South Florida had been almost non-existent in the early 90's, but in the last two decades alone, the known gang activity had bubbled almost 200%, spreading the follow-the-leaderesque, brainwashing, type of gang propaganda, all over South Florida, and by choosing young and easily impressionable kids, they got a lot of their numbers up very quickly. In these two decades, gang activity and violent crimes had more than tripled even the 1980's 'Cuban Crime Wave' era's crime statistics, and that was saying something.

It had most definitely caught the attention of the last 3 governors of Florida, the Police Commissioners, Sheriffs from all over the state, as well as the state Senators and Representatives who voted to use any and all tools at their disposal to deal with the many millions of gang members that had overrun the beautiful tourist state. All separation of powers during any of the gang investigations would cease to exist, and all agencies and municipalities were expected to cooperate. It was all about any means to an end, and all borders would be ignored, lines would be crossed, and grievances and petty beefs overlooked, all for the greater good, a means to an end to gang violence.

As could only be expected from someone already struggling with racial tolerance, Mike Chambers, of course had developed an attitude towards young black men ever since his daughter had been caught at school underneath the bleachers with a young black Zoe Pound gang member, and had been getting trouble in school ever since. It of course had been like throwing gasoline on a fire for Mike Chambers, or giving an intolerant asshole any reason at all to hate

320

another race. So, although Shelby never actually heard Mike say anything racially offensive, he had it inside of his heart, and therefore he definitely had given off that vibe before.

As Shelby continued to walk down the alley and look for where the authoritative voice had come from, she observed many coke, heroin, and flaka baggies all over the place, and beer cans, condoms, and other random little trash here and there. It was definitely a ghetto here, almost a 3rd world country.

Right then she heard the voices again, loud as ever, then some shouts, and then some loud pops, like popopopopop, pop, pop, pop. Then, around the corner, there were several young black kids coming from where she had assumed the shots or pops had come from. The pops, to her, had sounded hollow, no depth to them at all. They were either .22 or .25 caliber shots, but then again, they were too close together, and she didn't know of any automatic, well fully automatic weapon, with either of those small calibers in that large of a capacity. She had heard at least a hundred shots, so that was telling to her that something was wrong. Something didn't add up to her about the whole situation. Being as such, she was especially on guard for anything out of the ordinary, something that could make sense.

She rounded the corner to reach a T-shaped intersection of the alleyways and two little boys running towards a fence away from her, and none other than a fat, out of shape, Mike Chambers, gun drawn with his finger on the hair trigger, ready to take a life. Shelby was still far enough away that in the darkness of the alleyway, she was not at all visible. She was trying to run and get there as fast as she could, but she was still about 30 feet away when the whole scene unfolded in front of her. It was like a bad dream, a movie. Every person of color's worst and common fear, when dealing with anybody of the law enforcement community. Fear of being unarmed to protect themselves, yet shot by the police anyway. Something that could happen to any of us, that *did* in fact happen to us, all the time in innocent interactions with the police and anyone of authority.

It all happened so fast, and yet it seemed like slow motion to her, as she came closer, and finally had to make the split decision to chose right or wrong. Her choice had nothing to do with good or evil. It was all about what was right and *who* was in the wrong. She didn't know these two kids before her. Didn't judge whether they were gangbangers or not, whether Mike Chambers was a racist or not. She only had two eyes, one gun, and a split second in which to choose. Her choice would ultimately mark the end of her career as a homicide detective, and in a way, she was grateful for that. It was the best thing that could have happened to her in the end of it all. The best outcome to all involved.

She saw it all so clearly, as the light from the street light on the other side of the fence produced a backlight, causing the two teenagers to be placed in a silhouette as they jumped towards the fence. Mike screamed, "Stop or I'll shoot!" Shelby could see one of the teens had a black touch screen phone in his left hand. All in a split second, the first kid grabbed onto the fence with both hands, as the second one hesitated slightly. He turned, almost imperceptibly towards Mike, as he took his hand that was holding the phone, and began to move it towards his pocket in order to have his hands both free to climb the fence and flee. She knew and could see all of this from her vantage point.

Just as she knew that Mike couldn't possibly see the kid's phone in his hand at that angle, she knew the kid could not see Mike to know how his body movements could possible be interpreted by an officer with his adrenaline pumping on full blast and a gun pointed in his direction. Shelby screamed as loud as she could: "Hold fire Mike! Hold your gotdamned fire!" But all to no avail.

§§§§

Mike Chambers could hear nothing but his own loud breathing, his heartbeat, and the sound of kids' feet hitting the ground as they all continued to flee the pops that they all had heard and assumed was gunshots. In slow motion he heard the rattling of the fence as the first of his two shooting suspects' hands and feet hit it, trying to flee their arrest, and jumping at least four feet into the 6 foot fence.

He heard a girl scream, "Hold Fire!" but it didn't compute as things were moving so fast in his adrenaline full mind, as he saw with his own eyes the little gangbanger reaching for a gun in his pocket to shoot him, Mike Chambers with. Mike knew that his gangbanging suspect had to have a gun, because all of these little gangbangers carried guns and also because of the many pops that he

323

had heard when they had first been shooting at him and into the crowd. Mike had been inside of that crowd asking some random gangbangers what they knew about the shooting, and then he, like everyone else, had ducked down upon hearing all of the gunshots, automatics is what Mike figured, and probably an AK-47 at that, since these gangbangers always liked to use those fully automatic assault rifles. Now they even went farther and had made the Draco a popular item. A Draco is just a shorter and better version of the AK-47. He knew it was these two punks that he was in pursuit of too, since they were the farthest away, which to him meant that they had been already in motion while everyone else had been ducking down. That was an obvious tell to him.

After shouting a warning to the suspects to stop or he would shoot, he received a negative response, as they continued to disobey his instructions. Mike took his trigger finger off of the side of the slide, and put it into the trigger guard, pulling the tension tightly on his four pounds of pressure trigger. He narrowed his eyelid on his left eye, the side from which most of the available, yet dim light was coming from, to allow himself to concentrate all of his right eye's vision and attention on top of his Glock, model 22, onto the gunsights. As he lined up the front barrel single sight, with his rear dual sights on the back of the Glock, he was suddenly lifted off of his feet right when his Glock's firing pin hit the bullet, activating the primer, which in turn fired the gunpowder which propelled a .40 caliber Parabellum round at the kid. Confusion took over his mind.

This was his last and only thought being that something had

made him miss the little gangbanger.

§§§§

For Shelby, it was quite different. She was at an angle sort of sideways from both suspects, but head up and to the left of Mike, which gave her a perfectly clear shot. As she watched the whole thing play out in the slowest of slow motion, she screamed once again, "Mike! Hold Fire!" But he continued along as if he were in a daze, a dream, some type of Alice in the Wonderland and he had fallen down the rabbit hole. Maybe he was Doris and just wasn't in Kansas anymore.

As the kid put his phone in his pocket, and Shelby saw Mike's finger tighten on the trigger, she stopped her run and all in one motion, she took a knee on the ground, supported her right hand holding her gun, onto her left, and made her last split second decision as a homicide detective. She went ahead and took the shot.

Shelby went down in history as being the first Palm Beach County Sheriff's Office Homicide Detective that had shot her own partner. She shot Mike Chambers, her Senior Homicide Detective, Palm Beach County Sheriff's Office, and at the same time, she saved the life of 13 year old Jovan Mills, an unarmed black kid in the West Palm Beach Whitehouse Projects. But saving Mills didn't matter to anyone but Shelby, but the shooting of Mike Chambers did. It made all of the difference to her life and career and reputation.

325

Chapter Thirty - Four

Lil' Fade was on his last day of the 72 hour hold for suicide watch and he couldn't believe that this could even have happened to him, not like this. He had never felt as low as he felt right now on suicide watch. It was like, if you didn't want to kill yourself, being buck naked with a shroud in an empty cell, or bathroom really, would definitely make you consider it. Fade had no intention of killing himself though, had never once even considered it. His little sister, Anika, was 9 years old and autistic. He could never even consider leaving her alone. Not in the same way that their father had left them both, he knew that she needed him and would not survive long without him. So, he would fight. He would get home to her.

He couldn't begin to comprehend how just cussing out a piece of shit cracker guard, could land him in a solitary cell, buck naked, and him being under constant guard, or observations for potential suicide attempts. The guard he had gotten into it with must have had some pull, maybe from seniority, and apparently thought that this was funny, or just that it would be more of a punishment than the box for the fight, by putting him on suicide watch. Real funny, thought Fade. Ridiculous. Fade hated to admit it, but the cracker was right, this suicide watch sucked. He has no bed, no sheets and blankets, no clothes and shoes, basically nothing but his own thoughts in his own head, and that also sucked.

He thought back to the fight and was satisfied that at least he had not only earned his respect in there, but that he also had won the actual fight against the much older, bigger thug. It definitely gave him more of his confidence back, after the cracker guard had "slapped fire out of him," as the saying went. That had been so unexpected and so demeaning, that it had definitely hurt his pride. He wanted nothing more than to catch that cracker one day, and on the outside, where he could really let his gun do the talking for him. That cracker would respect him then. It would be the last thing that he would do though.

"St. Clair, let's go! You're being moved!" said another cracker guard, as he opened the door to his suicide watch cell, which was nothing more than a real live fish tank, being that the only one wall that wasn't a glass wall, was the one that had the sink and toilet on it.

"Yea, yea, yea," grumbled Fade, stepping out of the cell finally, after three days of absolute indignity. "Where I'm gone to officer?" The cracker guard just laughed and kept walking, leading the way. "You'll see soon enough jit, hope you can fight just as good against a bunch of jits as you did against that one guy in the intake cell," he said and continued on laughing.

Fade had nothing to say, so he just played it cool, staying strong and silent in order to convey his indifference. The truth of the matter was: He was scared as hell and he didn't want to allow the emotion, or the fear in his voice, to betray the fact to this cracker guard, who he knew was escorting him into the belly of the beast. The guard then walked to the elevator and pressed the Up button. The elevator's door jamb had a 3 on it, so he knew that he was on the third floor.

Nine floors to go, he dreaded to himself.

"Face the wall, Jit!" said the cracker guard, suddenly slamming Fade's face up against the wall roughly. "The fuck!" shouted Fade. "Can't you read, Jit?" asked the dumbass cracker guard, and in that moment Fade could see the "Attention: All Inmates Must Face The Wall!" notice that was posted there on the wall with him just not having seen it before this moment. What kind of shit was this? he wondered. Face the fucking wall? For what? He was outside of his comfort zone and none of this made any sense to him. Was it some sort of power trip? Face the wall, give up your humanity? he wondered. It was ridiculous.

He let it go as the elevator doors opened. The guard grabbed his elbow and pushed him in. Looking around and then to the elevator's control panel, he noticed that all of the floor numbers above 3 were all even numbers. There were 4, 6, 8, 10, and then 12 were the only choices. The guard stuck a circle shaped key, like the one for the soda machines or bike lock, into the key hole and pressed the 12 button. He turned, and seeing Fade looking, he pushed his face into the wall again. "Damn jits, y'all don't never learn, damn you!" Again, too late, Fade saw the notice on the wall inside of the elevator again.

"Fuck!" Fade muttered as he was absolutely livid. He had earned his confidence in his fighting, then this whole dehumanizing process was killing him all over again. He again thought back to all of the lyrics and hood movies that he had seen growing up as an even younger kid, and he couldn't ever remember being given this kind of expectations. The rappers and hood heroes never warn you or give

328

you the game about this type of fear that you might develop on this elevator to the top of the South Tower, where the deuces, or body alarms, are hit the most. Where all of the violence is, and where you would begin in this gladiator school of sorts. It wasn't just being the new kid on the block, or about new rules of how he would be required to constantly fight in order to establish himself in the pecking order, it was more about the fear of being alone. He was a social creature, and he always had been. He had thrived on the admiration of his other peers.

Well, here was his great awakening, as they exited the elevators, turned to the left and was faced with a clear plexi-glass door that started immediately opening, somebody somewhere watching on the many cameras that were located everywhere that you looked. He looked into the cavernous U-shaped room, about 30 feet high with a wall that was completely plexi-glass. It had a big booth in the middle of the room, with two separate patios on either side of it, and a basketball court on each of the sides. Just in case the 12 stories of height wasn't enough to prevent some over-eager inmate from trying to escape, the huge patio areas were all fenced in, also preventing a drone from dropping off any possible contraband.

Once the guard led him to the big booth, or bubble, as it was known in the Gun Club County Main Jail, Fade could see a dorm with many rooms located on each side of the patios, so one basketball court for each unit. At least there was that, thought Fade, he would at least be able to show out on the courts and show how he balled. He saw there was a small police desk in the middle of each of the units, and all of the cells were in a V-shape with the desk there in the middle manned by a young Deputy Sheriff who looked as if he could be Terry Crew's twin brother. His name, Fade came to find out later, was Zeke.

The guard escorting him put a white flash card, with Fade's picture and his information printed on it, into a little metal box, and the guard in the bubble opened the other side of the box and took the card from within it, and began looking at it. "A Unit," she said.

"To your right Jit, good luck, you gone need it," he said laughing as he walked away from Fade, leaving him to fend for himself and see if he could make it.

"Get fucked, pussy ass cracker," mumbled Fade as he walked over towards the door that led into the A unit dorm.

The guard walked off, back through the door that they had come through and the elevators located beyond. As Fade walked up, he could see the whole unit because the outside wall was made of plexiglass meant for the bubble officer to be able to see and observe the activities therein. There were two big and heavy doors, the first, a slider, and it slid open as he approached. He passed through it, entering into a sally port of sorts, or a vestibule. The door behind slid shut as he awaited permission to enter.

It was obvious to him that the outer door was controlled by the bubble because the dorm guard was walking around while this door closed, and the inner door wouldn't open. This was a point where Fade had no choice but to give some great contemplation about his life. As big as the dorm was, he was surprised to find only a few kids out in the open dorm coming towards the front to look at him, try to feel him out, as he expected that they would at least attempt to put down on him, or bully him, just like the first day of school, and find where his place would be in their already established vision of the hierarchy.

Fade immediately understood why only eight or nine inmates approached the vestibule; plexi-glass wall, that he was currently imprisoned in. These few inmates had on gloves and were cleaning up. All of the many other inmate population were all locked inside of their cells. He could see because every cell door was made more of plexi-glass than of steel, so all of the many bodies and faces were glued to their respective windows, trying to get a good look at him, Fade, the new kid.

That was okay with Fade though. He had made his own mental agreement with himself not to take any shit from anybody. He had learned that quickly from T-Zoe and Light Skin, and he had found that his resolution made sense. The first of these kids that would try him would be the first one that he would put down just as fast, and with prejudice.

"I want you first jitt! You comin' in my cell first!" shouted the tall black kid with the long dreads that were pulled up and standing on top of his head like some palm trees, the top overflowing with the palm branches. Fade surprised them all by smiling at the comment, looking directly into Palm Tree's eyes.

"Oh, so you think it's funny then jit?! I'ma beat you then fuck

331

you like you's my bitch! Then I'ma pass you to da homies and let them have a turn! I wanna see you smile then jit!" said Palm Trees, trying his best to get the reaction that he really wanted to see from Fade, his new possible victim. He would not get that.

"Okay, okay, back off and let him in!" said the dorm cop stepping up to the dorm guards horse shoe desk. The inmates turned and got back to their mops and brooms, continuing to clean up the unit. The guard turned and hit a button on his desk, and the inner door made a buzzing sound, allowing Fade to push open the inner door and walk into the unit. As Fade stepped in, the dorm guard walked over to him holding a bedroll, which contained a blanket, sheets, towel, toilet paper, deodorant, toothpaste, toothbrush, and soap. Fade didn't even break his stride and passed by the bulky muscled guard ignoring him completely. He immediately walked towards the back of the unit where he saw Palm Trees, as he had silently named him. All of the other inmates had stopped their screaming conversations in the air conditioning vents and through their cell doors, as they noticed that something was amiss. Something was about to go down and they all wanted to make sure to witness it. Palm Tree's co-workers had all stopped their cleaning duties and become silent statues. All watching to see what would happen. Palm Tree turned around, the last to see Fade coming, as he noticed the silence that had spread across the dorm. He then watched as Fade walked toward him.

"Okay then! Whassup den? Let's get it in!" said Palm Tree, throwing up his set and preparing himself for the fight.

When Fade had gotten close enough, he ducked Palm Tree's first lazy left hook and came up inside of his long reach with a right uppercut. Palm Tree's whole body tensed up and he fell backwards, frozen in his stance. Fade could feel the victory, and began to smile again until he felt the first punch of many to the back of his head. He had finally got a first punch knock out, and it was being ruined by Palm Tree's friends, who were now jumping him. Fade was trying to turn, trying to stay on his feet, amid being punched from all directions. His eyes had automatically reacted and closed upon the first hit involuntarily, but he knew that it was a mistake, and opened them in time to see the floor rushing up to meet him, trying to save him and give him some rest. Finally some rest. His head hit the floor. It hit very hard and it had hurt him. It was lights out for Fade, though he was still being kicked and stomped, long after consciousness had left him and had taken him to dream land. What he thought were so many claps in his dream, for either his basketball, boxing, or rap career taking off, was in reality, all of the other jits on that floor, in that unit, South 12-A, banging on their doors, or clapping to root for the fight to keep going and for things to get even more rowdy.

With what were just one on one fighters at first, were now numerous combatants against one. Lil' Fade. They were all now just stomping on Fade, who was unconscious, and not even able to defend himself or comprehend what was happening to him. The Terry Crews looking guard couldn't stop six or seven jits from stomping on one jit, and so, he just hit the deuces and waited for the doom squad, as they were called in Gun Club County Jail, or SRT, which is the Special Response Team. SRT was what the Terry Crews looking guard used to be, as he was big and muscled like them, but they had ended up putting him back on regular duty because he wasn't violent and mean enough to stay on the SRT team.

Once they had gotten Fade down to medical and given him an MRI, and CAT scan, he was found to have a serious concussion, which was causing his brain to swell, filling with blood and causing pressure between his skull and the brain. They were going to have to transport him to the outside hospital where he would be treated by a surgeon. They knew that it was a life or death situation at this point.

The main problem was that although he did have state charges pending, he also had the Federal hold on him for the gang RICO, RICO meaning Racketeer Influenced, Corrupt Organization Act, and racketeering charges because he had been screaming about being Haitian Sensations at the club while he was drunk and high on the Everclear and Kush that they had snuck in. So, not only was he property of the Palm Beach County Sheriff's Office, but they would also need to get the Marshals involved, since he was also a Federal Inmate. The US Marshals would need to be present no matter where they were going to be taking him or what the circumstances might be with him. US Marshals did their own transport.

"He is going to die if we don't get him to the operating table at St. Mary's and drill into his skull to reduce the brain swelling," said the doctor on staff at Gun Club County Jail's inside hospital to the Captain, trying to convince him of the seriousness of the situation and Fade's actual condition.

334

"I've left a message with the Marshal's Office and I'm waiting to hear back, but that's all that I can do, Palm Beach County Sheriff's Office can't transport a Federal Inmate without the Marshal's approval," replied the Captain sadly, who was in charge of the whole jail at the moment.

"Man we've got to do something! This kid is dying!" said the doctor almost begging for Lil' Fade's life, and wanting so bad, just to drive him in his own damn car, to the hospital himself. He knew that he was between a rock and a hard place, but they couldn't just let this kid die, could they? No matter what crimes he might have committed and was charged with, he is only a 14 year old kid and surely he didn't deserve to die.

Just as Doctor Samuels was about to suggest something very unorthodox, like drilling it himself, to the Captain, a solid BEEEEPPP could be heard down the hall and the nurses started running towards the room that Fade was in carrying the CRASH kit, for resuscitating patients in cardiac arrest. The nurse yelled, "Doctor Samuels! Code Blue! Room three! Code Blue!" she said.

Doctor Samuels rushed over, but what could he do? The boy needed a hospital.

Chapter Thirty - Five

Jonny was dead, slumped over his computer desk, shot in the back of the head by his most trusted cousin, the only one he would allow himself to turn his back to. A big misjudgment on his part, thought Iggy. There was no chance of Jonny making it into this new era the new Gulf Cartel run by Ricky Felix officially, but he would be the one who would be mainly in charge of everything and running the day to day business. The new Gulf Cartel wouldn't just be on the Gulf of Mexico and Tamaulipas anymore, it would enclose the whole border with the U.S. and a total of 1,954 miles across that whole border. They would, along with the Haitians, bring a new way of taking over the drug trade in the U.S. Higher prices and the ability to choose their clientele was their biggest goal. More efficient corruption of the police and officials, as well as an almost franchise of the police departments. Also, there were so many of their tunnels that had been closed down after Vincente Fox had left office, and now even the new Mexican Government wanted to re-open them, so that the bribe money can go back to flowing as they were used to.

Iggy's phone rang then. It was El Senor. Well, he thought, here goes nothing.

"Si, Jefe, como estamos?" asked Iggy answering the call. Yes, Boss, how are we?

"I just received a call from Liz! What the fuck is going on down there?" asked El Senor heatedly.

"Well, I'm dealing with a lot Senor, I been communicating with all of our friends in the police departments and not getting much for the effort, Jonny is missing, so I been communicating and coordinating, trying to run shit, but honestly Boss, it's a big mess and I am on my own over here dealing with this shit in the best way that I can. What is Liz doing? You said that she had called, but I thought that she was staying away from here?" asked Iggy deflecting and pretending not to know what was going on.

"No, you idiot! She called because she was attacked and they attempted to abduct her! Now she won't answer when I told her to immediately get on the jet back to Mexico, where I can assure her safety. She said that some guy was following her, Jonny's guy, but then he disappeared! Now, do I have to come all the way there?" he said, allowing the silence to reinforce his seriousness. "Listen Iggy, you get my fucking niece on a plane home, now! Or I will."

"I understand about Liz, Senor, " replied Iggy, and then he tried to redirect the conversation, "but I am all alone here, I'm not getting any help at all without Jonny, maybe it's best that you come here, because I am not even sure if the Haitians are involved. The cops are saying that it's not them who attacked us, but I'm sure that if you came into town and had a sit-down, we could then get to the bottom of this ..." Iggy trailed off hoping to entice El Senor enough to come to South Florida where they would be able to make their move. Getting El Senor to come out of his comfort zone was the most crucial element in the plan.

"Am I to understand that you are losing control of this situation in Florida, Ignacio?" asked El Senor calmly. So calm in fact that it was scary in the deliverance. But of course that had been the intention all the while.

"Senor, I only just came here, Jonny has all of the contacts in the police department, and of all of these people that work for him, very few of them even know who I am. This is his area, Senor. I think that with your influence, they will all see that El Gulfo is taking this seriously, and as such, they will as well, and I think that your coming here and having a sit-down will definitely make the difference," said Iggy to El Senor, trying to use everything at his disposal to convince him.

El Senor didn't say anything for a few seconds. Iggy knew that this was how his mind worked. Patient, calculating, and cold. But he was definitely smart. Iggy had to be extra careful of that, he wasn't the Gulf Cartel's leader for almost three decades for being stupid or impatient. He was not going to be fooled easily. If he was, El Chapparo of the Sinaloa Cartel would have won in one of their many assassination attempts. But instead, the FEDs had finally gotten Chapo, and here stood El Senor, still strong, and incredibly smart, almost immune to the Federal Government of America. Iggy could take nothing away from him there.

"I will be there shortly, I have to tie up some loose ends here first," said El Senor as he pointed, out of sight from Iggy, to another tall Mexican with a rope around his neck. He nodded to his favorite sicario, Carlos Reyes, one of his grand nephews, and Carlos pushed his uncle off of the chair that he was standing on, breaking his thick neck, immediately.

"Take him down," said El Senor after hanging up, full of sadness, "he is still my son, and I will still give him a proper burial, if only for his mother's sake."

Carlos began taking down the body of his uncle, El Senor's second youngest son, a son that he would now mourn, only minutes after hanging him from the 20 foot vaulted ceiling and his $100,000 Tiffany & Co. chandelier in his own mansion outside of Reynosa. Many people around would think that El Senor was heartless for taking the life of his own son, but to him, El Jefe, he could only see it as self defense. For his life he might not have taken the life of his beloved son, but for control of the Gulf Cartel, he would continue to reign, and he would kill anyone that would get in his path and do anything to keep his position. El Gulfo, the Gulf Cartel, was his, and his alone, and would be until he was well into his grave.

After allowing Carlos and some of his choice Dos Zetas, to take down the body and remove it from his presence, preserving his dignity, he dialed Liz on his phone, hoping and praying that she was okay and would answer his call. She did so on the first ring, to his relief.

"Tio? What in the hell is going on over there?" asked Liz with panic in her voice, not sure what to do or say.

"Mija, I am going to fly down there tonight, but everything is going to be alright, okay? Are you somewhere safe?" asked El Senor calmly.

"Si, Tio, estoy con amigo mio y tio de el," she said. Yes, uncle, I'm with a friend of mine and his uncle, she said this in Spanish so

339

that EJ wouldn't hear Liz telling her uncle about him.

"Okay, stay where you are and stay armed, I'll be there soon,"

He hung up after that was said, and went back to going over his son's financial records as well as his contacts. It was really crazy how his own son had been working in collusion with the other cartels and trying to work deals on the side and make trades, selling out the Gulf Cartel allies to their enemies to gain more border territory. El Senor saw that his son was vying for border territory and was actually gaining it, but why was the question that he really could not quite figure. It just didn't make any sense, he had to look outside the box.

In any case, El Senor could have claimed most of the border territories years ago. Well, all of them except the Sinaloa, those territories held by El Chapo, were never going to be taken. Well, not without any American support. But everything else El Senor could have had, he just didn't want them because to own too much border territory was to spread one's self way too thin. The whole state of Tamaulipas, sure, but to cover a horizontal border that runs across Texas, New Mexico, Arizona, and California for 1,954, was just too much, too far of a distance for his cartel to control. On the other hand though, if his son were doing it, it would most likely be possible. The problem with his son had been his lack of patience. If you indeed stretch the cartel so thin as to do this, he would then, for all intents and purposes, be leaving his back door open. So, now any of the southern cartels, or even the MS-13 cartel, could move in on their home territory, because they would be stretched so thin between the borders across the other three states. Not having the man power, that was the dilemma. It just simply wasn't worth it, is what he concluded. Yea, he could have a monopoly on the introduction of drugs into America, but that was a crazy thing in itself as well. Wasn't worth it.

Patience. It was most definitely a virtue, thought El Senor. If his son would have expressed his interest in procuring something territorial-wise, they could have come up with a plan. Come up with a way to work it. He only had been at it for a couple of hours, and yet he already had a good idea of how to make it happen. The same question remains though, why? Why do all of this, when Texas itself makes up for about half of the border with the United States. Just in Tamaulipas alone, their Gulf Cartel had over 1,000 working tunnels and backups for their drug trafficking.

On the human trafficking side of it was a lot easier because of the coyotes and pathways across the desert areas, and the fact that there are no permanent locations for the FEDs to bust like there is with the tunnels. They had no problem whatsoever moving things across, so the why of it is what he had no answer to.

The how though, he knew that answer. El Chaparro had been indicted, convicted, and sentenced by the American Federal Government and so there was a great opportunity in the Sinaloa region. Because the Gulf Cartel had the man power to eliminate all of the other border cartels except the Sinaloa Cartel, the best move would be to do so, then offer a partnership to Sinaloa. With Chapo out of the picture, his many sons would be falling all over each other to fight for the control. All he would need to do is find the weakest link. The weakest son, of course. He would then offer his support, back him in a civil war, then make them fight and kill each other, and put the weakest son on the Sinaloa throne. A temporary partner. Then, when he had the man power and the allies, he would eliminate the one on the throne and take Sinaloa. He couldn't deny that the prospect was appealing, and he might actually pull it off, but he wanted to know why, before doing anything. He already had more than enough territory and could hold that, but anything more would stretch his men thin, and that he didn't want. El Senor got ready to take his jet to the Palm Beach International Airport to deal with the rest of his irresponsible son's mess. Good idea, he could agree that it was. But a bad plan when it came to a double cross of El Senor. Not even his son can double cross El Senor in anything.

Chapter Thirty - Six

Antoine had been bidding his time and stringing along Big Head to keep his suspicions to a minimum. The 400 Mawazo were literally driving him crazy with all of their antics. For example, there was a club called Scalleywags a few blocks away from Steff's trap house and the abandoned house that the Mawazo had taken for their personal use and were hiding in. They were constantly sneaking out and trying to go hang out at the club, which normally wouldn't be a problem, but they just drew so much damn attention. It was infuriating to Antoine. Not only were their accents a big drawback, but there were already four police reports of some women being grabbed and one even having been raped there in the parking lot, and that was definitely attention that they didn't need at this crucial time in the plan. Antoine was pissed but wasn't there to control them. He couldn't watch them with all that he had going on in his side of things.

He kept telling Steff to control them, but even Steff's own cousins had joined forces with the out of control Mawazo. Steff's cousin Pookie was constantly partying with them, smoking boot joints, marijuana laced with coke or crack, and then Mookie, the other cousin, actually bought them a little Toyota Supra from the 90's, and had some of them actually making runs for him with GPS and a Metro Phone to their regular customers. He thought that it would be able to keep them out of trouble and on the grind. He just couldn't control them without Buju, but he needed Buju exactly where he was, with Big Head. The last thing that he could afford is having Big Head think for himself instead of asking Antoine what he should do as he had always done. Antoine was the brains and Big Head the brawn, as well as the title.

Antoine's burner phone was ringing. He looked at the display and saw the 956 area code from the valley in Texas, right on the border. He knew who it had to be, but he wasn't sure, so he had to be careful. He couldn't start to get sloppy now.

"Who is this?" he asked answering the call.

"Well, you know who it is, and I'm sure that you are fully aware of why I'm calling. If I had bad news I wouldn't have called at all, I would be dead, and most likely, so would you ..." said the Mexican accented voice on the other end. Iggy. Based on his message, it could only be him, as nobody else would be able to pick up their conversation where they had left off on it.

"Okay," said Antoine, "How is our timeline looking?"

"Well," answered the voice, "I would imagine tomorrow, I left it up to El Senor, but luckily he will feel the need to come and deal with shit himself. My original plan to grab his niece failed, but as a residual effect, it spooked him enough to think that he needs to come himself to get his niece safely back home, and I also suggested a sit-down since I told him that I didn't think that the Haitian Sensations were even responsible, so ..."

"A sit-down? That's actually a good idea, we can do that and take care of our business there, usher in a new era to both of our Cartels, as well as demonstrate a cooperation between our people

344

and to kill two birds with two bullets," said Antoine with a vicious smile on his face.

"I'll be in touch, we will have our plan my friend, it is inevitable, and success as well as progress, will be ours, and the complete 1,954 miles of the border mine, ok, till tomorrow my friend," said Iggy.

As soon as Antoine had hung up with Iggy, he drove his favorite Toyota to Big Head's house on Manalapan and knocked on the door. "Come," said Big Head's voice from the living room. Antoine let himself in and came to the living room where Big Head was alone, watching the soccer game on his beloved new Curve TV screen.

"I have word, I've spoken to my counterpart in the Gulf Cartel and they wish to have a sit-down, possibly tomorrow. They have some doubts about our involvement in the deaths of their two family members at the Toro Loco, and robbery at the Taqueria. I think that it's a good idea, and maybe we find out what's going on," said Antoine, trying to be a mediator, but only on the surface.

"Dem be fucked! Me bring dem 400 Mawazo and me kill all but da leader dem. Him we fa go torture wit machete! Then him tell us what dem do wit Richy Rich and Big Meet, dem!" said Big Head, pointing excitedly at the machete by the front door, yet saying so with a finality that betrayed his seriousness.

Antoine needed to get Buju away from Big Head and to do so would take some of his maneuvering. He wanted it to be Big Head's idea though.

"Okay, Head, I will go back immediately and start readying the 400 so that they can be prepared for what is going to go down at the sit-down," said Antoine baiting.

"Nah, not fah worry Antoine! Me send Buju to go wit ya, dem only gwan listen to Buju, so him gwan wit chu, and you arrange dis meetin somewhere we fah gwan have control. Me neva trust Mexican dem, so make a good place!" said Big Head.

I most certainly will, thought Antoine with a smile. More than Head can even know or guess.

Chapter Thirty - Seven

EJ, Jean, Shelby, and Liz, were all comfortably lounging around on the Love Sac sofa couches in EJ's condo. Shelby and EJ had began to bring things from the night raid that they had done on Lemonhead's house up to the apartment to put away, and to do some further investigation into who Lemonhead really was and exactly where he might be found, but were taking a break after seeing the seriousness of the ongoing conversation between Wicks and Liz.

Apparently, Liz had opened up a little bit to Wicks while EJ and Shelby were at the van. Really Wicks, who was a self proclaimed "street nigga through and through", had called her on her bullshit. Wicks had known instantly that she was someone connected just by the professionalism of the team that had been sent to abduct her. Then you add to it, her calmness, as well as her training that EJ had described to him when he had first met her, and her education, that is not to mention, her wardrobe.

Jean was a smart enough individual to know that Liz really liked EJ and was worried about his opinion of her. Jean had reassured Liz that EJ wasn't one who would hold anything against her, wouldn't judge her. After all, he pointed out to her, remember who his uncle is, on top of that, that they both worked at the Youth Center trying to help kids from going in the wrong direction. The same Youth Center in fact, that she herself, had expressed an interest in getting involved with, for the very same reasons. He also pointed out, when Liz vocalized her concern of Shelby having been a cop, that he was Shelby's man.

Because Shelby had just been released from her debriefing an hour before, she was too emotionally and physically drained to even talk about the shooting, or her future at her job, so Jean had smartly let it go to address it at a later time. He had instead brought her up to speed with what was going on with EJ and Liz. Jean had put together the fact that Liz hadn't yet even told EJ about what had been in her past that might have caused the attack on her, so he orchestrated a brief encounter to have a quick dialogue with Liz to ascertain why it had happened.

After he shared with her a small bit of his past, she decided to do likewise and had almost caused him to choke on his Heineken that he was sipping on at the time. It had definitely taken his breath away.

"You are a part of the Gulf Cartel?" he asked incredulously, "as in you are a member of El Gulfo? Or you just know them? What?"

"No! Of course I'm not a member, I don't want anything to do with them! I've been down in Boca Raton, going to FAU and working hard on my plan, to sort of merger my La Victoria brand with the Publix Supermarket brand. To cut the long story short, I was fucked when this stupid gang war at a night club was televised on the news, and my connection within the Publix chain saw it, and immediately terminated all of our negotiations with this deal. This was my brain child for as long as I can remember ..." she said sadly and mournfully.

"But why would any gang war terminate any negotiations on

any of your franchise merger talks? There is something that you aren't telling me here," said Jean.

"Because all of my businesses have my family name attached to them, and in the news reports, they mentioned my family name in connection with ..." she left the rest of her thought unsaid, but the implications were obvious.

"But I saw that news report! It only said the 400 Mawazo were going to war against the Felix Family Cartel and ... oh shit! You're Elizabeth Felix?" he asked incredulously.

The dialogue had ended then temporarily when EJ and Shelby had brought in the rest of the things in the CIA van. Nothing more needed to be said actually, but at least Jean could fully understand why Liz would be so nervous about EJ finding out about her. She was an heir to a whole drug empire! A multimillion dollar weekly revenue, and the Boss of the Gulf Cartel's niece at that? This would not end well for EJ. Or for Liz for that matter.

Jean needed to think. Liz was a really nice girl. She was everything that her family was not, and even here, she was trying to bail her family out of the drug game and get them into a legal business. Jean hated the fact that she was naive enough to think that her family would ever be willing to make that transition to being good citizens. They never would be willing, it was almost like the ridiculousness of a Jew becoming a Muslim, an impossible thing to imagine. No matter how hard Liz could try, the power that her family had, it was just not a very likely thing to expect or even think could happen. It was unrealistic to even think it possible, and he even

349

expressed that to her. All to no avail.

When Shelby and EJ had finished and finally sat down, she collected her thoughts. Shelby had gathered the whole story about the attack on Liz through EJ while they had been dealing with all of their winnings from the Lemonhead raid. The drugs, Shelby had led EJ into the bathroom and asked him to help her to flush them all down the toilet out of ear shot of Jean. She was already in love with him, already trusted him, but there was no logical reason to keep hardcore drugs around when they could so easily be disposed of. She knew Jean and Wicks didn't care either, but just wanted to quickly be done with the part of illegalities that she had participated in. She, after all, was still a cop. She also had a moral dilemma with the money taken from there as well.

But it could be used for good, so she would revisit that subject with EJ and Wicks together, in a different atmosphere.

"Liz, you are going to stay here, nobody will find you here and you will be safe. I'll go get you whatever you might need, but until we figure out what is behind this attack, I want you here where I don't have to be worried," EJ had said at the time, hoping that she wouldn't take offense.

Liz put her head down. She felt ashamed keeping secrets from EJ when she liked him so much and knew he was crazy about her as well, but she couldn't face him. She had spoken to her uncle and told him about the Jonny Tapatio angle, his number and connection with the situation, so he had immediately assumed the worse, and hired another P.I. firm to investigate. Liz had received a call a couple of hours later in which her uncle shared his new P.I. firm's preliminary findings, as well as his many suspicions, Iggy being at the top of the list because of his relationship to Jonny, just as much as the relationship that he had with Ricky, El Senor's own son, who they knew Iggy was loyal to a fault to. A son whom he had already killed without a second thought, after extreme interrogation, he had admitted his involvement by duress, only that they could not understand his reasoning behind it. He would be able to eventually get that from Iggy. He hoped so at least.

She knew that EJ would keep her safe, she could feel that, but yet she knew that her uncle was also working every angle on his end as well, and so this would be soon over and done with. She would then share her very embarrassing family connections with him, and on a 'take it or leave it' basis, she truly hoped that he would be willing to take it, and be able to get to know her for who she was inside, and not who her family was, and the reputation that they had.

"Okay, EJ, I'll stay with you for as long as I can, but I might have to go at some point, so ..." she left it unsaid that he wouldn't stop her.

§§§§

Later on, when EJ went to return the government van that they needed back, Jean and Shelby were all alone with Liz and tried to get her to talk about it. Liz finally relented once they pointed out that he was an ex-drug dealer, and Shelby had, only hours before, shot a cop. Her senior partner.

"Okay, okay, I just spoke with my uncle, basically, his head of security down here is Jonny Tapatio, that's whose number had been calling the bad guy's phone. So, his younger cousin, named Iggy Rodriguez, my uncle's right hand man, who my uncle had sent down here to help with this problem. It's an unrelated problem, doesn't even bare mentioning. Anyways, Iggy is best friends with my uncle's son, Ricky Felix, but he has also been working for Ricky to take power from Senor and give it to Ricky, basically a coup.

So, what he thinks, and I believe him, is that Iggy had his cousin Jonny, hire those guys who tried to kidnap me, so they could ransom me to my uncle, acting as they were the other group that is actually the unrelated problem down here. They will lure my uncle here, knowing that he cares a lot for me, and then kill him, that clears the path for Iggy and Ricky to run the businesses and actual Cartel, from there with my uncle out of the way, you see?" she asked, finally finished with the whole story and explanation.

"Who is this other party?" was the first question that Jean asked, but then answered it himself. "The news story? 400 Mawazo and Haitian Sensations?" He was incredulous about the whole story.

"Are you fucking serious right now? The 400 Mawazo are here now? In South Florida? And what? Like they are joining forces with Haitian Sensations against your own family?" Shelby asked, pissed off now.

"Yes, and what's more, Ricky Felix and his team are working

352

on a movement with the Haitian Sensations, one that is going to try to oust my Grand Uncle from power."

"We've only made shit worse!" said Shelby clearly aggravated about it.

"Not necessarily true Shelby, we still have all of the control, as well as the element of surprise ..." said Wicks smiling.

Chapter Thirty - Eight

"Victims of Justice"

Once they had figured out what was really the reason, and who had been behind the attack on Liz, they had finally gotten a grasp on what could be done in order to protect her, as well as plan a preemptive strike to answer the attack that they had made on Liz.

Once Shelby had the ability to sit and talk openly with Liz about her family, her life, and her goals and dreams, Shelby had silently considered Liz one of the good guys. Shelby didn't outrightly tell Liz about their secretly declared war on the Cartels, because then that would be implicating to her participation on the Renteria's deaths and the money that was lost at the Taqueria, but she made sure to make it known that she had no love lost with what had happened to them.

Liz made it clear to Shelby that she was an ordinary citizen, going to FAU for her College degree in business, and had never participated in, or even condoned the illegal activities of her family. She told her all about her La Victoria venture, as well as her dream to take her family completely legit. Shelby listened respectfully, but had to interrupt her a few times to fully be able to understand her motivations. Her family would never be satisfied being legal, Shelby told her. It was an addiction like anything else would be, somewhat like gambling or drug use. It would take motivation and dedication to be able to break such addictions. Liz had never developed the addiction, and thus, she wouldn't need to break it, nor could she understand the addiction itself, without carnal knowledge of it. Some people couldn't change, it was simply who they were. Facts.

Shelby and Liz's conversation had been cut short when EJ had arrived back after returning the van that he and Shelby had used for the Lemonhead raid. Shelby had then got a call from Sacioa Johnson anyways, so she would have to leave to go meet up with her. Sacioa was her one and only ally in the whole law enforcement community. Shelby was actually very grateful that she had asked her to meet up with her at the Starbucks downtown and not the police station or IAD offices. It made her feel trusted, valued and respected, which were all of the feelings that she hadn't felt from her co-workers ever since the shooting had occurred. Sacioa definitely had been completely understanding and considerate about Shelby's feelings.

"So, how are you holding up, Nash?" asked Sacioa once they were seated. Shelby observed with irony that this was the same Starbucks that had introduced her to all of the most recent events, as well as the beginning of her relationship with Jean. She couldn't complain, she thought.

"I've definitely been better, but I'm just glad to have not had to take a life to protect another life. I feel better than the day where I *did* take the life, even though that life I took had just taken the life of my husband. I'm just glad that the kids, as well as Mike's life, are all spared. I wouldn't want to do it any other way," Shelby said with great conviction. Shelby sipped her coffee after the pretty blonde server set it down in front of her. Sacioa was smiling deeply.

"I couldn't have asked for any better answer, Nash," said Sacioa, as she set her coffee down and set both palms on the table. "I have to talk to you about something important, something that you have control over making a big difference or being a newspaper article. I'm talking about your future."

"What about my future?" asked Shelby, confused.

"You can make a difference in your future, or you can not. Now, it is your choice, but I'm here because I want you to make the right one."

"What choice is that? I've got no idea what you mean by that."

Sacioa leaned in real close, voice low, yet very serious. "I mean that we are all impressed down at Internal Affairs Division, or IAD as we call it, it took a lot of guts to do what you did, and whether you know it or not, or if you regret it or not --"

"I don't," said Shelby, interrupting quickly.

"Well, be that as it may, what you did took balls, and it was incredibly brave. But, more than anything, it was the right thing to do, and you did it for the right reasons at that. So ... we want you to come and work for us in the IAD, work for me, with Eddards as supervisor and in charge, which is funny because before you, he had never backed my play before, but we both are in agreement about you coming aboard. You are in if you want to be. You're an honest cop, a good cop, and I know that you can do a lot of good here. Judging by your appearance in Congress' Judicial Committee meetings, that is your goal as well. So, what do you think?"

Shelby was simply speechless. This was not at all what she had

356

been expecting.

"You've heard my testimony on Capitol Hill?" she asked.

"I've examined everything to do with your life, from your meager Haitian upbringing, to your shooting of the Romeo & Juliet killers, and then the fall backwards that you had from the very undeserved guilt, if I'm to be honest, and now, to this selfless course of action that you took to do the right thing, you risked your job, career, your very life, just to save one kid. It's admirable. I don't know many people who could, or would, do the same in your position," Sacioa said looking deeply into her eyes to convey her seriousness.

Shelby was impressed and a bit shocked. She hadn't at all thought of what she had done, she just did it. She said as much, which only further impressed Sacioa by her heartfelt sharing.

"Well, Nash, that is exactly why I want you on our team. It's so hard to find someone who doesn't think about it, yet her natural reaction is to do the right thing, like I said, it's admirable, so, what do you say Nash?" she asked her.

"I don't know, I would have to think about it and it would have to depend on the outcome of this shooting investigation. I really just made detective and I -- why are you looking at me like that?" asked Shelby surprised.

"Nash, it's over at Palm Beach County Sheriff's Office, they aren't investigating anything. It is for things to look proper, but behind the scenes, the brass has already tentatively decided to ask for your resignation, I'm sorry. But look, Nash, this is a good thing overall in the scheme of things. It -- " started Sacioa.

"This is a good ... you have no idea, do you? I've worked so hard to be able to accomplish what I have and to make detective in a good ole boys environment and you tell me just like that, I've lost all I've worked for ... I, I'm just -- "

"What I'm trying to get you to see is that all of your hard work was for this moment! What I'm offering you is a chance to make a difference here! What would happen next time you did this and saved an unarmed black kid from getting killed? How many times before someone shot you? How can we make a difference when we play by their rules? Do you really even believe that you can make a difference in Palm Beach County Sheriff's Office? They didn't accept you Nash. They never would have, I'm giving you the chance of a lifetime, make a difference, Shelby," she finished.

Shelby was taken aback. Everything Sacioa was saying had the ring of truth to it, but Shelby didn't want to be so cynical as to believe that there was no way to make a difference from inside. She had dedicated her life to making a difference from the inside of a broken system, and believed that it could be fixed.

"I, ah," Shelby started, "I just don't know --"

"This is your chance, Shelby! There are so many dirty cops in South Florida and we need your help to start bringing them down! There's just been too many victims of justice in this jurisdiction --" Sacioa started.

"Where did you hear that at?" asked Shelby. "That phrase, 'Victims of Justice', I want to know where you heard that at ..."

"*Si vis pacem, para bellum,*" said Sacioa staring off cryptically. "If you wish for peace, prepare for war. Yes, well, there is that. But to answer your question, Victims of Justice were the women at the Salem witch trials, the starving kids over the years back in Europe and South America; Portugal; Africa, that had stole a loaf of bread just to survive. Getting caught, they had the hand that they had stolen it with, cut off. The Victim of Justice was the ten year old girl who had to marry a 60 year old merchant in muslim countries, just to feed her starving family. Victims of Justice are *you*! A thousand time over, who try over and over to do right, yet are fired from your job because of your gender, or even the color of your skin. Victims of Justice are those who are victimized by the so called Justice System, the ones who are set up by dirty cops, prosecuted by corrupt prosecutors, and sentenced by money and power hungry judges who play along to get into the next best office with a view that is available. They bribe or blackmail their way for the campaign money for the next election from big business. Victims of Justice are the ones that we, in my office, strive to help, we fight for them. The ones who need our help. We are the ones who police the police, and sometimes execute them, just as you almost did with Mike Chambers. It's up to you Shelby. I pulled a lot of moves in order to get you on board, and I know that together we can make a big difference, I know you're good Shelby, come and join the side of the Angels. What do you say?" asked Sacioa.

Shelby could do nothing but smile. This was the thing that she had been waiting for all of her life. "I say yes, Sacioa, thank you very much."

Chapter Thirty - Nine

What in the fuck is this non-bowling ass idiot doing with a fucking bowling ball bag? Antoine thought to himself walking into Big Head's mini-mansion east of Lantana on Manalapan, with Buju there to answer the door. Things were moving too fast now. Antoine felt like a speeding train. Full speed ahead with too many cars behind him, all full, making Antoine's train weigh so much that it would soon be almost impossible to stop it now. It was just moving damn too fast. That, Antoine didn't like. Buju noticed Antoine's look, then went and got Big Head for him.

"I thought you was watching da meetin' place, dem? Fa why ya come ova here with so much to do?" asked Big Head as he walked in with Buju following behind him. Big Head was so stupid that it literally drove Antoine crazy. Here was this asshole, supposedly in the middle of a war with a billion dollar murderous Cartel in Mexico, yet he is in his unlocked house, wearing the ugliest Versace robe and slides, with his gun, nowhere in sight. Stupidity has to be hereditary, not contagious, because Big Head's own mother wasn't much smarter than him. She was an idiot in fact.

"Well, for starters, this," Antoine said, producing a .22 revolver with a long barrel. It was the same gun that Buju had supposedly killed his own father with. He pulled a potato out of his jacket pocket and fitted it on the end of the three inch barrel like a make-shift silencer, and pointed it at Big Head's chest.

"What ya fa do wit dat? Ya fa kill me? Ya fa kill da badman

361

dem? I's da badman! Fa no human can kill he! Buju!" said Big Head looking back to Buju questioningly. "Buju?" he asked, all the sudden humble. All in one look, he knew the truth of it. His time as head of Haitian Sensations, head of the 400 Mawazo, and just being Big Head, was over and done with. He knew eventually that the day would come, he just never suspected that it would be this day, and he definitely never suspected that it would be by these two individuals. One, a child he had given a purpose to, a life to, a position. The other, a kid that he had played with for his entire childhood, came and went from Haiti to Jamaica, Cuba, and Bahamas. Their own Caribbean neighborhood, the Atlantic Ocean had been their playground. But now this. He knew that it was his time, but had always vowed that he would never "go gentle into the night" as the old poem he suddenly remembered from his school days had said.

Antoine knew that this was where his mind was going, knew Big Head well, and so he kept his gun aimed at Big Head's wide chest. He wouldn't shoot his old friend in his face. Not for any sentimental reasons, or because he now knew that he was his blood brother. No. He needed the face as a trophy. It was a ridiculous ritual, but one that would grasp the Mawazo's attention, as well as pay the debt owed to the Matamoros Cartel for the assumed treachery on the Mawazo's behalf, for the killing of the Reterias as well as for Kiko and Juan's deaths.

"So, me done fa, ay?" Big Head smiled his last ugly smile that he ever would, and then made a dive towards Antoine, but just as fast as Billy the Kid, with his revolver, Antoine began dumping all 8 of his .22 caliber rounds, deep into Big Head's chest. Three of them punctured his lungs that were already black from the continual use of cocaine laced marijuana blunts and Black & Milds cigars. Two of them actually entered into his heart. One stopped in the left ventricle, the other pierced the aorta and was stuck on a rib on the way out. The last three bullets were spread out. Two of them went into his lower abdomen, one of which struck his lower spine which would have made him into a paraplegic if he wasn't already dead from the other two earlier bullets that had stopped his heart from pumping the blood to his brain, housed in his large cranium. The last bullet did the least damage to Big Head's body, as it had struck his collar bone, but that same bullet did the most damage to the house, as all of the other bullets had stayed inside the corpse. This one grazed his collarbone which redirected it upwards and straight into the 80 inch 4k Curve TV that Big Head seemed to have loved so much, after he had killed his previous TV before this one.

Now that Big Head's body matched his TV, being completely ruined, the beef with the Gulf Cartel and Felix Family was now a dead issue. Since Antoine's father had disappeared 20 years ago, Big Head had always assumed that Antoine would never find out the truth of how Big Head had blackmailed his father into leaving by using his own mother against him. Antoine was not his actual son. Jean Keys Jean couldn't have children of his own, but had raised Antoine as his own son. Antoine's biological father had been Dio Jean Joseph, who was also Big Head's father. Big Head had always known Antoine was his brother. But since Antoine's mother had died giving birth to him, Keys had raised Antoine as his own, and loved him just as if he were from his own flesh and blood, finally giving his last bit of love with the act of selflessly leaving. Big Head had been threatening to let Antoine know about, not only his terrible and secretive beginnings, but also the truth about his mother, and that, Keys couldn't allow. He loved his stepson so much that he agreed to give up everything to keep Antoine's innocence intact, his mother's memory alive for him, although she had died before he ever got to meet her, and keep him from even being hurt in any way because of his birth.

It had taken years and years, plus hundreds of thousands of dollars to find him, but three years ago, he finally did. After about six days of crying and reuniting, Antoine finally convinced the only father he had even known into telling him the truth. So, in a Costa Rican mansion that Keys had banished himself to, the current plan began its formation. Antoine had, since then, been planning and plotting to complete this take over, even losing his father Keys along the way. He was the one who had recruited Buju, and gave him the cover as the assassinated fall man's son. Buju had indeed played his role to perfection. So, now with Antoine in control of Haitian Sensations and then Buju taking control of the 400 Mawazo, they could start back to their business of getting money and being done with this beef that only causes the loss of money. Beef would only end up slowing money up and for that reason they would have to settle this and squash it.

Prices on things would go way up, bringing the same money with yet less transactions, more importantly, less risk taking. There will be less drug usage. It's the exact effect that it would be if the drugs were only legalized and taxed, as the government would surely be open to doing one day in the future. More expensive means less access to the lower class, making the poor unable to afford it, and more usage by the upper class, which would end with the re-distribution of wealth. Of course there would be variations of that effect, but overall it would leave the country better off than before the plan, of that Antoine was sure. Antoine's plan was more than just some scheme. It was a New World Order of sorts. He wasn't only trying to capitalize. He knew the damage that drugs did to the community, but he was also realistic in his knowledge that you couldn't make people change if they didn't want to. So, if they wanted to get high, they would find a way. But if the prices went up all around, and it was simple inflation, the availability would go down, then so would usage. Like when the prices of cigarettes had gone up in the year 2010, many millions of people had made the effort to quit. Antoine was counting on a similar effect with his plan.

So, not only could he force users into a lower level of consumption, he could also capitalize immensely off of the new change in direction that the United States would be forced into. He knew, after heavily researching the history of certain droughts, he could force a permanent drought.

Antoine grabbed the machete Big Head had so arrogantly left by the front door and brought it back over to the body with him. He grabbed Big Head's thick dreads and pulled his head up, exposing the neck, and began swinging the machete, chopping Big Head's enormous head off. Pun intended. It was a lot of work to chop through somebody's neck. A lot more work than Antoine suspected, but finally the head came loose. Antoine raised the head up in the air, and looked into his brother's still opened eyes, and he spat in his face, as Buju took a picture with Antoine's phone. Buju then handed back the phone and Antoine sent the picture to Steff and one other recipient. Steff texted back, having already expected the photo, "I'll show the 400, have Buju with you when you come."

The other person that he had texted the photo to, texted him back just as fast as well, "Bring it with you tonight, everything is set. I will handle my end when we meet, good work. Your Father would be proud."

Antoine had just earned the respect that he had always yearned for, always wanted. His real father had only died about a year ago, which was two years into these plans, but he had made sure that Antoine would be left as the king, and he had done everything in his power to ensure it. Alliances were made, old debts settled, and new debts incurred for Antoine's future benefit. Because Keys had been thought dead years ago, not only by everyone, but also by Big Head, he or anyone else could never see him coming. When everyone found out about the lengths that Keys had gone to and the planning Antoine had undertook, it would be too late.

Antoine took the bowling ball bag, dumped the bowling ball out of it onto the marble floor, crushing it into pebbles, and placed the head in the bowling ball bag. Now this is a big fucking head, thought Antoine, hefting the bag, trying to zip up the zipper on it. He felt kind of proud. His father would be proud, would be impressed even, with all that had been accomplished with simple mind over matter. Planning. Thoroughness. Ambition.

Buju and Antoine calmly left the house and got into Antoine's favorite Toyota. They were headed to the abandoned house right now. The 400 Mawazo needed to see their new leader, as well as their old leader. Betrayal. Antoine had killed not only his own best friend, but also his blood brother as well. But he had avenged his father, and made his father proud today.

Chapter Forty

Liz and EJ were back at the Youth Center, and they were now unpacking the boxes of the photography equipment and trying to match things together. They were also trying to make sense out of what the Director of Activities at the Youth Center had told them. Sammy had already contacted Wicks apparently and had asked for his help as well. Now he was asking for theirs. EJ now knew that Liz could help with this problem.

EJ and Liz had spent an amazing night together, the previous evening. It wasn't even sexual in nature at all. They had been laying in bed all night, looking into each other's eyes, probing and learning each other's most hidden secrets. Falling in love. If that was even possible that fast, and without physicalizing it at all. But the main thing was that Liz had come clean about her family ties. She was scared to death when she did so, but she was delighted and impressed even more at EJ's reaction and the way he was immediately supportive and understanding. He shared with her about the nightmares, his body count and the times that he had felt broken, holding his many dead friend's dog tags, and even wishing to God that it was him instead of them in that body bag. Wishing he could've saved his friends' lives.

While they had been in the new photography department room there, Sammy had come rushing in saying that he had received a call from the Captain that was in charge at Gun Club PBSO main jail, and that there was some rioting and inmates barricading themselves in on the 12th floor in there. The infamous Jitt floor. The jail guards were not deep enough to make a difference in the situation, so they had to call in all of the street patrol officers to come and assist the corrections officers in getting control of the whole 12th floor, which they did end up doing, but now, as a result, the whole Gun Club County Jail was on full lockdown.

"It wasn't just the one side either," said Sammy incredulously, "the one side of the Jitt floor was actually communicating with the other side through the use of their jailhouse sign language."

"So, what's the problem, Sammy? What's this got to do with us?" asked EJ.

"Um, well, I thought that you already knew about this ongoing war that has been between the Haitian Sensations and the Matamoros Cartel? Well, it's gone well beyond that now, as they were just kids fighting but now the whole Gun Club is in on it. They are making kids in that Jitt floor pick sides. So, it had broke out in the Jitt dorms, and they were forcing every kid in there to choose a side, then once they had both got their numbers up, apparently they all coordinated attacks on the guards, and expelled them from their respective dorms. Then they both turned on each other, both sides attacking the other, and the forced kids taking the brunt of the violence. They've killed three kids in there already and they are all saying that they are going to continue to attack each other on sight. It won't be good, EJ. They've got the whole jail on lockdown as well as the Belle Glade jail too. They need us to get down there and help calm things down. It's mostly kids that have at one time or another, passed through this Youth Center. Now many of them are shot callers, and the Administration believes that they might listen and we can work out a truce of some sort. A lot of these kids aren't even involved in this gang shit, and yet being in there, they were forced to join and pick a side."

"I don't get how this happened, Sammy, these kids ain't even gang bangers, that's more for the older kids. How these gangs get into it all of the sudden?" asked EJ.

"Well, the Special Investigations Supervisors, or SIS, have talked to some of the kids, individually, after they were separated from the others when they were taken to medical to be treated, and the ones who would talk, basically said that the fight at Chance's night club started it, and they said that the Zoes started it, and the speaker for the Zoes, who was one of the ones charged with the deaths at the club, said that the Mexicans were the ones that started it when they took Big Meet and Richy Rich, so there really is no compromise to be had, as far as the SIS are concerned, but we have to do something here EJ. Jean is on his way there already. They are trying to find somebody from the Matamoros Cartel to come and represent the Mexican kids, so then they can try to squash the beef, we gotta go EJ. These kids need us, we have to stop this!" said Sammy passionately.

EJ and Liz looked at each other. "We might already have a rep for the Matamoros Cartel here ready to go. What do you say, Liz?" asked EJ, already knowing the answer. She nodded imperceptively and walked off, dialing on her phone. She had wanted to help these kids in some way too, she wanted to be involved in the Youth Center, but she didn't know how. She now had her chance. Finally she felt needed and knew she could help. She called her uncle, El Senor, and explained the situation and listened while he sat on the phone explaining his whole plan, and what was required of her to ensure her safety, as well as the safety of the kids. She agreed to his plan, and immediately walked back to EJ. She nodded affirmatively to him.

"Well, let's get going then!" said Sammy, seeing that they were all ready.

Chapter Forty - One

His phone rang finally. He checked the display and then answered the call, seeing who it was on the other end. "Senor, como estamos?" asked Iggy with hope in his voice for some good news.

El Senor, on the other end, sat looking at his phone and the picture that was depicted on it, saying evenly: "Everything is set, I'm landing at the Signature gate off of Southern Boulevard at the Palm Beach International Airport around 8 o'clock, have them meet us at the closest bar by the airport," said El Senor before hanging up the phone. Signature is a private terminal, where someone of great influence, such as El Senor, could land his private jet and have a bit of privacy and leniency with the customs and such. They had been flying millions of dollars of their drug proceeds on his jet back to Mexico every month for years using Signature, driving the money straight into their private hanger at El Senor's disposal, and loading his jet all the way to the maximum capacity with big two feet by two feet blocks of hundreds. That was why most of Palm Beach County had such a shortage on hundreds, because they used all of the twenties and fifties to pay bills, workers, or even to buy things with, but all of the 100 dollar bills went back to Mexico, in order to keep the flying weight down.

Iggy was excited now. El Senor was finally stepping out of his comfort zone in Matamoros, where he was always surrounded by his most loyal sicarios and Dos Zetas soldiers, and could not be touched by anyone. He was going to grace South Florida with his presence and Iggy would be able to kill him right away. Finally.

Ricky Felix would be the boss technically, but in reality, it would be Iggy controlling the whole Cartel and running the day to day operations. It was Iggy's imagination, along with his connections to Haitian Sensations, with Richy Rich, which had gotten them so far with as much as he possibly did from his position, and El Senor didn't even appreciate that much. Everything was all about Liz. His Grand Niece who was so special and spoiled. So important to him. Iggy had been building resentment over the years, and it was beginning to over-flow and start showing, despite his own feelings for her.

His phone rang, the damn Little Princess Liz herself, he laughed to himself but he still didn't answer the phone call, sending her to voicemail instead. He didn't even suspect a connection between El Senor's aloofness on his call, and her call out of the blue not even five minutes later. She still wasn't bad in his eyes, only spoiled and misled, he thought. Instead, he dialed his Haitian Sensation connection, Antoine, to let him know how their plan could now move forward. His main concern now was Antoine's part and their agreed upon terms, and the benefits of them.

"Who is this?" asked Antoine carefully, suspiciously even.

"Can we just skip it this time, Papa? I've had a long day and you know exactly who this is and why I'm calling, " said Iggy, quickly losing patience.

"Alright, what do you have for me, partner?" asked Antoine.

"He's flying in round 8 o'clock, so let's go ahead and meet at

The Shack, it's a bar right across the street from the Palm Beach Kennel Club, the other corner on Congress and Belevedere Road, next to the Airport. Be there early, and do me a favor Papa, huh? Don't bring a bunch of those crazy ass 400 Mawazos with you, try to get Big Head close to me as you possibly can, and I'll take care of the rest, okay?" asked Iggy deviously.

"Alright then, I don't want to see a bunch of those Dos Zetas and shit either, amigo, try to limit the calvary, huh? I'll see you tonight," said Antoine and then hung up the phone. He's an asshole, but he's smart, thought Iggy, he's going to help us get into the new era of drug distribution. A whole new way and with it the 1,954 miles of the border with the United States as well.

As Iggy pulled off from the Checkers fast food drive-thru spot, he had been sitting in while having his conversation with Antoine, his phone beeped. He stopped before turning back onto Australian Avenue and checked the incoming text message. "I am going to Gun Club, our ppl are at war with HS in the jail and need us to talk them down. Tio says 4 u 2 come immediately 2! Something about a truce? Call me!" The text was from Princess Liz herself, Royal Pain in his ass, as well as his heart, if truth be told. Now, what was all this bullshit with her? El Senor had involved her in this shit too? he wondered.

She picked up on the first ring. "Where the hell are you? I'm right here in the lobby of Gun Club, waiting to go upstairs, you have to be here to explain the truce to our members here!" she practically yelled at him. She's inside of the lobby, where I can't get to her, otherwise I'll ransom her privileged ass myself right there, he thought to himself. "I'll be right there," is what he replied though. "Hurry, they are taking me up now, ask for Sergeant Sanchez when you get here and he will bring you upstairs. And don't forget to leave your weapons in the car because they search you here," she said back to him, always wanting to have the last word. Little Bitch, he laughed as he hung up and turned Jonny's truck north to Gun Club. Time to put the act on.

Chapter Forty - Two

Wicks and Shelby were in the open area, below the visitation booths but in front of the bubble, on the 12th floor of the South Tower at Gun Club County Jail. EJ and Liz joined them along with 16 SRT members there to ensure the safety of this meeting, this sit down, so to speak. The SRT team were masked up and had oxygen tanks on their backs just in case there would be any need for them to use chemical agent. All of the big wigs, the Captain; Lieutenant; SIS Lieutenant; Psychologists; and a few of the jail medical staff, as well as the local hospital EMTs, were all present there. They were all given simple corona type masks with the straps that loop behind the ears. Wicks declined this offer. EJ, Shelby, and Liz followed suit, just for the simple purpose of proving a point.

"Okay, we ready?" Captain Lee asked SRT Sergeant Alvarez, who then nodded in the affirmative. "Okay then people, Sergeant Alvarez and his team are going to secure the unit. These civilians are going to talk to selected members of their respective groups, once they are all reasonably safe, I will give the word and then I will order everyone back, everyone with me? Okay? Okay then good, let's go," he said the last part with deep sarcasm. "No more prisoners out of their cells than is absolutely necessary. Shot callers, even street level kids, but I don't want just anyone coming out from their cells! SIS can monitor, but keep your distance, I don't want them spooked, I'm not trying to build a case against anyone, I'm only trying to calm my jail down so that we can come off of lockdown, Ok? Psych services and medical are all on standby, so stay by the front door! Okay then, let's get this shit calmed down in here!"

With that, Captain Lee waved at the bubble and the door to 12-A began to slide on its track and opened up for the group to enter.

"We covered all of the windows with newspaper when they had first barricaded the inner door so they wouldn't see us coming," explained Captain Lee to everyone's curious gaze as to why the windows were all covered. Wicks only nodded. After 13 years in a Federal Penitentiary, there was little that he hadn't seen. COs, or Corrections Officers, would use anything and everything that was at their disposal for psychological warfare. Anything could be used and weaponized to keep inmates off of their balance and under control.

The officer inside the dorm hit the button that popped open the inner door to the vestibule and they all filed in. The dorm was a mess, mattresses everywhere, half burned tables on their sides, broken chairs and televisions dominated the bottom floor of 12-A. It looked almost as bad as a hurricane had hit and destroyed everything in its path, similar to Katrina. A natural disaster. Only that this disaster wasn't a natural one. It was a war time one.

The SRT officers fanned out, 8 on top, 8 on the bottom, and spaced themselves out, holding their non-lethal paint ball guns loaded with mace balls, held down, but at the ready. Medical staff stayed in the entrance as the outer door slid shut and secured them all into this Gladiator Dorm, as it was known to most.

"Here's the roster," said Captain Lee, handing Shelby the clip board that listed every member of every gang, their names, and the

377

cells that they were located in. "SIS will also be selecting certain inmates that they've determined to be 'high influence' examples in their groups. 'Shot Callers'. Basically, the ones that have displayed overall violence, put in work, and just bucked us all the way. We believe those are the hardest to control. Those are who we need your help with. Basically, they've got the juice in here." Shelby began reviewing the names on the clip board and looking for a candidate for her to pull out.

They began to pull out the Mexican inmates first. Some of them were aware as to what was going down, but still mean mugged their Haitian rivals through their plexi-glass windows, and even more so at the SRT team. That was who had attacked them first mercilessly, then eventually got them all back into their respective cells by taser and mace balls. They walked over to where Liz and EJ stood. They first looked at EJ distrustfully, and at that moment, some showed recognition on their young faces when they started to recognize who exactly he was from the Youth Center. Finally then, Iggy was led into the cavernous room that was the inmate's day room, where they watched TV and played cards. There was also a TV room, but the Captain had wanted all the locked down inmates to see the peace talks while they were happening, and so it had been decided that the middle of the day room would be appropriate for that purpose.

When the young shot callers who recognized Iggy observed him walk straight through all of the others present and go to Liz, hugging and then kissing her hand, they all looked anew at her, wondering who she was. This had all been choreographed to have this same desired effect. She immediately took the initiative and began to address the ten inmates that they had pre-approved to come out first and began the negotiations. She had all of their full attention immediately.

"Hello Chicos," she began, speaking in Spanish. "I am Elizebeth Felix, I am the niece of El Senor, and he has sent me, as well as Iggy here, to let you know that the continuous war with the Haitian Sensations has not been approved and will *not* be backed by El Gulfo, or Dos Zetas."

"This is fucking America, why don't you fucking speak English or go back where you came from," said one of the SRT members as she was about to start speaking again, but she dealt with this ignorance all the time in Boca, while at FAU.

"No, actually, if you were smart enough to know history, Florida was colonized by the Spanish first! So, English is actually Florida's second language," said Liz to the amazement of everyone present.

The Captain pointed at the SRT member and quickly said, "Out! Now!" All of the kids watching were now all in awe of this amazingly smart and powerful woman, who the likes of, they had never before seen. Liz spoke to Iggy in his ear and he immediately went to the Captain and spoke quickly, while Liz and the boys waited.

The Captain said, "PBSO staff! Back off a ways and give them some privacy!" and immediately a circle of guards and SRT backed off at least 50 or 60 feet away. Out of ear shot of Liz and her gentle voice. All of the kids were now even more in awe. This was all by design of course. It was to give the psychological effect that they were very important, and that PBSO staff respected them, which in turn, made the kids more comfortable. More responsive. Sometimes that was all that it would take, to be respected and appreciated.

"Now may we talk without being interrupted? I want you to know that although I don't know you, that you are all better than this lifestyle. You can do better, and I think that each and every one of you knows and realizes this fact. I was born into the Felix Family, yet I chose hard work and school to run a business and not the Gulf Cartel. Now I know that some of you grew up in broken homes. Poor, alone, abused or hurt, and I wasn't. But I still believe in you and know that if you choose to, you can change your life and be successful at any thing that you put your minds to, and if you so choose, I will help you no matter what you choose to do. The Youth Center is open to you." She paused her speech and yet hardened her look at that time. This in itself made her look even more incredibly powerful.

"But if you turn your backs right now on this offer, my offer to help you make something positive of yourselves, pay for school, which El Senor had agreed to, to help you kids to go in the right direction, then you are going to be with Iggy. Want to sell drugs, be fuckups all your lives? Your fate will be sealed with Iggy's. He is your boss and contact. There is one rule though, if you do select to continue on this road, from now on, the Youth Center is off limits. No business is allowed to be conducted there, understand me? This comes directly from El Senor himself, if you disappoint or disobey El Senor, you know what will happen. Now, before I get into the truce, does anyone have questions?"

A hand went up. Francisco. She saw his name on the clip board and knew that he was important in his group. A leader. She nodded at him. Inviting him, and hoping that he will back her plan in front of the others. But he doesn't commit. "Juan and Kiko were my cousins, what about avenging their deaths?" he asked respectfully. Iggy took this one.

"It is my understanding from seeing the news and the interviews of the witnesses there, that it was one kid, on his own, that attacked Juan and Kiko, and he did so alone. Number one, he wasn't a Haitian Sensations member. I talked to Antoine Jean myself," said Iggy jumping in, "Number two, he is dead. Three, it wasn't sanctioned by Haitian Sensations, and El Senor and Big Head are about to meet right across the street when this is done and we leave here, to seal an alliance between us. Not my choice, but at least we will stop the beef, and a hands off policy will be in effect from now on. So, it's over, okay? Any more questions?" There were none.

Liz started again. "I mean what I say for those of you that want to start a new and positive lifestyle." Liz then put her card on the table in front of Francisco. "I will take care of everything and help you in any way that I can. Leave this shit alone or you will end up like Iggy here, ok?" She looked at the confused look on Iggy's face, then looked back at Francisco and said, "Call me if you're out and want help. The ones who chose to stay in, call Iggy," she looked to

381

Iggy. "Give them your card Iggy, we'll be in touch chicos, thank you." With that she walked away. If only one called her, it would be worth it, but she was hoping that they would all reach out to her and take her up on her offer to help them out of their terrible lifestyle.

Chapter Forty - Three

Wicks and Shelby went into the vestibule after Liz and Iggy were done speaking to the kids in their group. It was up to them now to convince all of his beloved kids, his Haitian kids, to drop this war and to try to work on themselves. To try to make a change, to better themselves. He needed some help, so he had called in a favor that he knew couldn't turn him down. Someone whose family owed him. Well, he didn't see it as them owing him, but they most certainly had. Not snitching was a life he had signed up for. He didn't turn rat because of who he was, not because of who Haitian Sensations were. That, he didn't regret, couldn't regret.

From the elevator, stepped Los and Leo Fuentes. Although Los was still a kid at the Youth Center and not truly Haitian Sensations, he wanted to show respect, as well as support for his best friend's uncle Wicks. As for Leo, he was the one Wicks had called on for the favor. Though he was only in his early 20's, he was still a hood legend from the way he had earned his Golden Gloves. By killing his opponent in the ring with a stupid strong left hook. He had had plenty of KOs since then when he was only 17 years old. Everyone had heard of or knew Leo, and all of them had great respect for him, and if not for him, at least for his mean infamous left hook.

"Thank you for coming, Leo," said Wicks embarrassing Leo. He dapped up Los too.

"Of course, Wicks," said Leo, "you know I be reaching out for you man. Just cuz you out the game don't mean that we ain't still

383

brothers. I'ma always have your back, and you always gone have a place in Haitian Sensations."

"Man, that time is long ago gone, you don't know the whole story, but Richy Rich is a snake, and so is Big Head at that, man. I'm just not Haitian Sensations anymore. I got a 9 to 5, and I'm good bruh, I don't need to be involved with Haitian Sensations anymore, I'm all about helping these kids man, and if you don't wanna help or can't help or can't respect that, I'll do it myself," said Wicks as he looked Leo directly in his eyes and made sure to get his point across.

"Man Wicks, I'm here bruh, that's what my actions say. I support you and got your back till da wheels pop off this bitch, real talk," answered Leo, just as serious staring right back into Wicks' determined eyes.

"Okay then, Leo, so you see my mission now and you see what I'm tryin' to do with these kids, so I need you to; number one, back my play by telling them that from now on, the Youth Center will be off limits for business purposes. Nothing is to be done at the Youth Center's property. Nothing. The Felix Family Cartel has already committed, so we are in agreement there. Secondly, since I can't kill some kids who shot my lil' nephew, he gets a fair match with Lil' Fade for shooting him. Win, lose, or draw, I want it to be a dead issue with them. We also have to talk these kids out of warring with each other when this beef is for the adult members, and even they are having a sit-down now, are we on the same page? Leo? Los?"

"Done and done, as long as Los fights the other kid involved cuz Matt is dead, so Los and Lil' J go, after Fade and Ray, and I will put the word out immediately that no business be conducted at the Youth Center, and there will be repercussions for those who violate this new rule. I got ya Wicks, I'll always have your back," said Leo as Los was nodding his head in agreement behind him. What was big to Wicks was just a small favor to them because of the respect that they had for him.

"Okay, then, let's go talk to these jitts and get this shit calmed down."

Shelby allowed Wicks, Leo, and Los to take the lead as they went to the other side of the jitt floor, 12-D. It had the same hurricane and riotous look, just as 12-A had. The SRT team and other deputies did the same number that they had done in 12-A and spread out. SIS were taking some of the inmates out that they deemed to be high influence and Leo picked a few himself whom he knew to be leaders of their age group and they were brought to them and placed surrounding their small group of Haitian Sensations representatives.

"My name is Wicks," he said starting to address the group, but paying extra hard attention to Lil' Fade. "I am here because I work at the Youth Center after doing 13 years on a 66 year sentence for being Haitian Sensations. I say 'for being Haitian Sensations' cuz I was specifically targeted so that they could gain intel on HS. When I wouldn't rat, they stacked 924(c) charges on me, and over-sentenced me to 66 years. No victims. No violence. Those cops were later indicted and me, released. Long story short, is that I've been where you are. I've been a victim to their so called justice, and I persevered. I overcame. Just as all of our strong ancestors did. I made it out and I made the changes I had to make to never come back. I want the same for you, yet without having to go through what I went through. I want you not to have to go through what I did. To *choose* not to. So, I'm here for you. If you want my help, I'm going to help you in any way that I can. If you want to keep fucking up your life in this revolving door, that's your choice. I'm only for those who don't wanna be in and out of this shit forever. I'm sure that you all know Leo here, so I'll let him speak to you about the current events that are important now.

"Sup, y'all, I'm Leo, from Southside L-Dub," he said, letting them know his city and hood. "I see a few of you that I know from round the way, and some I don't know. But da Big Homie Wicks here called me to speak to y'all, and I'm here to support his move and to let you all know that the Big Homie here has put in work, paid dues, and done time, all in the name of Haitian Sensations. So, he deserves all of our respect, and he's more than earned that. So, first things first, those of you that go to the Youth Center and hang out there, there will no longer be any business conducted there by HS, at all, period. Nothing. It's all a part of the truce too, so don't forget that one." He looked to Fade in that moment, made eye contact, and saw Fade break eye contact with him first.

"Second, Fade, you have to see Lil' Ray in the ring. Los will see Lil J after that, and we not going into details, y'all know what's up and after that it's a dead issue, and then y'all stay away from the Youth Center, I -- "

" -- Wait Leo, I ... how come I can't go to da center? Look man,

Wicks, Los, I'm sorry for what I done man, I ain't mean it, I want to change and to be better and ... " Fade looked devastated and his eyes started to water up.

"Like I need this shit?" asked Leo, looking at Wicks. "Man, don't fucking interrupt me again, Fade. You can talk to Wicks afterwards, but right now, this is way more serious and more important than all of that. Man, y'all got SRT up the ass in here, y'all jitts got the whole Gun Club locked down. The fucking head of Gulf Cartel is finna meet with Antoine Jean right now man. Listen, this shit is over and done with. Y'all got lil' personal beefs? Y'all know what to do. One on one in da cell, and wait a couple weeks till shit cool down, ya know? As of right now Antoine is the head of the Haitian Sensations. Me, Steff, Michel, Johnboy, and Lucrecia are all under him. The war with Matamoros Cartel, Gulf, and Felix Family, is over and done with. In fact, things are going to be very good with us from now on. Thing is, y'all just worry about squashin' this beef and stayin' off the Youth Center property, and its surrounding area if y'all gone do some dirt, ya heard? Nothing! Now, are there any questions about this shit?"

All of the jitts stayed silent, mostly shocked. A hand went up finally. Lil' Post. Another one of the ones that started the whole thing at Chance's Club.

"What 'bout them that's homies with Kiko and Juan? They all know that we jumped in to try to help out Matt when shit went down over at the club, are they holdin' beef or what?" asked Post, clearly worried.

"After the meeting between Antoine and El Senor," started Leo, "y'all goin' to hear 'bout it tomorrow, but debts will be paid and a 'hands off' policy will be initiated between us. You don't do shit to them, and they can't do shit to us. But it's in their interests to leave shit alone, okay? Anything else?"

Nobody said anything. "Okay then, good, be happy, fighting is over, we's all gone be friends now, ok?" he said sarcastically. "Anything more? Wicks?"

Wicks put his number on a paper and handed it to Post. "I meant what I said about helping any y'all get out the game. Call me if you need some help and want to do right, I'm here for -- " but he was interrupted by Fade.

"I want to get out man. Will you help me too? I just almost died man! Look at this hole in my head, they had to drill it to let out the blood that was swelling inside of my head against my brain, man Wicks, I want to change, can you help *me?*" asked Fade in the most sincere way possible.

This was the most unexpected turn of events, yet the biggest, and most challenging thing. Wicks was frozen where he stood. He was at a loss for words. This was a kid that he had demonized in his mind, wanted to kill in his heart, yet wanted to fix for his soul. What could he do? He couldn't turn him down, could he? He had to start somewhere, didn't he? It was a conundrum though.

He believed in his heart that helping kids was his mission on this earth, so how could he not help this particular one? How many others will feel turned away if he turned this kid away? What if this *was* the only kid that he could save? Would he give up this opportunity to save him because of his past? What of his own past? Jean was back now. Jean wouldn't allow himself to be the judge of this kid. "Sure, kid, I'll help you however I can ..." answered Jean.

Chapter Forty - Four

When Jean and Leo had finished their respective speeches with all of the Haitian kids, the ones from South 12-D anyways, they were asked to stay until the administration had worked out a way to spread the word about the truce. Due to the truce being a real agreement between the elders on opposite sides, SIS, and in turn, the administration had nothing to hide. No tricks up their sleeves. So things should be worked out rather quickly, each side moving on to the other things. Allowing the jail to open back up, ending the lockdown.

The administration worked out a plan. The Haitian kids from South 12-D would all be allowed to go to the D-side recreation patio for them to update their other members, who had stayed in their rooms during Wicks and Leo's speech. They would have an hour to update those of their friends who weren't up to date on the truce.

Likewise for the Mexicans on South 12-A. They were all out on A-side recreation patio and were updating their own cohorts about Liz and Iggy's positions and the pending truce with the Haitians. There, the conversations veered more towards Liz and how they all agreed that she was the new Queen of the South, and how amazingly beautiful and powerful she was. They were all in love at first sight.

SIS and the administration listened to the microphone located on the "box", which was a two-way call system meant for emergencies, located on the wall outside both of their respective patios. They were having a laugh at how in awe the Mexican kids were of Liz's "power", since the whole thing with the SRT guy making the "speak english" crack, was all set up by the administration on the recommendation of the in house psychologist. It had worked in making Liz seem all so powerful in front of the kids, which succeeded in making her credible in their eyes, which made them more likely to listen and respect her all the more. Kind of like the all powerful OZ in the movie.

With Wicks and Leo though, SIS had stayed out of it because they had both already established street cred, and been known to the kids. But better believe that these people were most definitely listening to all of their conversations as well, trying to learn as much intel as they could from the kids, however they can.

Once these kids sounded like they were all in agreement, SIS took all of the Haitian kids from South 12-A and put them on D-side's recreation patio and vise versa with the D-side Mexicans, putting them with their fellow Mexicans on A-side recreation patio. Now that both sides were out with their fellow car members on the respective sides, they brought all the officers into the units to clean up all of the debris and do a light search of their cells for any shanks, or prison made knives carved out of the metal on their bunk beds or tables, since the lockers couldn't be used as they were made out of plastic.

SIS had made sure that Wicks and Leo both had hugged and kissed Liz's hand as well as shook hands with Iggy, just to reinforce the idea as they left in the main corridor in full view of both patios where both of the group of kids could see the mutual respect and be reassured about the whole truce and get more comfortable around their no-longer-rival's group. They were to see and appreciate the elders on either side knew more than them, and were making a truce for a good reason.

Liz and Iggy left with a lot of clapping and shouting and even a little bit of the banging on the windows. It was all the reassurance that Liz wanted in order to know that she had been of tremendous help on this day. She was now committed as well as addicted to helping the kids straighten up their lives and to be more involved at the Youth Center. EJ, Jean, and Shelby might have been there first, but she planned on making every bit of a difference. Now she would have to deal with the plan El Senor had set before her.

EJ and Shelby had stayed with Leo, Los, and Wicks just to give the moral support, and to see this thing through. SIS ended up leaving the Mexicans on A-side patio and Haitians on B-side patio for an hour and a half. So long in fact, that some of the Haitians, who were actually friends with some of the Mexicans, had began to talk through the closed doors that separated the two patios. Some even did sign language through the bubble window that allowed them to see each other through the glass, and communicated their final agreement with the truce.

It was at this time that SIS decided to tentatively allow them to come back inside of their respective units, and see what happens. Everything ended up going well and smoothly, the TVs being the kids' only complaint. The Captain quickly had them replaced, as they all knew that televisions are the best baby sitter in the whole prison system.

It was finalized. The truce was intact and the war is over. All looked as if it would all work out just fine from now on. The Youth Center volunteers had been the ones who were able to make the turn in the events. It was extraordinary.

Chapter Forty - Five

Liz already knew what would be waiting for her and Iggy upon leaving the Gun Club County Jail catwalk. It was a very long walkway that extended from the visitation lobby, all the way down to the parking lot at 30 feet in the air, passing over a road that leads to the intake section, as well as a canal. It had a natural effect of making your very own freedom feel even that much more important and magical as you walked an almost football field long walk of silence, high up in the air, with wind just blowing in your hair because of the draft. It was something.

It put into perspective as well, that the dirty mother-fucker walking next to her down this catwalk had tried to have her kidnapped and possibly murdered. She was mad as hell, especially at the fact that she needed to stay quiet about it the whole time they were inside of Gun Club, in front of the kids. She knew what was next, so she could hold it no longer, she had even told the kids who rejected her offer of help, rejected her, to call Iggy, "that their fate was tied with Iggy's fate." Even then she knew she would end up killing him. When the kids who wanted to follow his footsteps heard about his fate, as well as who did it to him, she prayed that they might then, finally want to change their lives and do good with themselves. It was her last ditch effort to pull the kids away from Iggy's way of life. Show them why they should change.

"I knew you were behind those mercenaries maybe 10 minutes after I killed them. There had been calls," she explained, "from your cousin Jonny's phone going to their burner. They couldn't answer. I had already killed them all."

She searched Iggy's body and face for any tell, some kind of reaction. He gave away nothing. He had always been very smart. They walked a few more steps until they could see that a stretch Hummer limo, all black on 28" Giovanni rims, pulled up to the bottom of the steps. He wasn't supposed to fly in until 8 0'Clock, yet here was a limo that could only be El Senor's limo.

"That could mean that my stupid cousin was involved. I don't see how that might implicate me in anything, in any way. You gotta come better than that. He was a rapist and fiend. In fact, there is no telling how much he might have wanted you ..." Iggy trailed off.

"Was? So, he's dead then?" asked Liz. "Why though Iggy? That's all I really want to know, is why? Let me at least understand your reasons behind it ... you had everything ---"

"I didn't have *you!*" he said to her frozen expression, snapping loudly in the quiet windy elevated catwalk.

"After I killed that filthy photographer *pimp,* you finally started coming back around more and ..." he said, trailing off, seeing her eyes getting as big as saucers hearing this unexpected revelation.

"Killed? You had my boyfriend killed? Why? How?" she asked stunned. She had never known or even suspected, but after hearing it, everything all clicked into place, finally making perfect sense. Phil had never taken the train, and he was no clutz, so he wouldn't just fall in front of one anyways. He was coordinated, he had to be with his profession, being a photographer. She couldn't believe it,

395

couldn't even begin to comprehend this.

"Because you were just so damn into him, you stopped coming around me, didn't even talk to me anymore, I was always there for you, and you just treated me like the fucking help. You don't know what that did to me, I *loved* you! I always have!"

"First of all, you're old enough to be my father, so eww! Second of all, you *are* the fucking help! And I loved PHIL! We were going to be married! And you killed him? How could you!?" She began to walk again, even more angrily, if that was even possible. She wanted to push him right off of the catwalk right here and now.

They had got about 20 feet from the stairs which led down to the parking lot when two of El Senor's most favored sicarios, Carlos Reyes, and Leticia Felix, who was Liz's older sister, stepped up to the top of the stairs at the end of the catwalk. Both of them held silenced Sig Sauer P229s, and had murderous looks on their faces.

"You're being traded to the Haitians, they are giving El Senor Big Head on a platter in exchange for you. Quite literally in fact. So, fortunately, I will never see you again," said Liz trying her best not to betray her feelings in front of this monster. She knew that she had to keep it together, see this thing through, and cry for Phil later. She just couldn't believe that Phil had died because of her, because of who she was. She passed the sicarios, even her own sister, without so much as a word. She just couldn't think, couldn't speak. She got into the limo as she heard a lot of knocking on the jail windows, many stories, high into the air, her fans banged as loud as they could for her. She hugged her uncle and sat back, mentally preparing herself for what task lies in front of her. She didn't like it.

Iggy was fitted with plastic zip ties and sat facing El Senor and Liz. He still held his head high, no shame at all. "Ricky will avenge me," he said with some self importance and indignation.

"I've got a surprise for you Ignacio, I've known about you for a long while and I killed my son yesterday," smiled El Senor.

"No! No! No! Nooo!" screamed Iggy, as Leticia handed Liz a gun. She used it.

§§§§

Going to The Shack bar had always been Antoine's idea since he knew the owner, Cashwell. He called ahead of time to verify that he could rent her bar for $10,000 for the whole day. She agreed, and added the unspoken rule out loud, that: "I ain't see shit, Twan!" Antoine had laughed about how well she knew him.

He had showed up around noon, and had placed his bowling bag right there on the bar. Cash wasn't even curious, didn't even look. She just brought him a Captain Morgan & Coke, so that he could calm himself for the upcoming meeting. His most trusted men were there with him, and woman. There was Steff, Buju, Michel, Lucretia, and also Leo, who would be there shortly.

Lucretia, or Crea to her friends, was shooting pool with Steff. Buju just watching. It almost seemed as if he had a little bit of a crush on Crea. Michel was just observing everything. He was a good guy. Family man, very hard worker. He would be something one day, Antoine was glad to promote him into his inner circle. He had definitely earned it.

Antoine had some hurtles to jump, but the worst was well behind them all. As soon as his new permanent drought was initiated, there would be a lot more money and a lot less traffic. EL Senor had been skeptical about his plan at first, but if anyone remembered last December and January, well it wasn't really a drought. It was Antoine's test run to prove to El Senor that it would all work and what the economic effect might be on the whole of South Florida.

El Senor couldn't have been more impressed. The only thing that Antoine didn't tell Ricky and Iggy, was that they wouldn't even need the border belonging to the Sinaloa Cartel. That, in itself, had proved their disloyalty to El Senor, so Antoine and El Senor's truce and agreement had stemmed all from this understanding. El Senor could've supported El Chapo's weakest son against his much stronger brothers in a civil war, but he had been shown by Antoine that he wouldn't need to. That had been the difference between El Senor and his son, Ricky. Impatience ruled Ricky.

Antoine heard a car door being slammed as well as voices outside, and this brought him out of his thoughts. "They're here," said Michel by the window in front. Antoine walked over to where Michel was watching. "Jesus Christ! They just doing that in the parking lot?"

"Doing what in my parking lot?" asked Cash, alarmed.

"Nothing, Cash," said Antoine reassuring her. Cash caught on quick and went back to wiping down the bar top that was already spotlessly clean.

What Michel had seen and Antoine was now watching live, had been, two sicarios, one holding an arm each, and pretty, petite Liz, chopping at the neck, trying to remove the head from the rest of the body of Iggy. She looked determined and very pissed off. She was really going. Finally with one final chop, she pulled the head free and threw it to the ground silently. She kicked the head once and walked towards the backdoor to the bar out of breath, yet seeming somewhat satisfied with herself.

The two tattooed up sicarios were starting to play soccer with the head as the soccer ball, until El Senor finally stepped out of the beautiful stretch Hummer truck, the sort of truck Antoine had never seen before. Both sicarios straightened up and stopped playing soccer, which he figured was more for his benefit than for any other reason. The female assassin helped El Senor as the male picked up the headless corpse and brought it around the back of the truck. The female grabbed the head as she passed it and walked with El Senor to the rear door that had opened directly to the parking lot.

After pushing the corpse into the trunk of the stretch truck, he quickly caught up to El Senor and escorted him to the club's door, alone with his female look-alike. They appeared to really adore the old man. It was quite an amazing scene actually, regardless of the class of people they were.

Liz walked into the bar first. "Bottle of Patron, and a dirty glass," Liz said to Cash sardonically. "I've always wanted to say that like I was in a movie, so what better time then now?" she added under her breath, but still allowing Cash to hear as she placed the bottle alongside a noticeably clean glass on the bar. Liz poured the glass full, an equivalent of about ten shots and took a tentative sip of the clear Tequila as she tried to drown out her worries. To clean her head of the memories, all of the lies that she was told. All of her life she was trying to be better than her family, trying to be a good person. But even in her relationship with Phil, where she had thought that she could be a normal girl, a wife one day maybe, she had only succeeded in getting her man killed. All for some unbalanced jealousy fueled fantasy by a man that she looked at as family. She took another gulp of the smooth Tequila. She had avenged Phil. She had shot Iggy in the same heart that he had claimed belonged to her, and then chopped the same head that had plotted her boyfriend's murder off of his neck. El Senor walked in dramatically with Iggy's head in his hand. To all those present he seemed like he was a Mafia Don of old. He walked towards Antoine, placing the head on one of the tables as he met Antoine halfway there and quickly embraced him to everyone's astonishment. Nobody there was aware that the two of them were even acquainted, much less that they seemed to have some kind of a bond, a friendship of sort, or at the very least a friendly business relationship. But the one thing that was obvious to all was that they were both happy to see each other.

"My friend, Antoine, it is so great to finally see you again! It has been far too long, my friend, your father would be so proud of you ..." said El Senor, holding Antoine still, at arms length, to get a good look at him, maybe even to memorize him just like this.

"You've put on some weight I see!" He smiled.

"Yes sir, Senor, I've been in the gym a lot since daddy died ... But you know, he's gone but since our plan has come to fruition, you know how grateful he would be to you right now, for all of your help. Senor, I am, well, *we* are grateful," said Antoine emotionally.

"Of course, of course, but you know very well that this was all the work of your father and you, I was only glad to be of some small assistance after all that your father had done for me three decades ago, when he helped me to seize control of El Gulfo and took out many of my enemies. He was an incredible soldier and an even better friend ..." El Senor walked to the bar where according to Antoine's instructions, Cash had placed glasses and also bottles of El Presidente, a Mexican made Brandy that was both delicious and smooth, on a generous drink tray atop the bar. El Senor took the drink tray and brought it to the table, placing it right next to Iggy's head. Steff chose that moment to approach as El Senor was pouring generous cups of the brandy. Steff opened the bag and grabbed a handful of dreds and placed Big Head's enormous cranium on the table next to Iggy's head.

"A toast, first of all," said El Senor, handing Antoine a glass filled with the amber colored El Presidente, "to your father, and my dear friend, to be always remembered fondly. To Jean "Keys" Jean, always with us." Antoine touched glasses with El Senor, "To my dad," said Antoine with El Senor.

"Now on a brighter note, bring it in fellas," said El Senor, as if he began to fill all of the glasses and pass them out as everyone approached. He introduced them all and raised his glass, "To our mutual conquest, to a truce and more, a friendship with our people. To us having each other's backs and helping each other mutually grow. To the Haitian Sensations and 400 Mawazo, our friends and partners. To the new us, Zoes & Zetas, the Double Zees, toast to us," said El Senor.

"Double Zees," said everyone together in unison.

"Antoine, my niece, Liz. That's the one to watch out for, I am betting that she is the one to run El Gulfo the best, she has the brains --" said El Senor happily, before Liz interrupted him.

"No, Tio! I will never run El Gulfo! How could you kill him Tio? I was in love with Phil! I just -- I can't believe --" said Liz heartbroken.

"No! Mija, I had no idea! I'm sorry, but Iggy said, well it wasn't my doing, Iggy had an agenda. It's best not to talk about it here. I'm so sorry though, I would never hurt you my princess ..." said El Senor.

"I have to go, I'm sorry, I'll call you, but I need some time to myself to think and to get my head right. I can't deal with this right now." She left.

Steff and Leticia came in together to let them all know that the scene was indeed set. Outside, Carlos Reyes had one head under each tire of the big stretch Hummer. He was yoking the gas to get it on top of the heads. Once he finally did, the pressure crushed both of the heads, dramatically beneath the tires. It was a gruesome mess.

He ran back and forth on top of the bloody grey mess that was left until they became a mushy pumpkin looking mess. Cash came out of her bar with the long hose in her hands, mumbling about how "this shit is crazy" and began hosing off her parking lot. It took almost an hour because of the size of Big Head's, well, head. It was during this time that Wicks, Shelby, Los, and Leo showed up, and EJ picked Liz up from the bar.

As everyone else was inside, enjoying drinks and celebrating the truce, Cash finally got all of that mess cleaned up and again ready for another day as a South Florida bar and club owner. Another day of being a citizen. But in this new world, with dirty cops, conspiring task forces, corrupt prosecutors, and judges, a normal citizen is only a step away from becoming a 'Victim of Justice'. So, there was Wicks and Shelby now. The ones that can help the ones that the police won't or don't want to help. They wanted to make their community a better place. They would stop cops and crooked prosecutors and judges, and they didn't care who it was or what their power or official job was, they weren't going to allow any of their people to become the next 'Victims of Justice'.

Epilogue

Taboo,   12-12-21

    What's good bruh? I hope you in there keepin' ya head up! I wanted to drop you a line and give ya an up date to what's been goin on round here since all that shit be done went down at Gun Club, the Youth Center, and finally at Cossi's Bar, "The Shack." Knowin that you in a maximum custody U.S. Penitentiary in da feds, I'll watch what I be sayin, but I gotta keep it blood raw, ya dig?

    So, first off, that cop that died at El Toro Loco was some big wig. Shelby ended up taking down his whole dirty team when she started working for Internal Affairs Division. She also has been taking down some over-zealous cops, ones shooting unarmed civilians, planting evidence, and basically making ordinary citizens into "Victims of Justice."

    I'm really proud of her, bruh. She definitely found her niche, taking down bad police, prosecutors, and judges. Giving them the justice they are due. Real justice. She got some help for that girl she found at Lemonhead's house, and we are still after him. Lemonhead has connection with Lil' Haiti, so we'll find him eventually. Or maybe I will with my P.I. license and access to Lexis-Nexis! Shelby is helping me to start my own private investigations firm, so I'm going to help defense attorneys save their clients! I also filed to get my record expunged, so soon, I'll be a normal citizen again!

    I've talked to Sammy and I'm trying to get another youth center going across from John Prince Park, on Lake Worth Road. I can't wait, it's going to allow us to help so many more kids! The PBSO found a body in his trunk at the Youth Center. Juanito. So now they've agreed to send out more patrols, so things like what happened with Lil' Ray won't happen to any other kids.

The patrols will be properly trained too. None of that trigger happy shit, like Mike Chambers. Shelby is starting a police "Explorers" program too, for lil' girls who are interested in becoming good cops. She will help them to become good people first, ya feel? Now, I don't eat cheese, and even Master Splinter gotta die, but we don't need no more bad cops out here, and she's definitely on track for that

shit! The fight! Lil' Ray is 12, and Fade is 15 now, and Bruh you'll be so proud of Nephew! He trained like hell and got a draw, in spite of Fade's age and size! It was amazing! Now Fade spends alot of time with Lil' Ray training, and I know what you thinking, but Fade is good now. I've been working with Fade alot since he asked for my help, and he's come a long way. He even helps alot with the younger kids, so don't count him out yet, I think those kids that jumped him did some good and knocked some sense into him, that or my damn speech did it! Lol! For real, no cap!

ET and Liz still counting each other, but she's been distant since she found out about Phil Flash's murder, she's been in Mexico alot, dealing with La Victoria. ET been either in training or off on missions, so they've been enjoying the lil' time they do have together. I think they finna make it though! I guess we'll wait and see.

But J is now running the Yoo Mawazo. Him and

405

ANTOINE ARE STILL TIGHT, BUT MAWAZOS HAD TO GO! TOO MUCH ATTENTION, DEM! ANTOINE SENT THEM BACK TO PORT AU PRINCE! SO, THAT'S THE END OF THAT. HOPEFULLY. EL SENOR HAD ISSY AND JONNY'S FAMILIES HUNG FROM BRIDGES IN REYNOSA AND MATAMOROS. ALL THE WAY DOWN TO THE FAMILY DOG, STRANGE ENUFF.

EL SENOR AND ANTOINE SHOOK HANDS ON THE AGREED ON PRICES ON COCAINE, HEROIN, AND FLAKA. THE PRICES WERE SO DAMN HIGH, THAT IN THESE LAST 6 MONTHS ALONE, UNEMPLOYMENT WAS DOWN SO LOW, THAT INFLATION WAS CUT BY FIVE. SOMETHING NOBODY WAS PREPARED FOR. WITH RISING PRICES ON IMPORTED DRUGS, ADDICTS COULDN'T AFFORD CRACK OR HEROIN ANYMORE. FLAKA USE WENT TO METH AND MOLLY, BUT THEN PRICES ON THOSE WENT UP. BIG PHARMA CAUGHT ON AND JACKED UP THE OPIODS AS WELL.

ANTOINE IS A ECONOMY GURU IN MY MIND! ALL OF HIS THEORIES AND PREDICTIONS WERE PROVED RIGHT. BOTH CARTELS WERE STILL MAKING MONEY, YET ONLY THE RICH CAN AFFORD IT. THE ADDICTS IN THE HOOD BEGAN TO SELF RE-HABILITATE, CAUSING THE ECONOMY TO BOUNCE BACK. WHAT USED TO BE BUMS AND ADDICTS, WERE NOW MAKING UP MOST OF THE WORK FORCE, PAYING TAXES. ITS A COMMUNITY REHABILITATION FORCED BY DRUG DROUGHT.

STAY TUNED HOMIE, MY FIRST CASE AS P.P.I. IS A TEEN GIRL BEING PIMPED OUT, AND HER FAMILY WANTS ME TO GET HER BACK FOR THEM. I'M A DO WHAT I CAN, AND IF I GET SOME BLOOD UNDER MY FINGER NAILS, YOU KNOW WICKS IS BACK. DON'T WORRY BOUT ME HOMIE, I'LL SEE YOU SOON WHEN CONGRESS FIX THE STACKED 924(c) SENTENCES AND GET THEM 91 YEARS OFF YA! STAY TUNED, I GOT TO GET CECLIANE HOME TO HER FAMILY! STAY UP!

JEAN
WICKS

Book Club Questions

1) What do you think about the ability of Jean and Wicks in either empathetic or violent situations, to be the dominating personality?

2) What do you feel that the difference between Jean and Wicks actually is, emotionally when based upon the necessity or the propensity for violence?

3) How do you think that Jean or Wicks' family and friends feel about his dual personality disorder? How do you think that Shelby deals with it?

4) How long do you think that Jean has had Wicks as his alter ego or personality? If Jean didn't have Wicks at all in his life, would he still have been imprisoned, and how would his life possibly be different?

5) Do you think that Wicks is all bad, and Jean all good? Or is there some bad in Jean and some good in Wicks? How do they relate?

6) Do you think that Janel was more in love with Jean, the man, or with Wicks, the gangsta? What about Shelby's feelings?

7) Do you believe, as Jean did when he explained it to Shelby, that

he is responsible for what happened to Janel? How could he have prevented that?

8) Do you feel that Shelby was responsible for Tomas' death? What could she have done to prevent him from dying or even the Romeo & Juliet killers from their own terrible fate?

9) Do you think that Shelby was right in shooting her own fellow officer, even if he was a superior and partner?

10) Do you think that Wicks did the right thing by allowing Jean to agree to helping Lil' Fade with changing his life? Would, or could you have done the same, even though he was the one who had shot Lil' Ray three times?

11) Who do you think that the cop was at the scene with the Renterias when they were killed? Do you think he should have been revealed?

12) Do you think that EJ was righteous in all of his actions, or do you think that he was just gone off of Liz and in love? Do you think that she fell for him as well? Do you think that their relationship could possibly work in real life?

13) Do you feel like Liz will stay true to her plan to help the kids at the youth center, or will she take over the Gulf Cartel as her uncle

wants?

14) Do you think that Iggy and Ricky Felix could have actually accomplished their plan and getting the whole 1,954 miles of the border under their control? Why do you think that El Senor didn't go through with it?

15) In a real world situation, do you feel like Antoine's idea of helping the community by creating a drought and raising prices to cause the poor people to start to self rehabilitate could have worked?

16) Why do you think that drugs are so popular in our urban culture? Do you think that they were right in starting a war and killing drug dealers in order to stop the flow of drugs to the youth center? Was there a better way to do so?

17) Do you think that Lil' Fade's autistic sister was his motivation, or did almost dying from the beating that he suffered dominate his decision to finally seek help from Wicks to make a change?

18) How many of the kids on the Jitt floor do you think chose to accept Wicks offer to help them change? What about the kids in which Liz spoke to?

19) Do you think that there was anything more that Wicks or Liz could have said while addressing the kids to motivate them more?

What might you have said to convince them to stop this and make a change in their lives?

20) Do you believe that Jean and Shelby can actually make their relationship work with her as an officer at IAD and him being a convicted felon? What do you think will happen at her job once the powers that be finds out about their relationship, and Wicks past mistakes?

About the Author

Taboo, or Brian Micko Yeary, is a Federal Prisoner who has been sentenced to die in prison for non-violent, victimless gun and drug possessions charges. Being an advocate for Criminal Justice Reform and while waiting for retroactivity to apply the First Step Act to his stacked 924(c) sentences, Taboo started FREE TABOO PUBLISHING, LLC to bring attention not only to his own situation, but to also help to publish other talented authors and poets who are also Victims of Justice incarcerated in this criminal INjustice system.

Sentenced to 91 years for a draconian 924(c) sentencing enhancement that has since been corrected by Congress, Taboo still sits under this unfair and ridiculous sentence. Convinced by Tom Cotton of Arkansas, Congress decided that the 924(c) law is only unfair to those who were sentenced AFTER 2018 and not those who are actually still suffering right now from the unfairness of it, so they withheld retroactivity from older cases sentenced before the First

Step Act.

Most convicts in Taboo's position would become a product of their environment in a Maximum Security Penitentiary overrun by gangs and violence, but this author instead persevered and established FREE TABOO PUBLISHING in April 2022 and introduced his debut novel, "A Victim of Justice" shortly thereafter. He has two new authors to introduce and a trilogy of his own coming out soon. He lives in Lee County US Penitentiary with no cats, dogs, yet a lot of hope in Congress to pass legislation for retroactivity and equality in sentencing reform.

Made in United States
Troutdale, OR
08/09/2024

21876357R00229